Escape to...

a glamorous world of sun-drenched passion, rising temperatures and romantic destinations...

Revel in those long, lazy summer days...

Lose yourself in hot, balmy sunshine by a sparkling Mediterranean sea, with a very attentive Spanish male.
Escape to Spanish Seduction
two entrancing bestsellers
in one romance-filled volume.

Available in the

Escape to

Collection...

19th May 2006

16th June 2006

21st July 2006

18th August 2006

Escape to...
SPANISH SEDUCTION

Containing

Mistress of La Rioja
by Sharon Kendrick
&
A Spanish Practice
by Anne Herries

DID YOU PURCHASE THIS BOOK WITHOUT A COVER?
If you did, you should be aware it is **stolen property** as it was reported *unsold and destroyed* by a retailer. Neither the author nor the publisher has received any payment for this book.

All the characters in this book have no existence outside the imagination of the author, and have no relation whatsoever to anyone bearing the same name or names. They are not even distantly inspired by any individual known or unknown to the author, and all the incidents are pure invention.

All Rights Reserved including the right of reproduction in whole or in part in any form. This edition is published by arrangement with Harlequin Enterprises II B.V. The text of this publication or any part thereof may not be reproduced or transmitted in any form or by any means, electronic or mechanical, including photocopying, recording, storage in an information retrieval system, or otherwise, without the written permission of the publisher.

This book is sold subject to the condition that it shall not, by way of trade or otherwise, be lent, resold, hired out or otherwise circulated without the prior consent of the publisher in any form of binding or cover other than that in which it is published and without a similar condition including this condition being imposed on the subsequent purchaser.

*M&B™ and M&B™ with the Rose Device
are trademarks of the publisher.
Harlequin Mills & Boon Limited, Eton House,
18-24 Paradise Road,
Richmond, Surrey TW9 1SR*

ESCAPE TO SPANISH SEDUCTION
© by Harlequin Books S.A. 2006

Mistress of La Rioja and *A Spanish Practice* were
first published in Great Britain by Harlequin Mills & Boon
Limited in separate, single volumes.

Mistress of La Rioja © Sharon Kendrick 2002
A Spanish Practice © Anne Herries 2001

*ISBN 10: 0 263 85083 8
ISBN 13: 978 0 263 85083 3*

108-0806

*Printed and bound in Spain
by Litografía Rosés S.A., Barcelona*

MISTRESS OF LA RIOJA

by
Sharon Kendrick

Sharon Kendrick started story-telling at the age of eleven and has never really stopped. She likes to write fast-paced, feel-good romances with heroes who are so sexy they'll make your toes curl! Born in west London, she now lives in the beautiful city of Winchester – where she can see the cathedral from her window (but only if she stands on tiptoe). She is married to a medical professor – which may explain why her family get more colds than anyone else on the street – and they have two children, Celia and Patrick. Her passions include music, books, cooking and eating – and drifting off into wonderful daydreams while she works out new plots!

Sharon Kendrick has a new novel available in August 2006. Look for *Bedded for Revenge* in Mills & Boon Modern Romance®.

For my darling TK, who has inspired more
passion and romance than he will ever know...

CHAPTER ONE

THE phone chose precisely the wrong moment to ring. Up to her eyes in spreadsheets, Sophie gave a little groan of irritation as she clicked the button up. She still had masses to get through, which was why she had been in the office since the crack of dawn.

She normally worked from around eight until late—however late she needed to be to get the job done; no one could ever accuse Sophie of a lack of dedication, but for once she wanted to leave early. To spend an outrageously indolent time getting ready for a date. A hot date, too—with Oliver Duncan, owner of rival ad agency Duncan's.

She wriggled her shoulders with anticipation—because she was about to spend the evening with one of London's most eligible men and was currently the envy of all her single girlfriends!

'Now, I *did* say I didn't want to be disturbed, Narell,' she joked in mock-stern tone, knowing full well that Narell was the best assistant in the world, so maybe it was important. It had better be!

But Narell's voice sounded strained. 'I'm afraid that this man wouldn't take no for an answer. He insisted he speak to you.'

Sophie pulled a face.

'Insisted, did he?' she mused aloud. 'I'm not sure I like men who insist! Who is it?'

'It's...it's...' Narell cleared her throat, as if she

couldn't quite believe the name she was saying. 'It's Don Luis de la Camara.'

Luis.

Luis!

Sophie gripped the desk as if holding on to it for dear life. How mad, how crazy—that just the mention of his name was enough to bring her out into a cold sweat.

She felt excitement. Gut-wrenching and stomach-melting excitement. And then, hard on the heels of excitement came guilt. She felt its icy heat pin-pricking at her brow.

Just what was it about Luis de la Camara? She knew what kind of man he was. Shallow and sexy and completely out of bounds, and yet here she was now, calm and rational Sophie—Sophie who was supposed to be excited at the thought of dating Oliver—only now her heart was racing like a speeding train as she stared at the phone. Oliver was forgotten, and in his place exploded the dark presence of the most formidable man she had ever met.

But she pulled herself together, wondering why the arrogant Spaniard was ringing her here, at work, and *demanding* to speak to her, no less!

Ruing the day that her cousin had ever married him, Sophie gave a reluctant nod. 'OK, Narell. You can put him through.'

'Right.'

There was a momentary pause and then Sophie heard the unmistakable voice of Luis de la Camara, pouring like rich, sensual honey down through the intercom, and despite her good intentions she felt the slow wash of awareness creeping colour across her pale cheeks. He's married, she reminded herself, and he's married to your cousin. A man you despise, remember?

But animosity was an acquired skill she had learned along the way. She had had to teach herself to hate him. Far better to hate a man than to admit that he excited you in a way which was as frightening as it was inappropriate. And how could you feel anything other than hate for a man who could look at a woman with pure, undiluted lust in his eyes—just days before he was due to be married to her cousin?

'Soph-ie?'

He said her name as no one else did. The slight lilt to the voice, the faintest idiomatic Spanish accent which could send goosebumps all over your skin. She hastily clicked the switch down and grabbed the receiver—the last thing she wanted was the amplification of those dark, richly accented tones filling her office.

'This is she,' she answered crisply. She put her pen down. 'Well, this is certainly a surprise, Luis.' And how was that for understatement?

'Yes.'

His voice sounded unfamiliar. Heavy. Hard. Burdened. And Sophie suddenly felt some ghastly premonition shiver its way over her skin as logic replaced her first instinctive reaction to hearing him. Her voice rose in fright. 'What's happened? Why are you ringing me at work?'

There was a moment of silence which only increased her foreboding, because Sophie had never heard Luis hesitate before. Indecision was not on his agenda. Some men were never at a loss for words and de la Camara was a prime example.

'What is it?' she whispered. 'What's wrong?'

'Are you sitting down?'

'Yes! Luis, for God's sake—*tell* me!'

In another world, another country away, Luis flinched. There was no easy way to say it, nothing he could do to ease the painful words. 'It's Miranda,' he began slowly. 'I am afraid to have to tell you, Sophie, that there has been a terrible accident. Your cousin...she has been killed. *Murio en un accidente de coche,*' he finished on a note of disbelief, as if only repeating the words in his native tongue could make him believe the terrible truth himself.

A cry was torn from Sophie's throat, so that she sounded like a wounded animal. 'No!'

'It is true,' he said.

'She's dead? Miranda is dead?' she questioned, as if, even now, he still had the opportunity to deny it. To make it go away.

'*Sì*. I am sorry, Soph-ie. So very sorry.'

Buffeting against the sick feeling in her stomach, the words punched their way home.

Dead! Miranda dead? 'But she can't be dead!' Sophie whimpered. How could a beautiful woman of twenty-five be no more? 'Say it isn't true, Luis.'

'Do you not think that if I could I would?' he said, and his deep voice sounded almost gentle as he carried on with the grim story. 'She died in a car crash earlier today.'

'No.' She shuddered, and closed her eyes.

Until an even more horrific scenario reared its terrifying head and they snapped open again. 'What about Teodoro?' she cried, her heart clenching with fear as she thought about her adorable little nephew. 'He—he wasn't with her, was he?'

'In the early hours of the morning?' he questioned heavily. 'No, Sophie, he was not with her. My son was tucked up in bed, safely asleep.'

'Oh, thank God!' she breathed, and, just as a great wave of grief pierced her like a dagger, so did his words imprint themselves on her consciousness.

If Teodoro was tucked up safely in bed, then what was Miranda doing out in the early hours of the morning—and how come Luis had not been injured? Unless...unless he *had* been injured. 'Were you hurt yourself, Luis?' she questioned unsteadily.

In the fan-cooled air of the vast hacienda, Luis's hard, dark features set themselves into bleak and unforgiving lines. 'I was not in the car,' he said roughly.

Though her thoughts were fragmented by the enormity of what he had told her, Sophie frowned in confusion. Why not? she wondered. Why was Miranda travelling in the early hours without her family?

Her fingers clenched themselves into a tight little fist. The whys and the wheres and the hows were not appropriate—not now, not when the cold practicalities of death must be dealt with in as sympathetic a way as possible.

And Luis must be grieving—he must be. Despite the ups and downs of a marriage which Sophie knew had definitely not been made in heaven. His wife— the mother of his son—had met a tragically early end, and, no matter what had gone on before, Luis's world had imploded.

Her own feelings about him didn't count—not at a

time like this. He was owed her condolences and not her hostility.

'I'm...I'm so sorry,' she said stiffly.

'Thank you,' he said, his voice flat. 'I rang to tell you the news myself rather than having the police contact you. And to enquire whether you wish me to ring your grandmother...'

His words reminded her of the awful task which lay ahead—of telling her elderly and now frail grandmother what had happened. Sophie drew in a painful breath, thankful that her cousin's parents had been spared the ordeal of learning the fate of their beautiful daughter. For wasn't the premature death of a child the most terrible bereavement of all—even if they *had* treated Miranda with a kind of absent carelessness?

Miranda's parents had been nomads at heart, inveterate travellers who had journeyed to all four corners of the earth, greedily seeking out new experiences, never growing tired of the adventure of the unexplored. Until one day when their light aircraft had plummeted out of the sky and into the unforgiving mountains. Miranda had been just seventeen at the time, and soon after that, she had begun to live as though there were no tomorrow.

And now there never would be, not for her.

'No.' Biting back her tears, Sophie slowly let the word out. 'I will tell my grandmother myself, in person. It'll be easier...' She swallowed. She wouldn't break down in front of him, she wouldn't. 'Less painful, coming from me.' And try somehow to contact her own parents, who were having their own holiday of a lifetime, ensconced in luxury on some vast, ocean-going liner.

'You're sure?' he questioned.

'Yes.'

'It will be...hard,' he said, but his voice was uncharacteristically soft now, soft as butter. 'She is an old woman now.'

She steeled herself not to react to that murmuring voice, because it was vital that she remained impervious to Luis de la Camara—for all their sakes. 'It is thoughtful of you to care.'

Did she mock him with that cool, unfathomable tone of hers? 'Of course. She is family, Sophie—what did you expect?'

What *did* she expect? She didn't know, and she wondered how he could ask her a question like that at a time like this.

She hadn't expected her beloved Miranda to die so needlessly, or for her nephew to grow up without a mother, so far away from the land of her birth.

Teo.

Just the thought of him focused Sophie's grief into energy and resolution. 'Wh-when is the funeral?'

'On Monday.'

Which gave her three days.

'I'll be there. I'll fly out on Sunday.'

And, to Luis's appalled horror, he felt the stirring of triumph and the impossible ache of knowing that soon he would see her once more, and he cursed the body which betrayed him so completely. 'Contact my home or my office to let me know the times of your flight,' he said tightly. 'You will have to fly to Madrid and then take a connection on to Pamplona. I will arrange to have a car pick you up at the airport. Have you got that?'

'Thank you,' she said, thinking how in control he sounded, until she remembered that he was in control—always—and that, whatever happened, it was Luis de la Camara who was calling the shots.

'*Adios,* Sophie,' he drawled softly.

With a shaking hand, Sophie let the phone fall down into its cradle, and at the harsh finality of the sound reaction set in at last. She stared blankly at the wall in front of her, her mind spinning with disbelief as she thought of Miranda.

Her poor cousin—dying alone in a strange, foreign country! Poor, sweet Miranda—envied by so many women, solely because she was married to a man so universally desired. A man whose child she had borne, whose money she had enjoyed, but whose heart had always been tantalisingly locked away from her.

A man, moreover, whose black eyes glittered with such stark sexual promise that Sophie could not imagine that he would have been able to remain faithful for even the first year of marriage.

After all, *she* had ignored the unmistakable invitation she had read there, but that was because she loved Miranda. She doubted whether other women would have such scrupulous morals where Luis de la Camara was concerned.

And now a little baby would now have to grow up without a mother.

Sophie's gaze was drawn to the silver-framed photo which stood in pride of place on her desk and she picked it up and studied it.

It showed Teodoro and it had been taken just before his first birthday, only a few short weeks ago.

He was an adorable child, but Teodoro's looks owed very little to her cousin's exquisite blonde beauty. Instead his face was stamped with the magnificent dominance of his father's colouring, and as she stared at it the image of his hard and handsome face came flooding back into her mind with bitter clarity.

Gleaming black eyes, fringed with sinfully thick lashes and hair which was as dark as the moonless night she had first met him. When she had virtually bumped into him in the deli at the end of her road and he had stopped dead, stared at her intensely, as if he knew her from somewhere, as if he couldn't quite believe his eyes.

And the feeling had been mutual. When just for a moment her heart had leapt with a wild and unexpected joy. And an unmistakable lust which had set up a slow, sweet aching.

The kind of thing which wasn't supposed to happen to sensible city girls who were cool and calm in matters of the heart.

Was it possible to fall in love in a split-second? she remembered helplessly thinking as she gazed at the proud, aristocratic features she seemed to have spent her whole life waiting for.

She'd seen his eyes darken, the heated flare of awareness which moved along the angular curve of his high cheekbones. His lush lips had unconsciously parted and she'd seen a thoroughly instinctive movement as his tongue flicked through to moisten them, and outrageously she had imagined that tongue on her body...in her body...

She had never been looked at with quite such insolent and arrogant appraisal before. He wants me, she'd thought, with the warm flooding of awareness. And I want him, too. She had found herself wondering whether she would be able to resist him if he touched her, while at the same time asking if she had completely taken leave of her senses.

And then Miranda had appeared, carrying a bottle of champagne, her mouth falling open in surprise. 'Sophie! Good heavens!' she exclaimed, and glanced up at him, not seeming to notice the brittle tension in the air which surrounded them. 'What an amazing coincidence! We were just on our way to see you, weren't we, darling?'

Darling?

With a jolt which went deeper than disappointment, Sophie registered dully that Miranda was possessively touching the arm of the tall, dark man with the glittering eyes and the softly gleaming lips. And the champagne...

'Are you—are you celebrating something?' she questioned with a sinking heart as she quickly realised exactly what they must be celebrating.

'We sure are! Sophie—I'd like to introduce you to Don Luis de la Camara,' Miranda announced proudly and then smiled up into the dark, shuttered face. 'Luis—this is my cousin, Sophie Mills.'

'Your cousin?' he questioned with a frown, and his voice was as rich and dark as bitter chocolate. The predatory look had disappeared in an instant, and Sophie had seen the rueful shrug which replaced it, knowing that Don Luis de la Camara would never look at her in that way again. As the cousin of his wife-to-be, she was much too close to home to play around with. But a man who looked like that just days before his wedding *would* play around. Sophie recognised that with a blinding certainty and she hated him for it.

'Well, we spent all our holidays together—so we're more like sisters, really!' Miranda smiled her wide, infectious smile. 'Sophie—we're getting married! Isn't it wonderful? Luis has asked me to marry him!'

Sophie shuddered as she remembered the jealousy which had ripped through her. To be jealous of your own cousin! But she had forced a smile and hugged Miranda and given Luis her hand, all too aware of the warm tingle as their flesh touched. And he had bent and raised her fingertips to his mouth, in an old-fashioned and courtly style—faithful to the manner of the Spanish aristocrat he was, his black eyes seeming to mock and to tantalise her in tandem.

They had gone back to her flat and drunk champagne and chinked glasses and toasted the future. But while Miranda had fizzed with life the Spaniard had sat watchfully, choosing his words with care, looking so right and yet so wrong in Sophie's flat and her world. Because he was Miranda's, she had reminded herself. Miranda's.

With an effort she pushed away the disturbing memories and forced herself back to the present. Concentrating on the image of the child in the photo instead of the potent sexuality of his father.

At least Teodoro's face still had the softness of innocence and she could see little of the indomitable nature which so defined Luis.

She wondered what would happen to Teodoro now—whether his mother's memory would be allowed to fade until it was so distant that it was almost forgotten. Sophie bit her lip. What chance would he have of learning about his mother and the land of his mother's birth?

And suddenly a sense of duty dulled some of the raw edge of sorrow. Luis shall not take him from us entirely, she vowed. I will fight for the opportunity to get to know him as if he were my own! And he will know me, too. With a trembling hand, she buzzed through to Narell to ask her to book her flight to Spain.

And then she washed her face, dragged a comb through her hair and called Liam Hollingsworth into the office, who took one look at her and started.

'What the hell have you been doing to yourself?' he demanded. 'Are you OK?'

Her voice still trembling slightly, she said, 'Not really, no.'

'For God's sake, Sophie—what's the matter? What's happened to you?'

She framed the unbelievable words. 'It's my cousin, Miranda,' she told him. 'She's been...killed in an accident. I've...I've got to go and break the news to my grandmother—'

'Oh, my God.'

'And th-then fly on to Spain to the funeral.'

'Oh, honey!' He was round her side of the desk in an instant, staring down at her with a look of dazed concern on his face as she began to cry. 'Honey!'

'Oh, Liam!' she sobbed.

'Come here,' he said gently, and put his arms around her.

She allowed herself to cry a little more, but after a couple of moments she broke away and went to stand by the window, staring out at a world which no longer looked the same place. 'I still can't believe it,' she said dully.

'What happened?' he asked.

'I know very few facts. Just that she was in a car crash. I was too...too shocked to ask for any details, I guess.'

'How did you find out?'

'Her husband, Luis—he rang me from Spain to tell me.'

He frowned. 'That's the millionaire guy—the one you can't stand?'

'That's the one,' she said tightly, thinking how much more complex the truth was than a simple case of not being able to stand the man.

'And when's the funeral?'

'Monday. I'm flying out on Sunday.' She sighed. 'Oh, Liam, I don't know if I can bear it.'

He nodded understandingly. 'Well, it'll be hard, but at least after that you need never meet again.'

Sophie shook her head. 'But it isn't that easy. I wish it was. I can't just spirit Luis out of my life, however much I might want to. Don't forget—he's the father of my nephew, and I feel I owe it to Miranda, and to *Teodoro*...' The words seemed to come from an unknown place deep inside her. 'To fight for him.'

Liam stared at her. 'Fight for him?' he echoed. 'You surely don't mean you're going to apply for custody, Sophie? You wouldn't stand a hope in hell. Not if he's as rich and as powerful as you say he is. And he *is* the father.'

Tiredly, Sophie rubbed at her temples. 'I don't know what I mean—other than knowing I have to get out there. To let Teo know that he has relatives, and that we care.'

'And once the funeral is over? Will you come straight back?'

She met his eyes. 'I don't know. I can't commit to a time scale. But I'll still be able to do *some* work—I can always use my laptop, and you'll be able to manage here without me for a bit, won't you?'

'Of course we can manage,' he said quietly. 'We'll just miss you, that's all.'

'Thanks,' she whispered, and, gulping back more tears, she began to pack her briefcase.

She and Liam went way back.

They had met at university and discovered a shared sense of humour coupled with an ambition to make lots of money while having *fun*. Which had been how the Hollingsworth-Mills advertising agency had come about. Now they were tipped for the top. A combination of enthusiasm and employing bright young staff with similar high-reaching goals meant that Sophie and Liam were poised on the brink of unforeseen success.

But what did any of that matter at a time like this?

Feeling too shaky to drive safely, she took the train to Norfolk, her heart weeping for her grandmother as she walked up the path of her Norfolk country cottage, where she and Miranda had spent part of their school holidays, every summer without fail. They had walked for miles on the vast, empty beaches which were close by, and climbed trees and fed the fat ducks on the pond with pieces of bread.

And Sophie had watched as Miranda's beauty had become something more than breathtaking. Had seen for herself the bewitching power which that beauty gave her over men...

She rang the old-fashioned jingly-jangly doorbell, praying for the right words to tell her grandmother what had happened, and knowing that there were none which would not hurt.

But Felicity Mills was almost eighty, and there was little of life she hadn't seen. She took one look at Sophie's face. 'It's bad news,' she said flatly.

'Yes. It's Miranda—'

'She's dead,' said her grandmother woodenly. 'Isn't she?'

'How? How could you possibly have known that?' Sophie whispered, much later, when tears had been shed and they had sought some kind of comfort in old photographs of Miranda as a baby, then a sunny toddler and every other stage through to stunning bride. But Sophie hadn't wanted to linger on *that* photo—not when the dark face of Luis mocked her and stung her guilty conscience. 'How?' she asked again.

'I can't explain it,' sighed her grandmother. 'I just looked into your face and I knew. And, in a way, there was a dreadful inevitability about it. Miranda always flew too close to the sun. One day she was bound to get burned.'

'But how can you be so *accepting?*'

'How can I not? I have lived through war, my darling. You have to accept what you cannot change.'

She squeezed the old woman's hand. 'Is there—is there anything I can do for you, Granny?'

There was a long silence and Mrs Mills stared at her. 'There is one thing—but it may not be possible.

I'm too old and too frail to fly to Spain for the funeral—but I should like to see Teodoro again before I die.'

Sophie swallowed down the lump in her throat. Surely that wasn't too much to ask—even of Luis—not under these circumstances. 'Then I'll br-bring him to you,' she promised shakily. 'I promise.'

'But Luis might not allow it.'

Sophie's eyes glimmered with unshed tears. 'He must, Granny—he *must!*'

'It is a big favour to ask him. Tread carefully, Sophie—you know how fiercely possessive he is about his son and you know the kind of man you're dealing with,' her grandmother added drily. 'You know his reputation. Few would dare to cross him.'

'I'm hoping it won't come to that,' said Sophie, then stared up at her grandmother, her eyes confused. 'Don't you hate him, Granny? For making Miranda so unhappy?'

'Happiness is not the gift of one person to another,' answered her grandmother slowly. 'It takes two people to be happy. And hate is such a waste of emotion—and a total waste of time. What good would be served if I hated the father of my great-grandson?'

But if Sophie took hate out of the equation, then what did that leave her with? An overpowering attraction which she prayed had weakened with the passing of time.

All she wanted was to have grown immune to his powerful presence and his dark, unforgettable face. After all, she hadn't seen him since just after Teodoro's baptism, a year ago, when they had brought the baby over to England.

Sophie had deliberately kept her distance from

Luis, although she'd been able to feel those steely dark eyes watching her as she moved around the room. She'd wondered if he had broken his wedding vows yet, and when she'd had a moment had asked her cousin if anything was wrong, but Miranda had just shrugged her bare brown shoulders.

'Oh, Luis should have married a docile little Spanish girl who didn't want to set foot outside the door,' she had said bitterly. 'It seems that he can't cope with a wife who doesn't whoop for joy because she happens to live in the back of beyond.'

And Sophie had directed a look of icy-blue fire across the room at Luis, meeting nothing but cold mockery in return.

Sophie's plane touched down in Pamplona in the still blazing heat of an early Spanish evening and she hurried through Customs, her eyes scanning the arrivals bay, expecting to see a driver holding a card aloft with her name on it, but it took all of two seconds to see the tall and distinctive figure waiting there.

And one second to note the hard and glittering black eyes, the unsmiling mouth and the shuttered features. He was taller than every other man there, and his face still drew the eyes of women like a magnet. No, he hadn't changed, and Sophie's heart gave a violent and unwelcome lurch.

He stood in the crowd and yet he stood alone.

It seemed that Don Luis de la Camara had come to collect her in person.

CHAPTER TWO

Luis watched as Sophie walked through the arrivals lounge, unsmilingly observing the heads which turned to follow her as she walked, though she herself seemed completely oblivious of it. But of course she had the fair skin and hair which made the hearts of most male Spaniards melt, though none of the deliberately provocative style of her cousin.

He felt his pulse quicken and his blood thicken as she made her way towards him, her light cotton dress defining her slender legs and such delicate ankles that he was surprised they could support her weight at all. He remembered the very first time he had seen her, when she had captured his imagination with her natural beauty and grace, and such completely unself-conscious sexuality.

He had met her and wanted her in an instant and had despised the hot, sharp hunger she had inspired in him, a hunger which would never—could never— be satisfied.

And then she was standing in front of him, all honey-coloured hair and pale, translucent skin. As slender and as supple as a willow—with a look of almost grim determination glittering from the china-blue eyes.

Luis sensed danger in that determination, but he did not acknowledge it. Keeping his face a mask of formal courtesy, he inclined his head in greeting. To any other woman he might have given the traditional kiss on either cheek, but not this one. He had wanted to kiss her the first time he had seen her, but by then it was too late.

And now it was later still.

'Sophie.' A small, formal bow of his dark head. 'I trust that you have had a pleasant flight?'

He was so tall that she had to look up at him, and Sophie's heart sank as she realised that all that raw and vibrant masculinity was as intact and as potent as it had ever been. But the way he was speaking, he might as well have been enquiring about the weather. He certainly didn't sound like a bereft and newly-widowed man, and for the first time she wondered if tragedy had not, in fact, proved a convenient ending to an unhappy marriage.

She kept her face neutral—though God only knew how. 'It was smooth enough, thank-you.' Though in truth the hours had passed in a blur as she had tried to equip herself with the emotional strength to stay polite and impassive towards him.

She wondered what *his* emotional state was. Untouched, she would guess. There was no tell-tale red-rimming of the eyes, no hint that tears had been shed for the mother of his child—but then, whoever could imagine a man like Luis shedding tears?

Today, he looked remote and untouchable. His face was as cold and as hard as if it had been hewn from some pure, honey-coloured marble—but only a blind fool would have denied that he was an outrageously attractive man.

He stood at well over six feet and his shoulders were broad and strong. Lightweight summer trousers did little to conceal the powerful shaft of his thighs, and beneath the short-sleeved cotton shirt his arms looked as though they were capable of splitting open the trunk of a tree without effort.

But it was the face which was truly remarkable—it effortlessly bore the stamp of generations of Spanish aristocracy. Proud, almost cruel—with only the lush lines of his mouth breaking up the unremitting hardness of his features. A mouth so lush that it exuded the unmistakable sensuality which surrounded him like an invisible cloak.

No wonder her cousin had fallen for his devastating brand of charisma, Sophie thought, and a sudden sense of sadness left her feeling almost winded.

He saw the hint of tears which misted the Mediterranean-blue of her eyes. All the fire and determination had been wiped out, her sadness betrayed by the slight, vulnerable tremble of her lips, and he reached out to take her hand. It felt so tiny and cool when enclosed in his.

'You have my condolences, little one,' he said gravely.

She lifted her chin, swallowing the tears away, and removed her hand from his warm grasp, despairing of the not-so-subtle chemistry between them which made her want to leave it exactly where it was. 'Thank you,' she returned softly, letting her gaze fall to the ground, just in case those perceptive black eyes had the power to read exactly what was going on in her mind.

He looked at her downcast head and the stiff, defensive set of her shoulders. She was grieving for her cousin, he reminded himself—although the defiant, almost angry spark in her eyes on greeting him had little to do with grief, surely?

'Come, Sophie,' he said. 'The car awaits us and we have some drive ahead of us. Here, let me carry your suitcase for you.'

It sounded more like a command than an offer to help, and, although Sophie could have and would have carried it perfectly well on her own, she knew that it was pointless trying to refuse a man like Luis.

He would insist. Instinct told her that just as accurately as anything her cousin had ever divulged. He came from a long line of imperious men, men who saw clearly delineated lines between the roles of the sexes.

Spain might now be as modern as the rest of Europe, but men like Luis did not change with the times. They still saw themselves as conquerors—superior and supreme—and master of all they surveyed.

She could see women looking at him as they passed. Coy little side-glances and sometimes an eager and undisguised kind of hunger. She couldn't see into his eyes from here, and wondered if he was giving them hungry little glances back.

Probably. Hadn't he done just that with her, before he had discovered her identity?

And of course now, without a wife, he could behave exactly as he pleased—he could exert that powerful sexuality and get any woman he wanted into his bed.

The airport buildings were refreshingly air-conditioned, but once outside the force of the heat hit her like a velvet fist, even though the intensity of the midday sun had long since passed.

He saw her flinch beneath the impact of the raw heat, and he knew that he must not forget to warn her about the dangers of the sun. 'Why don't you take your jacket off?' he suggested suavely.

'I'll be fine,' she said tightly.

His mouth hardened. 'As you wish.'

Thankfully, the car was as cool and air-conditioned as the airport terminal, and she waited until he had driven out of the car park and was setting off towards the open road before turning to him.

'Where's Teodoro?'

'At home.'

'Oh.'

He heard the disappointment in her voice. 'You imagined that I would have brought him out on a hot summer's night to await a plane which could have been delayed?'

'So who's looking after him?'

Did her question hint at reprimand? he wondered incredulously. Did she imagine that he had left the child alone? 'He is in the charge of his *ninera*...' He saw her frown with confusion and realised that she, like her cousin, spoke almost no Spanish at all. 'His mother's help,' he translated immediately.

'Not any more,' said Sophie quietly.

'No,' he agreed heavily. There was a short, painful pause and he shot her a side-glance. 'How did your grandmother take it?'

Sophie bit her lip. Would it sound unfeeling and uncaring if she told him that, although the news had saddened her grandmother, it had come as no great surprise. What had she said? Miranda had flown far too close to the sun... But if she told Luis that then surely it would do a disservice to her cousin's memory.

'What happened, Luis? How did Miranda die?'

He pulled in a breath, choosing his words carefully, remembering that he must respect both her position and her grief.

How much of the truth did she want? he wondered. Or need?

'No one knows exactly what happened,' he said.

She knew evasion when she heard it. And faint distaste, too. She wondered what had caused it.

'There's something you're not telling me.'

He didn't answer, just kept his dark eyes straight on the road ahead, so that all she could see was his hard, shadowed profile, and Sophie said the first thing which came into her head. 'Had the driver been drinking?'

There was a short, bald silence. But what would be the point in keeping it from her? It would soon be a matter of public record.

'*Sì. El habia estrado bebiendo.*' He was thinking in his native language and the words just slipped out of their own accord.

She spoke hardly any Spanish, but Sophie could tell what his answer was from the flat, heavy tone of his voice. She closed her eyes in despair. 'Oh, God! Drinking very much? Do you know?'

'The tests have not yet been completed.'

A sense of outrage and of anger burned deep within her—and for the first time it was directed at Miranda instead of the man beside her. Her cousin had been a mother, for heaven's sake, with all the responsibility which went with that. She'd had a young child to look after—so how could she have been so stupid to have gone off in a car where the driver had been drinking?

Unless she hadn't known.

But Miranda hadn't been *stupid*. She'd been headstrong and impetuous sometimes, but she definitely hadn't been stupid.

Unless this man beside her, who drove the car so expertly through the darkened Spanish countryside—unless *he* had made her life such a misery that she hadn't *cared* about common sense and personal safety.

She shook her head. There was absolutely no justification for Miranda going off with a drink-driver. Whatever the state of her marriage, she had always been free to walk away from it.

She shot a side-glance at the darkly angled profile. Or had she? What if Miranda had tried to walk away, taking Teodoro with her? Couldn't and wouldn't Luis have used his power and his influence to try to stop her?

She turned her head and pressed her cheek against the coolness of the window and looked out, only half taking in the wild beauty of the silhouetted landscape beyond.

The air was violet-dark and huge stars spotted the sky with splodges of silver. They looked so much bigger and brighter than the stars back in England, and her home seemed suddenly a long way away. And then she remembered. She had responsibilities, too.

Through sheer effort of will she reached down in her briefcase to retrieve her mobile phone.

'Will this work out here?' she questioned.

His eyes narrowed as they briefly glanced over at

the little technological toy. 'That depends on what type it is.' He shrugged. 'But I have another you can use, if yours can't get a signal.'

'You have a mobile phone? Here? In the car?'

His mouth twisted into a grim smile. 'Did you imagine that I communicate by bush telegraph? You will find every modern comfort, even here in La Rioja, Sophie.'

And yet his words seemed to mock the reality of his presence. 'Modern comfort,' he had said, when with his dark and brooding looks he seemed to represent the very opposite of all that was modern.

He watched as she punched out a string of numbers. 'Is your call so very important that it cannot wait until we reach the hacienda?' he questioned softly.

'I have to let someone know that I arrived safely.'

'A man, I suppose?'

'Actually, yes. It is a man.' Not that it was any of his business, but let him draw his own conclusions, which he very probably would. And obviously if it was a man then she *must* be sleeping with him!

The connection was made. 'Liam? Hi, it's me!'

Beside her, Luis stared into the abyss of the road ahead, wondering if she shared the same sexual freedom as her cousin. His gaze wandered unseen to her legs, and he was unprepared for the sudden buck of jealousy at the thought of those slender, pale limbs wrapped around the body of another.

He reminded himself that he knew women like these—with their blonde hair and their big blue eyes and their gym-toned bodies. The bodies of women but with the minds of men. They acted as men had been acting for years...they saw something they wanted and they went all out to get it.

And she had wanted him once, before she had discovered that he was to marry her cousin, just as he had wanted her—a wanting like no other. A thunderbolt which had struck him and left him aching and dazed in its wake. And it had taken her as well, he had seen that for himself, as unmistakable as the long shadows cast by the sun.

He listened in unashamedly to her conversation as the car ate up the lonely miles.

'No, I'm in the car now. With Luis.' A pause. 'Not really, no.' Another pause and then she glanced at her watch. 'It's just gone nine. No, that's OK. Yeah, I know, but I can't really talk now. Yes. OK. Thanks, Liam. I hope so, too. OK, I'll do that. I'll call you on Saturday.'

She cut the connection and put the phone back in the glove box.

'Thank you,' she said stiffly.

There was a soft, dangerous pause as he saw her cross one slim, pale leg over the other. 'Does he hunger for you already, Sophie?' he asked silkily, and the blood began to pound in his head.

She couldn't believe her ears. It was such an outrageous thing to say that for a moment Sophie was left speechless.

'I *beg* your pardon?'

He gave a half-smile in the darkness. So beautiful and so unintentionally sensual, and yet she could turn her voice to frost when it suited her.

'Actually,' she said, 'Liam is my business partner.'

'Ah.'

Something dark and sensual conveyed danger in that simple word, and Sophie felt her heart race with something more than fear. 'Is—is there going to be anyone else staying at the hacienda?'

He heard the tremor in her voice and it amused him, even while it frustrated and tempted him. Was it him she wasn't sure she trusted? Or herself? Did she want him still?

'You mean apart from Teodoro?' he questioned casually.

'You know I do.'

'One of the women from the village comes in to help with meals. And Pirro, who is my cook and gardener, lives in the hacienda with Salvadora, his wife. She is Teodoro's *ninera*—as she was mine before, when I was a child.'

'Since...when?' asked Sophie, thinking that Salvadora must be getting on a bit if she used to look after Luis. 'Since before Miranda died?'

'Oh, long before that,' he murmured evasively. 'My son is devoted to her. You will see that for yourself.'

A wave of indignation washed over her, and something far more primitive followed on its heels. Had Miranda effectively been elbowed out of the way? she wondered. The Englishwoman pushed aside for the mummy-substitute—a fellow Spaniard who could teach Teodoro the language and traditions of his father?

Well, not for much longer, vowed Sophie. Somehow she would teach him something of his mother's heritage. She scrabbled around again in her handbag, this time for a hairbrush.

His mouth curved. 'There is no one here to impress with your beauty, *mia querida*,' he drawled. Apart from him. Because when she lifted her head like that he could see the long, pure line of her neck and the perfect curve of her breasts.

'That was not my intention.' She carefully brushed out the fine, honey-coloured hair, which felt all sticky through the many hours of travelling. 'I merely wanted to make myself presentable on my arrival.' She could see distant lights. 'Are we almost there?'

'Yes, we are just about to pass through the vineyards.'

She looked out of the window again. The famous La Camara vineyards. The largest and most impressive in the region, with grapes yielding a rich harvest which was turned into exquisite wines exported the world over.

She had once drunk La Camara Rioja herself, at a very smart dinner party in London where the host had brought the fine wine out with a reverent air and everyone had sipped it with avid and awed appreciation.

All except for Sophie. She had managed no more than a couple of mouthfuls, feeling that the stuff might choke her as she remembered the proud, arrogant face and the mocking black eyes.

'You aren't drinking, Sophie?' the host had commented.

It would have been a real party-stopper if she had explained that she was related by marriage to the owner of the vineyard, a man who made her blood sing and her temper flare in equal measure whenever she thought about him.

And she didn't want to think about him.

Muffling a little gulp, she sat back in the seat and closed her eyes.

Luis glanced over at her, frowning a little as he saw the tension which tightened her shoulders, wondering if she was about to cry, and instinctively his voice gentled. 'Did you eat on the plane?'

'No. It was horrible little bits of unrecognisable food in plastic trays. And I wasn't hungry.'

'We will have dinner when we arrive.'

'Surely it's too late for dinner?'

'But we eat very late in Spain, Sophie, did you not know that? Did you not know that the Spanish are more awake than anyone in Europe—and not only because they regard going to bed before three a.m. as a kind of personal dishonour?'

She shook her head. 'I've only ever been to Spain once, and that was for the weekend when Teodoro was baptised.'

'Then you have missed very much.' His voice had deepened now, was made almost kind with something which sounded like compassion. 'I wish this time it could be under happier circumstances, *querida*. It is a pity that you will see little of my country before you return home.'

There was an expectant silence and Sophie ignored it.

But Luis did not. 'By the way, you didn't tell me how long you were going to be staying?'

'No. No, I didn't.'

'And?'

She was glad of the darkness because the way he

framed that single syllable was nothing short of intimidating.

'I'm not sure.' Until she had reached a position of trust which ensured that she would be able to fly Teo back to England for a short holiday to see his great-grandmother. But now was definitely not the time to tell him *that*.

And then she reminded herself that as his guest he was owed certain courtesies. 'That is, I would like to stay for at least a few days, maybe longer, if that's OK with you. I'd like to see a bit of Teo.'

Unseen, his eyes narrowed. No, it was not 'OK with him.' He did not want this woman in his home for a minute longer than necessary—for reasons which were both simple and highly complex. He wanted her, but he could never have her. Not now. Not ever.

'Spaniards are famous for their hospitality, Sophie,' he said softly. 'And therefore my home is yours for as long as you wish it.'

Sophie nodded. Unless he made it impossible for her to remain, of course. 'Thank you,' she said stiffly.

'De nada,' he answered.

The car swept up a gravelled drive, and through the broad canopy of strange trees Sophie saw the welcoming lights of the large hacienda.

He opened the door of the car and she thought that she caught the drift of oranges and lemons, the soft night air thick with the scent of exotic blooms. She gazed at the imposing building which looked as if it had been there for ever. There was a sense of beauty, and of history, which she found impossible to ignore, despite the heartbreaking circumstances which had brought her here.

And then she was caught in the ebony glitter of those beautiful, mocking eyes.

'Welcome to my home, Sophie,' he said softly.

CHAPTER THREE

THE interior of the hacienda was cool and spacious, and their arrival must have been heard, because as soon as Luis had taken Sophie's jacket and put her suitcase down an elderly woman appeared from further down the hall. Her face creased into a warm smile as she looked up at Luis.

'*Buenas noches, Don Luis.*'

Sophie saw his hard face briefly soften with affection as he bent to kiss the woman on both cheeks.

'*Buenas noches, Salvadora.*' He said something rapidly in Spanish, and then, reverting to slow and careful English, he spoke again. 'Sophie, this is Salvadora, Teodoro's *ninera*. Salvadora, this is Sophie Mills, Miranda's cousin.'

'*Buenas noches,*' said Sophie politely, though her doubtful thoughts in the car were borne out by the woman's appearance. She really looked far too frail to be in charge of a boy aged just over a year.

Salvadora's expression was wary, Sophie thought. Her old eyes narrowed as she looked her up and down, but the wariness was replaced with a slight, formal bow.

'*Buenas noches, Señorita Mills,*' she replied slowly. 'I regret very much the sudden death of your cousin.'

Sophie bit her lip. No tears, she told herself. They could wait for later. 'Thank you.' And then, with an almighty effort, she gave a trembling smile. 'You speak very good English, Salvadora.'

Salvadora nodded in solemn acknowledgement. 'Thank you. It was always so. Don Luis had an English tutor when he was a very little boy, and so I learnt the language, too!'

Sophie tried to imagine Luis as a little boy, learning English, but it wasn't easy to picture him with the same soft, innocent face as his son.

'And, of course, it is essential that any *ninera* of Teodoro understands the language of his mother,' said a deep voice, butting into her thoughts, and Sophie turned to Luis, a question in her eyes.

'Why?'

'Because otherwise the two women would have been unable to communicate, wouldn't they?' he offered drily, seeing the look of genuine surprise on her face, and his mouth hardened. Did she imagine that he would wish to deny his son his English heritage? Did she think him some kind of devil, then?

Not for the first time, Sophie wondered why Miranda had bothered having anyone to help her with Teo at all. She hadn't had a job outside the home, nor had much to do inside the home, judging from her phone calls. She remembered how delighted her cousin had been on discovering the true extent of Luis's wealth and influence.

'He's not just gorgeous—he's *loaded,* Sophie! Absolutely loaded!'

Sophie had frowned, wondering if the financial insecurities of her childhood were blinding Miranda to reality. 'Yes, but money isn't everything. Honestly it isn't. As long as you're happy, Miranda—that's the most important thing.'

'Oh, I'm happy, all right!' Miranda had said. 'Who wouldn't be in my situation, with a man like Luis? And it's so *wonderful* having servants, Sophie, I can't tell you!'

Sophie hadn't approved of Miranda's attitude and approved of her own fleeting pang of jealousy even less. But she had said nothing. And even if she had, it wouldn't have made any difference. Miranda had always been determined to fight tooth and nail for what she wanted, and she had wanted Luis.

And who in their right mind could blame her for that?

His deep voice broke into her thoughts.

'Salvadora will show you to your room now, Sophie,' said Luis, who was watching her very closely and wondering what had caused her to frown like that, caused the tiny goosebumps that made her slender arms look so cold and so vulnerable.

That piercing black look distracted her, but she forced herself to remember the main reason why she was here. 'Can I...can I see Teodoro first? Please?'

He thought how pale she looked, and how tense—the faint shadows beneath her eyes making her lovely face look almost haunted. He shook his head decisively. 'First you should eat something.'

'But—'

'No buts, Sophie. You may shower and change first, should you wish, and then we will eat dinner.'

She wasn't used to such dominance, or to letting a man call the shots like that, and she was just about to protest when some warning light which glittered so imperiously from the jet-dark eyes told her that her protests would land on deaf ears. She would see her nephew when *he* chose to let her!

And a whole meal to get through first. 'You don't have to bother with dinner,' she said, unwilling to sit down alone with him. Suspecting that she would find it impossible to keep up pleasantries for an entire meal. Or to keep forbidden thoughts at bay. 'I could always have a sandwich in my room.'

Luis's eyes narrowed with irritation at her clumsy refusal of his hospitality. 'It is inconceivable that a guest should travel all this way and not be offered sustenance. And besides, you have a long and difficult day ahead of you tomorrow. You will join me in the dining room.'

There he went again—commanding her instead of asking her! What would he do if she insisted on staying in her room? Though wouldn't that be stupid? She could hardly hide away the whole time she was here. Better get used to eating with him, no matter how much the idea managed to appall and yet excite her at the same time. And surely it was inappropriate to even be *thinking* such thoughts at a time like this?

She nodded. 'Very well. I'll get changed and come down again.'

'I will be waiting.'

Sophie felt very slightly out of control as she followed the old woman upstairs, wondering how on earth you could get used to having your every wish catered for.

Although she earned a more than comfortable salary, she had always prided herself on her independence. Unlike most of her friends, she did not have anyone to clean her apartment for her, and she did not send her shirts out to be laundered. Her mother had always drummed into her that delegating life's unpleasant tasks made you remote from life itself.

How different life appeared to be here, with gardeners and cooks and women who cared for your children.

Her shuttered room was cool and dominated by a large, plain bed, covered with snowy white linen. A vase of white flowers which she didn't recognise had been placed on the dresser and a huge fan spun around from the ceiling to shift the warm and heavy air. She would have liked to just lie down and close her eyes, but she knew that her implacable host would be waiting.

'The bathroom is through there,' pointed Salvadora. 'Is there anything you need, *señorita?*'

Peace would be close to the top of her list. But there would be no peace for Sophie, not in the foreseeable future—not with Luis present, looking like some dark and alluring angel. But she put him out of her mind because there was something far more important she needed to know.

'How is Teodoro?' she questioned falteringly, and just the mention of his name brought a little warmth creeping back into her heart. 'Is he missing his mother very much?'

Salvadora did not answer for a moment, as if she did not understand, yet it was a simple enough question.

'Of course,' said Salvadora carefully. 'He knows that something is wrong. He cries. But soon we will make him laugh again.'

Sophie felt sick. *He knows something is wrong.* Something *wrong?* The child had lost his mother, for heaven's sake, and here was Salvadora making it sound as though he had thrown his rattle out of his pram! But Salvadora had power, too. Power over Teodoro, which came from being close to him. She needed to make the older woman realise that she cared about her nephew, and that was why she was here.

'I hope to help make him laugh, too,' she said softly. 'Thank you, Salvadora. Please tell Luis that I shall be down shortly.'

'*Sì, señorita.*'

Sophie carefully hung up her clothes, and it was a relief to strip off her travel-crushed things and to stand beneath the invigorating jets of the shower and wash away the grit of the journey.

She plaited her still damp hair and put on a fresh cotton dress. Drawstring trousers would have made her feel more relaxed, but she suspected that an evening meal in the de la Camara house would have a certain formality to it.

She was right.

When she entered the dining room it was to see Luis already seated at a long, polished dining table laid for two and that he, too, had changed—and there was absolutely nothing she could do about the sudden rapid beating of her heart.

Gone were the short-sleeved shirt and the lightweight trousers. In their place he had donned a snowy-white shirt, a filmy garment which tantalisingly hinted at the hard, muscular torso beneath. He had left the top two buttons of the shirt unbuttoned and on view was the soft, silken gleam of olive skin, and the sprinkling of dark hair. As he rose to his feet she could see stark black trousers which hugged the narrow jut of his hips and moulded themselves to the powerful shaft of his thighs. The overall effect was to make him look like someone who had just stepped out of one of the portraits of his ancestors which lined the walls, and Sophie's mouth dried into dust.

'Good evening,' he said formally as he stood up. 'I trust that you found everything to your satisfaction?'

For a moment the power to walk properly left her and she stood unsteadily in the doorway, her trembling fingers gripping the door handle for support as she realised that she was alone with this magnificent man she both desired and feared, and in such a magnificent setting.

He knitted his dark brows together, seeing the way that her face had paled to the colour of the whitest lily, making her skin look almost translucent in comparison. Afraid that she might suddenly faint, he swiftly moved towards her.

'Something is wrong?'

Something was wrong! Everything was wrong! She was feeling everything she wasn't supposed to feel, didn't want to feel. Dark, illicit thoughts which enveloped her with tantalising fingers, locking her into forbidden fantasies. She found herself praying for some kind of merciful release. She should be concentrating on Teodoro, and on Miranda's memory—not on the bone-melting effect of her host.

She shook her head. 'No, I'm fine.'

'Then please sit down.' He pulled out a chair for

her and then returned to his own seat. 'For you do not look fine to me.'

Sophie sank down gratefully and, in an effort to distract herself, looked not into the inky glitter of his eyes but at the formality of the setting instead.

The table was set with the finest silver and fresh with flowers and gently glowing with candlelight. It was the kind of table that you would probably need a pool cue to propel the pepper and salt from one end to the other, it was so long. She could see that some cold soup had already been placed there, and never had a sandwich in her room seemed so attractive. Or so safe.

'You shouldn't have gone to all this trouble for me!' She swallowed.

'Trouble?' A dark brow was arched in arrogant query. 'I can assure you that dinner is exactly as usual.'

She supposed it was—he didn't strike her as the kind of man who would eat his dinner on a tray in front of the television! 'Oh, I see,' she said, rather weakly.

Luis studied her. He had not been expecting her down yet, imagining her to be transforming her appearance in the privacy of her room. He noticed that her face was as untouched as it had been at the airport. She had not bothered to apply any make-up and her hair was still wet from the shower. The overall effect made her look fresh and clean and much younger than her years. Almost innocent. Luis's mouth twisted into a cynical line.

He was used to women using every weapon in their armoury in order to impress him. Carefully applied make-up and gowns designed to show off magnificent cleavages, or the length of their legs. At a time like this he would not have expected finery—but he had been anticipating that a little extra effort would be made.

Clearly, Sophie Mills was not trying to impress him!

Her cotton dress was as unassuming as it was possible to be, and yet its simplicity made the curve of her high breasts all the more beguiling. She was an unnerving combination of innocence and experience, and Luis felt the slow and reluctant flicker of arousal. Perhaps the effect was deliberate, he thought. Perhaps she knew precisely how a man would react to such an innocent woman look, with her bare, pouting lips which cried out to be kissed.

'Please,' he said coolly, 'drink your soup.'

She picked up her spoon and sipped at it, but in between sips her eyes were drawn irresistibly to her host.

How daunting he looked, and not just because he had seated himself at the far end of the table. No. There was something unapproachable in the cold magnificence and the warning light which gleamed in the unfathomable depths of his eyes.

'Señor?'

Sophie looked round as a beautiful young Spanish girl appeared at the door.

'You will have some wine, Sophie?' He gestured to a dusty bottle.

She needed *something* to help her relax. 'Please.'

He murmured in Spanish and the girl immediately

poured red wine into Sophie's crystal goblet and topped up Luis's own.

Sophie drank some. 'It's...it's lovely.'

'It is a bottle from one of our finest cases.'

'Then I am honoured,' said Sophie.

He raised his glass with a thoughtful look. 'I think we must drink a toast to thank God for the life of Miranda.'

It was too much! Sophie put her glass down with a shaking hand, wondering just how hypocritical a man could be. Didn't he have any idea that Miranda might have confided in her and told her that the devastatingly handsome Don had a heart which had been chiselled from ice?

'Her life in general?' she demanded. 'Or her life here? And if that is the case then it will hardly be a joyous toast, will it, Luis?'

How passionate she sounded, he thought as the anger sizzled off her like electricity, her eyes flashing hot blue fire at him, and he met the challenge there, feeling a pulse begin to flicker into life at his temple.

'Was it such a terrible life, then?' he asked seriously.

Her gaze didn't waver, the words coming out before she had time to consider the wisdom of saying them. 'I wish to God she'd never met you,' she said bitterly.

Luis nodded slowly. But if he had never met Miranda then there would never have been a Teo—and he could not imagine a life without Teo.

How much had Miranda told her cousin? he wondered as he put his glass down on the crisp linen tablecloth and stared at her reflectively.

'Do you know how my relationship with your cousin began, Sophie?' he asked slowly.

'I know that you picked her up when she was flying!'

He stilled. 'Picked her up?' Fierce pride clipped his words out like bullets. 'You think that I am the kind of man who goes around the world propositioning air stewardesses?'

'How should I know? You've never had any shortage of women, have you? Not from what I hear!'

She made him sound like some kind of indiscriminate alley cat! 'I am not promiscuous!' he ground out. 'And I never have been!'

She gave him a cool, disbelieving look. 'Really?'

'Sophie...' he began dangerously, but then drew himself up short. She was here for probably no longer than a few days—why taint her memories and risk making the pain of loss even greater?

'What?' she questioned as she saw the shutters come down again.

He shook his head. 'Nothing.'

What was he hiding from her? What couldn't he face telling her? 'I want to hear your version of how you met,' she said stubbornly.

There was a moment of silence. 'I was flying to New York on business,' he remembered softly, and gave a wry smile. 'Your cousin served me a drink and wrote the name of her hotel on the accompanying napkin, suggesting that we meet there for a drink.'

'Which was an offer you couldn't refuse, I suppose?'

'Why should I refuse?' he asked seriously. 'She was a beautiful and vivacious girl.'

Sophie took another shaky sip of wine. 'Any woman would do, is that what you mean, just as long as she was willing?'

He felt the implacable beat of anger. And of pride. 'If that were the case,' he shrugged, 'then I would spend my whole life in bed.'

Her heart beat faster, and she was shaken by how disturbing she found his statement. 'That's a very arrogant boast, Luis.'

'It is not a boast, it is simply the truth, *querida*.' But he saw the paleness of her face and relented. She was tired, and overwrought and full of sorrow. 'Come,' he said quietly. 'Let us drink our soup in peace, and talk no more on this subject.'

Sophie shook her head. She wanted to make some sense of her cousin's life here—which at the moment seemed like an out-of-focus picture. Miranda's contact with her had been erratic—and usually when she was in the midst of one of the many crises which had seemed to dog her all her life.

'I want to know. I want to hear your side of it.'

She spoke as if he were standing on trial, he thought bitterly. For the sake of his son and the de la Camara name, he would not be judged and found wanting! 'Very well,' he continued. 'I will not deny that I was flattered by her attentions. When a very beautiful woman makes no attempt to disguise her desire for you, what man wouldn't be?'

'But you intended it to be a one-night stand, I suppose?'

He stared at her uncomprehendingly. 'A *one-night stand?*' he repeated incredulously. 'What joy and pleasure and fulfilment can be gained from such a liaison as that?'

She heard the raw vitality in his voice and saw the passion which animated the proud, handsome face. And for one brief moment Sophie realised that by chasing Luis Miranda had flown *very* close to the sun. And had paid the price. To have known such a man intimately, and to have borne his child, must indeed have taken her to dizzy heights from which there could only be a plummeting descent.

For with an inexplicable but blinding certainty Sophie recognised the elusiveness which lay at the very core of Don Luis's character. A man who would only ever give a part of himself to a woman. His body, yes. But his heart? She wondered if a man like this actually had a heart. Or if, as Miranda had once claimed, it was made of ice and not of beating flesh and blood.

'So you were offering her a future, is that it?'

He shrugged as he took some bread and broke it. 'Relationships do not have two extremes,' he pointed out coolly. 'There is something midway between a one-night stand and marriage.'

'You mean an affair?'

'An affair implies that one of the partners is married to someone else, which was not true in our case.' He paused. 'I would have called it a relationship.'

'What a grown-up and yet cold-hearted word you make that sound.'

'I did not mean to. And it was a very enjoyable relationship—for a time, at least.'

'But a baby changed it, I suppose?'

There was a short, tense silence. 'Yes, Sophie,' he

said eventually, his voice expressionless. 'A baby changes everything.'

'And...and...if she hadn't been pregnant, would you have married her?'

He met her gaze unfalteringly, wondering just how he had been coerced into talking so frankly to a woman in this way. And recognising that much more of telling the truth would hurt her. And for what purpose?

'I think this conversation has gone on long enough, don't you, Sophie?' he said gently.

'Tell me,' she pleaded.

'I think you know the answer to your question, deep down, don't you?'

'So you didn't love her?' she breathed. 'You married her, but you didn't love her!'

'You ask impossible questions!'

'Not impossible,' she argued. 'Difficult, maybe—but not impossible.'

There was a long, fraught silence before he spoke. 'I do not think that I know what love is!' he said quietly. 'Do you? All I know is that Miranda was pregnant, and that it was my duty to marry her. And my responsibility.'

Duty.

Responsibility.

These were not the words of a man who had loved and lost, and with an aching heart Sophie accepted that the proud Spanish aristocrat had never really loved her cousin.

'And did she know that it was duty? Did you drive that message home to her, that she was only your wife because of circumstance? Is that why she was so unhappy?'

'The subject is closed!' he snapped. 'I will not discuss it further. Now eat your soup, Sophie.'

She opened her mouth to object, but the black eyes glittered tellingly and Sophie realised that she had said enough. More than enough. Why make him angry? A disconcerting enough thought in itself—but the fall-out from that anger would be self-defeating. She needed to have access to her nephew, and for that she needed Luis on her side...

'Eat!' he said once more, and then unexpectedly his voice softened. 'Please.'

With the brittleness gone from his voice, some of the fight went out of her, and she ate, hungrier than she had imagined. The gazpacho was delicious. As was the omelette studded with sweet herbs which followed and then a creamy little wedge of flan. Sophie ate every bit, and when she had finished she looked up to find him wryly studying her.

'You were very hungry,' he observed gravely.

'Yes.' She tried to remember the last time she had eaten a complete meal. Not since his telephone call, and that was two days ago. 'Well, I haven't had much appetite lately.'

'No. Of course you haven't.' He put his napkin down on the table. 'Come, Sophie. You should sleep now.'

She shook her head. 'Not yet.' She rose unsteadily to her feet and met the question in his eyes. 'Please, Luis,' she forced herself to say, recognising that in this, at least, he had total control, 'I would like to see Teodoro now.'

He would rather she wait until the morning. She looked too pale and too fragile at this time of night—as if when she stepped forward she might tumble into his arms at any moment, and he had to quash the thought of how much that would please him. But he could read the determination in the stubborn lift of her chin, and he gave a small sigh. 'Very well. Come with me.'

Breathing a sigh of relief, she followed him upstairs, feeling disturbed and guilty by the fact that she couldn't tear her eyes away from each movement of his body. She shouldn't be feeling this way. Not now and not with *him*—and especially not at a time like this. Wanting him should have left her a long time ago, been replaced with a feeling of detachment. So where the hell was the detachment now?

Through a maze of corridors they passed, until he stopped outside a door and turned to her.

'Now you must be very quiet,' he warned softly. 'He has been sleeping fretfully of late, and on no account must we wake him.'

'Is it any wonder he's been sleeping fretfully?' she whispered back. 'Babies are instinctive—he must be missing his mother like mad.'

He seemed about to say something, but then appeared to change his mind, putting one finger over his lips. 'Shhh! No more. Come,' he murmured.

They moved silently into the room like two people doing an impersonation of Santa Claus, and once they were by the large, old-fashioned wooden crib Sophie's heart flipped a somersault.

She had not seen Teodoro since his baptism, when he'd been a few weeks old. A few infrequent photos from Miranda had come her way, the most recent taken on his first birthday.

But nothing could have prepared her for the emotional impact of seeing Miranda's sleeping child lying there, oblivious to the world.

His rosy mouth was puckered and two angelic arcs of thick, dark lashes curved above the apple-plumpness of his cheeks. The curls of his hair looked jet-dark against the pillow and Sophie thought that she could see the faint trace of dried tears on his face.

So innocent and helpless, she thought, tears misting her eyes. And he would wake in the morning and be miserable for his mother and unable to articulate why. Poor, darling Teo!

Instinctively she reached her hand out to smooth away a lock of hair, but in an instant it was caught in an iron-fast grip before she could reach it.

'No,' he breathed, in a voice soft with threat.

And before Sophie could stop him he had hauled her unceremoniously out of the room and quietly shut the door behind them.

He still had her by the wrist and she could feel his strong fingers biting into her flesh, just as she could almost feel the palpable rage which lit angry fire behind the black eyes. He was too close to ignore. Too close for comfort and yet not close enough.

Every pore in her body seemed to scream out that he was within touching distance, and for one mad and delirious moment Sophie wanted to touch him above all else, just as she had done the very first time she laid eyes on him. To lose herself in the cradle of those strong arms, to rest her weary head on those broad shoulders, to feel the hard, lean power of his body.

'I told you not to waken him, *señorita*,' he ground out furiously. 'Did you want that we should have an inconsolable child crying for the rest of the night?'

'I...I wasn't thinking,' she protested, snatching her wrist away from his hand, feeling the frenzied flutter of her pulse beneath his strong, hard fingers and wondering if he had felt it, too. And wondering if he would guess that it was inspired by desire, and not by fear or anger.

'No,' he said grimly, and her trembling mouth and darkened eyes wakened a sudden pulse of need in him which only added to his fury. 'You didn't think. Well, try thinking now, *querida*. Teodoro is a child and not a toy—you don't just pick him up on a whim in the middle of the night, no matter what the circumstances, and especially not in *these* circumstances. Try thinking of him and of *his* needs, and not your own!' he finished bitterly.

Sophie stared at him. She had tried her best to keep her dislike of him hidden, but it seemed that he had no qualms about doing likewise.

She took a sure and protective step back. 'Goodnight, Luis,' she said coldly. 'I'm going to bed now.'

CHAPTER FOUR

LUIS stared down at the bent blonde head, thinking how ridiculously young she looked wearing black. 'Sophie?'

Sophie looked up at him blankly. 'What?'

He handed her a tiny cup containing coffee as ebony-black as his eyes. 'Here. Take this. Drink it!' he ordered softly.

In a daze, she nodded and took it from him. But then, she had spent most of the day feeling as though she was on autopilot, following the flower-decked coffin like a disbelieving robot. 'Thank you.'

He watched her sip it through frozen lips. She looked tiny—almost doll-like—as she hunched up in one of the oversized chairs he had gently sat her down on. Against the whiteness of her skin, her blue eyes dominated her face like saucers, the lashes feathering out like stars.

He gave a low sigh as some of the tension left him, relieved that the day would soon be over. The funeral had been both ornate and sombre, with four priests performing it out of respect for Luis's position, rather than because Miranda had been particularly religious.

'Are you feeling a little better now?' he asked softly.

'Yes.' Sophie was just glad that it was all over, another page turned, another ordeal behind her. Somehow she had survived the day. There had been a late arrival of a group of lavishly dressed, bright-eyed twenty-and thirty-somethings, who, Luis had informed her, rather grimly, were Miranda's own little clique. But mostly the church had been filled with friends and family of Luis—his mother and father had flown from Madrid for the service, and a car had just taken them back to the airport.

Luis's mother had given her a curious stare, but she had embraced her, and Sophie had been grateful for that. She knew from Miranda that their relationship had not been a good one— 'She thinks he should have married some cute little Spanish girl,' she had once said.

But the grief of Luis's mother had seemed genuine and Sophie had falteringly accepted her condolences.

She looked around the room. Everyone had gone, and now it was just the two of them left in the elaborate and rather formal sitting room. In his dark clothes, Luis looked impossibly formal, a black-haired and black-suited stranger—a few short steps and yet a million miles away from her.

'Where is Teodoro?' she asked.

'Salvadora is bathing him.'

'Isn't it a little early for that?'

'I think that I am the better judge of my son's welfare, don't you?' he responded blandly.

Sophie bit her lip in frustration. She had barely seen the child since she had been practically hauled from his room last night by his angry father, who seemed to imagine that she had been trying to wake him up on purpose.

And today he had been brought to the church in a

separate car with Salvadora, and had clung to her neck throughout.

Sophie met Luis's look of indifference with a sudden flare of defiance. 'Luis—are you trying to keep me away from my nephew?'

He raised his dark eyebrows, as though she had just said something completely incomprehensible. 'Why should I do something like that?'

'I should have thought that it was fairly obvious! You don't want me to get to know him, do you, or, more importantly, for him to get to know me?'

'*Dios!*' he said, heatedly now. 'The child is feeling lost and confused—'

'Well, of course he is—he's just lost his mother!'

He opened his mouth to reply and then seemed to think better of it, and Sophie looked at him in frustration. 'Haven't you got an answer to that? Can't you even begin to try to imagine what it must be like for a little child—one moment she's there, and the next...?' Her words tailed off and she expelled a long, low breath.

She was making it very difficult for him.

She looked up, her eyes bright. 'Well?'

'Sophie, it is not quite as you imagine it to be,' he said heavily. 'It could be worse.'

'How?'

He chose his words with care, picking them out as if they had been deep thorns embedded in his flesh. 'Miranda was not the kind of mother who was with Teo every waking hour.'

She heard the hint of something unknown in his voice. 'Are you trying to tell me she was a bad mother?'

'I am saying that she wasn't...around—not for a lot of the time. She left most of Teodoro's care to Salvadora—you must have seen the evidence of that for yourself today. Anyone can see that my son is completely devoted to her.'

She didn't want to believe him, but his words had a ring of truth to them, and Sophie bit her lip as she remembered Miranda talking about life as a mother. Hadn't her cousin said herself that motherhood wasn't all it was cracked up to be? Hadn't she told Sophie that you never appreciated freedom until it was taken away from you?

Sophie frowned. Had Miranda neglected her son by her absences—and could it have been Luis's behaviour which had driven her away? Her inability to cope with his regard for other women perhaps? She studied his impassive face. Even if that *had* been the case, was there any point in letting that deter her from her real objective for being here? What good would blame and reproach do Teo?

He stared at the indignant set of her lips, and sighed. 'What do you want, Sophie? Tell me, honestly, and I will give my consideration to your desires.'

But, to her startled horror, she felt little shivers begin to skitter across her skin, his murmured words reminding her that their meaning could be interpreted in more than one way. Was it just a trick of nature which was making her warm with the slow unfurling of need? she asked herself in silent despair. Nature's ruthless way of ensuring that the living carried on in every way that mattered? Didn't death only accentuate the life force?

She swallowed, focusing on facts and not on her body's weakness. 'I'll tell you what I want, Luis,' she said slowly. 'I want time for my nephew to learn to know me and to love me—'

'To *love* you?' he repeated incredulously.

'Is that such a crime?'

'No, no crime. But do you really think that these things can happen overnight?'

'Of course I don't. But neither do they happen if I am to be continually kept at arm's length. I would have liked to see him having his bath—'

'I thought that you would be tired,' he said coolly. 'And too upset today to cope with Teodoro's domestic routine.'

'Like you are, I suppose?'

He shook his dark head. 'I make no pretence, not even to you, Sophie. I grieve for a young life uselessly wasted, but I will shed no tears on my pillow tonight.'

'Have you—have you no heart?'

The black eyes narrowed thoughtfully. 'Who knows?' he answered softly. 'Some would say not. Women have said it for most of my adult life, but I will tell you this, Sophie—where my son is concerned, I most definitely *do* have a heart, and with it a determination that nothing or no one will ever harm him. Do I make myself clear?'

Crystal-clear. There was no mistaking the threat underpinning the rich, deep voice and a different woman might very easily have been intimidated by the sheer force of personality which he so effortlessly exuded. But she had something to fight for—or, rather, someone. And the knowledge that she was fighting for Teodoro gave her the strength to return the challenge of his gaze.

'I have no intention of ever harming Teodoro, Luis.'

'And no desire to paint his father as a black-hearted demon?'

'Even if I thought that...' She met the proud hauteur in that gaze without flinching. 'Even if I did—I would not dream of trying to warp a tiny child's perception. You may be no friend of mine, Luis—but our relationship is not what is at stake here. My relationship with Teodoro *is*.'

'But you have no real relationship with Teodoro,' he stated quietly.

'No, you're right, I don't,' she admitted. 'And I might never have done—more than the occasional family celebration.' She put her empty coffee cup down. 'But things have changed,' she continued quietly. 'What went on before is irrelevant now. Miranda is dead and I want her son to have the opportunity to get to know the other side of his family. To learn something of his English roots. Starting now.'

His eyes narrowed. *'Now?'* he echoed quietly.

'Right this very moment.' She nodded, and rose slowly to her feet, smoothing down the skirt of her black linen dress. 'Once Teodoro is bathed, I would like to read him a bedtime story. I assume that you have no objections to that, Luis?'

A shaft of sunlight had filtered through the shuttered windows and illuminated her hair to spun gold. With her white, untouched skin contrasting so markedly against the black dress, she looked so pure, he thought, and a slow pulse began to flicker at his temple.

'Of course I have no objections,' he answered huskily. 'But you will not object if I am there also?'

'You think perhaps I might attempt to spirit him away without your knowledge?'

He resisted the urge to answer with the logical reply that she had no passport for his son, because the principle here was far more important than the practicality. Sophie Mills needed to be very clear where he stood and where she stood.

'Try anything like that, Sophie,' he said in a soft voice of dangerous threat, 'and you will know what it is to enrage me. I am a de la Camara, and nothing which is truly mine will ever be taken from me. Do you understand?'

The hard features had tightened with some dark, atavistic emotion, transforming him into an adversary most people wouldn't dream of taking on, and for a moment Sophie despaired. Oh, why had her cousin chosen to hitch her star to such a man? Why couldn't she have settled down and been happy with one of the countless other men who had adored her?

Because Don Luis was unobtainable—that much was apparent. And hadn't Miranda always delighted in the pursuit of something which eluded her so completely?

The black eyes glittered. 'Do you understand?'

And suddenly a wave of reactive relief washed away some of the tension. The worst of the day was over—and she was going to read her nephew a story! 'Oh, for goodness' sake—don't overreact, Luis! I'll go and get a story-book from my room.'

For the first time that day, he smiled. 'Very well. I will bring Teodoro down here to wait for you.'

In her room Sophie took the opportunity to change out of the stark black dress and slipped into a pair of old jeans and a faded green singlet which had seen better days. But babies were babies, even if they were newly bathed! She didn't want to worry if he dribbled on her clothes or was sick. She wanted to relax completely and she badly wanted to cuddle Teo.

She picked up one of several books she had brought with her, and a brightly wrapped package, and closed the bedroom door behind her.

Quietly she descended the dark and sweeping staircase and walked back along to the sitting room, but when she reached the open door she stood completely still, her startled eyes taking in the scene which lay before her.

Luis was stretched out on the carpet, playing with his son. He must have discarded his jacket and his tie, and loosened the top few buttons of his snowy shirt, for a distracting glimpse of dark olive skin was on show.

He hadn't seen her—his attention was all on the pyjama-suited chubbiness of his young son, who was squealing with laughter and shouting, 'Papa! Papa!' And Luis was laughing too, throwing his dark head back with uninhibited pleasure.

She sucked in a raw breath of disbelief, because he was now pulling funny faces and was almost unrecognisable. Was this really Luis de la Camara? she wondered dazedly.

His black eyes had softened, and so had his mouth—curved into an indulgent and affectionate smile as a fat little fist curled over the hard definition of his shoulder. He threw his head back to chuckle again as small fingers moved up to graze over the shadowed jut of his jaw, and with that rich and sonorous sound something inside Sophie sprang to unwelcome life.

She had always understood his physical appeal—that would have been apparent to just about any woman on the planet—but this Luis, this soft and tender Luis, caught her completely off guard.

She had never seen him so relaxed, nor so at ease with himself. He looked...he looked almost *boyish* as he murmured something in Spanish into Teodoro's ear.

She tried to tell herself that it was just instinct which made the pit of her stomach begin to dissolve. Just like the instinct which made you swat at a fly if it buzzed too close to your eye. And instinct wasn't rational—it was random and cruel.

She shook her head as if to deny that it was anything more than physical attraction—because that was easy enough to hold in check. Far more dangerous was to start getting all dreamy about him and attributing qualities to him which he simply did not possess. He loved his son, that was all. *That was all.*

He looked up then, and his face changed as if by magic. It was almost as if some impenetrable shutter had suddenly descended, for his features stilled and his face lost something of its vitality and animation.

And maybe Teodoro sensed the change in his father too, for he suddenly turned his dark and curly head to stare at Sophie with wide, questioning eyes.

The innocence and confusion that she read in them

made a lump catch in Sophie's throat and she walked towards him, the hand which held the book and the present trembling with the emotion of seeing him again. Part her. Part *her* flesh and blood, too, as well as Luis's.

She dropped to her knees onto the floor in front of him, her delight at seeing him again making her impervious to the fact that Luis's long legs were sprawled only inches away from her.

'Hello, Teodoro, darling,' she said softly, but she could hear the break in her voice.

Teodoro continued to stare at her, his little face solemn.

Luis spoke softly in Spanish. 'Teodoro—this is your cousin Sophie. You met her once when you were very tiny.'

'Hello, darling,' she said again, and, to her mortification, the little boy's lips began to tremble and he buried his face in his father's shoulder, but not before Sophie had seen the tears which slid from between the thick black lashes of his eyes and the little shake of his shoulders as he gave a muffled sob.

'Oh, Teodoro,' she whispered helplessly. 'Please don't cry.'

'*Ssh, mi querido hijo!*' crooned Luis. Balancing his son in the cradle of his arm, he sat up and continued to murmur to Teodoro in Spanish, in the softest and sweetest way that Sophie could ever imagine a man doing.

And *she* had made him cry!

Luis glanced up to see her stricken face, and felt an unwilling tug of empathy as he felt his son quieten in his arms.

'Do not blame yourself, *querida,*' he said quietly. 'It is a difficult time for him.'

She met his gaze and saw a look of understanding there which took her breath away. 'Yes.'

'See.' His long, olive fingers wound themselves between the ebony curls on Teodoro's head. 'He cries no more.'

Sophie nodded, wondering if the child would ever cuddle *her* the way he was cuddling his father. It didn't seem likely.

Luis picked up the book, and then said something else in Spanish to Teodoro, who nodded against his shoulder and then slowly turned around.

'Shall we read the book together?' he questioned. 'With Sophie? Come. Come, Sophie.'

He gestured to one of the long sofas. Feeling suddenly almost stricken with shyness, Sophie followed him over to it, and he waited until she had sat down before sprawling upon it himself. He stretched out his legs with a kind of careless grace, with Teodoro clinging on to him like a little monkey all the while.

She perched on the edge of the seat, catching the faint scent which was a beguiling mixture of aftershave and masculinity, and fumblingly she opened the book.

Luis leaned over to look at it, and the aftershave became even more distracting.

'What is the story?' he asked.

'It's a book of nursery rhymes,' she said tentatively.

She had thought carefully about what to bring, deliberating and agonising over her choice of book, terrified of evoking painful memories of Miranda.

'I hope you like nursery rhymes, Teodoro?'

'Canciones infantil,' interpreted Luis, and Teodoro wriggled himself forward, his attention caught by a beautiful illustration of a silver nutmeg and a golden pear.

'Do you know this one?' asked Sophie.

'He knows only Spanish stories,' said Luis.

But surely Miranda must have read to her son in English?

'Well, this is an English story with a mention of Spain, so it seems perfect! Now, listen, Teo. "I had a little nut tree and nothing would it bear..."' As she began to recite the poem, her voice taking on a slow and rhythmical resonance, Teodoro listened, seemingly enraptured. And when she got to the bit about "the King of Spain's daughter came to visit me, and all for the sake of my little nut tree!", Luis laughed, and Sophie found herself laughing with him.

The laughter broke the ice completely and melted it away as Sophie read about ten of the rhymes, until there was a light brush of her arm, and she turned to find Luis's dark eyes fixed on her, their expression rueful.

'It is late, *querida,*' he said. 'See how sleepy Teodoro grows.'

She could see the boy rubbing his fist in his eyes and stifling a yawn as he struggled to listen to more rhymes, and she closed the book. 'I could read you some more stories tomorrow, Teodoro,' she whispered. 'Would you like that?'

Just for good measure, Luis repeated the question in Spanish and she was rewarded with the briefest of nods, which sent his dark curls dancing, and then he jammed a thumb into the corner of his mouth and snuggled back into his father's shoulder.

She looked up as Luis rose to his feet and scraped a silky handful of hair back from her face. 'Can I—can I help you to put him to bed?'

Luis froze, arrested by the movement which suddenly shattered his equilibrium. The way she scooped away her hair only drew attention to the breasts which danced beneath the faded T-shirt, and his eyes narrowed as he felt the unmistakable beat of desire. He felt the heat and the unwelcome hardening of his body, and silently he cursed her, even though the provocation had been unconscious, not deliberate.

'No,' he said flatly. 'Not tonight.'

She raised her eyebrows at him in question and this time he arrogantly mouthed the word no again, over his son's head.

Sophie shot him a defiant look. She wasn't about to start making a scene in front of Teodoro, but she wasn't going to let it rest, either. How dared he blow so hot and cold with her? Acting as though she had made an outrageous request, when all she had done was ask to help put the child to bed! And this after what she thought had been a very amicable reading session.

But she gave Teodoro a gentle smile. 'Goodnight,' she said softly, and then for good measure she added, *"Buenas noches!"* and was rewarded with a quick little quirk of a mouth which told her exactly what a young Luis's lips must have looked like.

Luis expelled a hissing breath as he carried his son up the stairs, waiting for the dull ache of desire to gradually subside.

Maldecir! he thought to himself. *Damn* her.

His body was hungry—his senses on fire with a clamour which made him feel weak. What did she do to him, and how? And why had time only sharpened his hunger, not dulled it, as time so often did?

In Teodoro's room he watched and waited and stroked the dark tumble of curls until the little boy had fallen into a slow and steady sleep. Only then did he allow himself to suck in a shuddering lungful of air as he stood watching his son.

Poor, innocent *niño,* he thought, with bitter sadness. His mother buried today and all his father could think about were the insistent calls of his own physical needs.

Sophie took her place opposite him at supper that evening in a headachy mood. She said little during the first two courses and ate even less, but she drank two full glasses of La Camara Rioja, and some of the tension left her.

'The chicken is good?' Luis frowned.

'It is very good.'

'Then why don't you eat a little more of it?'

But her answer was stalled by the ringing of the telephone, and moments later Salvadora came in.

'Don Luis?'

Luis glanced up. *'Sì?'*

'It is Alejandra,' she said quickly.

Luis nodded and rose to his feet, but not before Sophie had seen the thoughtful frown in his eyes.

'Will you excuse me?'

'Of course.'

She tried to listen to his conversation, just as he

had listened to hers with Liam, but she couldn't make out a word of the quick-fire Spanish. Whoever Alejandra was, he was certainly very intimate with her, judging by the way in which he spoke.

But when he came back into the room she thought he seemed edgy, the handsome face shadowed and tense. Several times she saw him glance down at his watch.

Eventually, she put her coffee-cup down with a clatter. 'Am I keeping you from something, Luis?'

'You do look a little tired, *querida*,' he observed.

'Yes,' she agreed. 'And so do you, for that matter.'

'Might I suggest that you retire to your room at the earliest opportunity?' he said, his eyes trying not to linger on the sleek, creamy column of her neck. 'It has been a long day.'

'And you? Are you planning an early night yourself?'

Luis's mouth hardened and a pulse began to work at his temple. Did she imagine that having houseroom gave her the right to question him about his arrangements?

'I have to go out,' he said silkily. 'If you have no objections?'

She wondered what he would do if she said that yes, she had. Would he cancel whatever was making him seem so distracted? And yet, perhaps, in a way it would be better if he went out.

She could phone Liam and check her e-mails. Do all the normal things which usually occupied her mind, instead of remembering this terrible day and trying to keep her thoughts away from this black-eyed Don who had now risen to his feet.

He stood looking down at her, with fingers splayed carelessly across his narrow hips, stretching the dark material of his trousers tautly over the powerful shafts of his thighs.

And, shockingly, Sophie couldn't tear her eyes away from him, feeling her throat dry to dust and forcing herself to pay attention as her fumbling fingers folded the linen napkin. Yes, much better that he went out, as far away from her as possible.

'Of course I have no objections,' she said thickly.

He took one last look at her. She looked as beautiful as any woman he had ever seen. The candle light was transforming her hair into bright, liquid honey which fell like angels' wings on either side of her face. Did she realise that when she spoke to him she sometimes snaked the point of her pink tongue along her lips? Making them gleam more enticingly than if they were painted with the finest cosmetics.

Had she come to his home with the deliberate intention of taunting him with what he could never have? And did she not realise that her obvious dislike of him was having no effect on him at all, making absolutely no difference to the tension which always seemed to pulse in the air whenever they were together. *'Buenas noches, señorita,'* he bade her, the courteous formality made meaningless by the sudden roughening of his voice. 'I will see you in the morning. Please don't wait up.'

She looked up, and her voice was as cold as her eyes. 'Why ever would I want to wait up for you, Luis?'

CHAPTER FIVE

THE room and the house seemed curiously empty once Luis had gone. And, even though Sophie knew that Salvadora and Pirro were still around, and that Teodoro was sleeping upstairs, shadows and ghosts of the past seemed to rise up to haunt her.

She tried to imagine Miranda sitting in here, eating the beautifully prepared food in the beautiful dining room, but it was a hard stretch of the imagination. The house was exquisite, but so isolated. And Miranda had always been such a people-magnet, always preferring parties to privacy. Had she bothered to think through the reality of Luis's lifestyle before she had married him? Sophie wondered.

She drank a small cup of the deliciously strong coffee which Salvadora had left on the table and then, when her yawns could no longer be stifled, she went upstairs and took a long shower before climbing into bed.

The bed was wide and welcoming, but sleep took a long time coming, and when it did come it provided no welcome refuge, because her dreams gave her no peace. For the nature of the dreams was as disturbing as the identity of the man who inhabited each and every one with such dangerous and sensual stealth.

Luis.

Strong and lean, his dark figure mocking her from afar, the black eyes tempting her as they always had done. She reached out for him, but the air was empty, the promise of him as false as a mirage.

She grew warm, then cool, and then warm again. Distractedly she touched her skin to find it bathed with the slick of sweat. Only half-awake, she pushed the linen sheet from her body, tossing and turning, moaning a protest against the rapid thundering of her heart, unable to rid herself of the powerful image of the proud Spaniard with the cold, hard face and the hot, hard body.

His face swam in front of her, and this time—this time surely she could reach him? For one moment he caught her in his arms, crushed her to his chest, a second away from kissing her, but then he shook his head in contemptuous dismissal, pushed her back down on the bed and turned away.

A heartfelt moan of protest was torn from her lips. 'Luis!'

Luis was tiptoeing past her room when he heard a startled cry coming from the direction of Sophie's room and he stilled.

He stood silently outside the door when another sound greeted him—only this time a kind of moaned sob. And his name. She was crying out his name! *His* name! Sweet God in heaven! His gut twisted and something in the quality of her cry made him ache unbearably.

Softly he twisted the handle and pushed the door open and then stilled, becoming as motionless as stone as his eyes grew accustomed to the light.

'Mi Dios!' he breathed, almost imperceptibly.

She must have opened the shutters, for moonlight spilled through the window with an incandescent light which painted her silver, like some creature from a fable. She wore a tiny scrap of a nightgown, some slippery pale garment which had ridden up over her knees.

Her hair lay gleaming across the pillow, while one arm was stretched with abandon above her head, and as he watched she moved, one slim and delectable thigh sending a tantalising shadow shafting across her body, so that she was all light and dark.

Luis felt the thick, honeyed pulse of desire as he watched her, saw her turn again, saw her frown, still in the throes of sleep, and he wondered what had caused that sudden look of distress.

Madre de Dios!

Was she dreaming?

Or was he?

He wondered if he should wake her, but could he trust himself to approach her pale beauty? What if she awoke to find him in her room, towering over her bed, his face tight with the tension which her unconscious sensuality had unwittingly produced—then might she not scream the house down?

Uncaring of the folly of his actions, he moved silently towards the bed, staring down at her, noting the faint sheen of sweat which made her skin gleam as if it was lit from within, and again he felt the aching heat of desire.

But it was nothing other than an unendurable torture to stand and watch her, and he bit his lip, preparing to take his leave of her.

Sophie's eyes flew open and she saw the lean, proud face, his eyes blacker than she had ever seen them as they stared down at her, and even in the moonlight she could see a dull flush darkening the aristocratic curve of his cheekbones.

'Luis!' she breathed in disbelief, as if her dream had suddenly taken living, breathing form.

He shuddered out the words, 'I heard you call out.' But he omitted to tell her exactly what it was that she had called. 'I thought that perhaps you were having a nightmare, *querida*.'

She sat up, oblivious to the spill of her breasts over her nightgown, aware only of their tingling, their ache, their growing tenderness as he continued to stare at her like that.

Her hand flew to her throat. 'What—what time is it?'

He swallowed. 'It is late—or, rather, it is very early. Four o'clock and the birds have not yet begun to sing. Go back to sleep, now, Sophie. Sleep. Sleep, *querida*. You need to sleep.'

She had never heard his voice so soft, nor so beguiling, and she settled back down against the pillows.

'Sleep,' he urged again, and she pulled the sheet up to her chin, for which he both damned and applauded her.

He stood there, watching the drift of her lashes as they curved down over her darkened eyes, heard her sigh—once, twice.

He waited until her breathing was steady, and then, with the aching which now seemed to have invaded every pore of his body, he moved stiffly away from the bed.

He shut the door as quietly as he had opened it and then, once he had checked on Teodoro, went to his bathroom and took a fierce, cold shower. He lay in bed, watching with empty eyes as the dawn crept in through the window.

Sophie awoke with a heavy head and a curious sense of disorientation which a long bath didn't quite banish. And, when she eventually went downstairs to where breakfast had been laid up on the sunlit and flower-filled terrace, it was to find Luis's place empty.

Half-heartedly she spread jam on sun-warmed bread and looked up at Salvadora, who was pouring coffee.

'Luis has already eaten breakfast?'

Salvadora hesitated. 'No, *señorita*. Don Luis has not yet been down.'

Had he come in late, then? Sophie stared unseeingly at her plate as fragments of a troubled dream came back to taunt her.

Salvadora deposited a dish of fresh fruit in front of her. 'You would perhaps like some eggs?'

'No.' Sophie shook her head. 'Thank you, no. Bread will be fine.'

But once Salvadora had gone Sophie ate very little, then pushed her plate away and sat looking at the beauty of her surroundings.

It really was the most idyllic place she had ever seen. The sky was unbelievably blue, and in the distance was the acid-yellow hue of the lemon trees, hung heavy and fragrant with fruit. She stood up and went to lean over the balustrade, staring ahead at the formal and beautifully laid-out gardens. It was a very peaceful place, she thought.

She thought of the solitude of the hacienda, the isolation of Miranda's position as a foreign wife, so far from home, and a great wave of sadness washed over her, knowing that her cousin had made the wrong choice in coming here.

And if Miranda had not done that—then might there not have been a chance for Sophie?

She sighed. Of course there wouldn't. It was only through Miranda that she had met him. Fate had never intended her to become involved with Luis de la Camara, and she must never forget that.

'Oh, Miranda,' she whispered helplessly as guilty tears began to slide from beneath her lashes. Would she have been shocked or surprised to know that Sophie had always secretly coveted her husband? Forgive me, prayed Sophie silently.

Luis saw her from inside the house, and knew she was crying even before he was close enough to see the faint glimmer of tears shimmering on her pale cheeks.

He flinched as if he had inflicted the tears himself, but maybe it was best that she cried, for these were the first tears that he had seen.

'Sophie?' he said softly.

She heard his footfall, but didn't turn her head, dabbing instead at her eyes with the napkin, not wanting him to see her looking so lost and so vulnerable. And dreading that those clever black eyes might guess at part of her guilty secret.

'Why are you crying?' he questioned, close enough to touch the silken gold of her hair, and he clenched his fist deep in the pocket of his trousers to stop himself.

She shook her head and swallowed down the last of them. 'Nothing. I'm—I'm OK now.'

'No,' he asserted gently. 'Tell me why you are crying.'

His softness dissolved all her defences. 'I was j-just...' her voice trembled '...thinking about Miranda. Wishing that it could have been—'

'Different?' he put in, and she nodded. 'Ah, Sophie,' he said softly. 'Sophie.'

His words drew her into his arms as surely as if they had been magnetic and she went into them, the tears streaming down her face.

'It's OK,' he soothed, and his hand went up automatically to smooth down her hair, his fingertips lingering on its silken softness. 'It's OK.'

But even in the midst of the storm his touch made her senses go into overdrive. The warmth of him. The lean hardness of him. His scent, so evocatively and so provocatively masculine. She could feel her breasts, first cushioning and then hardening against the muscular torso, and before the honey-rush of desire could overwhelm her, warning bells began to sound in her subconscious.

She had dreamed of him! 'You were in my room in the middle of the night!' she accused.

He wished she had not reminded him, for the memory began to produce an ache which was distinctly uncomfortable. 'I heard you call out,' he husked. 'I was concerned. I merely came in to check that you were OK.'

All of a sudden she felt acutely embarrassed as she remembered the dream and wondered just what she *had* called out, and it was easier and less disturbing to focus on what *he* had been doing there. 'You'd been out, hadn't you?' She frowned. 'It was very late.'

'Yes. I was on my way back to my room when I heard you.'

'And you'd been out to see a woman. The woman who called you during dinner. *Alejandra,*' she remembered.

'Alejandra,' he agreed. 'That is correct.'

Something in the tone of his voice alerted her. Had the events of the past few days heightened her perception? For Sophie knew with a breathtaking certainty that his relationship with this woman Alejandra was not one of innocent friendship.

'She's your mistress...' He didn't deny it. How could he? 'Since when?' she asked, her blue eyes piercing into him.

He was unable to look away and there was a long, heavy pause as he reluctantly answered the question. 'Since six months into my marriage,' he said eventually. He had told himself that he had no reason to lie to her, but even so he was surprised by her reaction.

She flung herself at him, blonde hair flying wildly, her nails flailing uselessly close to his impassive olive face as he caught hold of her wrists with a razor-sharp reflex.

'Rail at me to your heart's content,' he said. 'But do not mark me!'

'Why? Wouldn't Alejandra like it?'

'Stop it, Sophie!'

'Will you let go of me, please?'

'Once you stop trying to scratch me.'

'I won't scratch you.'

He let her go, but her nails came up again and he captured her once more. 'Ah, so you were lying, were you, *querida?*' he questioned softly. 'You promised that you would not attack me again.'

She stared at him, her heart thundering painfully in her breast. 'You...you spent *last night,* straight after the funeral, in the arms of another woman? Can that really be true, Luis?'

'You are the one demanding answers,' he observed quietly. 'Can I help it if they are ones you do not wish to hear?'

She felt like throwing something at him. Like pummeling her fists against that silk-covered chest. 'You...you...left your son sleeping while you made love to someone else?'

'Yes, my son *was* sleeping,' he hissed back. 'And safely in the care of Salvadora!'

'You unspeakable man!' she accused, rising shakily to her feet. 'Couldn't you have left a decent amount of time before you allowed your libido free range? Or maybe this is just par for the course? Maybe this is the kind of thing you used to get up to when Miranda was still alive!'

'Collarse!' he snapped, and when she stared at him in confusion he translated again into English. 'Keep your voice down!'

But she shook her head. 'What kind of man can possibly visit his mistress on the night of his wife's funeral?'

He felt all the fight go out of her and let her go, and this time she stumbled over to one of the chairs and sat down, her eyes dull.

'My God,' she breathed on a shuddering breath. 'No wonder Miranda was so unhappy!'

But Luis had had enough of her accusations and her judgements. He strode across the balcony towards her and levered her to her feet, his fingers biting into the soft, silken flesh of her arms as he gripped her. 'You know nothing of my marriage!' he accused.

'I know enough!'

'Will you be quiet, Sophie?'

'Never!'

He saw the defiant tremble of her mouth and something inside him snapped, like elastic which had been stretched to breaking point, and with a furious little moan of rage he pulled her hard against him, crushing his mouth down on hers even harder.

Anger and frustration and rage and a sense of injustice seemed to explode inside her like a devastating incendiary device as Sophie felt his lips capture hers as she had dreamed of them doing last night in bed. Only this time the dream was true. The fantasy real.

And, though it felt right, it was wrong. All wrong.

So why was she letting him kiss her—her breathing so weak and thready, but not so thready as to prevent the small, hungry sigh escaping from her lips? And why did the punishing pressure of his mouth make her feel as if she was melting? On fire with a need so fierce that she itched to burrow her hands up beneath the white silk of the shirt which did nothing to disguise the hard frame of his torso? As if no man had ever kissed her before? And, indeed, no man had.

Not like this.

Luis felt her arms wind up around his neck and the movement brought her soft, full breasts pressing into him, and his anger escalated, along with his desire. My God, he could ruck her skirt up and...and...

'Dios!' he ground out furiously. *'Mi Dios!'*

Through the hard, sweet pressure of his mouth and the aching of her swollen breasts Sophie felt the simmer of heat and hunger bubble up into an irrevocable burn.

Yet this was the man who had cheated on her cousin, who had visited his mistress only last night. A man whose sexuality was so explosively potent that it seemed he could reduce any woman he wanted into a compliant and uncomplaining partner, greedy for his kisses and his touch. Just as she was now.

She tore herself out of his arms to meet the hateful black mockery in his eyes but her breath was coming so quickly and so erratically that it took a moment before she could splutter out her own bitter accusation.

'That tells me everything I need to know!' she exploded. 'Just what kind of a man Miranda married. One who could kiss any woman so indiscriminately—just to shut her up!'

But Luis shook his head. It had not been indiscriminate. No, not at all. He had wanted to kiss her in the night and many times before that. And just recalling her softness and her warmth and the clean, innocent scent of her was enough to make him feel as though he could explode with frustration.

'That has been a long time in coming,' he said darkly. 'We both know that, so don't bother denying it to me, Sophie!'

Her breathing was still erratic, and her eyes blazing. 'Yes, I saw the way you looked at me the very first time you saw me—as if you would like to drag me off to the nearest bed!'

'And you did not look as if you would have objected if I had done,' he pointed out silkily.

The fact that he spoke nothing but the truth only increased her sense of shame. 'I knew then what kind of man Miranda was marrying—the kind of no-good Don Juan who would leap on any woman who wanted him to. If only I had told her,' she moaned. 'And if she hadn't been pregnant then I would have done!'

'I think that this time you have pushed me too far, Sophie,' he said in a voice which was dangerously soft. He had tried to protect the memory of his late wife out of respect, but he would not live a lie. Nor let Sophie jump to false conclusions which would forever damn him in her eyes; he had too much pride for that. 'You leave me with no choice other than to give you the true facts about my marriage.' His eyes glittered with challenge. 'And only then shall you have the right to judge me.'

'Knowing that it's in your interest to lie to me!'

He threw her a look of icy scorn. 'You think that I would protect myself with lies? Never!'

And, oddly enough, the fierceness and the unmistakable aristocratic contempt in his voice actually made her believe him. 'It is painful to recount,' he began slowly. 'You see, in the beginning I liked your cousin very much—she was funny and sweet and a little bit crazy.' He sighed, wondering how many lives would be lived differently if you were allowed a glimpse into the future. 'We enjoyed a mutually satisfying relationship.'

'How cold you make it sound, Luis!'

'Not cold—just how it was,' he contradicted. 'However different we might wish it to be. I am not a hypocrite, Sophie, you know that. And I would never admit to feelings that I did not have.' The warm morning sun beat down on him, but his skin felt cold. 'I was never "in love" with Miranda, Sophie,' he said softly. 'She knew that. I never made a secret of the fact. She was beautiful and sparky and we were good together. But she also knew that there was no long-term future in our relationship.'

She stared at him in frustration. 'But you *married* her! Why the hell did you marry her if you weren't in love with her?'

'I married her because, as you know, she was expecting my baby—a baby which was not planned...at least,' he added heavily, 'not by me.'

Sophie shook her head. She would not believe this; she wouldn't. 'If you're trying to tell me that Miranda deliberately got pregnant then I know that isn't so. She wasn't that desperate—*and* she was on the Pill! She told me!'

'What else did she tell you?'

'That it was true that the pregnancy wasn't planned, but that she'd had a stomach upset, and that—'

'Sophie!' he interrupted. 'I did not—do not—want to dishonour the memory of your cousin, but it was no accident when she became pregnant. Believe me. I was searching for some papers when I found her contraceptive pills. Untouched. I challenged her with it, and then she admitted that she had stopped taking them without telling me.'

'Oh, my God,' breathed Sophie. She remembered Miranda's excited chatter just after the wedding. She'd told Sophie how Luis was the most devastating man she had ever seen. How she had looked at him and thought, I've *got* to have him. Had she really planned it? The oldest trick in the book to get a man to marry you?

And with a sinking heart she guessed at the answer. 'She had a terrible childhood,' she said defensively. 'Her parents were never there for her—she was chronically insecure.'

'I am not blaming Miranda for her behaviour,' he said gently. 'I'm just telling you how it was.'

'But why still go ahead and marry her just because she was having your baby?' she demanded. 'Men don't have to do that any more, Luis. If you didn't love her you must have known from the outset that it wouldn't work.'

'I told you—because of my sense of responsibility. This was *my* child as well as hers! And Miranda did not want the baby to be born illegitimate. Indeed, neither did I. She decided that marriage could work and so did I. She wanted to enjoy the security which being married to me would bring, and which I was prepared to provide, and I would have the child which already my heart had begun to yearn for.'

'So it was a marriage of convenience, you mean?'

'Or a marriage of expedience,' he corrected.

'And were you honest with each other right from the start?' she demanded heatedly. 'Did you tell her that you couldn't possibly remain faithful and warn her that soon you would have to seek solace elsewhere? Was she prepared for you to have a mistress?'

There was another pause. 'No, she was not—and neither was I! I fully intended to honour my wedding vows, Sophie. I *am* a man of honour!' He narrowed his eyes as he remembered. 'And it would have been no hardship to remain faithful to a woman like Miranda. Marriage can be based on more than love, you know. Indeed, many cultures believe that it has a much better chance of survival if it is based on mutual respect, and trust.'

'But?' Because she sensed that there was a 'but' coming.

He chose his words carefully, not wanting to hurt her, but maybe hurt was the inevitable consequence of truth. 'I do not think that I offered Miranda the kind of life she was really seeking.'

'Oh, come on, Luis—she adored you!'

'No.' He shook his head resolutely. 'She liked what she thought I could offer her, but the reality fell far short of that. She adored the high life and the glamour of a playboy lover—which is what I was when we first met. Life as a wife and mother in La Rioja was not to her liking at all. She found the slower pace of life down here intolerable, and she wanted to live in Barcelona—she used to call it Paris by the sea—but that was not possible.'

'You could have compromised,' she pointed out. 'And gone there for weekends.'

'As we did. As we could have continued to do, even once Teo came along, but—as I once told you— a baby changes everything.'

'It doesn't have to,' she objected.

He sighed. 'That's what everyone who doesn't have one always says, but it does change things,

Sophie—more than you can know. When you have a baby then late nights out at clubs and sleeping until noon are no longer compatible.'

'That's what she did?'

'That's what she did,' he agreed evenly. 'In the end, she used to fly to Barcelona by herself, leaving Teo here while she partied into the small hours. I told her that if she continued to do so it was inevitable—only a matter of time—before we started leading separate lives. And so we did.'

'And that's when you found yourself a mistress?'

'No.' His expression became rueful. 'I did a very liberated and un-macho thing. I suggested we go for counselling. Miranda stuck to all of three sessions before she told me that she was having an affair. And *that* was when I began to look outside the marriage for what was being denied to me at home.'

She could hear the solemn ring of truth in his words, and in spite of everything her heart went out to him. 'Oh, Luis,' she whispered. 'It sounds awful. Why didn't you just get a divorce?'

He gave a bitter laugh. 'You think it's that easy? Maybe in England it is—but I had no intention of allowing Teo to be torn apart in some acrimonious custody battle. To have him living—at least for some of the time—with a mother who did not care for him properly. Many people have "empty" marriages, Sophie. It was tolerable.'

'And then she died.' She fixed him with a steady look, realising that the cardboard cut-out man she had thought he was simply did not exist; he was as complex as every other human being, perhaps even more so. And this rich, handsome and powerful man might not have given his heart to Miranda, but he had a strong sense of conscience, and of duty. 'I suppose in some way it must be a relief to be free from such an empty marriage.'

His mouth hardened. 'You think me such a black-hearted monster that I would wish the mother of my son dead?'

'But you didn't approve of her behaviour!'

'No, I didn't,' he agreed. 'And, yes, Sophie.' He sighed. 'I cannot deny that there was a certain amount of relief that there would be no more unhappiness. But, believe me, I felt guilt for feeling that.'

It must have been hard for him to admit that. But he had given her his honesty—didn't he deserve the same kind of honesty in return? 'I think I can understand it. None of us is safe from feelings we would prefer not to have,' she finished, with a note of bitter guilt in her voice.

'Thank you,' he said gravely.

She let out a long, sad sigh. Poor, sweet, misguided Miranda. Foolish Miranda. She had wanted Luis and, in a way, he had given her as much of himself that he was capable of giving—and she had thrown it all away in the mindless pursuit of life in the fast lane.

But with the knowledge that nothing was as simple as you thought it was came another, more frightening knowledge in its wake. She didn't want to think of Luis as an intrinsically good man, because if she did, wouldn't that make her want him even more? And he was not hers to have. With a history like theirs, he never could be.

Yes, that kiss had demonstrated that a powerful chemistry still existed between them, but she should not kid herself into thinking she was unique. When he kissed a woman it was probably always like that. What woman wouldn't go up in flames the instant a man like Luis touched her?

And besides, wasn't she forgetting something else? His behaviour during his marriage to Miranda might have been justified, but his behaviour this morning had not been.

'It doesn't change the fact that you kissed me just now, does it?' she demanded, conveniently forgetting that she had fantasised about just that during the night. 'And straight after your night of passion with your mistress! You must have little or no respect for either of us to do something like that!'

His mouth hardened, but this time he did nothing to correct her bitter allegations. The less she knew, the sooner she would be gone—and he *wanted* her gone. For what did he really know of Sophie Mills? Only that she had once gazed at him with a hunger which had temporarily sent him reeling, a hunger which had matched his own. And that her response to his kiss had spoken of a dangerous, sensual promise.

But that told him nothing of her true motives for being here. What did she really want? What was going on behind those bewitching blue eyes?

No, he needed her here like he needed a hole in the head.

He steeled himself. 'So what are we going to do about it, Sophie?' he drawled softly.

Sophie stared as the blaze from his eyes imprinted the memory of that kiss in her mind, so that for one horrifyingly tempting moment she thought that he meant...meant...

'You think...you think I want to carry on where we left off?' she demanded breathlessly.

His mouth hardened with tension and frustration. 'Is that what you would like, then?'

Part of her wanted to breathe that, yes, she would—more than she had ever wanted anything in her life. Knowing that if Luis led her up to bed right now he could give her nothing but pure and untold pleasure. Demonstrate to her that she was alive, and alive in the most fundamental way possible. And wasn't that what people often craved in the aftermath of death?

'Is it?' he prompted as he watched the slow wash of colour and the darkening of her eyes.

'I don't think I've ever received such an untempting offer in my life!'

'I wasn't making you an offer,' he countered insultingly. 'I was asking you a question. Though maybe the question that I *should* have asked was whether what has just happened has made you change your mind about staying?'

'Oh, now I see.' She glittered him a look. 'Is that why you did it? Because you thought I would be so outraged by your behaviour that I would storm out of here and leave without giving Teodoro a chance to get to know me? Well, if that's the case then I'm afraid you badly misjudged me, Luis!'

'You mean you still want to stay?'

She shook her head; all she knew was that she wanted to take Teo to England to meet his maternal grandmother—but instinct warned her that this was not the moment to ask him. 'I don't know if ''want'' is the word I would use. "Need" might be better. As I said, Teodoro needs to know that he has an alternative family.'

'Very well.' He gave her a look of cool appraisal, then shrugged. 'Finish your breakfast,' he said.

'As if nothing has happened?'

'And nothing has.' The black eyes lanced through her. 'Nor will it.'

'You mean you won't kiss me again?'

'Not through anger, no. There will be no need to silence you if you do not continue to make your harsh allegations against me, Sophie.' He curved his mouth into a cynical smile. 'Of course, if you invite me to then that is quite a different matter altogether.'

'Oh, don't worry, Luis—there's no chance of that!'

He lifted the coffee-pot and poured himself a cup. 'And if you intend to stay then I suggest that we should at least behave in a civil way towards each other. Do you think we could manage that, Sophie, to exist in harmony?'

Could they? Manage to ignore the niggling tensions which stubbornly wouldn't seem to go away?

He saw the indecision and reluctance on her face. 'You have an alternative suggestion?' he asked quietly. 'That we eat our meals in isolation? That we have no contact with each other during your stay? If that is to be the case, *querida,* then it means that you will see very little of your nephew. Whom you profess to want to get to know.'

'*Profess* to want to?' she echoed. 'Of course I want to get to know him! Why else do you think I am here?'

He shrugged and reached for a peach. 'I can think of a few reasons.'

'Such as?'

'Perhaps you wish to discover whether any of my fortune has been made over to your cousin, who in turn might have passed it on to you.'

Sophie sat down before her knees gave way. 'My God, how you constantly surprise me, Luis,' she said drily. 'There was I, thinking that your opinion of me couldn't get any lower, but how wrong I was! Sorry to disappoint you, but I am just not interested in your money!'

His eyes were lit from within, like ebony fire. 'No matter what we are thinking underneath, Sophie, you must force yourself to see reason,' he said softly. 'If my wife knew and accepted my relationship with Alejandra, then there is no earthly reason why it should offend *you*. Is there? And there is no point in us fighting. It matters nothing what I think of you, or you of me. For we are nothing to one another except in terms of our relationship with Teo, no matter how our bodies tell us differently.'

Strange how words could wound like arrows. 'Very well,' she agreed painfully. 'I'm sure I can manage to be civil for a few days.'

'Good. Oh, and before I forget,' he continued as he began to peel the peach with a small knife, until the skin fell into a voluptuous curl on his plate, 'I have a family wedding to attend in Madrid next weekend, and I shall be taking Teo with me. If you are still here you may wish to come along.'

'Seriously?'

'Why not?'

'Isn't that a little soon?' Surely even *he* would want to go through the motions of some kind of mourning ritual?

He continued to cut his peach, his knife piercing the soft, sweet flesh. 'Life goes on, Sophie, and especially life for my son. There will be family there, close family, who have not seen Teo for many months, and they will wish to embrace him and to comfort him.'

'And comfort you, too, I suppose,' said Sophie in a hollow voice. 'The grieving widower.'

He met her eyes with a calm look. 'It's up to you,' he said carelessly. 'Come if you wish, or stay behind, it matters little to me.'

'I—I don't have anything suitable to wear for a grand wedding.'

'I'm sure you will be able to find something—there are some very beautiful clothes available in the city,' he said, and gave a slow smile. 'I shall just have to take you shopping, won't I?'

It was a darkly proprietorial statement, the kind of careless statement that a man would make to his mistress, the kind of statement she could imagine him making to Alejandra, and it should have made her hackles rise.

So how come her heart had started racing as if in anticipation of some delicious, illicit pleasure?

CHAPTER SIX

Luis leaned forward. *'Palacio Santo Mauro, por favor!'*

The driver nodded. *'Sì, Don Luis.'*

The powerful limousine moved out of the airport towards the centre of Madrid and Luis settled back in his seat.

'Look at Madrid, Sophie,' he instructed softly. 'See her beauty for yourself.'

Sophie obediently stared out of the window, thinking that the city's beauty paled into insignificance when compared to the man beside her and reflecting on the turn-around in their relationship since he had told her the truth about his marriage.

Unbelievable, really.

There had been no more fighting, nor recriminations—both had been determinedly polite and courteous with each other, though they had warily circled one another, like two people determined to keep as much physical distance between themselves as possible.

And Luis had been right, Sophie recognised that now. She really was in no position to criticise him for having a mistress. It was his choice and his life and she was no part of it. But it still hurt more than it had any right to hurt whenever she thought about it, and so she tried not to think about it. Something made easier by the fact that, as far as she knew, he had paid no return visit to Alejandra—there had been no further nighttime trysts.

She guessed that he was waiting until she went back to England, and the return journey had been much on her mind, even though she had yet to come to a decision about when to leave. She knew that she could not stay indefinitely, but she still hadn't summoned up the courage to ask him about taking Teodoro with her. She was waiting for the right moment and that moment hadn't yet arrived. And she was still afraid of what his answer might be.

But she could not deny that the days before the wedding had been largely enjoyable days—almost too enjoyable, really.

In the mornings Luis went to work, leaving Sophie to help Salvadora with Teo, and now Sophie had gained Salvadora's trust, as well as Teo's affection— the older woman seemed eager to delegate more and more.

Not that Sophie minded—not a bit of it. Under Salvadora's watchful eye, she had begun teaching Teo to swim, and once Luis had come back from work unexpectedly early and found the two of them splashing around happily in the pool.

'What is this?' he had demanded, and Sophie had looked up, her wet hair plastered to her head and streams of water running down her face while Teo giggled against her cheek.

'I'm teaching Teo to swim!'

'Without my permission?' he questioned darkly.

'I won the county cup for breast-stroke!' she said. 'He's been perfectly safe with me!'

'I can see that for myself,' he responded softly,

trying to ignore the ache which her words had produced. Breast-stroke, indeed! Witch! 'But in future you will clear any activities with me, Sophie, is that understood?'

'Perfectly.' She nodded, and slid a little further down into the turquoise water, the swimsuit suddenly seeming just too revealing.

'Just in case you plan to take him rock-climbing,' he finished laconically.

In the afternoons, after the siesta, Luis seemed determined to show Sophie as much of La Rioja and the surrounding countryside as Teo's routine allowed.

And the more he showed her, the more she liked it. She loved the region's peace and its natural beauty, which made London seem very crowded and grey in comparison. She saw for herself the clear, deep waters of the wide River Ebro, the only river in Spain which flowed down to the Mediterranean, its banks frilly with vineyards and pinstriped with rows of garden vegetables.

There were beautiful mountains in the Sierra de la Demanda, and when she had said so he'd smiled, almost indulgently. 'Mmm, very beautiful, and high enough to ski down. Do you ski, Sophie?'

She nodded. 'I'm completely addicted to it,' she confessed.

'Me, too.'

She didn't want to discover the things that they had in common. If only he had told her that he hated skiing with a passion!

He had stopped the car so that they could look at the breathtaking gullies of Rioja Baja. 'Look down there,' he mused, his voice deepening. 'There dinosaurs once made the earth tremble—'

'Seriously?'

'They certainly did. Or at least left their curious tracks in a prehistoric bog, which petrified for posterity.'

He told her that, even today, tourists from all over the world came to the region to see for themselves the evidence of these huge and ancient beasts. It was a side of Spain she hadn't known existed.

'You thought we only had bulls?' he teased.

'I suppose I did,' she answered slowly.

'Shame on you, Sophie—for the gaps in your education!' But there was so much more than history that he wanted to teach her, knowing as well that it was forbidden. *She* was forbidden. And elusive and unknown, he reminded himself, and behind the wrap-around shades he wore his eyes hardened.

One rare and deliciously cool afternoon, the three of them had travelled to Navarra's 'magic' mountain of Aralar, wooded with beech and rowan and hawthorn groves.

Sophie had unpacked the simple picnic and looked around, while Luis hoisted Teodoro up onto his shoulders for the best possible view while he told of the legend of San Miguel, and Sophie lay back and listened, mesmerised.

'It's a beautiful story,' she murmured when he had finished. 'And this is so beautiful, too.' She waved her hand to encompass the lush green landscape.

He raised his eyebrows. 'You thought it would be harsh and inhospitable?'

'A little,' she agreed, thinking that once she had

imagined him both these things, but he was neither. There was a sensitivity and a soulfulness to his character which did nothing to detract from his unquestionable masculinity and innate sensuality. It became easier to understand with each minute that passed just why Miranda had been so determined to have him.

And in the evenings, after supper, Sophie would retire to her room to catch up with her e-mails and to read through documents which Liam had forwarded to her.

Oliver had texted her and rung her and her reaction to the phone calls had brought her close to something like despair. She remembered how excited she had been at the prospect of dating him. But that excitement seemed to have evaporated into nothing more than mildly interested friendship. At least on her part. And she was perceptive enough to understand the reason why.

'When are you coming back, Sophie?' he'd asked. 'And having dinner with me?'

'I don't know. I haven't decided yet.'

'You know how much I want to take you out,' he murmured. 'I should have asked you ages ago, but I guess your reputation stopped me.'

'*What* reputation?' she laughed.

'Oh, you know—for being cool. Unapproachable.'

Cool? Unapproachable? She would bet a month's salary that Luis was not of the same opinion.

Just once, she had sat and drunk wine with him on the terrace, late into the night, with the moon huge as a dinner plate in the night sky. Around them the sounds of the cicadas had echoed in piercing yet restful chorus while she'd told him all about her company—her hopes and dreams for it and how close they looked to being fulfilled.

'I applaud you your ambition,' he said softly, and Sophie had to stifle a sigh. The perfect setting and the perfect man. Except that he wasn't perfect, she must keep telling herself that. And he certainly wasn't perfect for *her*.

The car glided down one of Madrid's main streets. It was beginning to feel too much like a holiday, she realised uncomfortably, and at that moment he moved, and the fabric of his trousers flattened distractingly over the hard shaft of his thighs.

Sophie swallowed. 'So tell me about the bride and groom,' she said quickly as the car began to pick up speed again.

He turned his head to look at her. 'What do you want to know?'

'Oh, the usual things. Something. Anything!' Anything to make her stop thinking about the mouth which had kissed her with such sweet, angry thoroughness.

If only the baby would wake up and occupy them! Divert her attention away from the watchful black glitter of his eyes. But Teodoro, who had been playful and communicative during the flight, was now sleeping happily.

'Ramon is a cousin of mine,' he replied. 'He is marrying Estrella, whom he has known for many years.'

'So does he love her?'

He turned his head to meet the challenge in her gaze, his eyes narrowing. He knew the subtext beneath her question—was his cousin's marriage going to replicate his own? 'Ramon loves Estrella with a passion,' he said quietly, and for the first time in his life he found himself envying someone.

'Well, I guess that's something.'

'Yes, it is—and she is far too fiery to contemplate ever sharing her *marido* with another woman.'

'And that's something, too!' she added drily.

'So you're a romantic at heart, are you, Sophie?' he mocked.

'I just believe that marriage should mean forsaking all others. That's what the vows say.'

'That's what they say all right,' he agreed evenly.

This was getting too compatible for comfort. 'So there'll be lots of your family at this wedding?'

'Yes. Lots. My parents. My sisters. Countless other cousins.'

'And the cream of Spanish aristocracy, I suppose?'

He inclined his head. 'Of course.'

He said it carelessly, as if it was the natural order of things, which she supposed it was. He was so sure of himself and his rarefied, exalted position in the world. And maybe that was the major part of his attraction. Would a woman look at him twice and lose her head over him if he were—say—a farmworker?

But then Sophie imagined the reality of that scenario, could picture it perfectly in her mind's eye. Luis engaged in hard physical labour, yes—that took no great leap of the imagination. His physique suggested that he could accomplish any such thing with ease. She could visualise tiny beads of sweat glimmering, burnishing the dark skin of his broad shoulders, the ripple of muscles as he worked the land, and her breath caught in her throat. A man like Luis would be desired by women no matter what he did.

'Won't they think it rather strange that you're bringing your wife's cousin along to a family wedding?'

'But it is precisely *because* you are family that they will accept it unthinkingly,' he murmured, noticing that her pupils had dilated and her lips had parted into a little pout, and he felt his body begin to harden with tension. 'The Spanish people put great value on a sense of family.'

She stared out of the window as the magnificent buildings of the capital passed them by, telling herself that she should consider herself lucky to be flown across Spain in the lap of luxury. But she didn't feel lucky. She felt...sad. Yes, sad, stupidly enough. Because soon she would leave this place and this man, and although she knew that it would only be for the best—part of her ached hopelessly to stay.

'You are excited to be in Madrid, Sophie?' questioned Luis softly, seeing the sudden tense set of her profile and wondering what had caused it.

'Kind of.'

'Oh, to be damned with faint praise! If Madrid were a woman she would now be shedding tears!' he murmured drily.

'Oh, I have nothing against the city.'

'Just your travelling companion, is that it?'

She turned to face him, arrested by the inky glitter of his eyes and the lush, kissable lines of his lips. 'Given the choice, I don't think I would have settled for a weekend away with you, no.'

'My ego is severely wounded,' he murmured.

'That makes a change.'

'Indeed it does,' he agreed gravely.

Sophie pressed her lips together, hating it when he teased her like that, or, rather, liking it too much, because it conjured up an intimacy which didn't really exist. They were just two people thrown together through circumstance and making the best of an awkward situation.

But at the moment it didn't feel like an awkward situation. She felt as excited as a schoolgirl on her first trip abroad—being with him and Teo in a glamorous city, with the prospect of staying at one of Spain's finest hotels.

Perhaps a more sensible woman would have refused to accompany him on this trip, but what would have been the point of that? To wander aimlessly around the beautiful villa on her own, with Teodoro miles away—when getting to know him was her sole reason for being here? And as she kept telling herself, she couldn't stay on indefinitely…

Liam and the others were coping perfectly well back at the office, but the fact remained that she had a pivotal role in the company and she could not leave it unfilled indefinitely while she luxuriated in Spain.

As if on cue, the mobile phone in her bag rang, and she heard Luis click his tongue impatiently against the roof of his mouth.

'Don't you ever turn that thing off?' he drawled.

'There wouldn't be a lot of point in having a mobile phone if people can't reach me on it, would there?' she replied serenely, clicking the connection and reading the name which flashed up on the screen. 'Liam! Hi! What's happening?'

Luis raised his eyebrows as he smoothed back a black curl from Teo's cheek. She had told him that Liam was her partner—but perhaps her 'partner' wanted more than a business arrangement, judging from the amount of times he seemed to ring her!

And what of this Oliver—who also seemed very fond of phone calls and sending her a series of text messages.

What, he mused, would either man say if he knew how much she was trying to fight her attraction towards him? An attraction made all the more obvious by the way she constantly tried to hide it. From herself, he suspected, just as much as from him.

He wondered if she knew how transparent her face could be. If she was aware that her pupils always darkened when their eyes met, only to be followed by cheeks being flushed by a telltale guilty pink, as if she was afraid that he could read her thoughts.

Not her thoughts, no; at least, not always. But her body, yes—that was easy enough to read. And a lifetime of being finely tuned to the desires of women convinced Luis that Sophie was by no means immune to him.

'No, I'm in Madrid,' she was saying. 'With Luis.'

'Madrid?' Liam echoed. 'You mean you're at the airport? Does that mean you're coming home?'

'Er—no. Not yet. I'm...I'm actually on my way to a family wedding.'

There was a short, disbelieving silence. 'With *him?*'

Sophie shot a glance at Luis's profile, but even though he could hear every word she was saying it was as expressionless as if it had been carved from some golden-olive marble. She watched as he absently smoothed the dark curls of the sleeping child.

'That's right,' she agreed, thinking that as a father he couldn't be faulted. He was a wonderful father.

'Are you listening, Sophie?' questioned Liam, and to her horror she realised that she had switched off, letting her thoughts run away—and lately they seemed to be running in a very predictable direction indeed.

'I thought the whole point of you going over there was to be with your nephew,' he objected. 'Not gallivanting around the place with a man you're supposed to despise.'

'Teodoro's with us.'

'That's not what I meant—'

'Listen, Liam, I can't really talk now,' she said rather pointedly, because Luis's mouth had hardened into a brief, hard smile and she was worried that Liam might say something *really* insulting about him and that he might hear. 'Was there something in particular you wanted to speak to me about?'

'What? Oh, yeah. It's Ted Jacobs—'

'I e-mailed him first thing!'

'He wants to see you.'

'Well, he *can't!*'

'But he said—'

'Listen, Liam,' she interrupted, because Teodoro was now beginning to stir, 'you're perfectly capable of dealing with Ted yourself.'

'Yeah, but he prefers you.'

'I know he does,' she sighed. 'But you'll just have to explain to him what's happened. I need to be here; my nephew needs me.'

'And what about Luis?' questioned Liam slowly. 'Does he need you, too? Sounds to me like you're conveniently slotting in where your cousin left off, Sophie. Cosy, cosy, cosy! Is that it?'

If only he knew that Miranda had spent the majority of her time at the opposite end of the country! Sophie knew Liam was only asking out of concern for her, but she couldn't really start explaining patiently to Liam that Luis hardly needed a replacement wife—not when he had a mistress waiting patiently in the wings.

'Ring me on Monday,' she sighed. 'I'll be back from Madrid by then! OK?'

'OK,' he echoed. 'I'll talk to you on Monday. Have a good time.' But he didn't sound as though he meant it.

She broke the connection to find Luis looking at her, and the deep voice was full of a lazy amusement which matched the expression in his eyes. 'So, they cannot cope without you?'

'I suppose I should be flattered that they miss me when I'm not there.'

'But you are not flattered?' he observed.

She stole a look across to where Teodoro's eyelashes were just beginning to flutter. Funny how you could suddenly find you were changing your mind about certain things. Sophie had two god-daughters, whom she adored, but she had never been one of those women who put having a baby at the top of their wish-list.

Yet the time she had been spending with Teo had been a real eye-opener. She had discovered that cajoling a smile out of a toddling infant could be just as rewarding as landing a big business deal.

Or maybe it was just Teo himself, and the effect he had on her. Dreamily she smiled down at his sleeping head, until she remembered that Luis had been talking to her, and she looked up to find his black eyes sizzling into her.

'Not particularly flattered, no,' she said, dragging her thoughts back to the present. 'It makes me wonder if I haven't bothered to delegate effectively if they can't do without me for a couple of weeks. Or maybe we should just think seriously about taking someone else on. It had crossed my mind that the staff quota hasn't kept up with company expansion.'

In the evenings he had heard the blip of her computer while she worked in her room. 'You work hard,' he commented.

'Well, so do you.'

'Not too much just lately,' he answered flatly.

'You've had your hands full with Teo.'

'Yes.' He gave a wry glance at his son. And not just with Teo, with Sophie, too. Mountain picnics weren't supposed to be on his agenda. He had tried telling himself that their excursions were solely for his son's benefit—except that wouldn't have quite been the truth, because he enjoyed showing her his country. And, let's face it, he thought, she has proved to be a very enthusiastic and decorative recipient.

'And the vineyards haven't ground to a halt without you, have they?' she teased.

He laughed. 'Not yet they haven't.'

'Nobody's indispensable, Luis. Not even you.'

'Nor you either,' he mused.

Teo woke up then and jabbed a finger against his father's mouth and giggled—as if wanting his father to laugh some more—and the car glided to a halt in front of a vast building.

A uniformed doorman pulled the door open and Sophie looked up at the magnificent façade. 'Good heavens,' she said faintly. 'Is this where we'll be staying?'

'Not just us. Most of the family have taken rooms. Do you like it, Sophie?'

Like it? How could she not? 'It's lovely.'

'Just wait until you see the interior,' he promised.

He was as good as his word. Inside was a wood-lined interior of mirrors and paintings, and enormous potted palms. The vaulted ceiling seemed to go on for ever and the air was cooled by old-fashioned fans.

It was difficult not to be slightly overawed at such an unashamedly luxurious place, but Teodoro was grizzling by now, squirming in his father's arms while Luis was speaking in rapid and incomprehensible Spanish to the receptionist, a whole mass of baby equipment at his feet.

'Come, Teo,' whispered Sophie, holding her arms out tentatively towards him. 'Come to Sophie.' And to her delight he wriggled inside them, snuggling up comfortably against her breasts. She buried her nose in the sweet fragrance of his hair and held him very tight, and Teo giggled and began to play with her hair.

Unseen, Luis had watched the whole little scene, and his dark eyes narrowed. He was reluctantly moved by the way she was around his son. Her reaction was not feigned; he could tell that—and Teo would have seen through it if it had been. Children could always tell whether affection was genuine.

It perplexed him.

It was unusual for a woman of her independence to invest so much time and emotion and commitment in a child who would never be more than on the periphery of her life.

So why? Was it simply love and loyalty to her cousin which made her act in this way, or did she have an ulterior motive? Some hidden agenda which might later become clear? But the bellboy was standing waiting and Luis nodded. Now was not the time to dwell on 'what ifs' which might never happen.

'Come, Sophie,' he said softly. 'They will show us to our rooms.'

The rooms were more like individual suites of the penthouse variety.

'All this, just for me?' asked Sophie as she stood in the middle of a floor the size of a ballroom, still holding Teo in her arms and resisting the urge to dance around with him.

'You sound like a little girl,' he murmured, watching her uninhibited pleasure as she looked around the room.

'I *feel* like a little girl, let loose in the sweet shop!'

He imagined her in pigtails and had to stifle a groan as she bent and put Teo gently down on the carpet and he immediately began to crawl.

'Where will he sleep?' she asked him.

'I have arranged to have a cot in my room.' He pointed to a door at the far end of the room. 'Through there.'

Sophie swallowed. 'A-adjoining rooms?'

'It's a family suite—there is usually a connecting door.' His eyes glittered with a mocking challenge. 'Why, does it bother you?'

It most certainly did. The thought of such a thin divide between them. Of Luis in bed only yards away. At least back at the hacienda there had been a whole long corridor between them, and the knowledge that Salvadora and Pirro were also in the house acting as unseen chaperons.

But she met his eyes with a gaze as coolly mocking as his own. 'Not at all. Should it?'

A small smile curved the edges of his lips. She was lying. She knew it and he knew it. How would she respond if he challenged her?

But Teo had now set off at speed around the room, and already Luis could see several objects which needed to be moved out of reach of an inquisitive little hand.

He picked up the bin just as Sophie whisked away the bowl of complimentary sweets.

'I think we'll lose the candy,' she said, and reached up to put it safely away on the top of a bureau. 'Er—Luis.'

'Mmm?' He had been watching the lithe movement of her body as she stretched up. She had twisted her hair up and pinned it to the top of her head, leaving her long neck bare, save for a stray silken wisp, and he recalled the night he had walked into her bedroom, the way her hair had streamed down over her breasts, thick as honey.

She turned round, and wrinkled her nose as she picked Teo up. 'I think Teo needs changing. Do you want me to do it?'

He frowned. 'You think I cannot?'

'I don't know. Can you? I notice that you usually leave that side of things to Salvadora.'

'She seems happy enough to do it.'

'She probably can't imagine the sight of Don Luis de la Camara doing such a thing. Women's work,' she added drily.

'But you think it's a man's work, too?'

'Of course I do! Baby care has to be shared—you can't just delegate the less pleasant parts and keep all the best bits for yourself, otherwise how would you ever bond with him properly?' She smiled up at him, enjoying the rare moment of perplexity which made him look disconcertingly approachable. 'Would you like me to show you how?'

The perplexity vanished and was replaced with a look of outrage. 'I do not need lessons from you, Sophie!' he growled.

'You've done it before, have you?' she questioned doubtfully.

No, he hadn't. But, by the hand of God, surely it could not be difficult to change a nappy?

It appeared that it was.

Which was why Luis's mother found her son kneeling on the ground, trying to attach a clean nappy to a wriggling Teo, with Sophie, having fought desperately hard not to laugh, eventually losing the battle and dissolving into a fit of the giggles.

'You're hopeless!'

'Por Dios!' he exclaimed.

'Luis?'

He turned his head and saw his mother standing at

the door, her elegant features set into a look of bemusement. *'Buenos dias, Madre!'*

'Here.' Sophie crouched down beside him. 'Let me. You go and greet your mother.'

He sizzled her a frustrated stare. 'You will teach me later,' he murmured, and then he was on his feet, embracing his mother as they kissed on both cheeks.

'You did not bring Salvadora with you?' questioned his mother in Spanish.

He shook his head. 'She is getting old, Madre. And besides, Sophie said that it would do me good to have sole responsibility for him.'

'Oh, *did* she?' asked his mother, her dark eyes looking questioningly at her son. But by then Sophie had scooped up a happy and contented child and was holding him out towards his grandmother, who immediately took him and began to rain kisses on his ebony curls.

'My beautiful, beautiful grandson!' she exclaimed as Teo began to play with her exquisite pearl necklace.

'Isn't he?' Luis smiled and then began to speak in English. 'Mother, I need to take Sophie shopping to buy a dress to wear for the wedding—'

His mother smiled. 'And you want to leave Teo with me, is that it?'

'You don't mind?'

'Mind? Leave him with me for a week if you wish! Even longer!'

He glanced down at his watch. 'We'd better get going if we're going to make it in time.'

He hailed a cab outside and ordered it to drive to

the Salamanca region, where the city's finest shops were situated.

'Do you think your mother minds me being here?' asked Sophie as the door of an upmarket shop slid open. 'You said she wouldn't.'

'No, I don't think so,' he murmured. 'Why should she?'

'I just thought she looked at me a little strangely back there.'

He suspected that the look had something to do with his revelation that Sophie had offered him advice. And that he had taken it. 'It was probably the sight of her oldest son on his knees, changing a nappy,' he commented wryly. 'Come, now, Sophie, and tell the young lady what it is you are looking for.'

The clothes were out of this world, and Sophie was torn between an ice-blue floor-length sheath in clinging silk, with a matching coat which could be worn in the church, and a starker, more chic outfit in sophisticated grey.

'I can't decide! Which?' She turned to the salesgirl.

'Turn around,' came Luis's deep, velvety voice.

Slowly she twirled, acutely aware of the dark eyes appraising her.

'Get the blue,' he said carelessly, though his mouth was dry with desire. 'It matches your eyes.' And the dress clung like a second skin.

But when Sophie emerged from the changing room it was to find Luis charging the outfit to his account.

'What the hell do you think you're doing?'

'What does it look like, *querida?*'

'I am perfectly able to buy my own clothes!'

'But it is an unexpected expense. You were not expecting to have to purchase something of this value. Come, Sophie, let me buy it for you.'

'No! Definitely not!'

His black eyes glittered. 'I can afford it!'

'I know you can, and so can I! Here—' With a polite smile she gently removed his credit card from the fingers of the bemused sales assistant, and replaced it with one of her own.

There was a moment of highly charged silence. 'You are very stubborn, *querida*,' he said silkily.

'You're pretty stubborn yourself,' she returned. 'Or is it just that no woman has ever turned down a gift from you before?'

'But why should they?' he asked seriously. 'When I am happy to give it?'

Sophie stared at him. Had he never been with a woman who tried to meet him on equal terms? 'It's to do with something called pride, Luis,' she said quietly.

Pride.

Orgullo.

He gave a cynical half-smile. It was not a word he usually associated with the women in his life. Women wanted him; they had always wanted him—and to that end a gift would have been seen as a symbol of their importance. So why was Sophie Mills looking at him with such disdainful scorn?

'Why do you refuse?' he husked as the salesgirl turned away to wrap up the outfit.

'Because it would make me feel like a kept woman!'

He guessed that now was not the time to point out

that 'kept' women usually provided favours in return for gifts—because with that mutinous look on her face he could not trust her not to deliver an almighty ringing slap to his cheek in the middle of the department store!

He shrugged in impatient and uncharacteristic capitulation. 'Very well! You may pay for it if you insist!'

'Oh, thank you very much,' she returned sarcastically. 'I fully intend to.'

He itched to subdue her in a way which would have her sighingly accept his offer. To have her make such a scene and to refuse his offer in front of the sales assistant! She spoke of pride—did she not consider that she had offended his own masculine pride?

He simmered quietly in the car on the ride back to the hotel and Sophie sighed as she looked at his unforgiving profile.

'Of course, if you're going to be in a bad mood for the rest of the day—'

'Why should I be in a bad mood?' he questioned airily.

'Because you didn't get your own way! I thought that we were emphatically *not* going to judge each other during this trip. So humour me in my independence, won't you, Luis?'

He stared into her eyes and met the glint of amusement there. 'Very well, stubborn Sophie,' he sighed. 'The subject is closed, forgotten. Now sit back and enjoy the city.'

CHAPTER SEVEN

THERE was only just enough time left for Sophie to shower and change for the wedding, and she had just finished applying a final slick of lipstick when Luis knocked on her door.

'Sophie? Are you ready?'

A final glance in the mirror and Sophie nodded. She would do. She would have to. 'Yes. Come in!'

Carrying Teo, Luis entered the room, and he stilled when he caught that first sight of her, his black eyes narrowing like those of some jungle cat who had stumbled upon some unknown predator.

Sophie swallowed and dabbed her fingertips to her face. Had she inadvertently missed her lashes and smudged mascara all over her cheek? 'Is something wrong?'

Wrong? *Madre de Dios!* Had anything ever looked more right? The woman looked like a goddess brought to golden and gleaming life. Luis felt a pulse begin to beat heavily in his temple. And even more heavily in his groin. He shook his head. 'You're wearing make-up,' he commented throatily.

'Well, of course I'm wearing make-up! I'm going to have to stand next to numerous beautiful members of the Spanish aristocracy, so I have to look my best.'

'But you don't usually bother.'

'I know. Only for special occasions. It always

seems slightly mad to me to spend ages slapping the stuff on, only to have to take it off again!'

And the delicacy of her features and the huge blue eyes meant that, unlike most women, she could get away with the scrubbed look. But with make-up... He sucked in a raw breath of longing... She looked utterly magnificent!

Her eyes seemed to dominate her face, the darkening of the mascara emphasising their saucer-shape, while the shiny lipstick made her mouth all provocative pout. Her skin gleamed, softly golden, smooth as silk and just as sensual.

And the dress...

Luis couldn't keep his eyes off it.

The sensual fabric of the silk clung like syrup to her breasts and her hips, making the most of their slender curves. Sweet heaven! he thought heatedly. If it had been anyone else but Sophie, he might have suggested caressingly that she let her hair down, but that was most definitely not within his remit.

'You look extremely beautiful, *querida*,' he said haltingly.

So did he, if the word beauty could be applied to such an unequivocally masculine man. And somehow, yes, it could, for beauty could be angular and lean and hard as well as soft and luscious and curved.

She couldn't stop her eyes from drinking in the vision he made, his lean body defined by the formal cut of the dark suit, drawing attention to the length of his legs and the narrow jut of his hips. He must have just shaved, because for once the strong curve of his jaw was without its usual faint shadowing and the thick black hair gleamed with tiny droplets of water, fresh from the shower.

It took an almighty effort, but somehow she dragged her eyes away from him to Teo, resplendent in a snowy-white sailor-suit trimmed with navy blue. 'And you look utterly gorgeous, Teo,' she whispered. 'What a handsome boy!'

Teo cooed and suddenly the huge room seemed far too small, and, God-forbid him, Luis wished that they were alone, unbearably tempted to take her into his arms, and to kiss the soft pink lips clean of all that lipstick. He swallowed.

'Come. Let us go,' he said thickly.

A car was waiting to take them to the ancient flower-filled church and Sophie could feel curious eyes on them as they walked up the aisle to take their places with his family. Did she imagine it, or could she hear whispered voices murmuring in Spanish as they entered the church? Were they wondering who was the blonde woman who accompanied the Don and his young son?

It was an emotional ceremony, but then weddings were supposed to be emotional, weren't they? Except for Miranda's, Sophie realised suddenly. A colourless register office on a hot summer day, with Miranda pale and wilting and newly pregnant. But there had been an unmistakable note of triumph as she had made her vows and Luis's accented response had been faultless. But without passion.

Not like this. The bride's voice shook as she made her vows and the look of adoration in her new husband's eyes made Sophie feel breathless with a wishful kind of envy.

I want that too, she realised. If ever I marry it must be to a man who loves me with that fierce kind of passion. I want love, she thought wistfully. Real, enduring love. The kind of love which could move mountains.

And the man who stood beside her could never give her that. Never in a million years.

She glanced over at Teo, who had been surprisingly quiet and was now sucking his thumb as the choir gave a soulful rendition of some haunting Spanish hymn.

He was growing to know her, yes, and even to like her—but how long would it take before Luis would entrust Teo into her care and allow her to take the child to England?

She was going to have to discuss it, and soon, she decided as she stood up for the final blessing.

The reception was held in the ballroom of the hotel and was the most lavish occasion that Sophie had ever been to. They were serving exquisite regional delicacies and fine de la Camara wines, and the overpowering scent of the white lilies which adorned the room was decadently heady.

Teo was whisked from relative to relative while Luis introduced Sophie to various aunts, cousins and uncles.

Their eyes were curious enough, but they asked no questions about her presence—she supposed that generations of aristocratic breeding kept their conversation strictly neutral, though what they were thinking was anyone's guess.

And what was Luis thinking, as female after beautiful female sought his attention? His eyes gave nothing away, other than a slightly indulgent inky glitter as one woman after another attempted to monopolise him.

Then the music began. Soft, beguiling strings to lure people onto the dance floor. The bride and groom. Parents. Cousins. A middle-aged uncle whirling Teo around and an exquisite young Spanish woman who glanced up at Luis with eager shyness. He nodded, almost imperceptibly, as he took her into his arms.

'Such a—handsome couple they make,' murmured one of Luis's aunts in halting English as they danced past.

'Don't they?' Sophie agreed, but her heart was racing and she cursed the stupid, sharp and unrealistic pang of jealousy. He was not hers to be jealous of. Shaking her head at her own weakness, she went over to fetch herself a glass of water, quite prepared to be a wallflower but not prepared to watch while Luis moved with such careless grace with a succession of different women in his arms.

She sat it out for three numbers, sheltering behind a large potted plant, until she heard his deep, rich voice penetrating her mixed-up thoughts and felt herself tremble.

'Soph-ie?'

She glanced up and the watchful blaze from his black eyes dazzled her.

'Why are you hiding over here?' he asked her softly.

She forced a smile. 'I didn't hide well enough, did I, for you found me easily enough?'

He sat down in the chair beside her. 'Was that your intention, then, Sophie—to hide from me?'

She wondered what he would say if she told him the truth, that it hurt, it actually physically *hurt* to see another woman in his arms.

'I just wanted to rest my feet,' she lied.

'And now that you have rested them...' he allowed his gaze to travel to where the sexy little shoes rested beneath two such delicate ankles; she wore no stockings and he found himself wanting to remove the shoes, to massage the smooth and gleaming flesh, to rub the nub of his thumb round and around the instep of her sole '...are you going to dance with me?'

'I—I don't think that's such a good idea.'

'Oh?'

'People might think it rather strange—and I have no desire—' liar! '—no wish to monopolise you,' she breathed. 'Come on, Luis—there are any number of women here who must be dying for you to ask them.'

'But I am asking you, Sophie,' he persisted. 'And people will think it strange indeed if the Don does not dance with the woman who is his guest here. Come, Sophie—it is *my* wish. And if you do not desire—' he smiled as his voice lingered deliberately on the word '—to be discourteous you will do me the honour of dancing with me.'

She had never been asked to dance in quite such an irresistible way, but then she had never been asked to dance with a man quite so irresistible as Luis. It is courtesy, she reminded herself as he drew her into his arms. Simply courtesy.

But oh, the reality was heartachingly different. The sensation of being in his arms, with his hands resting lightly on her hips was such a delicious experience that she could scarcely breathe.

He pulled her against him and instantly his head was full of the scent of lilac. His fingers splayed possessively at the indentation of her narrow waist, the thin fabric of her dress making her seem outrageously accessible, almost as if he could feel her skin itself. But he wanted her closer, and closer still, and as he turned her round he drew her even tighter, watching her reaction and seeing the startled dilatation of her eyes as she made first contact with the inevitable evidence of how much he wanted her.

'Luis,' she said weakly.

'*Sì, querida?* You like to dance with me?'

She liked it more than was decent, but wasn't it just tantalising her to an unbearable pitch? Did he know what he was doing to her? He was so hard, and so magnificently unashamed of his arousal. Did every other woman he had danced with have the same effect on him? And were they, in turn, just longing to press themselves even harder against the jut of his hips and to feel the very cradle of his masculinity?

'You move very well.' She swallowed, praying that this wanting would go away.

He stifled a groan of frustration. So, sweet torment—so did she move very well. How much longer could he endure such temptation, and how long she?

She was starting to care, Sophie realised, and to care too deeply, for she wanted more than just his body—she wanted to see deep into his quick and clever mind, to find out for herself just what made Luis de la Camara really tick. But such wanting would bring her nothing. He already had a mistress, she reminded herself painfully, and so what the hell was he doing dancing with *her* like this?

The longer she stayed, the stronger the possibility that she would fall completely under his spell, and there was no future in it, no future at all. Could she bear that?

No, she could not. It was time to leave. And the sooner the better. 'I've had enough of dancing now,' she said shakily.

And so had he. Much more and he would find it impossible not to heatedly move his fingers across the satin surface of her back, and then to let them curve round to cup the luscious swell of her breasts.

He let his hands fall from her waist. 'We will find Teo,' he said flatly.

She knew that she could not put off telling him any longer, but she waited until later, when they were back in their rooms and a tired but happy Teo had been put to bed.

She rapped lightly on his door.

Luis was just taking off his cuff-links and trying to shake off the deep ache of frustration which had not left him all evening.

'Come in!'

The door opened and he turned around to see Sophie standing silhouetted in the doorway and his breath caught in his throat. He saw that she had let her hair down and that it gleamed in silken and golden array around her shoulders, and his eyes narrowed. Did she not know the danger in which she placed herself, or was she unaware that the light from behind her had turned the dress almost transparent, outlining the long, slender length of her legs?

Through the bodice he could see the tightened nubs of her nipples and the frustration inside him built up into an unbearable pitch.

He could hear his voice sounding unfamiliarly thick. *'Sì?'*

She stood in the doorway uncertainly. It was too intimate—far too intimate—to catch him in the act of undressing. How could she speak—when the words caught like dry pebbles in her throat? How *did* she? 'May I—may I speak to you for a moment, please?'

He glanced down at the sleeping child, and nodded, even though the words which must next be spoken sent all kinds of fantasies exploding into his mind's eye. 'But next door, in your bedroom,' he grated. 'Where Teo will not be disturbed.'

She nodded, her heart crashing against her ribs as he followed her into the room. It was like every dream she'd ever had come true. Except that it wasn't—it was going to be nothing more than a matter-of-fact talk which was long overdue.

Luis was almost driven crazy by the sight of her bottom as she walked in front of him. Sweet heaven—but the faint hint of a thong clearly outlined as the silk stretched over each high, curved buttock would have stretched any man's endurance.

And he knew then that he could not sleep, nor even live with himself if he did not do this...

'Luis!' she cried as with a sudden, unexpected movement he caught her in his arms and turned her around to face him, his mouth hovering deliciously close to hers. 'What are you doing?'

'What we have both wanted me to do all night,' he said unsteadily. 'To kiss you.'

'You promised that you would—'

'I promised that I would not kiss you in anger,' he agreed unsteadily. 'But there is no anger in me now, *querida*. Nor in you. I see nothing but sweet invitation in your eyes, and what kind of a man would I be if I ignored that delicious, silent message?'

It means nothing, she told herself. Just lust, that was all. But it didn't seem to make any difference, because nothing could have stopped her from succumbing to the raw passion which gleamed from his eyes, and the provocative promise of his parted lips. He bent his mouth to hers, her own automatically opening beneath his, the sharp tang of longing made satisfied and yet more hungry still with that first sweet contact.

She clung to him helplessly as he kissed her with a thoroughness which made her melt even further against his lean body, and with a groan he cupped her breasts and Sophie's knees threatened to give way.

'*Querida*,' he breathed as he incited a tiny nipple with the tip of his thumb.

She was on fire where he touched her with mind-blowing provocation. His hard thigh was pushing insistently against her and she felt her own legs parting of their own volition. And now he was impatiently rucking up the silky fabric of her dress, his fingertips feeling heated as they tiptoed over the cool flesh of her inner thigh. She squirmed in anticipation, wanting to beg him to touch her, and once he touched her...

Somewhere deep in the recesses of her mind, cold and inescapable logic acted like a bucket of icy water tipped all over her. She had to stop this and she had to stop it now, before it went too far—before either of them was unable to stop. How could she forget that this cold-hearted and distant man was a philanderer—and one who had made Miranda's life a misery?

Her body screaming out its protest, she stopped kissing him and pushed his hand away from her panties, trying to ignore the frowning look of frustration on his face and wondering if she looked just the same.

'Have a few days of abstinence from *Alejandra* made you long for a substitute mistress?' she gasped as she smoothed her dress down. 'If she's not around, then will anyone do?'

He shook his dark head impatiently. 'Alejandra is *not* my mistress!'

'As of when? As of now? You had sex with her on the night of the funeral. Surely you haven't forgotten *that?*'

'I did not have sex with her!' he ground out.

'Then why did you rush off to see her? To play backgammon?'

Did she imagine that he was capable of giving nothing other than sexual pleasure? he wondered heatedly. 'I went to see Alejandra because I realised that our relationship was over.'

'Convenient timing,' she volunteered drily.

'Not really.' He shook his dark head. 'Death forces you to confront reality—and the reality was that Alejandra was demanding far more than I was prepared to give her.'

'And what was that?' she questioned unsteadily.

He let out a heavy sigh. 'Our affair was never meant to be more than that—but she had mistakenly come to believe that because I was now "free" there was no obstacle standing in our way. And that we would soon be a couple—in every sense of the word.'

'She wanted to marry you?'

He gave an odd kind of smile. 'Alejandra has sensibilities, Sophie,' he said softly. 'And marriage was not actually mentioned, but, yes, I believe that was her true wish.'

So that was why he had dumped her—because she was getting too demanding, and Luis was not the kind of man who could cope with emotional demands.

She felt the slow sizzle of anger. Was this the way he treated all his mistresses? Discarding them once they were no longer satisfied with their tiny and limited role in his life?

And here he was, trying to make love to *her*—while she, stupid fool that she was, had very nearly fallen captive in his sensual snare!

She had to get out—and get out *now!*

'You insult me with your attempt to make love to me,' she said icily. 'And you treat women as second-class citizens! I'm going back to England, Luis—and I want to take Teodoro with me!'

CHAPTER EIGHT

LUIS'S eyes narrowed, all his frustrated desire for her melting away in the light of her unbelievable statement.

'Say that again,' he purred dangerously.

'I want to take Teo back to England. My grandmother wishes to meet him.'

'You will take Teo nowhere!' he snapped.

'I don't mean permanently—'

'Temporarily isn't even an option!' he said furiously. 'How dare you even suggest it?'

Oh, God—why had she stumbled it out so baldly? 'Please, Luis—'

But he hardened his heart against the appeal in her eyes. His instincts had told him not to trust her but he had let his desire dictate that those instincts go unheeded. 'What kind of fool are you, Sophie—to think that I would allow you to remove my son from his native land? Is it your intention to keep him there? To gain custody of him for yourself? Is that it, Sophie? Has that been your plan all along?'

'No, of course it hasn't!'

'There is no "of course" about it! We both know how notoriously difficult it is to extradite a child from another country,' he cut across her, still in that same, steely voice. 'You must be crazy if you thought that I would agree to such a scheme!'

Maybe she was. Too crazy for her own good.

Minutes ago she had actually been contemplating falling into bed with him—the man who could break her heart and chew it up and spit it out again. And instead of throwing herself on his mercy, of explaining her grandmother's request, she had issued what had sounded like an unreasonable demand. Had she really imagined that because he had proved to be a delightful partner over the last few days he would allow her to get on an aeroplane with his beloved son?

'Listen, maybe I phrased it badly—'

'Badly, perhaps—but at least truthfully,' he ground out. 'Is that why you've been so sweet and approachable lately, I wonder—because you wanted to lull me, to lure me into agreeing? Is that why you responded so beautifully in my arms while we danced tonight? Did you think that you might even make love to me, to lure me further still, to procure exactly what you wanted? Only at the last moment you couldn't go through with it, could you? Could not bring yourself to make love to a man you despise, no matter how much you wanted to get your hands on Teo?'

'Luis! You can't possibly believe that!'

'Oh, but I can! You have never made any secret of your real feelings for me—you just happen to be a consummate enough actress to be able to disguise them for a while.' His eyes glittered with rage. 'Perhaps that is also the reason why you were so accommodating towards my son?'

That hurt more than anything else he had said so far. 'Y-you honestly think that I manipulated Teo for my own ends?'

'How the hell do I know?'

She tried one last time. 'Luis, please—'

'Oh, spare me your pleas!'

She stared at him, this black-eyed stranger who was almost unrecognisable as the man who had just kissed her with such sweet, wild passion. 'And that is your final answer?'

'It is,' he agreed implacably.

'Then there is nothing more to be said.'

'No,' he agreed tightly. 'Not a single word.' His black eyes seared into her one last time, and then, with a final hardening of his mouth, he turned and left the room without another word.

Sleep was a long time in coming and Sophie awoke late to find that Luis was already up and dressed. He had left her a curt note to say that he had taken Teo downstairs for breakfast.

She showered and dressed and made her way to the dining room, seeing him seated at the far end of the room, his dark head bent and his mouth smiling as he spooned something into Teo's mouth.

Did he hear her footfall, or did he simply sense her presence in the room? Because he looked up as she approached, and his face grew hard and stony.

'Sit down, Sophie,' he said, the glitter in his eyes belying the courtesy of his words. 'Did you sleep well?'

'Not really, no. Did you?'

His rage had lasted long into the night, only fuelled by the thoughts that he had misjudged her badly, and further still by the fact that he had not made love to her. He ignored her question and parried with a mock-pleasant question of his own. 'Do you have your passport with you?'

'My passport?' she echoed blankly. 'Yes, it's upstairs in my handbag.'

'Good.' He spooned Teo another mouthful and nodded carelessly towards the dish of fruit, the basket of fresh pastries. 'I suggest that you eat your breakfast.'

There was something so very daunting about this icy, implacable Luis. 'I don't want any breakfast.' She wanted to know why the hell he was asking about her passport.

'So be it.' He shrugged. 'You will eat on the flight.'

'Flight? What flight? What are you talking about.'

'Your flight home.' He gave her a cold smile. 'I phoned the airline first thing. There is availability on the London flight from Madrid later on this morning. After all, I think you will agree that there is little point in you returning to La Rioja now.'

He was sending her away. As if she were nothing more than an unwanted parcel! 'But what about my things?'

'They will be forwarded on to you.'

'Just like that?'

'Just like that,' he agreed coolly.

She opened her mouth to argue with him, but the look in his eyes told her that there was no point. He was implacable in this. In everything. And he was right, she *was* a fool. She had let him get close— dangerously close—forgetting that he was offering nothing more than his body. And then she had blown everything—blurted out her intentions in a frustrated state of anger and hurt, and made him think the worst. But surely even Luis didn't really imagine that she wanted to steal his child away?

She registered the look of censure on his face, and realised that yes, he did—and that such a crime would never go unforgiven. Or unforgotten.

The rest of the morning passed in a blur, only brought into sharp and painful focus when he announced that he would not be accompanying her to the airport.

'I am spending the morning here in the city, with my mother and Teo.'

'Oh. Oh, I see.'

'So I will say goodbye now.'

She nodded, barely able to speak, but he let her hug Teo one last time.

'Goodbye, darling,' she whispered into his dark curls, and wondered when she would ever see him again.

A car was waiting outside the hotel in the warm sunshine, ready to whisk her to the Aeropuerto de Barajas, where she boarded her plane.

Luis had booked her into first class, but Sophie might as well have been on a cattle-truck for all the notice she took of the sublime service.

And when she landed back in England, to a cold and rainy day, she felt like a foreigner in her own country.

There were tons of messages on her Ansaphone and a whole stack of mail to catch up with, and before long she rang her grandmother.

'I'm back, Granny.'

'And Teo?'

'Oh...' She had been about to say "wait until you see him" but she bit the words back. 'He's...lovely...just lovely. I've taken millions of photos of him for you. I'll bring them down once they've been developed.'

There was a pause. 'But you won't be bringing him?'

'Nope.'

'Luis refused, I suppose?'

'Yes, I'm afraid that he did.'

'I suspected he would,' sighed her grandmother, and Sophie heard the sadness in her voice and wondered if she should have tried to fight harder for him.

Uneasily Sophie settled back into the busy routine of work. Of running for the tube and going to noisy pubs on Fridays, and lazy Sundays spent wandering round the shops and the galleries. But she missed Teo more than she could ever have imagined—nighttimes just didn't seem the same without his splashy bathtimes and bedtime story and then the sweet, baby smell of him. His little squeals of laughter when she tickled him, and his flailing, chubby arms while she taught him to swim.

The world and the life she had here in London was so different from the one she had just left behind. Almost too different. She missed the warm heat of the Spanish sun and the scent of the lemons which hung from the trees.

And she missed Luis, too. How strange was that? As if something fundamental to her life had been ripped from her, leaving her gaping, and aching— longing to hear his deep, softly-accented voice and see the enigmatic gleam of his black eyes.

So many miles away from him, it was easy to ignore the reason her head was trying to insist on and listen instead to the insistent clamourings of her heart.

Distance and time blurred the memory into only remembering what it wanted to.

Something had happened along the way, and it wasn't just sexual attraction because that had always been there—though she had ruthlessly quashed it when Miranda had been alive.

But it had proved impossible to be immune to the man who had been revealed to her—a man so at odds with the husband Miranda had described.

The Luis she had observed in Spain—the caring father, the intelligent and engaging companion—could that honestly have been enough to make her fall in love with him? Because it felt like love, or, rather, it felt as painful as only unrequited love could be.

She had never experienced emotions like this before. She felt like a drowning woman trying desperately to grab hold of a slippery rock which gave her no security. As if her old world was not real any more. She was just an outsider looking in—as if the people who made up her life were merely ghostly figures flitting through it like shadows.

She sent Teo a book, and two postcards of London, and said that she hoped she would see him again, and very soon, though part of her wondered whether Luis would pass the messages on.

Please, yes, she prayed. He might mistrust her motives, but surely, despite his angry words at the time, he could not really doubt the genuine love she had for his son.

And then, one evening, just when she had almost given up hoping, she got a phone call.

She had arrived home late, after a busy but rewarding day at the office. She and Liam had spent the week pitching for the biggest deal of their lives—taking on the advertising for a car company, and in particular for the latest must-have, upmarket sports model.

And to their astonished surprise they had clinched the deal and with it a multi-million-pound contract.

There had been champagne in the local wine bar afterwards and then Liam had suggested that they all go out for supper. Sophie had declined, pleading a headache, because you couldn't really tell your workmates that your heart was aching so much that you worried you would bring everyone's mood right down.

'You OK?' Liam had frowned.

'Of course I'm OK!' she had lied. 'I'm going to be a very rich woman!'

But what was money—what was anything, really, if you couldn't have the thing you wanted most of all?

What *had* happened to her? The cool, successful career woman had been slowly transformed into a woman who longed for the everyday pleasures of the family unit. And not just any family unit—there was a ready-made one with an unfilled vacancy of wife and mother.

Which was not on offer.

Definitely not on offer.

She picked up the phone.

'Soph-ie?'

And very nearly dropped it again.

'Luis?' she questioned breathlessly.

'Of course.' There was a pause while he relaxed,

half imagining that she might have slammed the phone down on him. And wouldn't he have deserved that? His voice softened. 'Would you like me to bring Teo over to see your grandmother?'

She closed her eyes tightly. 'Oh, Luis, really? Honestly? Do you mean it?'

'I do. Of course I do.' He sighed. Saying sorry had never come easily to him. 'Sophie, I was impetuous and blind to your own sense of duty. I should not have said to you the things I did. Once you'd gone I realised that your request was not an unreasonable one—'

'I should never have suggested I take him with me on my own.' But it would have been bizarre and inappropriate, surely, to ask Luis to accompany her back to England. As if they really *were* a couple.

'No, you shouldn't,' he agreed quietly. 'But that is done with now. Shall I come?'

'When?'

The urge to see her again consumed him. 'This weekend?'

It felt like the answer to every prayer she'd ever had. But he was just fulfilling his duty as a father, she reminded herself, not offering anything more. And even if his relationship with Alejandra was over there would be other women prepared to step into her shoes. Some beautiful Spanish woman who would make a far more suitable partner than the English cousin of his late wife.

'I'll meet you at the airport,' she promised unsteadily.

She put the phone down and rang her grandmother.

'Granny,' she said in a shaking voice, 'h-how would you like to see your grandson this weekend?'

On Saturday morning her fingers were trembling so much she could barely button up her dress, and the minutes dragged by like hours until Luis's flight touched down.

He came through the arrivals lounge, carrying Teo, his black eyes searching for her, and he felt the hot beat of desire when he saw her standing there, her blonde hair gleaming and lustrous, falling over the pale linen dress she wore.

He remembered her in his arms, the soft feel of her lips against his and the scent of her perfume bewitching him.

Sophie stood stock-still, unable to move, scarcely even able to breathe, the renewed sight of him sending her senses into overdrive. She had thought of little but him, yet the reality of his hard, lean body and proud, handsome face was a million times better than any memories.

And then Teo spotted her. 'Tho-thi!' he squealed, and she bit her trembling lip very hard as she held her arms open and the child went straight into them.

'He has missed you,' observed Luis.

Over the top of Teo's head she met the understanding dark gleam of his eyes.

'We both have,' he added softly.

It doesn't mean anything, she told herself fiercely. It doesn't.

'I've hired a car,' she managed. 'It's waiting outside. Oh, and I've bought toys and a big jigsaw for you, Teo.'

'You spoil him.'

'Why not? It's my pleasure.'

'I know it is.'

With Sophie still carrying the baby, the three of them left the airport.

'You don't own a car?' questioned Luis, once he had strapped Teo into the baby-seat.

She shook her head. 'There's no need to, really, not in London. I can walk, or get the tube—or taxis if it's raining.'

'And it is always raining?' He smiled.

'Certainly more than in La Rioja,' she agreed gravely.

Her grandmother was waiting by the door when the car drew up and the old-fashioned cottage garden looked just the same as it had done when Sophie had been a little girl. Hollyhocks and roses and clematis scrambled in profusion over the stone walls of the house.

'Hello, Luis,' smiled Mrs Mills, and then she looked long and hard at the black-haired child, her lined face lighting up in delight. 'And you must be Teo.'

It was warm enough to eat lunch in the garden, and Teo sat playing happily on a blanket on the lawn with his brand-new multi-activity centre, which made all different kinds of noises.

And afterwards he began to yawn, and they drank their coffee inside while he snuggled down happily on the sofa and eventually fell asleep.

Now what? thought Sophie, but to her surprise Luis and her grandmother began chatting together quite happily. She doesn't hate him at all, Sophie realised as she began to stack the plates and carry them through to the kitchen.

She loaded everything into the dishwasher, and when she came back her grandmother looked up.

'Why don't you take the opportunity to show Luis around the village?' she suggested. 'Teo is out for the count.'

Sophie looked at Luis. 'Do you want to?'

'Sure, why not?' he agreed evenly. 'You know for yourself that he will sleep one, maybe two hours.'

They walked down the lane, past the church. 'They have the most beautiful bell-ringing in there,' she said, though her breath was coming erratically. 'And up here is the post office. We were always allowed an ice lolly if we were—'

'Sophie,' he said suddenly, 'Salvadora is moving away.'

'Moving?' She stopped in her tracks. 'Moving where?'

'Back to Salamanca, where her family live. Pirro, too. She is getting old—far too old to care for Teo now. I realised that once you had gone. And she is happy to leave—the child is too much for her, I realised that, too, and I saw for myself the difference in the way you had been with Teo. Young enough to play with him as he should be played with.'

Her brows criss-crossed in confusion. How on earth would he be able to cope without Salvadora? 'What will you do? Who is going to look after him from now on?'

'I will have to advertise for someone.' He watched carefully for her reaction. 'Someone young.' A pause. 'Someone like you.'

She met his eyes, her heart leaping in her chest as she dared to ask the question without questioning the folly of doing so. 'But not me?'

He paused. 'You have your life here,' he said deliberately.

Did she? What kind of life was it now? A life she would willingly swap to be with the man she ached for. But he wasn't asking her to be with him.

'You mean you don't want me,' she said painfully, the wrench in her heart sending the words spilling out of her mouth of their own accord.

His mouth lost some of its habitual tightness as he relaxed. 'Oh, Sophie,' he drawled, pulling her into his arms without warning, his black eyes blazing with ebony fire as he stared down into her face. 'That is just the trouble, *querida*. I do want you. Believe me, I want you in every way that a man wants a woman.'

'Luis...' But she didn't move. Couldn't. In his arms was the place she most wanted to be.

'I want to make love to you, Sophie.' His rich voice caressed her like the fingertips which were tracing tiny paths over the peachy bloom of her cheeks. 'You have set me on fire,' he whispered. 'A fire which burns in my veins, filling me with thoughts of you and desire for you, a desire which can no longer be denied, no matter how hard I try. And yes, I want you to come back to La Rioja and to care for Teo as you have already done so beautifully, but most of all—God, forgive me—I want you in my bed.'

And she wanted to be there, more than anything else in the world, but... 'But what about Miranda?' she whispered, and guilt was as strong as it had ever been. 'What would she say?'

'Miranda is dead,' he said, a note of sadness making his voice soft, and quiet. 'And we are living. Do you not think she would want us to be happy?'

Happy? It was an interesting choice of word. Was he guaranteeing her happiness, or merely the see-sawing of violent emotions and passion which would bring her no lasting peace?

She sighed. 'I don't know.'

'Deny yourself this and you will regret it for the rest of your days,' he breathed. 'I know how much you want me, Sophie. I can read it in your eyes and on your lips. And your body tells me in no uncertain tones that your desire matches mine. Tell me that is not true.' His black eyes bored into her. 'No,' he finished on a small note of triumph. 'You cannot.'

No, she could not, but there was more at stake here than mere desire. Her life. Her career—and, most importantly of all, her fragile heart. She raised her face to his, staring with concentration into his eyes. 'It isn't that simple, Luis.'

'It's as simple as you make it,' he contradicted softly. 'And this easy.'

His mouth came down to meet hers and her gasp of protest was stifled by the sheer pleasure of his kiss. She heedlessly tried to tell herself that this was sheer madness. That he was offering her nothing more than his body and his companionship, while she, as a woman, wanted so much more from him than that. But her reasoning dissolved into nothing as his mouth explored hers. 'Luis,' she said brokenly against his mouth and opened her lips to his.

That first intimate contact of the flesh awoke an explosion of need in him so powerful that he could have pinned her to the ground, loosened her clothing and thrust himself into her sweet, ripe flesh right there and then. He felt the warm, moist cavern of her mouth, the flicker of her tongue against his, and he grew painfully hard in an instant, wanting to spill his seed and go on and on spilling his seed.

They each broke the kiss at the same instant, though for entirely different reasons.

Sophie ran her hand distractedly through her ruffled blonde hair. 'You're asking an awful lot of me, Luis.'

'I know I am.'

To give up everything she had here, in her safe, comfortable and predictable life in England—with nothing offered in return other than his body and his son and to live with him in the beautiful hacienda which nestled in the valleys of La Rioja. No declaration of love—but he has never been a hypocrite, she reminded herself. Nor a long-standing promise of commitment.

He was offering her more than he had offered Alejandra, it was true, but was she allowing herself to forget how conveniently he had discarded her? Wouldn't only a desperate fool grab at an opportunity like this?

But then she thought of the alternative—of the grey reality of life without the charismatic, vital Spaniard, and she knew then that sometimes in life you had to take risks. Emotional risks.

Sure, she had taken risks when she had started up the fledgling company with Liam, but that had been different—financial. She'd had a lot less to lose.

She thought about it some more.

She was twenty-seven years old and he had spoken

nothing but the truth when he had said that if she denied herself this then she would regret it for the rest of her days. And if it did go wrong, she could rebuild her life in London again. She could even start another advertising agency. She'd done it once, so she could do it again. But this might be her only chance with Luis.

What if she ended up bitter and unfulfilled—a woman who asked herself the heartbreakingly unanswerable question of what would have happened 'if only'?

Did he guess at her momentary weakness; was that why he moved in for the kill with his velvet-voiced question, like a matador moving in to claim the stunned bull for his own?

'Will you, Sophie, will you come and live with me in La Rioja?'

There was a heartbeat of a pause while she considered the alternative. 'I will,' she said in a low voice, thinking with a kind of poignant longing how much like a wedding vow that sounded. But he was not offering her marriage. He had been honest to a fault. He wanted her, yes, and he was entrusting her with the care of his son. But not love. Not marriage. His mistress and his son's carer.

It was not enough and yet, in a mad and inexplicable way, it was more than enough. Certainly more than she had here, without her proud, arrogant Spaniard who dominated her thoughts as no other man had done.

Nor would again, she recognised painfully. He was right. If she lived to be a hundred no sweet, tantalising opportunity like this would come her way again. She must seize it. Live it and relish it, day by day and night by night. She would give it a year—if it lasted that long—and then she would rethink her future. 'I will,' she said again.

But he needed to be sure. 'You would leave all this behind?'

'I would.'

'Why?'

'Because of T-Teo,' she faltered, and saw his face suddenly become shuttered, the eyes narrowing as he nodded almost imperceptibly.

'*Sì. Por Teo.*'

Something had made his voice colourless, and she sought to put the passion back. 'And...and for you, Luis.'

'But what for me, exactly, *querida?*' he questioned softly.

'I want you,' she admitted simply, struggling to elaborate in a way which would not terrify him into retracting his offer.

For wouldn't a man like Luis run a mile if he suspected that her heart was already lost to him?

'I want to sh-share your bed. I want you to make love to me,' she said shakily, because in this, at least, she would be as honest as it was in her power to be. She lifted her fingers and touched them to his black hair. 'I want what you can give me, Luis. What a man can give a woman.'

But not any man. Only this man.

He stared down at her, seeing the fleeting look of vulnerability in her blue eyes, unable to give her the reassurance he knew she needed and deserved. Maybe he *did* have no heart—but surely it would be unfair to express an emotion he did not feel?

He told himself that he had been through a lot lately—and that Sophie herself came with all the baggage of being Miranda's cousin.

He wanted her, yes—more than he could remember wanting any woman—but was what he felt for her nothing more than dressed-up lust? And wouldn't it be unforgivable if he could offer her nothing more than that?

But then her lips parted in silent invitation, and he was lost. Lost.

He gave a small groan as he lifted his hand and caught hers, drawing it close to his lips and slowly kissing each fingertip while his eyes captured hers in their ebony glitter.

'And can you just walk out on your company without a backward glance?'

'I'll have to think about that.' Maybe she could work part-time from Spain in some kind of executive capacity. Or would it be kinder to Liam and the company to sever her ties with it completely? Would the release of her equity free her from worry—the interest from her capital allowing her to continue to be independent? For she would not, she realised fiercely, be a kept woman. Not under any circumstances. She smiled up into his frowning eyes, and shrugged. 'As I've said before, Luis—no one is indispensable.'

But she had come pretty close to being indispensable to Teo, he recognised, not for the first time. She loved him and cared for him in a way that Miranda had not been able to do, God rest her soul.

'Do you know, I would like to take you somewhere

now and to seal this agreement with my lips and my body?' he said thickly. 'Shall we do that, Sophie? Is there somewhere...private...for us?'

Seal this agreement. How coldly he expressed himself! But even the pragmatic words could not dampen her hunger for him, and for one insane moment she considered taking him further up the lane, to where her childhood hideaway lay hidden within the wooded copse, where they would not be disturbed...

'And I would like that more than anything else,' she whispered, trying not to conjure up an erotic vision of him making love to her outdoors, right now. And then imagined what a sight they would make, returning to the house, covered in twigs and little bits of grass, their faces flushed and their eyes hectic! 'But we can't,' she groaned. 'My grandmother is waiting. And Teo, too. We have responsibilities, Luis.'

How ironic that what he admired in her he also resented! But she was right—they *did* have responsibilities.

'*Sì.*' His body ached as much as he suspected hers did, and yet he admired her cool restraint, the step back she had now taken to distance herself. Keeping him waiting and waiting, and wanting even more... 'Then let us go,' he agreed unsteadily. 'For unless we have a chaperon I will have to kiss you into submission, *querida.*'

'What makes you think you would be able to?' she teased.

'Shall we put it to the test?' he challenged provocatively, and moved closer, his dark, haunting features mocking her with their beauty.

But she shook her head, not trusting her own resolve in the face of such an offer. She tried and failed to imagine any other man getting away with such a masterful and silken boast, and shivered, wondering if she had taken on more than she could ever have anticipated with Luis de la Camara.

'You'll have us arrested,' she said, only half joking.

CHAPTER NINE

'SO YOU are here at last,' Luis breathed. 'At long last.'

Sophie's mouth dried as she gazed back at him, dressed in a billowy shirt of snowy-white and fitted jet trousers which made him look as though he should be bull-running in the nearby city of Pamplona.

'Y-yes,' she agreed shakily. 'Here at last.'

Once more he had met her at the airport, and they had just endured a car journey of almost unendurable tension. She had badly wanted him to kiss her, but he had not, and now that Teo had been put to bed he seemed reluctant still, and she did not know why, nor dared to ask.

Surely he was not now regretting his decision to ask her here, not after she had spent the last month tidying up her life back in England to accommodate an arrangement which was seeming increasingly bizarre by the second. Why did he stand so far from her, such an intimidating and untouching distance away from her?

He savoured the moment—the anticipation and the expectation—for just a little while longer. His hunger was unbearable, aroused to such a pitch by the fact that something denied to him so long was finally to be his.

He had not dared touch her at the airport, nor in the car, and not simply because this time he had brought Teo and his presence was inhibiting, but because Luis feared that once he touched her he would explode. And it was no fitting way to begin if he pulled over on some deserted stretch of the highway and made love to her in the cramped conditions of the car, with his small son in the back.

No, it would not be fitting.

He wanted a bed—and once he had her in it he feared that he would never be able to get out of it again.

He poured her a glass of wine and handed it to her. 'So, was it easy to leave?'

She took the wine, grateful and yet slightly resentful. He sounded as though he was interviewing her for a job—which in a way, she reminded herself painfully, he was.

'Not what I'd call easy,' she admitted, and sipped the de la Camara Rioja.

'Oh?' He raised his dark brows in imperious question.

She would not admit that almost everyone had tried to talk her out of it. Her parents had asked her worriedly if she knew what she was doing. Liam had told her frankly that she was 'mad.' And her grandmother had looked positively worried.

'Oh, Sophie, are you *sure?*'

'I love Teo,' said Sophie doggedly.

'Just Teo?' Mrs Mills queried perceptively.

'What do you mean?'

'Just what exactly is your role going to be? As sole carer for Teo?'

'Not sole carer, no, of course not. Luis will be hands-on whenever he isn't working. And there's a girl from the village who can babysit, apparently. Oh, and a new cook and gardener, and a housekeeper,' she added almost vaguely, and saw her grandmother raise her eyebrows fractionally.

'And that's all?'

Sophie sighed, not knowing whether to tell her grandmother the truth or not—but how could you possibly tell a woman of nearly eighty that you had agreed to become the mistress of a man you had always affected to despise?

'It's hard to explain,' she said falteringly. 'I don't know what's going to happen—'

'You're in love with him, aren't you?'

Sophie bit her lip, unwilling to lie, but even more unwilling to cause her grandmother disquiet. And besides, who could say? She thought that yes, she *was* in love with him, but maybe love was a word women used when they wanted to dress up the fact that they desired a man with a ferocity which left them slightly dazed?

'I don't know what I really feel.' She turned her eyes beseechingly towards her grandmother. 'I know that you think he did Miranda wrong, and that he's all bad—'

'I never said that,' interrupted her grandmother firmly. 'No one person is all bad, and no one person is all good, either—but two people may not be good for each other, and I think that was the case for Miranda and Luis.' She rubbed at the knuckles of her fingers. 'Just be careful, dear, that's all I'm saying. I can see the obvious attraction in a man like Luis, but he may not be good for you either.'

Sophie had remembered her words on the flight

over, recognising that her grandmother was probably speaking a truth she did not really wish to hear, but recognising also that she was in too deep now to back off. She had committed herself to Teo, and she had committed herself to his father, except that his father now stood like some gorgeous but unapproachable stranger on the other side of the high-ceilinged sitting room of the hacienda.

Well, she was damned if she was going to make the first move. Hadn't she given up enough to be here—did he want total capitulation into the bargain?

Luis could see the tension which had stiffened her shoulders. She looked uptight and brittle—as if she was regretting her decision to come. But she was bound to have doubts, and if he leapt on her with all the finesse of a teenager then might she not feel used, as women sometimes did?

'Sit down.' He gave a glimmer of a smile.

This was worse than unendurable. Was this what she had left her life in England for? This brittle expectation? The air was tight with the tension of knowing precisely why she was here—that they were going to make love at last, after a wait which seemed to have gone on for a lifetime. He knew it and she knew it, and suddenly she felt a little like a commodity.

She put her glass down with a shaky bang. 'I don't want to sit down. I think I might go upstairs to freshen up. I'm—I'm tired.'

But the thought of her disappearing was unendurable. *Madre de Dios!* He had tried to play the perfect host and gentleman, and not the would-be lover whose groin was on fire with need—but it seemed that Sophie Mills wanted none of these.

He put his own glass down and moved towards her with the stealth and grace of a panther. 'You want to go upstairs, *querida?*' he questioned silkily.

She studied her shoes. 'That's what I said.'

'And which room were you planning to use?'

'The room I had before.' Of that she had been sure. Mistresses kept some kind of distance, didn't they? And keeping her distance might be the only way she could put some kind of barrier around her vulnerable heart.

'No, you move into mine,' he negated implacably. 'You sleep with me. Only with me. Sophie.'

She looked up into his face, some honeyed quality of his words making it impossible not to. 'Luis?' she whispered.

'I have waited for too long now.' He kissed her then, because nothing in the world could have kept him back any longer.

And she too had waited for more than long enough. Was that his intention—to hold her at arm's length until she would be so filled with need for him that she would become a melting, responsive mass in his arms?

Because that was exactly what happened.

'L—' She tried to say his name, but his mouth blotted the word out and she clung to him as he enfolded her, smoothing his hands down over her hair, and then moving them down to cup her breasts, making a small groan against her lips as he did so.

'Oh, God!' She swayed against him, feeling her nipples peak against his palms in a blatant signal of need, feeling his hand now moving to the slight curve of her belly, brushing carelessly down over her dress and alighting very deliberately over where she was beginning to ache very badly indeed.

She squirmed against him as he deepened the kiss until she could barely think. Her body was on fire and she seemed to be all glorious and aching sensation, when, abruptly, he stopped and she stared up at him in silent reprimand, seeing the hectic, inky glitter of his eyes and the soft wash of colour which accentuated his aristocratic cheekbones.

'You want me to take you here, on the floor, *querida?*' he questioned in a voice made husky with desire. 'Is that your intention?'

Her breath coming in short little bursts, she stared back at him. Why fight her needs, or her desires? She was here on his terms, yes—but also on her own. And, as a mistress, then surely she had the right to tell him exactly what she wanted...?

'Or on the sofa, perhaps?' she suggested.

His pulses leapt even more at her erotic suggestion, and he growled and caught her against him again, wondering if she was like this with all her lovers.

'The first time should be in bed,' he ground out, and simply picked her up and carried her out of the room.

This was ridiculous—like a crazy fantasy come true. No man had ever stridden with her held so effortlessly and so masterfully in his arms, and Sophie felt almost faint with pleasure.

'I think you've been watching too many old movies,' she joked weakly.

'I think not,' came the unequivocal reply, and as he mounted the stairs he bent his head to her breast, suckling her through the cotton dress she wore, and

Sophie scrabbled her fingernails in frantic pleasure against his back.

'Stop it!' she murmured.

He didn't move, just gave one deliberate lick of his tongue and felt her shudder in response. 'Why? Don't you like it?'

Her head fell back. 'Y-yes,' she gasped.

But her answer was redundant. As he lifted his head to look at her he could see that she liked it very much.

As did he. With a groan he opened the door to his bedroom, and softly kicked it shut before carrying her straight over to the bed and placing her down on it, standing with his hands on his hips while he steadied his breathing.

Madre de Dios, but she looked beautiful! Almost wanton, with her flushed cheeks and her honey hair spilling in disarray, even though the dress she wore was decent enough.

Too decent.

He sat down on the edge of the bed and began to unbutton it, and Sophie watched him, mesmerised, as he freed her from the constricting garment. The cool air washed over her skin as he peeled away the still damp fabric from her breasts.

He sucked in a breath as he slid the dress from over her shoulders, the sight of her in her underwear making his heart rate undergo a dramatic change.

He had seen her in a swimsuit, of course, but a swimsuit, no matter how revealing, was very different from a bra and some flimsy little panties.

He ran a questing finger thoughtfully over a breast

covered with apricot lace and trimmed with tiny rose buds.

'These are new?'

To her horror, Sophie found herself blushing as she nodded and nerves suddenly assailed her again. 'Yes.' Did it seem like the world's biggest cliché, then, to come to him in brand-new underwear? Wasn't it all just a little too obvious?

'You pay me a great compliment, *querida*,' he murmured, then narrowed his eyes as he saw her swift rise in colour. She seemed almost...almost... Surely she was not *nervous?* 'Do I frighten you, little one?' he asked, almost reflectively.

Frighten her? No, *he* didn't frighten her—but for some reason she felt utterly petrified. Shouldn't he have tried out the goods first? she thought, verging on the brink of hysteria. What if she disappointed him in bed; what price his mistress then?

But now he had gently begun to stroke her belly, and despite her misgivings, Sophie began to relax, all her reservations gradually dissolving into nothing as he incited a slow build-up of pleasure to replace them.

She let her eyes drift to a close, and sighed.

Luis watched her. She puzzled and perplexed him. One moment she was writhing passionately in his arms, while the next, staring up at him almost nervously, as if she was a virgin—and he was prepared to bet his entire fortune that she was not.

'Unbutton my shirt, *querida*,' he urged softly, and dipped his finger into her belly button in an erotic mimicry of the ultimate possession.

Sophie opened her eyes and looked at him sitting beside her, so dark and so beautiful. She let her gaze wander to where he still stroked her belly, his fingertips tracing such erotic pathways over its slight swell. Eagerly she lifted her hands up and freed the first button of his shirt, then the next, scarcely able to resist a gasp as his torso was made bare for her delight.

His skin was bronze and roughened with dark hair, and his stomach was flat and hard. She freed the final button and he shrugged it off with an arrogant gesture of dismissal, staring down at her with a look of unashamed hunger and a fierce kind of tension.

And his hunger matched her own and gave her strength. Courage. Confidence to play the role he would expect. His lover, his *equal*.

She teased her fingertips over the buckle of his belt and then withdrew them, glancing up at him from between half-slitted lashes. 'Shall I?'

But he had anticipated her question before she uttered it and he caught hold of her hand, transferring it to where he felt he might explode with hardness and then deliberately moving it away again. 'No,' he whispered.

'No?' She stared at him in confusion. Maybe he only liked passive women—women who would lie back and do nothing?

He shook his head and stood up. He felt so aroused—unbearably aroused—and he was afraid that she might injure him, however dexterous she was. *'Querida.'* He gave a rueful smile. 'I will have enough difficulty taking the damned things off myself!'

Some of the tension left her and she watched him, enjoying the show as his body was gradually revealed.

Wincing slightly, he unzipped the black trousers and stepped out of them, roughly pulling off the dark socks and silk boxer shorts until he was left in nothing at all, and Sophie thought that she had never seen a man more magnificent, nor more at ease with his nakedness.

He came to her and lay down beside her, smoothing her hair back as he took her in his arms. He unclasped her bra, letting out a little cry of delight as her breasts fell free and unfettered against him.

'At last,' he breathed, and dipped his head to their lush swell, burying his face in their swollen splendour. '*Madre de Dios*—at last!'

He took one rosy nub into his mouth and licked it and teased it with his teeth, a sensation so exquisite that Sophie cried out with the pleasure of it, clutching at his shoulders in helpless surrender.

'Luis,' she whispered. 'Oh, Luis.'

'I know, *querida*,' he said in an unfamiliar shaky voice. 'I know.'

He could feel her slender curves contrasted against the angular planes of his own body and the rough brush of lace against the hard cradle of him seemed too much of a barrier. He lifted his head from breast to mouth and his hand drifted downwards, hooking into the delicate fabric at her hips. 'These I no longer wish to see, or to feel,' he husked, bringing his lips down to hers, and sliding off the tiny lace panties.

Sophie shivered uncontrollably, unable to keep her body still as he tracked his hand down her thigh.

But he shushed her. '*Querida*, don't move,' he said, with a slight note of desperation in his voice. 'You are driving me crazy.'

She tried, but it was hard not to squirm with excitement as he manoeuvred the delicate wisp down until it lay forgotten, coiled like the tail of a kitten around one ankle. Luxuriously, she touched his back, kneading her fingers possessively against the silken skin, and then moving them round to trickle through the thick whorls of hair at his chest, feeling him shudder in response when she feather-lighted her way over each tiny nipple.

He closed his eyes briefly, begging his body for control, then tipped her head back and looked down at her, his black eyes glittering sternly, though his lips held the trace of a smile. 'You test my patience, Sophie,' he said unsteadily.

'I don't want to test anything,' she whispered.

For answer, he slipped his hand between her thighs and smiled as her mouth opened in startled pleasure.

Sophie's eyes widened as he began to touch her. 'Luis,' she swallowed. 'Luis, please...'

He felt as if he might explode when he found her wet, wild heat, felt her move her hips in instant response. His erection pushed insistently against his stomach. Had he ever felt so hard before? 'What is it?' he beseeched her. 'Tell me what it is you want?'

It was difficult to get the words out when he was touching her intimately like that, his face so close to hers, so that she was unable to hide from him what she wanted most of all. 'You,' she choked. 'Now. Please.'

Their eyes met in a moment of complete understanding.

Her fears were gone, he recognised, but those fears might build again if he played with her. He wanted to tease her and take her to the very brink, so that her pleasure would be all the more intense, but he recognised that enough was enough.

She needed no games, nor demonstrations of his finesse. She was ready for him and all she needed was him—deep, deep inside her.

With a groan he moved away and reached to his locker, so that in a moment all he was wearing was a condom.

Sophie quickly closed her eyes in case he saw her reaction as he slid it on, for Luis needed no boost to his already well-developed ego. She swallowed, thinking that his ego wasn't the only part of him which was well-developed.

Oh, perfect man, she thought, almost despairingly. How could any other compete with Luis de la Camara?

But then he was back beside her, kissing her until she thought that she might faint with pleasure. He murmured to her in Spanish—hauntingly soft and huskily evocative phrases which made her even wilder for him. And that was when he moved on top of her.

She had longed and prayed for just this, and now that the moment was here she felt physically excited yet emotionally...well, emotionally she was as mixed-up as she had ever been. But why allow her insecurity to get in the way of such long-awaited pleasure? What purpose would it serve other than for one to cancel out the other?

His hardness was daunting—beautifully daunting—pushing teasingly against her, and, though part of her wanted to prolong the delicious anticipation, she couldn't. Please, she begged him silently. Please.

Did he read her mind, or was the waiting just too much for him as well? For suddenly he thrust into her, filling her with warmth and with himself, and her eyes flew open to find him looking down at her, his face tight with tension, as if he was reining himself in only with the most monumental effort.

He bent his head and kissed her, blotting out everything other than sensation as he began to move inside her, and Sophie had never felt so alive before, so at one, their bodies meeting and joining and moving in perfect synchrony, as if they had been designed only for each other.

So that when she felt the beckoning of pleasure she gave a little cry of disbelief and disappointment, for it was too soon and she didn't want it to end.

He stopped kissing her and stared down, his eyes completely black. 'What is it, *querida?*' he questioned unsteadily, but he didn't stop moving, and because of that it was too late, and she...she...

'Luis!' His name was torn from her lips as the delicious spasms caught her up in their indefinable dance.

Still thrusting into her, he gazed down at her enraptured face, wanting to watch her and enjoy her pleasure, but it was not to be. For just as she arched her back and flung her head back, just as her legs stiffened and the slow flush of orgasm bloomed like a flower on her pale skin, he felt his own release coming.

She fluttered her eyelids open and saw the tension

leave the dark, sculpted face, heard him groan as he drove himself into her over and over and over again.

Only when he was spent, and had dropped a kiss onto the tip of her nose, and yawned, and withdrawn, did Sophie wonder what on earth they did now.

Imperceptibly she shifted away from the dark olive body. 'Shall I—shall I sleep here tonight?' she asked.

He frowned. Was this her idea of a joke? One trip to heaven and back was enough for her? Granting him the ultimate intimacy whilst denying him the pleasure of holding her in his arms during the night?

He lay back and stared at the whirling fan above his head. 'If you wish to.'

He sounded as if he didn't care one way or the other. Maybe in the circumstances a little protective space might be just what they needed. Or what *she* needed. 'I could go next door,' she suggested. 'You'd get more sleep that way.'

She pushed the sheet aside, revealing her long, pale limbs as she began to swing them over the side of the bed, and in that instant Luis knew that he was not letting her go anywhere. And he would pleasure her so much that she would never make such an outrageous proposal again.

'But I have no wish to sleep, Sophie,' he said, pulling her back towards him, his fingers idly beginning to stroke at her breast.

The sensation was bewitching, but she wondered what had put that odd kind of note in his voice. If she asked him what he was really feeling right now, would he tell her?

But that was when he cupped her breast and took

it between his lips once more, and Sophie turned with a little moan, forgetting the questions in her mind and giving herself up to the renewed demands of her body instead.

CHAPTER TEN

SOPHIE moved across the sunlit garden towards the swimming pool to the sound of echoing laughter, and as she made her way through the shaded canopy of the trees and saw Luis rubbing suncream into Teo's back her breath caught in her throat, just the way it always did. She sighed.

She had thought it impossible that her feelings for him should grow even stronger, but in that she had been proved completely wrong.

Three months of living with him as his mistress had done nothing to diminish the earth-shattering effect he had on her. Though maybe that wasn't surprising. Didn't making love night after night with a man only heighten your emotions when you were in love with him?

If only...she thought wistfully...if only he loved her back. But he didn't and he wouldn't and she would just have to learn to live with it. And she couldn't really complain—because he treated her with all the true, innate courtesy she would have expected from his aristocratic upbringing.

He laughed at her jokes and she laughed at his. They read the newspapers over breakfast and discussed world affairs just as if they were a real couple. Sometimes he taught her words and phrases in Spanish, so that she might gradually learn to speak his native tongue.

So what was missing? Words of undying love and devotion? She had known from the beginning what the score was, and if she expected those then she was doomed to be disappointed. He wasn't breaking any promises to her, because he had not made any.

Luis lifted his head and saw her, his black eyes narrowing as he observed the striking vision she made, before a slow smile lit up the hard, proud features. *'Buenos dias, Sophie,'* he murmured, his soft voice carrying across the still air.

He was just too devastatingly good-looking, she thought as she grew closer, and not for the first time it seemed to her unfair that one man should have been given quite so many attributes.

Tiny beads of water glistened like diamonds on the burnished muscles. His skin was an even deeper olive colour now, tanned lightly by the sun, as smooth and luxurious as oiled silk, broken only by the dark hair which spattered his chest, arrowing down in an enticing line towards the black trunks.

Not skimpy trunks, like those worn by so many men on beach holidays, but in a way these were even more provocative. They hugged the curve of his buttocks and caressed the hard shaft of his thighs. The body she knew so well, the body she could never have enough of.

Composing her face so that it was free of any giveaway yearning, she smiled.

'Tho-thi!' squealed Teo in delight as he caught sight of her.

Sophie sped up and ran the last short distance towards him with her arms outstretched, as delighted now as she had been the first time he had managed his own distinctive version of her name!

'Buenos dias, Teodoro!' she beamed. *'Como estas?'*

As usual, her attempt at Spanish made him giggle uncontrollably and she ruffled his hair affectionately. 'You wait!' she teased, waggling a finger at him. 'Soon my Spanish will be better than yours!'

Luis sucked in a breath as she crouched down beside him, the fall of honey-coloured hair resolutely hiding her expression as he silently cursed and applauded her for her choice of swimsuit. He had never known a woman so modest!

Not for her the minuscule combination of three tiny triangles linked together with nothing more than a wisp of string. In his experience, most women used swimming as an opportunity to show off as much of their bodies as possible, but not Sophie.

Yet the blue of her suit enhanced her eyes, its high cut emphasising the long, long legs—and, although most of her breasts were concealed, the thin fabric did nothing to disguise their sinful curve. Breasts which pillowed his head at night when he slept...

'Vamos a nadar?' asked Sophie tentatively as she flapped her arms around in a swimming gesture.

'Sì, sì!' giggled Teodoro and held his arms up to her.

Sophie picked him up, breathing in the gorgeous baby scent of him as he wrapped his little sun creamed arms trustingly around her neck, yet she was aware of the black eyes following her every movement.

'Are you coming in?' she asked.

Luis frowned, distracted. 'Mmm?'

'Swimming?'

He shook his head, not trusting himself to move, he was so aroused. 'I'll stay here and watch.'

But sitting on the sidelines and observing her uninhibited splashing around with his son did little for his equilibrium. He stifled a groan and turned onto his stomach.

He had always longed for a woman who did not make impossible emotional demands on him, but now that he had found one he discovered that he was becoming increasingly frustrated.

Just what was it about Sophie? She never sought compliments, nor tried to engineer bouts of jealousy by flirting with his friends on the occasions when they had gone out to dinner as a couple. Nor did she demand to know how he 'felt' about her.

She adored Teo and never seemed to get irritated at the increasing demands he made on her. She was both cool and passionate, analytical and clever—everything a man could wish for.

So what was the matter with him?

'You looked miles away.'

A soft voice broke into his reverie and he looked up to see Sophie standing with water streaming in rivulets down her body, reaching down to pick up a towel to dry the wet toddler in her arms.

And treating him to a heart-stoppingly clear view of her cleavage, he thought savagely, wishing that they had a babysitter right now, so that he could take her off to bed and...

'Luis, what *is* the matter?'

'Why should anything be the matter?' he demanded shortly.

'I don't know. You were scowling, that's all.'

He closed his eyes. 'I'm just tired.'

No wonder, she thought lovingly as she watched the slow rise and fall of his back. By rights, she should have felt tired, too, seeing as how they had barely snatched any sleep last night. A smile curved the edges of her mouth as she dabbed at Teo's curls. The amazing thing was that she didn't feel tired in the least—she felt as if she could go out and run a marathon!

Later that evening, at dinner, he stared at her through the flickering light of the candles. 'Do you want to go to a party?'

Sophie blinked. 'When?'

'Tomorrow night.'

'That's a bit short notice, isn't it?'

'I was…undecided,' he said slowly. 'But I think you might enjoy it.'

He seemed in an odd mood tonight, she thought. Distracted. Tense. The black eyes looking even more enigmatic than usual.

But a party might be fun. 'OK, that sounds good,' she smiled. 'Shall I ring for dessert now?'

He felt infuriatingly disappointed at her lack of questioning. Why wasn't she quizzing him about where the party was and who was throwing it, and who would be there? Almost, he thought with another frown, as if she couldn't care less.

In truth, Sophie was nervous inside, but she was damned if she was going to let Luis know. She found the wives and partners of his friends unbelievably gorgeous and impeccably groomed. Most of them looked as though they had spent an exhausting day going from gym, to manicurist, pedicurist, hairdresser and then home, for some intensive work in getting ready to go out.

Not that she was a slouch in the dressing-up department, but she just felt on the wrong side of sophisticated in comparison. For a start, her nails were short and unvarnished—mainly because she seemed to spend a good deal of her day sitting beneath the shade of the lemon trees and playing in the sandpit with Teo, and sand tended to play havoc with anything approaching talons!

The following evening she opened the door to her wardrobe and surveyed the contents. No shortage of smart new clothes for her smart new life.

Selling her share of the business had left her a wealthy woman—well, only very relatively rich when compared with Luis, she supposed wryly.

Luis had taken her shopping in Pamplona for clothes suited to the hot La Rioja summer and once again she had thwarted his attempts to pay for her purchases.

'I can pay myself,' she had said stubbornly. 'I've sold the business, remember?'

'Madre de Dios!' he had exclaimed. 'You are a stubborn woman! You know that it is quite different now!'

'How?'

'You look after my son,' he had asserted. 'For which I would have to pay anyone else!'

'Maybe some day I'll ask you to,' she had said

serenely. 'At the moment I don't need it. And besides, I'm doing it for love, not money.'

He had opened his mouth and shut it again, unable to argue with her logic, and she had seen both frustration and admiration sparking from his eyes. Good! For she had long since decided that Luis de la Camara had stereotyped women for far too long now. Let him realise that there were many variations of a woman and they weren't all out for what they could get!

She took from the wardrobe a dress which she had not yet worn—a filmy, floaty scrap of pink with spaghetti straps which made the most of her light tan, and a just-above-the-knee skirt which made the most of her long legs.

Just as she had done for the wedding, she wore more make-up than usual, not just for the effect, but because make-up sometimes provided a mask you could hide behind. And she was well-aware of the eyes which would be watching her, the eyes which longed to ask just what was really happening between her and the Don, but didn't dare.

Luis was waiting downstairs for her and when she walked into the room he wondered why in God's name he had agreed to go to the damned party after all. They could have stayed here. Eaten finer food and drunk infinitely finer wines. He could have slowly undressed her and made love to her here, and then taken her upstairs and carried on...

A pulse beat insistently in his cheek. 'You look very beautiful, *querida*,' he murmured, and beckoned her. 'Come here.'

His eyes compelled her, as did the sultry note of command in his voice. But the hectic glitter in his black eyes warned her that it would be dangerous to do as he suggested, especially when—she took a quick glance at her watch—when they were due at a party.

'Luis—'

'Come here,' he repeated, and a small smile lifted the corners of his hard mouth as she came and stood before him.

'Luis—' she protested weakly as he lowered his head to kiss the skin of her bare shoulder, sending little shivers of sensation tingling over her body.

'Come and sit down,' he purred, and led her over to the sofa.

'But I thought we were going to the party—'

'We are.' He kissed her neck again and felt her shudder as he drifted his hand over her breast. 'In a minute.' His fingers began to trace feather-light paths over her nipples. 'Do you remember the night you arrived, and suggested making love on the sofa?'

'Stop it—'

'You don't want me to?'

No, she didn't, but if *someone* didn't put a stop to it then she knew exactly what was going to happen. And her heart started thundering against her breast as her body began to greedily anticipate just what that was.

'Stop it,' she whispered again, but this time her voice was slurred with a deepening note of desire.

'No, let's start it.' He took her hand and travelled it to where he was so hard that he knew he would be unable to set foot outside this house unless he rid himself of the unbelievable ache.

Her legs felt weak and her hands were shaking but

somehow she unzipped him, her fingers faltering as she felt the enormous power of him springing free, and she saw from the tightening tension on his face that he was close to losing control.

With a slow, sultry smile she took control, pushing him down on the sofa and edging his trousers down, before deftly stepping out of her panties and dropping them carelessly to the floor.

'Querida!' he gasped, and then gasped again as she sat astride him, taking him deep inside her and wrapping her arms tightly around him as she began to move.

It was all over very quickly, too quickly, he thought with a pang of regret as he waited for her fluttering little spasms to subside.

Eventually he lifted her from him, a rueful smile touching his lips.

'Come, *querida*, or we're going to be late for our party.'

She wondered what she must look like—flushed and warm and sticky and replete. 'You still want to go?' she asked uncertainly.

His mouth hardened as he forced himself to remember that what had just happened had been nothing more than a sweet diversion. 'Yes.'

She swallowed. 'Give me five minutes.'

She took ten, but when she reappeared, with her hair brushed and smelling of soap and scent—sexy, yet demure—it was hard to believe what a little wildcat she had just been. He held her pashmina out for her. 'Let's go,' he said shortly.

Sophie sat in the car, muddled and confused. Sex was supposed to bring you closer, wasn't it? So why did Luis suddenly seem like a million miles away from her?

She struggled to lighten the inexplicable tension which had descended on them.

'So whose party is it?'

'Oh, so you *are* interested.'

'Of course I'm interested!'

'It's a very old friend of mine—we grew up together. His family also own one of La Rioja's finest vineyards.'

'And does their wine rival the de la Camara vines?' she teased.

'What do you think?' he drawled.

Well, *let* him be in a bad mood, she thought defiantly. She certainly wasn't going to pander to it! He should be purring with delight—not grouchy like this. She remembered in breathtaking detail what had just happened on the sofa, but his attitude dampened the afterglow of their erotic encounter.

'I think you should wipe that frown from your face!' she said crossly.

And he would like to wipe that furious little look from *her* face with his lips, but by now they were sweeping up the drive with another car close behind them.

Outside, there were brightly coloured lanterns illuminating the house in rainbow-coloured hues, and when they stepped out into the warm night air they could hear the sound of music and laughter coming from the direction of the swimming pool.

'Ready?' he questioned, and held his arm out for her to link it, but Sophie ignored it. She was certainly not going to appear on his arm looking like some kind of *trophy!*

'Let's go,' she said instead.

He introduced her to Laurent Gomez, their host, and his beautiful pregnant wife, Maria.

'What will you drink, Sophie?' Maria asked, with a genuinely welcoming smile on her face.

Sophie relaxed. 'Some wine, please.'

'You will try some Spanish champagne?' asked Laurent. 'Though strictly speaking we are not allowed to call it that, for our French rivals have the monopoly on the name—but I can assure you that you will find it just as delicious.'

'Sounds lovely,' said Sophie, and glanced up at Luis, but his face was unsmiling as he met her eyes. What was *wrong* with him this evening? 'When is your baby due?' she asked Maria.

'In time for Navidad—Christmas,' dimpled Maria.

'And it is your first?'

'My fifth!'

'Good heavens,' said Sophie weakly. 'You look about the same age as me!'

'She is,' commented Luis drily. 'Just that some women start young and then never seem to stop, is that not so, Maria?'

'This is my last!' said Maria fervently.

'Last what?' enquired Laurent, who was returning with a tray of champagne.

'Nothing, *querido*,' murmured his wife, and winked at Sophie.

Sophie began to relax even more. Luis's friends were charming and they seemed to accept her—the close friends, in any case. As usual she was aware of the more quizzical looks from the unattached females, but she didn't really care. They could ogle him as much as they liked—*she* was the one who was with him!

After two glasses of delicious champagne, all she cared about was why Luis seemed so stern and so solemn, but she didn't get an opportunity to ask him, since they were never alone.

She had just been given a plate of paella, and was preparing to go and find Luis, to eat with him, when Sophie became aware of a split-second silence, followed by an unmistakable buzz of excitement. She looked up to see what or who had caused it.

It was a woman of such outstanding beauty that for a moment Sophie was certain that she had seen her on the front of a glossy magazine. And maybe she had.

She was tall—almost as tall as the tallest man at the party, who, naturally, just happened to be Luis. Her silver dress clung like a mermaid's tail to every slim curve of her show-stopping body and her thick dark hair was piled high on her head in an elaborate confection of curls, studded with jewels which glittered so brightly that they might very well have been real diamonds.

But it was her face which was the most extraordinary thing about her, and it seemed to personify all that was magnificent about Spanish women. An oval face, with enormous black eyes and a soft, luscious mouth painted red. A face which contained passion as well as beauty.

'Who's that?' whispered Sophie.

There was a slight, awkward pause. 'That is

Alejandra,' replied Maria carefully. 'Have you not yet met?'

No, of course they had not met—for why on earth would Luis introduce his current mistress to his former one? Wouldn't that put him in a more than precarious position if, say, the two women began comparing notes?

And what would she hear? Sophie wondered painfully. Would Alejandra describe a relationship just like the one she was currently enjoying with Luis?

Maybe it was time to stop deluding herself that what they had between them was something special. Luis treated her with respect, yes, and maybe their affair would continue for longer than his previous one, but that was only because she had ensured a secure position in his life by offering to care for his son.

'No,' she said slowly, and put the plate of untouched food back down on the table. 'We haven't met. Excuse me, please, Maria, I must go and find Luis.'

But Luis was nowhere to be found, and in the end Sophie grabbed a glass of fruit juice and went over to a shaded corner of the pool, unable to face anyone or make anything which would pass as conversation.

She sat down on a lounger, and gave a long, heavy sigh. She was either going to have to toughen up or get out while she still had the strength to do so. She had said that she would reassess after a year, but tonight her insecurity was threatening to swamp her. They had been happy these three months, yes—but he had been happy with Miranda once. And Alejandra, too. So was it going to happen all over again? Would Luis tire of her once the lust had burnt itself out?

The sound of a footstep disturbed her troubled thoughts and she looked up to see Alejandra standing there, looking like a shining, ethereal moonbeam in her clinging silver dress.

'You must be Sophie,' said Alejandra in perfect, accentless English which held a faint transatlantic drawl. 'Do you know who I am?'

'Of course,' said Sophie staunchly, but the hand that put the glass down onto the table beside her was shaking. 'You're Alejandra.'

Alejandra didn't say anything for a moment, just studied her without embarrassment. Then she said, almost ruefully, 'You are very beautiful.'

'And so are you.'

'He likes blondes,' said Alejandra reflectively. 'He always has done.'

She made her feel like one in a long production line of blondes, thought Sophie indignantly! But maybe she was. She opened her mouth to utter some meaningless platitude to the woman who had shared Luis's bed for who knew how long, when a dark figure appeared out of the shadows and the tall Spaniard stood there, as still as if he had been carved from stone.

His eyes were watchful, but that was all she could read in them in this dim evening light.

'Ah, so you two have met.'

The master of understatement, thought Sophie, and she gave him a cool look.

Alejandra took a step forward, her cheek held towards him for a kiss, but to Sophie's surprise he merely inclined his head in a more formal greeting. 'Alejandra,' he said calmly. 'You are looking well.'

'And you, too, *querido*,' she murmured, but her mouth curved in a swift, almost painful smile, as if she acknowledged the bitter fact that something fundamental in their relationship had changed. 'Domesticity clearly suits you.'

Was that designed to ruffle him? Sophie wondered. To make it sound as though the latest blonde had him in her clutches?

'Indeed it does,' he agreed, and looked at Sophie. 'You have eaten, *querida?*'

As if food would have done anything but choke her! 'I'm not very hungry,' she said truthfully.

'Then you would like to dance?'

'Actually, Luis, what I would like most is to go home. I hate to be a party-pooper, but I'm really very tired!'

'Ask Laurent's driver to run you home,' suggested Alejandra, imperceptibly drawing her splendid shoulders back so that the full impact of her breasts could be seen through the stretched silver fabric.

'I'm tired myself,' said Luis blandly, though his eyes glittered a secret, shining message to Sophie. 'Come along, Sophie—let's get your shawl and go home. Goodnight, Alejandra.' Once again he inclined his head with faultless courtesy. 'It's good to see you again.'

'Goodnight,' she answered tonelessly.

Sophie didn't say a word until they were back on the road to the hacienda, and then it all came spilling out of her mouth like poison.

'You *knew* she was going to be there, didn't you?' she accused.

'Of course I knew.'

'But you didn't see fit to tell me?'

'You didn't ask.'

'So what if I didn't ask? You should have realised that I would have wanted to know!'

'I didn't think you'd care,' he commented drily.

But Sophie was too caught up in her own rage to analyse the meaning of his words. 'I would never have gone if I'd known she was going to be there!'

'Why ever not?'

'Oh, don't be so naïve, Luis!' she said furiously. 'Don't you think that everyone must have been sniggering into their drinks to see your past and your current mistress together at the same party? Was that your intention? To humiliate me?'

He swore softly in Spanish as the car bumped down the drive towards the hacienda. 'You think that?' he demanded. 'You honestly think that?'

'What else am I supposed to think?'

'I offered you my arm on our arrival,' he accused, 'to show the world that you are the woman in my life, but you refused it, didn't you? Cool, cold Sophie and her don't-touch-me quality which would freeze water on the hottest day!'

'I'm not staying around to listen while you insult me!'

She jumped out of the car door and slammed it, marching straight into the house and storming into the sitting room with Luis hot on her heels. Once the door was closed behind him and they were alone she turned on him furiously.

'You were trying to make me jealous, weren't you, Luis?'

There was a long pause, and then he nodded. '*Sí*. Maybe I was.'

She stared at him. 'Why would you want to make me jealous?'

He gave a short laugh. 'Now who's being the naïve one?'

'I don't—I don't understand.'

And suddenly everything which had been bubbling away inside him for weeks now came to a violent boil. 'Don't you?' he demanded. 'Don't you really? I suppose that I must be grateful that you *do* appear jealous—at least that shows me you feel *something* for me!'

'Luis—'

'Do you have any idea what it is like to be made to feel nothing more than a stud?' he stormed.

'A *stud?*'

'A man who pleases you in bed, but is fit for nothing more!'

'Luis, that is ridiculous,' she protested. 'We do all kind of things together; you know we do.'

'I know that you do them while keeping me at arm's length, with those witchy blue eyes and that cool, mocking smile! But the only time I feel close to you is when I am making love to you.' He gave a snort of derision. 'And you wonder why I say that I feel like a stud!'

She had never seen him so het-up before, nor quite so *Spanish,* and she realised that for all his aristocratic upbringing and his fluent English, this man who stood before her now was a living, breathing Latin, with all the passion and the turbulence which went along with his heritage. But her confusion was genuine as her anger began to seep away, replaced by a desperate need to know what she should have asked him a long time ago. 'What is it that you want from me, Luis?'

Black fire sparked from his eyes. 'Nothing that you are not prepared to give,' he answered proudly.

And suddenly the thought that she might lose him became horribly and frighteningly real. 'I...thought that I was a good mistress,' she said haltingly.

Again he swore in Spanish. 'And you are! The very best mistress in the world!' he raged, and his eyes lanced into her as though they were black lasers. 'But I do not want a mistress! Not any more.'

Her mouth fell open and her heart began beating with distress as she bit out the painful words. 'You mean...you mean you want me to go away?'

'*Madre de Dios!* Must I spell it out for you in words of one syllable? I want to know what goes on in that mad, crazy, cool English heart of yours! No, I do not want you to go away—I want to know how you *feel!*'

'About what?'

His eyes blazed. 'About what?' he demanded incredulously. 'About *me,* of course!'

She turned away. He wanted too much! He wanted it all, and more besides.

'Sophie?' he said, on a note which came as close as Luis ever would to pleading.

'No,' she said stubbornly.

He looked at the defiant set of her shoulders. 'Why not?' he asked quietly.

'Because feelings were not part of the deal! I came here on the understanding that I would look after your son and share your bed. That was the agreement—your words, Luis, not mine.'

'And what if I told you that I was no longer content with the present agreement?'

She turned around. 'Just what are you getting at?'

'That feelings change, or maybe I was just too blind to see that they had been there all along. You see—' He bit his lip, as if trying to work out how to say words which were foreign to him. 'I love you, Sophie. I love you with all my heart—'

'But you don't know what love is,' she protested weakly, though her own heart was beating fit to burst. 'Remember?'

'How could I ever forget?' he said bitterly, wondering if he had been half-crazy himself to have ever said such a thing. But she was still standing an arm's length away, and her eyes were still wary and unconvinced. He struggled to put his own feelings into words, something which really *was* foreign to him.

'What would you say if I told you that I think I fell in love with you the moment I saw you? Sophie, it was a feeling so strong that it rocked the very foundations of my world—'

'Please don't!' she interrupted before he could say any more. 'That was wrong—you know it was! You were due to be married *to my cousin!*'

'You cannot help the way that someone makes you feel,' he argued sombrely. 'It is what you *do* about those feelings which makes it right or wrong. And I did nothing. Nothing at all. And neither did you.'

'I wanted you, too,' she whispered. 'And I felt so guilty about it. That's why I taught myself to hate you, to convince myself that you were looking at every other woman the way you looked at me that day.'

He shook his head. 'Never,' he said softly. 'I have never looked at another woman in such a way, but then no other woman makes me feel the way you do, Sophie. Women have plotted and schemed and made demands on me, but not you—and you see, I have grown to love you very much, and I still don't know how you feel about me.'

Sophie suddenly felt as though she had drunk a glass of champagne too quickly. 'Luis,' she said weakly. 'Will you hold me? Please?'

He needed no second bidding, just reached out and pulled her against him, his strong arms supporting her, protecting her. He closed his eyes and rested his cheek against the silk of her hair.

'Anyway, you do know,' she said indistinctly against his chest.

He lifted her chin, both moved and disturbed to see the tears which glittered in her blue eyes. 'Do I, *querida* mine?'

'Yes,' she sniffed. 'You must do. Of course I love you! You must be used to women falling in love with you all the time.'

Diplomatically he ignored that. 'You didn't act like you loved me,' he mused instead. 'Emotionally you kept me at a distance, Sophie; you cannot deny that.'

'Because love makes you vulnerable, that's why.'

'Don't I just know it?' he commented drily.

She stared at him as if he had just told her that the sun would shine at night. 'You? Vulnerable? Never!'

'Yes, sometimes. With you.' He smiled. 'You see,

with you it's different—different from anything I have ever experienced, or expected to.'

But the past came thudding down, like a dark and heavy thundercloud, and all Sophie's fears came spilling out. 'I can't stay with you, Luis—'

He stilled. 'Not *stay* with me?' he repeated incredulously.

She shook her head, knowing that she must confront her fears head-on, not leave them festering beneath the surface, where they could eat into her confidence and her life.

She shook her head. 'Not if I thought you were ever going to take another mistress—*ever,*' she emphasised fiercely, and turned her blue eyes up to him. 'And how do I know you won't?'

'Because I make that vow to you,' he said softly. 'Never, ever, ever—and have I ever lied to you, Sophie?'

She shook her head.

'How can I look at any woman ever again?' he said simply. 'Do you not know that you hold my heart in the palm of your hand, Sophie?'

It was the most wonderful thing anyone had ever said to her. A tear began to track its way down her cheek, and he made a reprimanding little sound as he wiped it away with his lips. 'Ssh,' he soothed. 'No more tears. No need for any tears. Come, Sophie, come and sit beside me over here.'

He led her to the window-seat and sat her down as tenderly as if she were a child, then raised her hand to his lips and kissed the fingertips thoughtfully.

'When did it happen?' she asked, loving this new reverence and homage. 'When did you know?'

He shrugged. 'Who knows? When you went back to England I missed you like crazy, and at first I tried to tell myself that it was just frustration. But frustration does not usually eat into your very soul. I wanted you,' he said simply. 'Here. With me. Always.'

'You took long enough to come and ask me,' she complained.

He nodded. 'But of course—because I needed to be sure. Because what I was asking of you was a big thing, *querida*. I could not risk Teo's happiness if I thought it would not work out, that you would have to leave him again. And anyway—' he gave her a rueful look '—I did not know what your answer would be. How did I know that you would agree to give up your high-powered life in England to come and live with me? It was my wildest, sweetest wish come true.'

Now feeling more than a little content, she also felt secure enough to bat him a look from between slitted lashes. 'And what if I had not agreed?'

'Then I would have come to get you,' he said darkly. 'Some way. Somehow. I knew I would have you in the end.'

Sophie shivered, thinking that she rather liked the sound of that. 'And now?'

The kiss to her fingertips became a little nip, and then a voluptuous lick of his tongue, and he smiled, seeing her pupils dilate in response. 'Now we go to bed, *querida,* and we make beautiful love together—'

'No change there, then?'

'And then you will tell me exactly when you will agree to marry me.'

EPILOGUE

SHE kept him waiting for almost a year, until Luis was almost climbing the walls. He had thought that he had felt frustration when she was far away from him in England but he had been wrong. This, he thought distractedly, *this* was frustration!

Did she expect him to beg? Because if so she was in for a big disappointment—for, although she had captured his heart for more than a lifetime, a de la Camara would never *beg!*

But he asked her to be his wife from time to time, usually when he found her especially irresistible, and her answer was always the same.

'Not yet, Luis. Not yet.'

'Why do you make me wait, *querida* mine?' he growled.

She touched her fingertips to his mouth. 'Because it isn't the right time.'

'When, then?'

'You'll be the first to know,' she whispered, and kissed him. 'And it's probably the first time you've ever had to wait for anything in your life!'

This much was true. Life's pleasures and rewards had always dropped with astonishing ease into the lap of Luis de la Camara and he was discovering for himself that delayed gratification could be a potent aphrodisiac! Sophie had laughed when he told her *that*.

'As if *you* had any need of an aphrodisiac!' she gurgled.

She was now learning Spanish and Luis arranged to have a tutor visit each afternoon while Teo had his nap. She took her studies seriously—so seriously, in fact, that Luis had wondered aloud if she would end up with a larger vocabulary than him!

'Very probably,' she said serenely.

And Teo had grown from a plump baby into the most enchanting toddler, who now called Sophie ''Mama''. The first time he said it she had felt her eyes filling with tears and had looked over at Luis and seen the responding telltale glitter in his own.

'It would be nice to give Teo a brother or a sister one of these days,' he commented in bed that night.

Sophie was still basking in the aftermath of an earth-shattering orgasm. 'Would it?'

'Mmm.' He leaned back over her and trickled a finger down to where she was still wet and pulsing with him, and she shuddered. 'We could have a lot of fun together, making babies, Soph-ie.'

'We have a lot of fun together now,' she protested weakly, but then he started kissing her, and she was lost.

Then one day, in his study, she put the phone down and turned to him expectantly.

'My parents want to come and stay,' she announced.

He looked up from his paperwork. 'So I gathered. I'm delighted,' he murmured. 'When?'

'Late next week.'

He nodded. 'I'll clear my diary.'

Luis had met her parents twice, when he had taken

Sophie back to England with Teo, and once he had dispelled their initial wariness with his obvious love for their daughter they began to think him the greatest thing since sliced bread.

They had visited her grandmother, too, and her London-based friends, and even Liam had grudgingly begun to accept that the aristocratic Spaniard made her happy.

'Darling Luis,' she murmured.

He feasted his black eyes on her extravagantly. 'Mmm?'

'You know my parents are coming out?'

'Well, since you told me that just moments ago, yes, I do, *querida,*' he commented drily. 'My memory is not quite that defective!'

'Well...' She drew a deep breath, knowing that she had put the moment off for as long as it needed to be. Miranda's memory would not be sullied, nor would any of their families feel any emotion other than happiness for them. 'It sort of seems a pity not to make the most of it,' she said slowly.

'You want me to throw a party for them?'

'*Us* to throw a party,' she corrected. 'Yes, I do.' She looked at him from between slitted lashes. 'We could make it a wedding party, if you like.'

He gave a lazy smile. 'Come over here.'

She did as he asked, went and sat on his knee and put her arms tightly around his neck.

'You're going to marry me at last, are you, Sophie?'

'Yes, please!'

'And you're quite sure?'

She gazed down at the black eyes which glittered

at her with such love and longing that a lump rose in her throat, and it was a moment before she could speak. 'Oh, yes, my beloved Don Luis,' she whispered. 'I've never been more sure of anything in my life.'

A SPANISH PRACTICE

by

Anne Herries

Anne Herries, winner of the Romantic Novelists' Association's Romance Prize 2004, lives in Cambridgeshire. After many happy years with a holiday home in Spain, she and her husband now have their second home in Norfolk. They are only just across the road from the sea, and have a view of it from their windows. At home and at the sea they enjoy watching the wildlife and have many visitors to their gardens, particularly squirrels. Anne loves watching their antics and spoils both them and her birds shamelessly. She also loves to see the flocks of geese and other birds flying in over the sea during the autumn, to winter in the milder climes of this country. Anne loves to write about the beauty of nature and sometimes puts a little into her books, though they are mostly about love and romance. She writes for her own enjoyment and to give pleasure to her readers.

CHAPTER ONE

'I ENVY you, Jenny, I really do,' Dr James Redfern said to his colleague. 'Six months in Spain, away from the English winter and the grind of the NHS.'

'I happen to feel a lot of affection for the NHS,' Jenny said, her soft brown eyes avoiding his as she tried not to let him see her sharp disappointment at his casual acceptance of her notice. She had hoped he would say it wasn't possible, that he simply couldn't manage without her in their busy practice in the heart of Norwich—that he would beg her to stay. 'I'm merely taking this appointment for my mother's sake. As you know, my parents went to live in the Costa del Sol when my father retired. Now he's suffering from the after-effects of his stroke, which thankfully wasn't fatal, and Mum begged me to go out there for a while. She even found me the job.'

'It sounds interesting,' James said, looking at her oddly. 'You'll be looking after people like your father, Jenny, as well as holidaymakers. It must be difficult for expats, people who have retired to Spain and don't speak the language very well—frightening, too. To have an English doctor on call will be wonderful for them.'

'That's what Dr Miguel Sanchez seems to think,' Jenny said. 'Though he speaks immaculate English himself. However, from our brief phone calls, I gather he's a very busy man, and most of his own time is spent working in the hospital nearby. He believes that having an English doctor with some years of practical experience at his clinic will be an advantage.'

'Do you speak Spanish?'

'Yes, just a little. My parents were always keen on taking holidays there so I learned the basic stuff. It wouldn't be good enough for me to work in the Spanish equivalent of the NHS, of course, but I could manage to find a bed for a patient in the hospital if I needed to. I've no intention of staying there for ever. I've promised Mum I'll go out for six months, and then we'll have to see how my father is getting on. If he's finding it difficult then it might be best for them to come back to England in the end.'

James nodded, looking at her thoughtfully. He would be sorry to lose her. She was an excellent doctor, about twenty-eight or so and clearly dedicated to her job as, to his knowledge, she hadn't had a serious relationship since leaving college. Sometimes he'd wondered why. Jenny was an attractive woman, though not what he would have called pretty, and certainly not his type. James went for rather more lively girls, and he was still playing the field even though he was approaching his thirty-fourth birthday. As yet, he hadn't thought of settling down.

'Well, don't feel guilty about making the change,' James said, and glanced at his watch. He had a heavy date that evening. 'You've worked hard, Jenny. Perhaps too hard. I've noticed you've seemed a bit down recently. It will do you good to have a break—and if you want to come back to us we'll be pleased to take you on again.'

'No, I shan't come back,' Jenny said. 'I'm not sure what I want to do after my six months abroad. There was a time when I thought I might specialize in paediatric medicine. I might go back to my old hospital and retrain.'

'Well, I wish you luck in whatever you decide,' James said, and offered his hand for all the world as if they hardly knew one another. Not even a kiss on the cheek! 'The profession is lucky to have dedicated people like you, Jenny.'

So that was that, Jenny thought as she walked out of the practice she had worked at for the last two years. She'd burned her boats and there was no going back. She hadn't even had to work out a notice period because she'd managed to locate a locum to take over from her almost immediately. She felt a slight ache somewhere in the region of her heart and for a moment the temptation to weep was strong, but she blinked hard and told herself not to be a fool.

'He just had no idea,' she murmured to herself as she unlocked her car. 'And he would have been embarrassed if he had.'

Jenny smiled wryly as she started the engine of her almost new Golf. She'd been carrying a bit of a torch for her boss for the past year—ever since he'd flirted her when he'd been slightly drunk at the practice dinner-dance—and he hadn't even noticed!

Of course, Jenny knew she wasn't his type. She had seen the glamorous women he escorted out to dinner and the theatre, and she'd told herself over and over again that she was a fool to let herself care. James Redfern was undoubtedly handsome, charming, a brilliant doctor—and he knew it!

He had the classic good looks that made him look as if he had stepped straight out of the pages of a magazine, and he exploited them to the full. Jenny hadn't particularly admired the way he treated women, which made it all the more frustrating to know that she was attracted to him herself. At least she had managed to keep her secret, and that was a source of relief. She would have hated it if he'd guessed how she felt.

'You're love-starved, my girl, that's your problem,' Jenny told herself as she drove back to the old house she shared with two other friends, both of them nurses at the local hospital. 'You should take Moya's advice and go out and find yourself a man!'

Jenny's mouth curved in a cheeky smile, a smile her colleagues at work had seldom seen. In fact, it had been a long time since anyone had seen it, apart from Moya and Angie—and her parents, both of whom she loved dearly. Her mother and father had supported her through medical school, even though her father had been longing to retire. He was some years older than Jenny's mother and they'd had their only child late in life. She had been thoroughly spoiled by them, which was why she felt she must give something back now even though it did mean giving up her own life for the time being.

Jenny wasn't sure she wanted to work in the coastal region of Southern Spain, even for a few months. She was a very conscientious doctor and felt that she had a duty to the NHS, which had trained her. Besides, which, she imagined she would be dealing with small injuries quite often, which wasn't really what she wanted to do—but her mother needed her and six months wasn't a lifetime, for goodness' sake! She could surely give up her own ambitions for that short period.

And Mrs Talforth's request had come at a time when Jenny was beginning to realize that she ought to make a move for her own sake. It had been painful to meet James Redfern every day, knowing that she wanted something she could never have. This temporary job in

Spain was something in the nature of a sabbatical while she made up her mind what she was going to do with the rest of her life.

Jenny wasn't really sure what she wanted. She had spoken of specializing to James more as an excuse to explain why she wasn't going to return to his practice than anything else. She did love children, of course, and returning to train in paediatric medicine was one option—though in her heart she knew that what she really wanted was a child of her own. Make that several! Being an only child wasn't much fun.

She had hoped that by becoming a GP she would be able to combine a career with raising a family. She would have needed to take a few years off, but if she had been lucky in her choice of a husband she could have gone back to medicine one day.

It didn't look as though she was having much luck in that department, Jenny reflected ruefully. She had been madly, wildly in love at medical school, but it had ended in tears. After that, she had dated for a while, but as her work had become more and more time-absorbing she had somehow got into the habit of going out in a crowd with friends and having only casual dates. No man had touched her inner being until that dance...and then James had kissed her under some mistletoe and suddenly she had wanted him to go on kissing her so badly that she had found herself unable to sleep that night.

In a moment of despair, she had confided her passion to her friend Moya, who had declared she was mad.

'What you need is some red-hot sex,' she had told Jenny. 'I'll fix you up with someone if you like—no strings attached.'

Jenny had shaken her head, laughing at Moya's no-nonsense attitude to the whole thing. Moya was a professional nurse and had no intention of marrying, but that didn't stop her having fun when she wanted it. However, she was a sensible woman, and knew what she was doing. Jenny had no need to worry about Moya, either physically or emotionally. However, Moya's way of life wasn't for her. She wanted the kind of marriage her parents had or nothing at all, and it looked as if she was going to have to settle for the second option.

Jenny parked outside the small supermarket at the end of the quiet road where she lived and popped in to pick up a few bits and pieces for her supper. She was about to leave again when a woman with a young child in a pushchair stopped her.

'I hoped I might see you here, Dr Talforth,' the woman said. 'I wanted to thank you for what you did for my husband that night. If you hadn't recognized the symptoms as an early warning of a heart attack he might have died. He had quite a nasty one when he was in the hospital, but because he was already there they managed to pull him round. He's out of Intensive Care now and feeling much better.'

'I'm so glad, Mrs Jackson,' Jenny said, and looked at the child. 'And how is Susan today? Over that chestiness, I hope?'

'Yes, she's fine,' Ann Jackson said. 'The medicine you gave her was wonderful stuff. I don't know what my family would have done without you recently.'

'I'm sure someone else would have treated you just as efficiently.' Jenny hesitated, then said, 'I haven't had time to let my patients know, but I'm leaving the practice. My father is ill and I'm going out to be with my parents for a while.'

'Oh, I am sorry—about your father and the fact that you're leaving us. We shall miss you.'

'I'm sorry to be leaving,' Jenny replied. 'But I know that Dr Redfern will look after you. And I'm very pleased your husband is feeling better.'

'Oh, he's talking about going back to work—but he thinks he may change his job to something less stressful.'

'That sounds like a good idea—and he might think about taking up some form of regular exercise. Cycling or swimming is very good.'

Jenny was smiling as she left the young woman and drove the short distance to her home. It was always nice to hear the good news, which was one reason why she enjoyed being a GP. There was more contact with the patients, unlike the hospital where you seldom saw them after they left. In the years she'd been at the busy practice Jenny had got to know a lot of people and she was going to miss that. She supposed it would be very different when she got to Spain. There would be very little chance of establishing a relationship with patients then.

'You've been so kind,' Beth Talforth said when the rather serious but extremely charming man came out of her husband's bedroom and handed her a prescription for new medication. 'I really don't know what we should have done without your support these past few weeks.'

Dr Miguel Sanchez smiled, his teeth flashing a brilliant white against the golden tan of his skin. He was generally thought attractive, though at times his features could seem harsh, his dark eyes cold and ungiving. At the moment they were warm and concerned.

'It has been a pleasure, Señora Talforth,' he said. 'Your husband is a sensible man. I have many patients for whom I fear being ill in a foreign country is more of an ordeal than need be—and it is I who have much to thank you for. Dr Talforth will be an asset to my clinic. At last I may have a little time for personal concerns.'

'We are both looking forward to having Jenny here. She would have hated to just sit around, twiddling her thumbs. That's why I happened to ask if it would be possible for her to work out here.'

'In a private clinic like mine there are no difficulties,' he replied seriously. 'Dr Talforth might possibly have to do some retraining if she wished to work in our hospitals, but for me it is not a problem. She will be dealing with English-speaking patients, which is what is needed here on the coast.'

'Well, I still feel very grateful,' Beth replied. 'Jenny has been rather unhappy for a while. I think there may have been a man involved. She doesn't say very much but, reading between the lines, I've an idea she wants to get away from an awkward situation—with one of her colleagues.' She sighed. 'Children can be such a trouble, Dr Sanchez.'

'Yes, I should imagine so. We must hope your daughter settles here for a few months, Señora Talforth.'

'I just want her to be happy. I'd like to see her married—but I think she's had one or two unfortunate relationships.'

'It happens.' He glanced at his watch, only half listening. 'I must go.'

'Of course. I'm chattering on—and you've already done so much.'

'It was my privilege.' Miguel smiled at her and went out into the quiet street where his car was parked.

His smile disappeared as he left the villa, which was situated on top of a hill overlooking the Mediterranean and in the heart of a popular holiday complex. It was past seven in the evening but the sun was still warm as he got into his car and reached for his mobile phone.

He was conscious of feeling tired, almost drained, emotionally and physically. It had been a long day at the emergency hospital, where he worked several days a week, dealing with both Spanish and English patients, most of whom couldn't afford to pay for expensive treatment at one of the private clinics along the coast. One of the English patients he had seen that day was a child who had cracked his head against an obstruction in the swimming pool and had been unconscious for some minutes.

Miguel was anxious about the boy, and he had asked that he be kept under strict observation for the night. It was likely that some intracranial swelling might occur, and he had made the surgeon on call aware of the possibility, but he was still unable to let go of the problem. He dialled the hospital number to check on the child's progress, then spoke to the surgeon again just to make sure he would keep an eye on the case.

Miguel frowned as he switched off his mobile and started the Mercedes' engine. He had three more house calls to make before he could go home. Unfortunately, his personal problems would begin then. A wry smile touched the mouth that could look harsh at times. He needed help to get through his heavy workload so that he could devote a little more time to Elena and Joachim. The boy was three years old, too boisterous for his mother to handle alone, and needed a father's influence. And Miguel just wasn't able to give him enough time.

Miguel knew he was taking a risk in employing an English woman he had never met. She had seemed sensible when he'd spoken to her on the telephone, and her qualifications were excellent. If things went well, he would be able to leave most of his casual private work to Dr Talforth while he concentrated on his hospital work—and perhaps he could take the odd afternoon off to be with Joachim.

'Mum, it's lovely to see you,' Jenny said, hugging her mother. She had driven herself from Malaga airport to the pretty resort halfway between Fuengirola and Marbella. It wasn't the first time she had visited her parents' villa, of course, but there was more luggage in the boot than she normally brought for her flying visits. 'How is Dad?'

'Tired—you know.' Beth Talforth tried to hide her anxiety as she hugged her beloved daughter back and struggled against the tears that threatened. 'It has been a bit of a worry, Jenny. I thought he might...well, you understand.' Her voice wobbled and her eyes misted. 'I've no idea how I would have managed if Dr Sanchez hadn't been so kind. He had your father straight in the hospital, and stayed with me until they had him stabilized. We couldn't have had better treatment if we'd been at home.'

'Was it expensive?'

'We insured for emergency when we came out here,' Beth said. 'We pay six thousand pesetas each a month. We've got the E111, of course, but that's all a bit of a rigmarole, though it's OK for some things. Your father prefers to pay the insurance to be sure—and he has such a good pension that we manage nicely.'

Jenny nodded. She knew her parents were financially secure, though far from rich.

'You haven't thought of coming back, then?'

'This weather suits us both,' Beth said. 'I was nearly crippled up with arthritis at home. Out here I hardly ever need a painkiller—and we've made lots of friends here. More than we had at home.' She frowned. 'Of course if anything happened to—'

'Don't think about that, Mum,' Jenny said. 'These days a stroke isn't necessarily the end of things. We can do an awful lot to help. Has Dad been having physiotherapy?'

'Some—but that's expensive,' Beth said. 'It wasn't covered, you see. Dr Sanchez spent some time explaining the exercises himself—and he never charges us anything extra. I've done what I could, but I'm not sure I've been of much help to your father.'

'Well, I'll be able to take over that side of things now,' Jenny said. 'I'll just take these cases in, Mum, then I'll go in and see him.'

'Yes. He's been looking forward to seeing you. We're both so grateful to you for coming. I know I shouldn't have asked, but I've been so worried.'

'Of course I came,' Jenny said, and hugged her again. 'I love you both—and you've been good to me. Besides, it was probably time for a change.'

'I haven't spoiled anything? No romance...?'

Jenny's cheeky smile peeped out. 'I did have a bit of a crush on someone, but it wasn't going anywhere,' she said. 'He hardly knew I was around—except in a professional way.'

Her mother looked disappointed. 'I keep hoping you're going to make me a grandmother.'

'One day I might—if the right man comes along.'

'Well, go and see your father,' Beth said. 'Then you can change out of those clothes and put something cooler on. You must be hot.'

'Yes, I am a bit,' Jenny admitted, looking down at her grey trousers and blue cotton shirt. She had taken off the suit jacket before driving to the villa, but was still warm. 'It was quite cool when I left home. You know what it can be like in England, even in May.'

'That's why I love being out here. You'll find a big difference. We're glad of the shade in the house most days.'

'Well, it is certainly lovely and cool in here,' Jenny agreed. 'When I've changed into something casual I might have a walk—take a look at the clinic.'

'Yes, that's a good idea,' Beth said. 'It will still be open, of course, though probably only the nurse will be there at this time in the evening. I think her name is Soraya. She deals with minor cuts and bruises from the holidaymakers, and telephones Dr Sanchez if any emergency comes in.'

'Yes, he told me a little of the routine when we talked on the phone,' Jenny said. 'He sounds very efficient.'

'Oh, he's a lot more than that,' Beth told her. 'But I won't say anything. I'll let you form your own opinions when you meet him.'

'Yes, well, that's not until tomorrow,' Jenny said. 'We have an appointment at nine-thirty. But there's nothing to stop me taking a look at the outside this evening, is there?'

It was a little cooler now, but still much warmer than it would have been at home. Jenny was wearing a pair of cotton shorts and a thin silk vest as she stood in the villa garden and looked down the hill. From here there was a gorgeous view of the sea, little white houses and apartments nestling amongst trees and flowering bushes.

The clinic was situated in the commercial area of the complex, near to the various supermarkets, tourist shops and cafés, but it was just far enough to make a pleasant walk on an evening like this, especially since most of it was downhill—at least on the way there.

Jenny passed the tennis courts and bowling greens, where holidaymakers were out enjoying themselves after a day spent on the beach or by the pools. She smiled as she watched two small children playing on the swings, and waved to their mother who was watching over them.

Continuing on down the hill, Jenny passed a Spanish bar she had visited for a meal on her last visit, and the owner lifted his hand in salute. The atmosphere in this complex was definitely friendly, like villages in England used to be once upon a time. Everyone knew you, and they all treated you like a friend. She could understand why her mother liked the life out here—it was certainly very different from the one she had had at home.

The clinic was set beside a rather attractive flowering tree, fragile mauve blossoms falling all over the place and their perfume seeming to fill the night air. From the outside the building looked small and rather like all the others in the complex, which made Jenny frown. Dr Sanchez had assured her that she would find the clinic well equipped and modern, but she had some doubts as she gazed at the place where she would be working for the next few months. If she found she couldn't work there it was going to be awkward.

Seeing that the door had been left open, Jenny wandered inside. The reception area was pleasant with dark plain ceramic tiles on the floor, black leather seating and terracotta pots with green plants to give it a welcoming atmosphere. So far so good, Jenny thought, and glanced round.

The receptionist's desk was empty, and the door marked as belonging to the nurse was firmly closed. She could hear a child's wails of anguish coming from inside and two or three female voices trying to comfort the patient. A smile touched her mouth. Jenny knew how much fuss a small child could make when hurt. She was about to leave the clinic when she saw a door with her own name on it and hesitated. She ought to wait for the morning, of course, but she was curious about her own room.

She walked towards it and was about to push it open when someone spoke from behind her. 'Please, don't enter the treatment rooms until invited,' a man's voice said harshly. 'You must wait until the receptionist has taken your details.'

Jenny swung round, her cheeks warm with embarrassment. She found herself looking at a man with dark, angry eyes, black wavy hair cut into a severe style as if he had tried to subdue the natural bounce and a mouth that was at that moment devoid of any softness. She was surprised somehow, having thought he would be older, but she recognized his voice.

'I'm sorry,' Jenny apologized. 'I know I ought to have waited until tomorrow, but I was curious. It was very rude of me.' She offered her hand. 'Forgive me. I'm Dr Jenny Talforth—and I believe you must be Dr Sanchez.'

'You are Dr Talforth?' His brows arched in disbelief. He seemed annoyed. 'But you can't be more than twenty-two at most. There must be some mistake...'

'I assure you I am nearly twenty-nine,' Jenny said, slightly offended at his tone. Did he imagine she had lied about her experience to get this job? He must rate his clinic highly! 'And my references are all in order. You may check them if you like—if you haven't already.'

'As a matter of fact, I have,' Miguel replied. 'Contrary to what you may believe, Miss Talforth, we have very strict rules and regulations here. Had you been straight out of medical school I wouldn't have offered you the job. It is your hospital and general practice experience that made me feel you would be suitable.'

Jenny bristled. 'I imagine I am over-qualified for the work I shall be required to do here.'

'Then you imagine wrongly,' Miguel replied, glaring at her. 'I've just come from the hospital. The day before yesterday I admitted a child with concussion after an accident in a swimming pool. Yesterday he was operated on for intracranial bleeding, which was putting pressure on his brain—this morning he is beginning to make a recovery. If you think such a case unimportant you are not the person for this job.'

'No, of course I don't!' Jenny was stung, as much by the scorn in his eyes as his words. 'But I don't expect that kind of thing happens often.'

'Often enough for me to require a full-time assistant,' Miguel said. 'I have managed with a nurse for the hours I was at the hospital, but that meant a lot of evening house calls. I was hoping that with you here I might be able to take a little time off now and then, but...' He left the sentence unfinished as if he felt cheated, which brought another hot flush to Jenny's cheeks.

'I hope you will feel able to do so,' she said. 'If I had the wrong idea about the work you do here I apologize. I imagined it was mostly sunburn and cuts, but I realize I was wrong. I should have known better. Please, forgive me—and for being rude enough to arrive here unannounced.'

Miguel ran his fingers through his thick, rather stubborn hair, studying her thoughtfully. Somehow Dr Talforth wasn't what he'd expected—he had seen her as an older woman, not as attractive. Something was triggered in his memory. What had her mother said about trouble with a man and an awkward situation? He hadn't been listening properly, but the difficulty had presumably been with a male colleague since she had been willing to leave her job at a moment's notice. She had appeared to be the answer to his prayers, but now he wasn't so sure. He hoped she wasn't intending to dress like this for work!

His disapproval was sharp and for a moment he was tempted to tell her that he had changed his mind about employing her. The last thing he needed was a *femme fatale* as a colleague. But, of course, he couldn't do any such thing! She'd given up her job on the strength of this one—and he was desperate for someone to help out at the clinic.

'I've had a difficult day,' he said, sounding apologetic. 'Personal problems as well as a death. I think I said rather more than was necessary. Shall we start again?' He offered his hand. 'Welcome to the clinic, Dr Talforth.'

'Thank you, Dr Sanchez.'

Jenny wasn't entirely reassured by his belated welcome. For a moment there had been a distinctly hostile look in those dark eyes, but now his expression had changed to that of a professional doctor.

'I hope you found your parents well? I've been a bit worried about Mrs Talforth.'

'My mother—why?' Jenny was puzzled. It was her father who had been ill.

'She seemed a little lost and disorientated for a while,' Miguel replied. 'It is natural, of course. Especially since she is in a country other than her own. Being ill out here is a terrifying experience for many foreigners. They come out when they are beginning to become more vulnerable, expecting to enjoy the lifestyle, and most of them don't mix with the Spanish population. They don't bother to learn the language—though your father is the exception—and then when they are ill they feel lost and frightened. I have a large number of such people on my panel, which is why I thought I would employ an English doctor—to give my older patients confidence.'

'Yes, I can understand that,' Jenny said, looking at him thoughtfully. At first she had thought she was going to dislike him, but now she wasn't so sure. 'My mother loves it here because she feels so much better—but if she lost my father I don't know what she would do. I suppose she would have to come back to England, even though she would feel much worse in herself.'

'Unless you decide to make your home out here, of course.'

His brows arched as he looked at her, and for a moment Jenny felt slightly odd, a little breathless, as if she had been running very fast. She took a deep breath and told herself not to be stupid. She had just escaped from one hopeless situation and wasn't going to fall headlong into another. If this man wasn't married, he had a girlfriend around—no man who looked like he did was going to be unattached. Not that it mattered to her. For goodness' sake! She wasn't even sure she liked the man.

She shook her head. 'No, I don't think—'

'Dr Sanchez.' A dark-haired girl with golden skin and a glorious figure came out of the treatment room. She spoke rapidly in Spanish, rather too fast for Jenny to make out more than a few words but she seemed to be saying they had been about to telephone him.

'Excuse me,' Miguel said. 'Apparently, I am needed. Please, feel free to look around wherever you please.' He glanced at the receptionist who looked as immaculate as if she had stepped out of a fashion magazine. And her clothes looked expensive! 'Isabelle, this is Dr Talforth. Please, help her in any way you can.'

The receptionist turned her liquid brown eyes on Jenny, their expression distinctly hostile as they went over her, taking in her long legs, which were shown to advantage in the shorts.

'You wish me to show you your room?' she asked, clearly not prepared to be friendly.

'Thank you, but I believe I shall leave that till the morning,' Jenny replied. 'Please, tell Dr Sanchez that I shall be here at nine-thirty as we arranged.'

She nodded to the girl, who made no answer, giving Jenny a hard stare as if to warn her off. Jenny imagined that she probably had some sort of crush on her boss and felt sympathy for her.

Miguel Sanchez was an extremely attractive man—or he might be if he ever stopped looking annoyed. He was also very busy, and would probably not have time to notice that his receptionist was carrying a torch for him. At least it looked that way to Jenny, though perhaps she was over-sensitive to situations like this because her own feelings had been bruised by James Redfern.

Poor Isabelle, Jenny thought. She ought to make the break and find someone else. Someone with more time to notice how lovely she is.

Women were such fools over men, Jenny reflected as she began to walk up the hill again after leaving the clinic. Breaking their hearts over men who didn't deserve it. Why was it that they couldn't help falling for men who just didn't know they were around?

One thing was certain, Jenny wasn't going to be foolish over Dr Sanchez. She wasn't at all sure he really approved of her, and she was going to have her work cut out to make him take her seriously.

It was a pity she had met him dressed like a holidaymaker. She would make sure she was wearing something more suitable for their appointment the next day!

CHAPTER TWO

'I HOPE you are satisfied with the facilities we can provide?' Miguel raised his brows as Jenny took her time looking round the clinic the next day.

'I must admit I'm quite impressed,' Jenny said. 'I didn't realize you would have the latest technology at your fingertips—not quite as much as this, anyway. I'm intrigued with your computer system—it's more advanced than the one I've been used to.'

'That is one benefit of private medicine,' he replied, and his eyes seemed still to hold that faint look of disapproval. Jenny was aware of an undercurrent between them, which she couldn't quite place—but he certainly was a disturbing man. 'As you see, I do have the capacity to do minor surgery here, but it is very rarely used. I have removed the odd cyst from someone's back under local anaesthetic or an ingrown toenail, and we stitch up quite a lot of cuts, but anything complicated is referred to the hospital, of course.'

'I wanted to ask you about that,' Jenny said. 'Where do I send emergencies?'

'I'll give you a number to ring for an ambulance,' Miguel replied. 'I work in the emergency department myself three days a week, and for the time being you can ring me there—just until you get used to the system. If the case is less urgent, where you send the patient will depend on the circumstances. Insurance cases that need investigation may go to the Hospital Costa del Sol or possibly one in Malaga. Emergencies are sent to Fuengirola, which is where I am going this morning.'

Jenny was surprised. 'You're not entirely private, then?'

'I work part time in what you would call the NHS,' Miguel said. 'But I also hold consultations in a private capacity—is that not what your consultants do in England?'

'Yes, of course.' Jenny felt herself in the wrong again. 'I wasn't implying there was anything wrong with private work. At home even the Government is beginning to realize we may need to rely on it more and more as a source of extra capacity. I suppose I imagined the clinic here took up most of your time, but now I see I was mistaken.'

'I had a partner at one time, and he did most of the routine stuff here, but he took a year off to work abroad. He is in Sri Lanka, doing minor surgery for a charity out there, which although admirable has left me rather at a disadvantage. I have had to work longer hours to keep up with my schedule. That was why I felt I could offer you a job here. I hope you will be able to deal with the majority of my private patients?'

'Yes, I imagine I should be able to cope.' Jenny found herself blushing like a schoolgirl again. What was it about this man that made her feel so inadequate? 'What hours do you open the clinic?'

'From ten to one in the morning and from three to six-thirty in the afternoon, but we do have a call-out service until nine in the evenings. After that the service transfers to a twenty-four-hour emergency agency.'

'I can see why you've been busy,' Jenny said. 'I thought I worked hard at home, but if you been combining those sorts of hours with your hospital work...'

'My nurse has been holding the fort on my hospital days,' he replied. 'Soraya will be relieved to have a doctor here again full time. I've only been able to come in for a few hours at a time recently, and that was awkward. She has had to make a lot of late evening appointments for me and send patients through to Emergency when they could have been dealt with here, though she handles more minor cases herself.'

Jenny nodded, finding that she was fascinated by the deep quality of his voice as he talked—and that mouth could only be described as sensual. She dragged her mind back to business. The work he was describing seemed more interesting than she had imagined.

'So—do you think you can manage?' Miguel glanced at his watch, showing an inch of tanned skin as his sleeve was pushed back. 'I have quite a list of people to see at the hospital today as well as any emergencies that come in.'

'Yes, of course, Dr Sanchez. Please, feel free to leave whenever you're ready.'

He hesitated for a moment, then said, 'It is better to stick to "Doctor" when we are at work,' he said. 'Patients feel comfortable with that—but I see no reason why you should not call me Miguel in private.'

'I'm Jenny to friends,' she replied, with a smile. She had twisted her long, rich brown hair into a practical pleat at the back of her head that morning, and the white linen trousers and loose top that had been recommended for clinic work gave her a businesslike appearance, but that smile was pure magic. Very few men could resist it—but, then, very few had been privileged enough to have it bestowed on them in a long, long time.

'Good.' Miguel's stern features relaxed in an answering smile. 'I must go. Soraya will make you coffee. I am sorry I have no time to share it with you.'

'I mustn't detain you,' Jenny said.

She watched as he picked up his briefcase and left, then continued her tour of the clinic alone, rechecking things she had seen only briefly on her first inspection. The treatment room was spotless, as was the rest of the clinic—gleaming and modern. Jenny felt pleased that conditions were so much better than she had been expecting. And the computers were the very latest, providing all sorts of new technology that might prove helpful if a difficult case presented itself. It actually had a direct link to a London hospital with facilities via the Internet for consulting specialists and transfers of patients by air ambulance.

Jenny saw a variety of minor ailments that morning, including a young mother with a child of three who was suffering from sickness and a temperature.

'I thought it might be meningitis,' she said, clearly anxious. 'Sarah has been crying for hours, Doctor.'

'No, it's just a rather nasty attack of nausea, Mrs Jeffries,' Jenny replied. 'Just keep her cool, give her plenty of fluids but nothing to eat for at least twelve hours and she'll soon be feeling better.'

'Aren't you going to give Sarah anything?' Mrs Jeffries frowned. 'I was hoping to see Dr Sanchez. He's always so good with children.' She looked at Jenny doubtfully. 'Are you quite sure it isn't meningitis? Only we were visiting a friend three weeks ago in England, and her teenage daughter has just gone down with it. Viral meningitis, I think she said. I was talking to her last night on the phone...and then Sarah started to be ill.'

'Yes, I can understand why you're anxious,' Jenny

replied. 'But if your friend's daughter has viral meningitis she's probably going to be all right. It's the bacterial form that's so dangerous and infectious. In that form the disease attacks the upper respiratory system, especially in young children and teenagers.'

'Oh, I see,' Mrs Jeffries said. 'Then you don't think Sarah is in danger?'

'No, I don't think so. She does have symptoms that are similar—but the thing you need to be aware of with meningitis is the rash. Sarah doesn't have one.'

'Oh... Well, I suppose that's all right, then...'

Jenny frowned as Mrs Jeffries left with her daughter. It was quite common for women with young children to worry about the possibility of meningitis, but something had been a little odd about Mrs Jeffries' behaviour. She wondered about checking Dr Sanchez's notes on Mrs Jeffries, but dismissed the thought as Soraya came to tell her that one of Dr Sanchez's elderly patients was experiencing pain in his chest and arms.

'That sounds as if it might be serious,' Jenny said. 'I think I ought to attend immediately.'

'I shall draw you a little map,' Soraya said helpfully. She was a woman in her mid-forties, well built and inclined to be friendly. 'Finding your way can be difficult in the complexes at first. You'll soon get used to it, and anyone will point you in the right direction if you get lost.'

'Thank you.' Jenny glanced at her watch. 'It will be too late to come back here after I see the patient, so I'll talk to you this afternoon.'

'You know where to ring for an ambulance if necessary?'

'Yes. Dr Sanchez gave me an emergency number— and his own mobile number. I've logged them into my own mobile so that I've always got them. I hope it won't be necessary to use either, but it's as well to be prepared.'

Jenny went out to her car. She smiled and nodded to Isabelle, who was wearing yet another fantastic outfit that day, but was ignored. She hoped that the receptionist wasn't going to become a problem. Thankfully, Soraya was prepared to be friendly!

Jenny looked at the patient lying on his bed. It was immediately obvious that he was experiencing a lot of pain and some difficulty with his breathing. After her initial examination, she decided it was probably a mild heart attack, but there was always the possibility of the spasm escalating and causing serious damage to the heart muscle. She opened her bag and took out a sterile syringe and needle, then damped a piece of sterile material with antiseptic to clean the skin.

'I'm going to give you a mild sedative to help calm you, Mr Dickson,' she said. 'Then I'm going to telephone the number Dr Sanchez gave me. I shall arrange for you to go into Emergency.' Hearing a little gasp from Mrs Dickson, Jenny gave her a reassuring look. 'I believe it's merely a warning. Don't worry, I shall arrange for you to go with your husband in the ambulance.'

'I'm so glad you were at the clinic,' Mrs Dickson said. 'If I'd had to wait ages for someone to come out from Fuengirola I should have been terrified. And it's so much better when you understand the language.'

'Dr Sanchez speaks perfect English. I think most of the doctors do along the coast. It's at the hospital that you may experience some language difficulty, particularly with the nurses—but I'll let Dr Sanchez know you're on your way and I'm sure he'll come and see you there if he can.'

Jenny made her calls. She discovered that once initial contact was established, the person at the other end responded in English. The despatch of an ambulance was arranged, and arrived in ten minutes, which was, considering the traffic on the main coastal road, very fast. Jenny spoke to the attendants, explaining what medication had been administered and what she felt about the patient's condition. She saw the couple into the ambulance, then dialled Miguel's mobile.

'Sanchez?' His reply was crisp, slightly impatient, as though she had interrupted something important.

'It's Dr Talforth,' she said. 'I'm sending Mr Dickson to the emergency unit with what I believe is a mild heart attack. I've given him medication to calm him, because he was experiencing a lot of pain, but I've left it for the hospital to administer corrective drugs. I've sent a few details with him, just to be certain you're in the picture.'

'I'll arrange to see him on arrival,' Miguel said. 'Thank you, Dr Talforth. I shall see you this evening.'

The call was terminated abruptly. Jenny looked at her phone and frowned. He had told her to ring him in an emergency, for goodness' sake! She could just as easily have alerted the emergency department herself. Her Spanish wasn't as good as it might be, but she knew enough to make herself understood. Besides, most of the Spanish people she had met so far spoke English as well as she did herself.

Jenny felt a little irritated as she drove to her parents' villa. She didn't enjoy being made to feel second-class in the medical department. She had enjoyed the respect of her colleagues at home, and expected the same here. Everything was very different here, of course, but she had coped with her first emergency easily. It was hardly her fault if she had interrupted Dr Sanchez at work.

Jenny ate a light lunch with her mother, then spent half an hour helping her father with his physiotherapy.

'It's my arm that's the worst,' Ronald Talforth said. 'My leg is a bit weak, but I can manage to stand on it if I'm careful. I think I could manage to get about if I had one of those walking frames. My shoulder is very painful when I try to lift my arm above a certain height.'

'Yes, that does happen sometimes after a stroke,' Jenny said. 'You were lucky there was no paralysis, Dad, but it's going to take time and effort to have you back as you were. We'll see what exercise will do first. If your shoulder remains frozen after a couple of weeks or so I'll get Dr Sanchez to give you an injection of cortisone. That often helps, though we shall need to keep on with the exercises.'

Her father smiled at her. 'Can't you give me the injection? Dr Sanchez is so busy. I've already taken too much of his time.'

'I'm not allowed to treat close family. You know that, Dad. Besides, I'm here to make things easier for Dr Sanchez.'

'It is lucky for us he was prepared to take you on.'

'I think he'll gain as much as we shall,' Jenny said, still a little annoyed by his attitude when she had rung him earlier.

'Of course he will,' her father said, giving her a loving glance. 'I know you're a good doctor, Jenny. It was good of you to come out. Your mother and I are very grateful.'

'You don't have to be,' she said, and laughed. 'Did I sound a bit grumpy? I'm not really. It's only that I'm not sure Dr Sanchez thinks I'm up to the job which is a little irritating.'

'You've imagined it,' Ronald said. 'Sanchez isn't like that, Jenny. He is one of the most considerate, caring men I've ever met. Your mother was frantic when I was taken ill. I don't know what she would have done if it hadn't been for Sanchez. He's done everything for us—far more than could have been expected.'

'Yes, I can understand how Mum felt. I was called to an emergency this morning, and the patient's wife was very frightened until I explained that I believed there was no need to be on this occasion as it was a mild attack.' Jenny frowned. 'Dr Sanchez was a little anxious about Mum—has she seemed all right to you?'

'She's better now you're here.' He squeezed her hand. 'We both are, Jenny. We've missed you. It's a good life out here, but we have felt we needed you with us. Just until I'm on my feet again.'

'I was glad to come.' She kissed his cheek. 'I'd better get back to the clinic in case we have another emergency.'

As it happened, the afternoon was very quiet. A young woman brought in a child with a nasty rash, which Jenny was able to treat with some antihistamine pills and cream, and a representative from one of the car-hire firms on a neighbouring resort came in with a pain in his side which Jenny suspected might be a grumbling appendix.

'It isn't an emergency yet,' she told him, 'but you might like to go for an investigation at the hospital. These things can turn nasty if they are left.'

'I'm going back to England next month. I'll probably get it checked out there.'

'Don't leave it too long,' Jenny advised. 'Sometimes

it can flare up unexpectedly and cause a lot of trouble. The routine operation is nothing to worry about—but a burst appendix can be very nasty.'

'I'll see a doctor at home,' he promised, and went out looking as if he wanted to escape.

Jenny wondered how long he had been having the pain. Sometimes patients hid the truth from themselves rather than face up to the possibility of surgery. Still, if he wasn't willing to go in for an investigation there was nothing more she could do at the moment.

Jenny was a little restless when she returned to her parents' home that evening. She was used to a much heavier workload and felt that she ought to be doing more. If she was going to stay out here for longer than the agreed six months, she would need to explore further possibilities.

But was she even considering such an eventuality? She had thought six months would be long enough to see her father through his recovery process, but now she realized that might not be enough. If her mother was feeling uneasy, Jenny wouldn't be comfortable leaving them out here alone. Mrs Talforth would never use her own health to keep her daughter here, but Jenny had begun to see that both her parents might be more vulnerable than she had thought.

After all, she had no ties at home, nothing to take her back to England. She could take a language course out here in her own time, and then, if need be, a refresher course to allow her to work in a Spanish hospital. It was a possibility.

After a delicious meal of fresh fish grilled outside in the open air, Jenny decided to walk down to the sports complex. She felt warm and sticky and thought a swim in the pool would be refreshing.

She took a quick shower then jumped in the deep end. The water was wonderfully cool and after six fast lengths of the pool, Jenny climbed out and towelled herself down. She was about to leave the poolside and return to the villa when a young woman spoke to her.

'Hi—I think I saw you last evening? I had the children in the playground and you walked by. Are you on holiday?'

'Not really. I'm working at the Sanchez clinic. I'm a doctor—Jenny Talforth.'

'Oh, yes, I've heard about you,' the young woman said. 'You saw my husband this afternoon. He's had that niggling pain in his side for ages. I've been nagging him to see a doctor, but he wanted to wait until we go home.'

'Next month?' Jenny nodded. 'You shouldn't worry too much. A grumbling appendix can go on for ages, but it does need to be investigated at some time. I don't think it's critical at the moment. Just make sure he does go to a doctor when you get home.'

'I don't want to leave, but Bob says he's had enough of being out here. I'm Sally, by the way.'

'How long have you been out here?'

'Two years. I love it, but Bob misses England. We have a much better social life here. Would you like to come to our party? We're having a farewell do next week.'

'It depends whether I'm on call or not,' Jenny said. 'It's a pity you're leaving, Sally. We could have been friends.'

'Well, I hope you can make the party—you'll meet a lot of people your age if you come. I'll see you round before then. I know Beth. We often stop and talk when we meet.'

'Yes, she seems to know most people. Like you, she

loves the life here—and I must admit I'm beginning to see it has advantages.'

'It's great. Everyone is so friendly—even the holiday-makers seem to come back year after year.'

She smiled and let Jenny go on her way, before going for a swim herself. Jenny checked her mobile phone to make sure it was switched on. She had brought it with her in case there was a house call, but there were no messages. She walked back to the villa, admiring the view of bright gardens and the sparkle of the blue sea. It was very pretty here, and she could see why her mother enjoyed the life—except for when she was worrying about her husband's health. But she wouldn't need to worry so much if Jenny was around.

A car had just drawn up outside the villa, and Miguel Sanchez was getting out. She thought he looked weary, as if the long, hot day had taken its toll of him. She was conscious of her beach wrap, which clung to her wet bathing suit and showed off her figure much more than the clothes she had worn that morning.

'It was warm,' she said, feeling some explanation was necessary. Why was he staring at her? Perhaps he thought she ought to have been at home by the phone. 'I went for a swim—but I took my mobile with me just in case.'

'I've done the house calls,' Miguel said. That look of disapproval was back in his eyes. 'Soraya rang me—Mrs Jeffries was worried about Sarah. I understand you saw her this morning?'

'Yes.' Jenny was puzzled. 'She thought Sarah might have meningitis. I thought I had managed to reassure her?'

'Did you tell her to look out for a rash?'

'I was trying to explain the symptoms—why?' Jenny

didn't care for this cross-examination. He was behaving as though she were a first-year student instead of a qualified doctor with several years' experience.

'Sarah developed a rash. Mrs Jeffries phoned the clinic last thing in a panic and insisted on seeing me.'

'Yes, I got the idea this morning that she really wanted to see you.' Jenny frowned. 'I was so sure it was just an attack of nausea.'

'It was,' Miguel replied, still frowning. 'If you had read my notes on Mrs Jeffries you would have discovered that she's neurotic where that child is concerned. Every time she gets a rash in future we're going to get a panic call-out.'

'Well, I'm very sorry, but I didn't have time to read all your notes—and I didn't think it was serious. Neurotic mothers are something we all have to cope with from time to time.'

'In Mrs Jeffries's case there is good cause. She lost her first child about two years ago.'

'Not from meningitis?' Jenny was shocked and upset.

'No—from an accident, but it hasn't made her a very confident mother.'

'I'm sorry. I didn't realize. I always try to keep my patients informed...' Jenny bit her lip. 'I did think she was a little over-anxious.'

'Well, it wasn't serious, just a bit of sun sensitivity,' Miguel replied. 'But next time she brings Sarah in, think about what effect your words may have on Mrs Jeffries, please.'

'Yes, I shall. I really am very sorry—and I'm sorry that you had to go on a wasted house call after a busy day.'

'I shan't expect you to do the house calls in the evening—at least, not until you are more familiar with the area. It can be difficult to find some of the apartments if you don't know them, especially at night.'

'I found my way easily enough this afternoon.'

'Soraya drew you a map. Without it, you could have wasted valuable time. I was grateful you were here, Jenny. Mr Dickson is being kept in for observation, but you were perfectly right—it was only a mild heart attack. Your prompt action helped avoid a lot of distress for him and his wife. Mrs Dickson stayed with her husband all day, but I brought her home this evening, and I shall let her know how he is first thing in the morning. She has phoned her son and he is flying out this weekend.'

Jenny nodded. She thought that he looked tired, and her earlier annoyance had evaporated. He was clearly a dedicated doctor, and careful of his patients' feelings. With his heavy workload it was understandable if he sometimes sounded harsh or impatient. Besides, they were going to be working together for a while. She would have to try to breach his defences if they were to have a good understanding.

'I'll do my best to learn my way about as quickly as possible,' she said. 'You shouldn't have to do all the evening calls. I've had an easy afternoon—you look as if you've had a hard day.'

'Yes, I have,' Miguel admitted, and then suddenly smiled. The smile changed his looks immediately, making him seem younger and altogether more approachable. 'But tomorrow I am taking the day off to visit the beach with Elena and Joachim. Do you think you can manage the clinic alone? I'll be back on call by six-thirty.'

'I'm certain I can.' Jenny wondered why she had a sinking feeling inside. She had known there had to be a girlfriend or wife around. Why shouldn't there be a child as well? And what was it to her, for goodness' sake? Nothing! 'You have a holiday. I am sure you can do with it.'

'It isn't exactly a holiday,' Miguel said. 'Joachim is a handful. His mother finds it impossible to control him. She has multiple sclerosis, which, as you know, is a debilitating illness. At the moment she is in remission, but I worry about what will happen if she ends up in a wheelchair. She wouldn't handle that well.'

'I'm so sorry,' Jenny said. 'It must be difficult to see your wife suffer from something like that.' Her throat felt tight suddenly and she wanted to stretch out and smooth that frown from his brow.

'Elena is my sister,' Miguel said. 'Her husband left her after she was diagnosed. Sometimes I have felt like giving him a thrashing, but it wouldn't help. Besides, Elena is still in love with him. She hopes he will come back to her.'

Jenny nodded, her eyes soft with sympathy. She wasn't sure what more she could say, but somehow it hurt her because she could see that it was painful for him. It was a sad story and explained why Miguel sometimes looked so grim.

'No wonder you've been at the end of your tether,' she said. 'Does Elena live with you?'

'No, but I support her and pay for the carers she needs,' he replied. 'That's why I need to keep the clinic going. I am not in financial difficulties, but Elena may need care for a long time—and I am not prepared to give her and Joachim anything but the best. It may be that she will need interferon B soon, and I may have to provide that myself. It would not necessarily be given through our national service. I believe you have a similar problem at home?'

'Yes.' Jenny nodded. 'It's the subject of a great deal of controversy at the moment. And sometimes it comes down to where you live as to whether you get it or not. It should, of course, be according to need, but I'm afraid it doesn't always work out that way.'

'It is a very expensive drug,' Miguel said. 'But if it was not available to Elena and I believed she needed it, I would pay for it myself.'

'She is very lucky to have a brother like you.'

He shook his head. 'I could not do less for her.'

'Not everyone would do that, Miguel. It takes a special kind of person to make that kind of decision.'

Instinctively, she put out her hand to touch his arm. His skin felt warm and she was aware of something passing between them at that moment. His eyes narrowed, seeming to become much darker, and Jenny gave a little shiver as she felt an odd heightening of tension in him.

What was wrong? Was he angry because she had dared to offer sympathy? She sensed a strong, churning emotion within him, but wasn't sure what had caused that stony expression.

'You are cold. I should have thought. Please, go in and change into dry clothes.' His voice was harsh, his manner becoming reserved as if he had intentionally drawn back from her.

'It is turning cooler,' Jenny said. 'Have you time to come in for a drink?'

'Not this evening. Perhaps another time. I merely wanted to apologize if I sounded abrupt this morning. Forgive me, I did not intend to burden you with my personal problems.'

Why was he so distant? What had she done to make him look at her so coldly?

'I was glad to listen,' Jenny said, and her heart ached

for him and his sister. 'We should talk if we are to be friends as well as colleagues. Perhaps I could meet Elena some time?'

'Yes, of course. She loves to have visitors. She is cheerful most of the time, though I think she weeps when she is alone. I shall ask her when it would be best to invite you.' His expression relaxed a little. 'Go in now before you take a chill.'

Jenny smiled and turned away. She was glad they had talked, if only for a few minutes. It had helped her to understand him.

She was thoughtful as she went into the villa and, after changing, joined her mother in front of the television. An English film was showing. Jenny had already seen it, but she was prepared to watch it again as it allowed her mind to wander.

Miguel Sanchez was not only devoted to his patients, but also to his sister. It wasn't surprising that he had looked tired that evening. Remembering the instinctive way she had reached out to comfort him, Jenny knew she was going to have to keep a strict watch on her feelings for this man—it would be easy to let them slip out of control.

She had been physically attracted to James Redfern, but she knew that was all it had been—just a need for human contact. It had been a long time since she'd been in a close relationship and she'd wanted that more than she'd realized. Now she knew that if she had become involved with James, she would have been settling for less than she deserved.

If she was going to have a relationship at all, she wanted it to mean something more than an affair.

Was she in danger of falling for Miguel? Jenny realized that it would be easy to do, but knew she must resist at all costs. They might develop a good working relationship, and even become friends, but it would be foolish to look for more. Miguel had enough to think about without emotional entanglements. And he didn't seem to approve of his new colleague much!

Besides, there was probably a woman around. She thought about Isabelle, who was so desperate for him to notice her. Obviously he hadn't or Isabelle wouldn't be so hostile towards Jenny, seeing her as a potential rival.

But there was probably someone…

'I am sorry I haven't phoned for a while,' Miguel said as he spoke to the woman who had just rung him. 'It has been hectic as you know, Maribelle.'

'You could have phoned,' the petulant voice answered. 'I've been patient, Miguel, but you can't go on the way you have been. I know you care about Elena…'

'She is ill. I cannot desert her. Your brother did that.'

'That wasn't my fault. I've told him he should be ashamed of himself. He said I don't understand—he can't face the thought of her becoming bound to a wheelchair or worse. He is a coward, Miguel—but that doesn't affect us.'

'There is no "us", Maribelle,' he replied. 'That finished six months ago. I told you it was over, and I don't change my mind. You should know that.'

'It was just a fling at a party,' she said, her voice catching with tears. 'I told you it didn't mean anything. I'd had too much to drink that night.'

'That makes no difference,' he replied harshly. 'I don't forgive betrayal, Maribelle. You slept with my best friend—and I lost a partner because of it. It became impossible for us to work together.'

'But it meant nothing…'

It meant a great deal to me.' Miguel sighed. 'I have had a long day and I am tired. I'm going to ring off now. It might be better if you didn't ring me in future.'

'But you promised we could still be friends.' She had a sob in her voice. 'Why won't you forgive me, Miguel? Anyone can make a mistake.'

'Not that kind of a mistake—not if they want to be my wife,' he grated harshly. 'You knew my feelings on the subject, Maribelle. I have no wish to cause you more pain—but I cannot forget. Nor do I wish to. Our relationship ended when you went to bed with Jorge.'

He shut down his mobile and got up to pour himself a drink of wine, cool from the fridge. Miguel was careful to ration himself to one in the evenings unless he was taking the following day off. This was his second glass of the evening, and as he sipped it he found that he was gradually unwinding.

Closing his eyes, he leaned his head back against the sofa, a smile touching his mouth as he remembered a woman in a wet bathing suit and clinging wrap. Dr Jenny Talforth had a good figure, and when she let herself be she was a very attractive woman. He wondered why she tried to hide it, then decided it was probably because she wanted respect at work.

He knew that they had got off on the wrong foot for one reason or another. He still wasn't sure what Jenny's mother had said about an involvement with a man. He ought to have paid more attention at the time, but he had been preoccupied. Something about some trouble with a colleague? Well, he wasn't looking for an emotional entanglement. He had too much to think about, too many responsibilities.

As for the physical reaction she had aroused in him, standing there in her wet bathing clothes, that was best forgotten. Miguel hadn't been in a physical relationship for six months and he knew that his body had instinctively responded to Jenny's femininity. She was rather sexy, though if she was the kind of woman who kept falling into messy relationships...

He couldn't afford to get involved! Jenny was a colleague, nothing more, even if the touch of her hand on his arm had made him want to make love to her. That was the way to disaster. He didn't have space in his life for any of this.

The arguments with Maribelle had started because he just didn't have enough time for her, and she had found someone else to amuse her. He wouldn't have minded quite so much if she hadn't chosen his partner, which had made it a double betrayal.

Crushing any feelings of bitterness, he decided not to dwell on the past. Because they'd been friends long before they'd been lovers, he hadn't been as harsh with Maribelle as he might have been. He had tried to be civilized about the whole thing, but now she was becoming a nuisance.

If she didn't stop phoning him, he would have to make the break final even if it meant saying things that he would find cruel and unnecessary.

CHAPTER THREE

THE following day was much busier at the clinic. Jenny started her morning with an anxious young woman wanting a blood test.

'I'm not sure what you call it,' she told Jenny. 'But I know it's to see if the unborn child could be suffering from spina bifida.'

'Amniocentesis,' Jenny supplied with a smile. 'Spina bifida is a birth abnormality in which there is a defective closure of the vertebral column during prenatal development. What makes you feel you need an investigation of this nature, Mrs Richards?'

'My sister's son was born with the disease,' Mary Richards explained. 'The doctors told her that in future she could have this test done, so I thought perhaps I should, too.'

'In case it runs in the family?' Jenny nodded, understanding her anxiety. 'Did your sister's doctor explain that there was a 0.5 increased risk of miscarriage with the test?'

The young woman shook her head, looking even more anxious. 'No. I don't know what to do now. We've been trying for this baby for so long...'

'There's another less invasive test we could do,' Jenny suggested. 'We could start by taking a blood sample. Higher levels of alphafetoprotein in a woman's blood during pregnancy can indicate the presence of spina bifida. We could take some blood and send it for sampling. After that we could do an ultrasonic test, which can reveal abnormalities, and then we'll have some idea of whether we ought to proceed to amniocentesis.'

'Could you do the blood test for a start?' Mary Richards was clearly relieved. 'I'd have to think about the rest if the tests were positive.'

'I'll take the bloods and print out some literature from the Internet for you,' Jenny promised. 'Come in again in ten days and I should have some results for you.'

Jenny smiled as her patient left. She saw several more patients and it was almost time to close the clinic for the evening when Soraya told her she had one last patient.

'It is Señora Marshall,' she said. 'You saw her husband yesterday afternoon. Can you fit her in?'

'Yes, of course,' Jenny said. 'I can always lock up if I'm late finishing.'

'Would you mind?' Soraya asked, a little hesitant. 'I have a dinner for the family this evening and...'

'You get off,' Jenny replied with a smile. 'Isabelle, too. I can manage.'

'I'm sorry to keep you late,' Sally said as she came in. 'But I've only just managed to park the children at their friend's house and I wanted to talk to you.'

'Privately or professionally?'

'It's a bit of both really,' Sally admitted. 'It isn't really for me—a girl I know thinks she may be pregnant. She's eighteen, Spanish and a Catholic, from a good family. She wants an abortion but her family would never allow it. She thinks her doctor would refuse if she went to him and asked me if I thought she could get it done in England. Apparently, she's going to college in London for a few months on some sort of exchange programme. She asked if I knew anyone she could talk to about this—so naturally I thought of you.'

'Yes, I can see that it would be a problem for her,'

Jenny said, and frowned as she heard a slight noise from somewhere in the clinic. For a moment she thought about going to investigate, but realized it must have come from outside as she heard some shouting. 'I'm not sure how the law stands here, but I do know that quite a few women from Catholic countries come to England for abortions. It isn't something I can generalize about, Sally. Even at home, I would advise a young woman to think very carefully about this. She may simply need counselling. Is she quite sure she's pregnant?'

'Well, she's had some sickness and missed a period—but she daren't buy a pregnancy testing kit in case her parents find out. It seems they would raise the roof. She says they're very strict and they didn't approve of her boyfriend—who incidentally is a thing of the past.'

'Look, why don't you ask her to come and see me? Does she speak English at all?'

'Very well,' Sarah replied. 'I think she has a brilliant future ahead of her, which is another reason why she wants the abortion. Yes, I'll tell Juliana to come in. You can explain what she would have to do if she decides to go for a termination.'

'Yes, that sounds good.' Jenny looked at her as she hesitated. 'Was that all?'

'I only wanted to ask if you could make the party. It's next Tuesday at eight in the evening.'

'Yes, I think that will be OK. I shall look forward to it. How's your husband—no more of that pain, I hope?'

'I think he gets it more than he lets on,' Sarah replied, and frowned. 'I'm almost sure it's the reason he wants to go home. He's such a coward about going into hospital, especially out here.'

Jenny laughed. 'He isn't the only one, Sally. There isn't really any need to worry more than you would at home, you know. If anything, the doctors out here are more highly trained than ours. Even the dentists do two years' longer training here than at home.'

'I didn't know that,' Sally said. 'But I keep telling Bob not to be such a coward—but, then, men always are, don't you think?'

'Sometimes,' Jenny said, and smiled.

'Well, I'm taking up your time,' Sarah apologized as she got to her feet. 'What do I owe for the consultation?'

'Nothing. It was just a bit of friendly advice.'

After she had gone, Jenny tidied up and checked that everything was locked properly. She noticed that one of the medication cabinets still had the key in it and removed it, slipping it into Soraya's desk where she thought it was normally kept.

She felt pleased with her day's work, and found herself wondering about her colleague again as she turned into the Riviera underpass and left the busy main road behind her. It wasn't surprising that Miguel had found it too much to cope with the clinic and his hospital work. She hoped they were going to work well together, though they hadn't had the best of starts.

He had seemed tired the previous evening. Perhaps he would be feeling better after his day at the beach.

Jenny relaxed with a glass of cool fruit juice, watching as the sun finally dipped into the sea in a ball of orange flame. There was a glorious view from up here, and she was feeling more satisfied with her day's work, at peace with herself.

She was lost in her thoughts and was startled as Miguel's shadow fell across her.

'Good evening. Your mother said I would find you here. It is a lovely view, isn't it?'

Jenny turned her head. He was wearing pale fawn chinos and a black shirt, which he had opened at the neck, showing a glimpse of his tanned skin, and the look of strain from the previous day seemed to have vanished.

'Yes, lovely,' she said. 'Have you time to sit down and have a drink—or is this work?'

'There were no house calls this evening.' Miguel accepted her invitation to sit down. 'Yes, I will have a drink, thank you. Your mother is bringing it now...'

Jenny saw her mother bringing a tray with a jug of iced fruit juice as Miguel sat down in a chair next to her on the patio, stretching out his long legs as if he needed to relax and felt he could there.

'Will you sit with us, Mum?' Jenny asked as Beth deposited her tray on the table near them.

'No, thank you, dear. You'll have things to talk about. Besides, I'm watching a serial on the TV. It's a period costume drama and you know I love those.'

'Your mother seems better since you arrived,' Miguel remarked as Beth went back into the house. 'I expect she enjoys having you around.'

'Yes, probably,' Jenny agreed. 'I'll have to see how she is when the six months are over.'

'Would you consider staying on?' Miguel arched his brows at her. 'I imagine you saw this very much as a temporary thing?'

'Yes, I did,' Jenny admitted. 'But I suppose I hadn't realized that my parents were getting older. I've been so busy working, and they were always bright and full of life when I came out for a visit. I might have to explore the possibilities further.'

'You have no plans for your own future?'

Jenny's cheeks felt warm. She kept her eyes straight

ahead as she answered him and wondered why she felt so very conscious of his eyes on her. 'I have no personal commitments,' she replied. 'Marriage and children are something I have considered, but only if I find the right person. I want the kind of relationship my parents have always had, you see. I'm not interested in moving in with someone for a couple of years and then simply walking out when I feel like it—or he does.'

'Yes, I do see.' Miguel's dark gaze rested thoughtfully on her face. She couldn't look at him, so she stared at his hands. His fingers were long and well shaped and something about them made her throat go dry suddenly. What was wrong with her, for goodness' sake? 'Commitment sometimes seems to be an outdated idea these days, but I must admit I feel much the same way.'

'And the job doesn't make it easy to find a relationship,' Jenny went on, desperate to keep her mind on safe topics. Why did she keep thinking that it might be nice, actually making babies with this man? She didn't know him! 'An urgent call in the middle of a romantic dinner seems to have an adverse effect on many a promising beginning.'

'But if you have children you will surely wish to stop working?'

Once again, Jenny sensed faint disapproval in his manner. Just why did he seem to have adopted this attitude towards her? She didn't think she had done anything to deserve it.

'For a while, of course, but I see no reason why I wouldn't be able to return to my job in time. Even if I'm limited in the hours I can work until the children are grown up.'

'I am not sure I agree,' Miguel said, his gaze narrowed and watchful. 'I would personally expect my wife to commit completely to her home and children—and to me.'

'Now, that *is* an old-fashioned attitude,' Jenny replied, a little sparkle in her eyes. 'The dominant male, lording it over his mate…'

'Good heavens! Did it sound that way to you?' Miguel gave her an incredulous look. 'I merely felt that I would prefer to take care of my family, that my wife should have a comfortable life and not have to work.' His dark eyes seemed to probe her thoughts. 'After all, your mother doesn't work, does she?'

'Touché!' Jenny laughed. 'I think she did for a while after I started secondary school, but she prefers to be at home—but, then, she didn't train for years to be a doctor. I feel it would be a waste of my training if I just gave it all up.'

'Yes, I can understand that,' Miguel agreed. 'The women in my family have never worked after marriage. I suppose it is a matter of pride—and family is important to us here. We love children, and expect to have several of them.'

'Yes, I see. How is your sister? Did she and Joachim enjoy their day at the beach?'

'Elena enjoyed being in a different environment,' he replied. 'My nephew had a wonderful time, getting filthy and playing in the sand.'

Jenny heard the indulgent note in his voice and felt pleased. It was clear to her that Miguel was devoted to his family, and she liked that. In fact, she was beginning to like him very much. He did have a few odd ideas about women and marriage, but perhaps that had something to do with tradition and him being Spanish. For many women the idea of being spoiled and not having to work might have seemed appealing, but Jenny wasn't sure it appealed to her. She would always want to keep a measure of independence.

'Will you be at the emergency department tomorrow?'

'Tomorrow morning I am in Malaga. I have a full list of private consultations all day—but you can still reach me there if you need me. And I shall join you at the clinic in the afternoon. I think we ought to talk over various aspects of our work, don't you?'

'Yes, I think that would be good. Soraya is very efficient,' Jenny replied. 'She helps me if I have a problem with referrals, but so far it's been fairly straightforward.'

She told him about the patient she had talked to about the various tests for discovering the presence of spina bifida in the unborn child, and they discussed the implications. Then they talked about aspects of the care they offered their patients, and Miguel asked if she had any suggestions as to how they might improve the service for their patients.

'I haven't really had time to get used to things yet,' she admitted. 'But if you really want my opinion I shall be glad to give it to you at a later time. Of course, I've been used to an NHS practice at home, where we run all kinds of clinics for people. I imagine we might be able to do something like that here—especially if we were able to offer them very cheaply. There must be a lot of people living here, or even on holiday, who would like to be able to pop in for a routine blood test—for diabetes or thyroid conditions. They probably feel it would be expensive to have a consultation, but if we had one morning a week for that kind of treatment...' She stopped speaking as his eyes narrowed. 'Perhaps that wasn't the kind of thing you were thinking of?'

'I was thinking it was an excellent idea—and I can improve on it,' he said. 'We could have a free clinic for anyone needing routine tests of that nature to attend—English-speaking or Spanish. Soraya could translate anything you didn't understand.'

'Well, if that wouldn't ruin your business,' Jenny agreed. 'I'm sure it would appeal to a lot of people who probably hesitate to see a doctor because of the expense.'

'I'll leave it to you to set up,' Miguel said. 'It was your idea so you can run it as you see fit.' He set down his glass and stood up. 'Well, I have enjoyed our talk, Jenny. I must go now, but Elena asks if you will come for lunch on Sunday at her home.'

'I should like that—if it isn't a lot of extra bother for her?'

'It will be no bother for her at all,' Miguel said with a wry look. 'Someone else will prepare the salad and I shall cook the meat on the barbecue. She has a machine to wash the dishes, of course.'

'Goodnight, then,' Jenny said. 'I look forward to seeing you tomorrow at the clinic?'

'Yes,' he replied. 'No, please do not get up. I know my way out.'

Jenny nodded, watching as he walked from the garden and round the side of the house. Miguel Sanchez was an interesting man, she thought. She would enjoy getting to know him better as a friend and colleague—but she would be careful not to get involved emotionally.

He was obviously a man who was used to getting his own way in many things, and Jenny was too fond of her independence to want to become too tied up with him, even if he were interested. And he probably wasn't. She would do well to remember that torch she had carried for James Redfern, which was beginning to seem more and more foolish, seen from a distance.

Heavens! She must have been lonely to imagine she

wanted a relationship with James. Comparison with Miguel showed just what a selfish man James actually was. It was lucky he had been too busy with his other female friends to notice Jenny had been interested!

She laughed to herself as she got up and went into the house. It was very odd but the Spanish sunshine was beginning to make her feel better about herself than she had in a long time.

Jenny was called out to an emergency just before lunch the next day. A diabetic child had fallen into a coma caused by low blood sugar after a strenuous session at the swimming pool, and his mother was frantic.

After administering an injection of glucose, Jenny saw the child pull round remarkably well, but she decided to send him to the hospital for further investigation.

'Peter needs to be balanced properly,' she told his mother. 'It may be that a new regime of diet and insulin would help to prevent another incident like this.'

Jenny spent some considerable time with her patient and saw them into the ambulance, which meant that after a hurried lunch she was a few minutes late at the clinic. As she walked in, she saw Miguel talking with Isabelle. He had his back to her, but Jenny had a clear view of the receptionist's face—and the look of adoration in her eyes!

'I should like that so much,' she was saying. 'It is so good of you to take me over...'

'I'll pick you up at nine-thirty, then.'

Miguel turned as he spoke, his smile disappearing as he saw Jenny. 'Ah, there you are, Dr Talforth.'

His tone implied that he had begun to wonder where

she'd got to, and Jenny flushed, stung by his disapproval once more.

'Yes,' she answered shortly, and walked past him into her consulting room. She didn't have to put up with this!

Miguel followed her in, closing the door behind him.

'I wasn't criticizing,' he said as he saw her angry face. 'Soraya told me you had had an emergency. Was Peter all right when you left him?'

'I sent him through to the hospital,' Jenny replied, shrugging off her annoyance as she adopted a professional attitude. 'I gather this has happened twice before in...about two months?'

'Yes.' Miguel frowned. 'My partner Jorge was here then. He saw the boy both times and said it was just a matter of too much exercise. Peter is a very normal boy and he loves sport.'

'Yes, I gathered that,' Jenny agreed. 'But he also suffers from a very nasty illness. Diabetes in children can, as you know, be very much more difficult to control than in adults. I think he needs a new assessment—that's why I sent him in. If he continues to have these comas frequently, one of them could be fatal.'

'I couldn't agree more. Peter doesn't accept his illness, but he does need to learn to control it.'

Jenny had been prepared for dissension and she was left staring at him without a ready answer. 'I'm glad we agree on something,' she said at last.

'I think we shall agree on most things when we've begun to understand each other,' he replied. 'Perhaps we got off to a bad start. I really think—'

He was interrupted by Soraya, who came in to tell them that a youth had just arrived at the clinic. 'He fell off a motorbike he had hired,' she explained, 'and is in some pain. There is also a mother with a baby running a temperature.'

'Right, I'll take the accident,' Miguel said, giving Jenny a rueful look. 'We shall continue our discussion later...'

Jenny nodded. She could hear the baby screaming as he hurried away. The untimely interruption was unfortunate, but it looked as if the ice might be beginning to crack at last.

Miguel suggested a drink that evening at a rather pleasant bar in one of the more exclusive complexes.

'I thought we would take alternate Saturday mornings,' he said. 'That will give us both a chance of a long weekend every other week, and it often isn't very busy because it's change-over day for the holidaymakers.'

'What happens about emergency calls on Saturday afternoon and Sunday?'

'They go through the answering service. Usually someone comes out from Fuengirola unless it is really urgent, then they contact me. But hangovers and minor cuts have to use the twenty-four-hour emergency service.'

Jenny nodded. 'At least we can look forward to a good night's sleep,' Jenny said. 'That wasn't always the case at home. I was on call three nights a week. My male colleagues shared the rest between them.'

'You sound a little regretful,' he said, arching his brows. 'Are you missing England—or someone in particular?'

'Neither actually. I may decide to settle here.'

'I think that might work out well for us both. And I am sure your parents would be happier with you living here.' His brows rose in inquiry. 'Shall you find your own house?'

'Not for the moment,' Jenny replied. 'The villa is big enough for the three of us, and very convenient. I shall just take my time and see how things work out.'

'Yes. Your parents may decide they wish to return to England after all.'

'No, I don't think so,' Jenny said. 'Mum told me she had thought it over and decided there's nothing left for her there. I know she would rather spend the rest of her life here amongst her friends—especially if I'm prepared to stay, too.'

'Not many daughters would give up their own lives so willingly.'

'When I think about it, I didn't have much of a life to give up,' Jenny admitted with a rueful smile. 'I do have friends—two in particular, Moya and Angie—but if I get my own place they can come and stay. We share a house in Norwich at the moment, and I've contributed my share of the rent for the next few months, but I know they can relet easily if I agree. And I can go back for a short trip to sort out my things. Most of my stuff can go into an auction. There are only a few personal things that I need.'

'You sound as if you've already made up your mind.'

'I have—almost. It, all of a sudden, seems the right thing to do.' Jenny said. She glanced at her watch. 'I had better get back or Mum will start to wonder where I am.'

'Yes. I have a call to do before I go to see Elena and Joachim—though he ought to be in bed. Perhaps one evening we could have dinner somewhere?'

'Yes, perhaps,' Jenny said. 'Anyway, I shall see you on Sunday.'

'Tomorrow I shall take the morning clinic,' Miguel said. 'I've had a holiday this week, thanks to you, and you might like to use the time to settle in. You've been working ever since you arrived.'

'Yes, but I've enjoyed it,' Jenny replied. 'I can't bear to be idle.'

Miguel smiled. 'Your mother said you would hate to sit twiddling your thumbs—what is this, please?'

'A very foolish English saying,' Jenny replied, and laughed as she realized he was teasing her. 'But, of course, you knew that. How is it that you understand English so well? Not just the words but the meaning of some of our more peculiar phrases.'

'My mother was English,' Miguel said. 'She would have liked you, Jenny. You are very honest and so was she. She met my father when he was on business in London and she was a student. They fell in love instantly and she gave up everything to be with him. They were very happy until he died of a heart attack. She lingered on for five years. She died three years ago of breast cancer. It was operated on, but unfortunately there were secondary tumours and they spread throughout her body.'

'I'm so sorry.' Jenny's heart caught and her eyes misted with tears but she blinked them away. 'When I hear something like that it makes me realize how lucky I am to still have both my parents.'

'Yes.' Miguel's austere features relaxed into a smile, and the result was stunning. Jenny was shocked at the way her heart suddenly started to thump as he reached across the table to lay his hand on hers for a moment. 'I know I have no need to tell you, Jenny, but you should always cherish family. To love and care for someone dear to you is more rewarding than anything else life can offer.'

Jenny gazed into his dark eyes. He was so sincere. To hear words so simply spoken was touching. Coming from many people she had met, she would have thought his sentiments merely platitudes, but this man meant what he said. She couldn't help thinking that Elena was lucky to have such a brother. Any woman who was loved by such a man would be fortunate.

'I should go,' she said, and stood up.

Her pulses were racing as she went out to her car. It would be much too easy to fall in love with Miguel Sanchez, and that was the last thing she needed!

Jenny popped into Marbella to do a little shopping the next morning. She had realized that most of the clothes she had brought with her were either too warm or too casual. She needed something cool but smart to wear for lunch on Sunday—and there was also the barbecue the following week.

Marbella had several trendy boutiques, especially near the Orange Square. Here there were orange trees growing between the various open-air restaurants, providing somewhere cool to sit and have a drink while the rest of the world strolled by.

Jenny bought a long cotton skirt in a hot pink, which she was told was very popular that summer, two rather skimpy tops and an embroidered shirt. Together they made a variety of outfits that could be smart or casual. She also purchased a pair of white jeans with lacing at the sides and some attractive leather mules.

It was odd, Jenny thought as she drove back to her parents' home after her shopping trip, but that feeling of being lonely had gone away these past few days. Of course, she was staying with her parents, and she loved them both dearly, and she was meeting a lot of new people...making friends.

With a flash of blinding honesty, Jenny realized that one in particular of her new friends was responsible for the warm feeling of contentment that seemed to grow as each day passed.

She had never met anyone quite like Miguel Sanchez before. Every other man she had ever known now seemed shallow in comparison.

He was a very special person.

CHAPTER FOUR

JENNY followed the instructions Miguel had given her, turning off the main highway via an underpass just before La Cala, and heading away from the coast. The villa she was seeking was tucked neatly away in a quiet area, only two or three others nestling beside it into the hillside. It was surrounded by high walls and had fancy wrought-iron gates, which stood wide open.

As she parked her car and walked towards the heavy wooden door, Jenny noticed huge terracotta pots spilling over with geraniums. The area in front of the door was tiled with slabs of a similar colour.

A plump, attractive Spanish woman came in answer to the pealing bell. She gave Jenny a pleasant smile and invited her in. She was led through a rather dark entrance hall into a large lounge with patio windows at the far end. Two sumptuous cream leather sofas dominated the room, but one wall had attractive mirrored cabinets running almost its entire length. Its shelves were filled with gleaming crystal, while enchanting Ladro figurines adorned the marble mantelpiece and stood in alcoves, giving the room both elegance and charm.

'Will you, please, go out and join the others, Señorita Talforth?'

'Yes, thank you.' Jenny nodded to the woman she assumed was Elena's carer.

She followed the sound of voices. Outside the long sliding window was a tiled patio backing onto a smooth lawn and then trees and flowering shrubs. Several chairs were set out beneath umbrellas, and there was a barbecue area with a long table covered by a heavy white cloth. It had been set with flowers, crockery and bowls of exotic fruit.

Miguel was standing talking to a man some years his senior, and a very pretty dark-haired woman was sitting in a cane chair with a high back. It was she who noticed Jenny first and said something to Miguel. He turned, saw Jenny and came towards her with a smile of welcome.

'You found your way all right, then?'

'It was no trouble,' she assured him. 'I simply followed your instructions.'

'Come and meet my sister—and our friend, Andrew Sinclair. He owns a rather pleasant restaurant just outside Marbella. We must go there some time.'

Jenny smiled but made no comment as she was led to the woman in the chair.

'This is Elena,' Miguel said. 'She has been looking forward to meeting you, Jenny.'

'Forgive me if I do not get up,' Elena said, her voice soft and husky. 'It is awkward for me, though I do try to keep mobile as much as possible. Miguel says it is good for me.'

Jenny nodded. Multiple sclerosis was a disease of the central nervous system, which attacked and gradually destroyed the white fatty substance that protected nerve fibres. Symptoms could vary according to the sites of the lesions in the nervous system. Some people suffered blurring of vision, tremor of the hands or spasms in the legs, with bouts of numbness, tingling or slurring of speech. The disease was in most cases intermittent, and could disappear, leaving the sufferer symptom-free for a long time, but if relapses were frequent the patient could become clumsy and progressively weaker.

'Please, don't get up for me,' Jenny replied. 'I think I shall sit next to you. It's horrible having to look up at someone all the time, isn't it?'

She had already noticed that an easy chair had been set close to Elena's, presumably so that someone could sit and talk to her.

'It was not too difficult to find us?' Elena asked, looking anxious. 'We are rather out of the way here.'

'Not at all,' Jenny said. 'It is a lovely villa and you have a large garden, which must be a pleasure to sit in.'

'Not as large as Miguel's own,' Elena replied, and glanced at her brother, who had moved away to bring their other guest over to meet Jenny. 'But he needs someone to share it—and to look after him.'

'Andrew, this is Jenny.' Miguel was introducing the tall, attractive and rather well-built man. 'She has come to work with me at the clinic.'

'Pleased to meet you,' the Englishman said, offering his hand. He seemed pleasant, and inclined to be friendly. Jenny decided she liked him. 'I understand your parents retired out here? My own came over fifteen years ago, which is why I decided to settle here. It's a wonderful climate, and a very different lifestyle from the one back home.'

'Yes, it is,' Jenny replied. 'I'm enjoying getting to know how things work and beginning to make friends.'

'Go and talk together,' Elena said, her manner towards Andrew Sinclair and her brother a little abrupt and, Jenny thought, petulant. 'I want Jenny to myself for a while.'

'To hear is to obey, majesty,' Andrew replied, and grinned.

He did not seem in the least put out by Elena's offhand manner. Something in the warmth of his eyes as he looked at her seemed to indicate that there was more to their relationship than mere friendship—at least on his side.

'I do not know why Miguel invited him today,' Elena grumbled as the two men went off towards the barbecue together. 'I did not want him here. I wanted only you.'

'Perhaps they had business to discuss.'

'Yes. Men always talk business.' Elena's mouth had a slightly discontented droop at that moment. She looked unhappy which, given her situation, wasn't particularly surprising. 'My husband was always talking business—before he left me. I travelled everywhere with him until Joachim was born. And then I began to be ill.'

'Yes, Miguel has told me,' Jenny said. 'You must feel angry—first you discovered that you have an unpleasant illness, and then your husband walks out on you. I know I would be angry.'

'I was bitter at first,' Elena said. 'I wanted to punish him, then I realized that Juan could not live with the knowledge that I was going to end up in a wheelchair…that I was going to die. So he had to leave. I have forgiven him.'

'We are all going to die one day,' Jenny replied. 'You shouldn't look at the worst scenario, Elena. You could stay as you are for years. You might never have another bad attack.'

'Or I might get slowly worse and end up in a wheelchair before I die, incapable of doing anything for myself.'

'But that isn't necessarily what will happen,' Jenny said. I've known patients who are stabilized by various treatments and who live quite happily for a long, long time. It's true that you could die, but so could I—or

Miguel come to that. No one ever knows what may be around the corner.'

'Miguel tells me I shall live for many years,' his sister said with a shrug. 'But if I do have to be in a wheelchair—to have everything done for me—I am not sure I want to go on for years.'

'You are in remission at the moment,' Jenny reminded her. 'Besides, what about Joachim?'

'Ah, Joachim.' Elena's frown lifted. 'You have not met my son—my reason for living.' She raised her head. 'Miguel! You have not asked Jenny if she would like a drink. And I would like Maria to bring Joachim out.'

'I'll fetch him,' Andrew offered. 'Back in a tick.'

He went off towards the house. Miguel asked Jenny what she would like and she asked for a white wine spritzer. She had just been given it when Andrew came back, leading a little boy by the hand.

Jenny thought at once that she had never seen such a beautiful child. His skin was slightly darker in colour than his mother's, his hair black and curly and his eyes a deep melting chocolate brown.

'Oh, he's gorgeous!' Jenny exclaimed. 'You are lucky to have him, Elena.'

She spoke simply from the heart, forgetting for the moment that the boy's mother had a very nasty illness which might, in its worst form, prevent her from seeing him grow to manhood.

'Yes,' Elena agreed. 'I am lucky to have Joachim—and also Miguel.' She held her arms out to the child, who ran to her and scrambled up onto her lap. She kissed him, then indicated Jenny. 'Say *hola* to Jenny, my darling.'

'*Hola*,' Joachim said, looking shy.

'*Hola*, Joachim,' Jenny replied and smiled. 'It's nice to meet you.'

Her heart ached for both him and his mother. It was sad that Elena should have an illness that prevented her from being as active a mother as she would have wished.

Elena seemed to have got over her moodiness. She talked to Jenny about her son, cuddling him and kissing him until he demanded to be let down. He then ran off to play football with his uncle and Andrew.

'Mr Sinclair seems to be fond of Joachim,' Jenny remarked as he picked the boy up, hoisting him on his shoulders.

'He wants to take the place of his father,' Elena said. 'I suppose I should let him. It would give Miguel more time for his own life. I tell him he should marry. He was serious about someone a few months ago, but I think it is over. I think it ended because of me, because Miguel spends too much time looking after me.'

'Oh…' Jenny wasn't sure what she was expected to say. She met Elena's dark gaze openly. 'He doesn't have anyone special at the moment?'

'Miguel says he has no time for a relationship.' Elena frowned. 'If it were not for me he would marry and have the children he wants.'

'Miguel is very fond of you. If he spends time with you, it's because he wants to.'

'Yes, of course,' Elena replied. 'We are family, but if I had someone to care for me…' She sighed. 'Andrew thinks he wants to move in with me. He says he loves me, but I think he feels pity.'

'He must care if he wants to be with you.'

Miguel was cooking chicken, steak and spare ribs over the barbecue. Elena's carer had begun to bring out covered dishes of salads and long crusty loaves. The smell of the roasting meat was tantalizing, making Jenny feel hungry.

'What should I do?' Elena asked. 'Would you try again if you were me?'

'I don't know,' Jenny admitted honestly. 'It is very hard to trust when you've been hurt.'

'I should not have asked,' Elena said. 'But there is no one I can talk to about this. Miguel would not understand. I cannot remarry, of course, but Andrew does not care. He says a piece of paper means nothing these days.'

'You are the only one who can decide, Elena.'

'Yes, of course.' She sighed. 'Go and help yourself to food, Jenny. I should not have burdened you with my problems.'

'If talking helps I'm glad to listen any time.'

'You will come again—on your own?'

'Yes, I should like to,' Jenny said, and smiled. 'Can I bring you something from the table?'

'Andrew will look after me. He likes to please me. I am not nice to him, but he still does everything for me.' Elena laughed. 'I am spoiled, no?'

'Perhaps a little,' Jenny said gently. She liked Elena's directness and her honesty. And she understood her moods. It couldn't be easy to face her illness, and the fact that her husband had left her.

Jenny got up as Miguel called to her. Andrew was already on his way over with a plate of salad and a piece of chicken for Elena. He arranged a table for her and then sat down in the chair Jenny had vacated, giving his attention to Elena.

Joachim was eating a ripe peach, having totally ignored Maria's offers to get him some proper food. She was watching over him, clearly used to caring for both the boy and his mother.

'What were you talking about for so long?' Miguel asked as Jenny approached. 'I have not seen Elena so animated for ages.'

'I was saying how lucky she was to have Joachim. He's gorgeous, Miguel. No wonder you're so devoted to them both.'

'He can be difficult,' Miguel said. 'Too much for Elena to manage alone. Some days she is much better than others—this is a good day.'

Jenny nodded, sympathy in her eyes. 'Yes, of course—but she has Maria, and I suppose cleaners come in?'

'Yes, naturally. Maria has her hands full...' Miguel turned a steak. 'What would you like, Jenny?'

'Chicken and spare ribs, please.'

He used a long-handled fork to put the meat on her plate. Jenny wandered over to the table to sample some of the salads, which were inventive and looked delicious.

'Try some of Maria's salad dressing,' Andrew suggested as he came to fill a plate for himself. 'It's very good—and so is this steak. Not having any?'

'Perhaps later,' Jenny said, and smiled at him.

She took her food to a table and sat down to taste the selection of salads she had chosen. It was all as good as it looked, as she told Miguel when he joined her a few minutes later.

'I thought you would prefer this to a formal Spanish meal,' he said. 'It is easier to talk in a garden somehow—don't you think so? Another time I shall invite more of our friends to meet you, but I felt just family for your first visit.'

'I'm glad you did,' Jenny replied. 'I am enjoying myself.'

'Good.' Miguel smiled at her and her heart suddenly started to race. 'I hope this will be only the start of a long and satisfactory relationship, Jenny.'

What did he mean? For a moment her mind played tricks on her and she saw herself living this way—surrounded by lots of friends and a growing family—but then she slammed the door shut on such thoughts. He was talking about a working relationship, of course. Friendship.

For the first time Jenny let herself wonder what it might be like if something deeper and more meaningful were to develop between them.

But she was only dreaming—wasn't she?

Jenny was just thinking about going home on the following Tuesday evening when Soraya came to tell her a young woman was asking to see her.

'She is Spanish,' Soraya explained, 'but she insists it is you she wants to see. She says her name is Juliana.'

'Ah, yes, I know who she is,' Jenny replied. 'Would you ask her to come in, please, Soraya? I may be a little time so you and Isabelle can go—just remember to put the catch down so that no one can wander into the clinic unannounced.'

'Yes, of course.' Soraya looked puzzled. 'Why do you make a point of that, Dr Talforth?'

'Because the last time I closed up a key had been left in the small medication cabinet, where we keep some of the stronger painkilling drugs. I locked it and put the key in your drawer, but we have to be careful about things like that—just in case someone wanders in looking for an opportunity.'

Soraya was frowning. 'I was sure I locked the cabinet. I wondered why the key wasn't where I usually leave it, but I thought you must have used it after I left.'

'No, I had no occasion to.'

'I wish you had told me then—it is too difficult to remember for certain now.'

'I'm not blaming you,' Jenny said. 'I told you I would lock up, and I did, but I just thought I would mention it.'

'I think I shall do a stock check tomorrow,' Soraya said. 'It should have been locked. I'm sure of it.'

Soraya went away and the next moment a very pretty young woman came in. She looked nervous and embarrassed until Jenny smiled at her and asked her to sit down.

'I understand you have a problem,' Jenny said. 'You think you may be pregnant and you're worried about what your parents may say?'

'They would be very angry,' Juliana replied. 'They would say I had ruined my life—and they would not permit an abortion.'

'I think we had better make sure you really are pregnant,' Jenny said. 'If you would go behind the screen and slip off your skirt and panties I would like to examine you. I should also like to do a pregnancy test of your urine.'

Jenny smiled at the girl as she slipped on latex gloves. She asked her a few questions about any changes she had noticed in her breasts and then began her examination. It took only a few minutes, then she nodded and asked Juliana to dress.

'I'll do the urine test,' she said. 'It's just the very simple one you can buy in any chemist, but I think I can already tell you that you aren't pregnant, Juliana. You aren't showing the symptoms I would have expected, such as tenderness in the breasts, increased frequency of urination, fatigue—and my preliminary examination seems to suggest there may be some other reason for the symptoms you have.'

The girl stared at her. 'But I have missed a period and I have pain in my abdomen and lower back.'

'Yes, I was going to ask you if you'd noticed any other symptoms,' Jenny said. 'That rather confirms what I had in mind.' She frowned. 'I think you may have an ovarian cyst, Juliana. Although often benign these can sometimes be cancerous, so it is best to check it out straight away. I'm fairly sure that it will be proved to be a harmless cyst. But we can make certain of that. We do that by blood tests and ultrasound scan. Now, I can take the blood tests myself and send the samples away, and I can arrange the other tests you will need—but it might be best if you go to your own doctor, as it may involve an operation.'

'Are you sure I am not having a child?'

Jenny glanced at the pregnancy test kit and saw the result was negative. 'Yes, quite sure, Juliana. I think what you have is probably a cyst, as I said, but I must stress that it does need to be checked out immediately. It isn't something you should leave, both because the pain may get very much worse and there's also the chance that it might be cancer. So I want you to promise me you won't just leave this in the hope that it will go away. You will see your own doctor?'

'Yes, I will do that,' Juliana said, her expression a mixture of both relief and a new apprehension. 'I can go to my own doctor for this. I was just so frightened that he would tell my parents if I was pregnant.'

'In the UK doctors aren't allowed to do that unless

you are under-age,' Jenny reassured her. 'I suspect it is the same here. If you requested the information be kept private, your request would be respected—but had you been pregnant your parents would have known in time. Because I don't really think you wanted an abortion, did you?'

Juliana smiled oddly. 'I didn't really know what I wanted. I just needed to talk to someone who wouldn't get angry and shout at me.'

'Well, had you been pregnant I would have advised you to think very carefully,' Jenny said. 'It's a decision that should never be taken lightly because it can cause a lot of regret on the part of the mother.'

'Thank you,' Juliana said as she got to her feet. 'I'll let you know how I go on, and thank you for seeing me at such short notice.'

'It was my pleasure,' Jenny replied, and smiled as she went out.

She had handwritten notes, but didn't enter them in the computer. Then she picked up her jacket and prepared to leave.

Miguel came in just as Jenny was checking that everything was locked. He looked surprised as he saw her.

'Working late?'

'I had a late consultation,' Jenny replied. 'It was a young Spanish girl. She thought she might be pregnant and wanted to discuss an abortion.'

Miguel's response was instant. His eyes snapped with anger. 'I trust you did not advise it? Abortion on demand is not legal here and in my opinion should never be, unless for a medical reason.'

Jenny glared at him. 'That isn't very professional.'

'When it comes to something like that...' He realized

what he was saying and shook his head. 'I know there is a very different attitude in England.'

'Not so very different,' Jenny replied. 'I would have advised her to think very carefully even had we been in England—but in this case it wasn't necessary. She isn't pregnant.'

'I see. Anything I need to know about?'

'No, I don't think so. She wasn't one of our patients. I advised her to see her own doctor because she may need treatment.'

'I seem to have been over-critical for something that is a personal opinion, not a medical one. Will you forgive me?'

'You are entitled to your own opinions.'

'But you think I am prejudiced?'

'Not necessarily.' Jenny sighed. 'You work with different rules and ideas here.'

He nodded. 'Do you have time for a drink?'

Jenny glanced at her watch, then gave a regretful shake of her head. 'Unfortunately, I don't. I've been invited to a barbecue…' She hesitated. 'I was told I could bring someone—I don't suppose you'd like to come?' She sensed he felt the need to apologize for his sharpness and gave him an opening.

'I have other commitments,' Miguel said, and frowned. 'I should like to have dinner one evening, Jenny—perhaps this Saturday? With any luck we should be able to get through without any emergencies.'

There was no sense in continuing this way. They needed to get to the source of his hostility towards her. She hadn't done anything to deserve it, had she?

'I'll look forward to that,' Jenny said with a smile. 'But I'm sure I'll see you again before then.'

'Yes, I'm sure you will.'

Jenny left Miguel to do whatever he had called in to do, and went out into the evening sunshine. It was still beautifully warm, the sea glistening and blue as she gazed down between the whitewashed buildings and a haze of greenery. She caught the scent of flowers on a gentle breeze as she paused for a moment, then got into her car and drove back to the villa, realizing that the magic of this place was beginning to weave its spell about her.

If only she knew what made Miguel look at her so oddly sometimes! Just what had she done to earn his distrust?

Miguel frowned as he began to key some case notes into his laptop. It would have kept until another time, and he knew there was no need for him to visit Elena. Andrew was with her this evening. In fact, Andrew had persuaded Elena to let him take her to dinner at a restaurant. Not his own, but a very prestigious one along the coast which had recently opened.

Miguel knew that his sister was very conscious of awkwardness in the way she walked. Her last attack had been severe, and she had been left with some weakness in her legs, though nothing that actually prevented her from walking, thank God! Perhaps because she had always been admired for her grace and elegance, Elena found the fact that she looked clumsy difficult to her. And her pride made her reject offers of help or sympathy.

Despite Elena's refusal to talk to him about it, Miguel knew that Andrew was in love with her. Andrew had made it clear that his intentions were to devote himself to her as much as she would allow—but could she forget her hurt pride and her pain sufficiently to accept his love?

Miguel wasn't sure. Until he could be quite certain that his sister and nephew were safely taken care of, he couldn't even contemplate beginning a meaningful relationship himself.

A little smile touched his mouth as his thoughts returned to the evening he had met Jenny returning from the swimming pool. The memory had been the source of more than one pleasant dream. If she had been anyone but his colleague at the practice, he might have considered a casual affair.

Was she the kind of woman who preferred that kind of a relationship? He had found himself becoming intrigued by her, despite his initial distrust. Their first meeting had given him the wrong impression, and he still had this vague memory of Mrs Talforth saying there had been some kind of trouble with a male colleague. Had Jenny had an affair with another doctor—one that had become messy and unpleasant? Miguel didn't need another complication in his life, though he did want children one day—with the right kind of woman!

His forehead wrinkled. Marriage didn't always have to be romantically based—he knew of some rather good ones founded on respect, mutual convenience and a desire for a family. It had once been normal for Spanish families to arrange such marriages, though these days young people expected to fall in love.

He supposed he had always imagined he would fall in love, though it had somehow eluded him in his previous relationships. He had for a time believed he might be in love with Maribelle. Theirs had been a stormy, passionate relationship at the start, though the heat had gone from it long before she'd betrayed him with his friend.

In the end, his pride had been hurt as much as anything else, but, like Elena, he was finding it hard to trust again.

If he were free to marry…would he? Miguel stared at the computer screen, seeing only a blank. He tried to concentrate on what he was doing, but images kept coming between him and the screen—images that could be altogether too erotic for his peace of mind. He certainly found some of the images his mind was conjuring up very appealing…

Beside him on the desk, his mobile had begun to shrill. He reached for it, bringing his mind back from the Elysian Fields where it had been wandering. Time to get back to work!

CHAPTER FIVE

JENNY glanced at herself in the mirror. She was wearing the white jeans she had bought in Marbella with a skimpy knitted cotton top. The overall effect was much sexier than she'd realized when she'd bought them, and for a moment she almost took them off again. But there was nothing else suitable in her wardrobe.

Frowning, she hunted for a plain cotton shirt. She slipped it over the skimpy top and tied it at the waist in front, which to her mind looked much more respectable.

'You look lovely,' Beth said fondly as she emerged from her room. Doesn't she, Ron?'

'Jenny always looks lovely,' her father replied. He was feeling a little better that evening and was sitting in a straight-backed chair in the lounge so that he could watch a cricket match on the TV. 'She looks a bit tasty this evening, though.'

'Ron!' Beth exclaimed. 'Take no notice, Jenny.'

'Is it too much?' Jenny asked anxiously. 'Shall I go and change?'

'No, of course not,' her mother replied. 'Everyone wears that sort of thing out here.'

'Yes, that's what I thought,' Jenny said. 'Well, I had better go or I shall be late.'

She kissed her parents and went out, and then drove the short distance to where the barbecue was being held. She could quite easily have walked, but it would be dark when she left and she would rather not walk back alone.

Jenny regretted that Miguel hadn't been able to come

with her. She had hesitated to ask, doing so at the last minute only because he had invited her for a drink. Perhaps if she had asked sooner...but he would probably have refused because he was too busy.

Taking her to his sister's or to dinner was probably as far as he wanted their friendship to go. A barbecue that promised to be rather lively would create a different atmosphere—and might cause them to step over a line she sensed he had drawn between them.

Jenny pushed all thoughts of Miguel aside as she was greeted by Sally and then by her husband Bob. Sally complimented her on her outfit, saying that she would kill for a figure like Jenny's, then asked what she would like to drink.

'Oh, fizzy water, please.'

'No way,' Sally said. 'You must have a proper drink, Jenny—this is a party.'

'All right, I'll have just one white wine spritzer,' Jenny agreed. 'But nothing strong, thank you. I may need to drive on the main highway tomorrow—and alcohol remains in the blood much longer than people think.'

The garden had been decked with balloons and festive lights, and a board had been laid on the grass to make dancing easier. A live group was playing popular songs from a few years back, and some of the younger people were dancing to the music in their own particular style.

Jenny sipped her drink and smiled as she was introduced to various people. Most were either couples or families with children ranging in age from about five to thirteen, but one man was on his own and had probably been invited for Jenny's benefit.

'Clive Jacobs,' he said, gravitating to her side soon

after she arrived. 'You must be the new doctor everyone is talking about.'

'Well, I'm not sure everyone is interested, but I'm certainly a doctor and new to this area,' Jenny said. Clive was tall, lean and fair-haired, and he had a pleasant smile—but something about him had set off alarm bells. 'So, what do you do?'

'You'll run a mile if I tell you.' Clive grinned at her. 'I'm a partner in a local estate agent's.'

'Ah...' Jenny appreciated the joke. 'Tell me, where should I buy if I decide I want my own place? I'm with my parents at the moment, but I may need to find somewhere of my own later on.'

'Depends on what you want—a holiday complex with all the trimmings and expense, or something residential.'

'I suppose the second option would be cheaper?'

'Much—but it's not for the faint-hearted.'

'No, I don't suppose...' Jenny was laughing as she turned just in time to see Bob Marshall clutch at his side in agony. As she watched, his knees buckled and he sank to the grass, bent double in pain. 'Excuse me...'

She hurried to Bob's side, looking down at him in concern. 'Is the pain very bad?' Jenny asked. She touched his forehead, finding it damp with sweat. He was clearly running a temperature. 'How long have you been experiencing pain this time?'

'All day, on and off,' he said between gritted teeth. 'I kept thinking it would go away as it has before.'

'Not this time, I'm afraid,' Jenny replied. 'I'm sorry but there's no alternative. I'm going to have to rush you into Emergency.' She turned to Sally as she came hurrying up to them. 'My mobile is in the car. I need to make a few calls. Get your husband to lie down if he can manage it. I'll be back in a moment.'

Jenny phoned for an ambulance first. She was promised it would be there in ten minutes. Next she rang the emergency centre and asked if they could deal with a suspected burst appendix and was told they had a surgeon on standby and would receive her patient. She then telephoned Miguel.

'I rang in case you were in the area,' she said. 'Bob is in a lot of pain and my bag is at the villa. I can't leave him to fetch it—I think he needs an emergency appendicectomy. 'I've arranged the ambulance and I've alerted Emergency. They have a surgeon on standby. Is there anything else I need to do?'

'It sounds as if you have it covered,' Miguel replied. 'I was just about to leave the clinic. I'll come straight up—whereabouts are you?'

Jenny told him and went back to the now silent barbecue. The guests were all standing around, looking lost. They parted as Jenny made her way back to Bob. Sally was in tears as she watched her husband writhe in agony.

'Can't you give him something?' she asked, sounding almost accusing.

'My bag is at the villa,' Jenny said. 'Miguel is coming. He should be here before the ambulance, but if he doesn't the paramedics will give Bob a painkilling injection then.'

Even as she spoke car lights flashed up the hill. Miguel was there unbelievably quickly.

'You were soon here,' she said as he came up to them a few moments later.

'I was on the point of leaving.' He looked at Bob. 'I'll give you an injection. It will ease the pain.'

Jenny watched as he took the syringe from his bag, injecting the medication swiftly and efficiently. Then she turned to Sally.

'You'll want to go with Bob, of course. What about the children?'

'Marian Moate says she will stay with them,' Sally said tearfully. 'Is he going to be all right?'

'We have everything on our side,' Jenny replied. 'But this isn't straightforward. If it has burst—'

'Burst? But you said it was only grumbling.'

'It seemed that way on my first examination,' Jenny said. 'But even if Bob had agreed to go to the hospital for further investigation, we might not have got the appointment before this happened.'

'He wouldn't go,' Sally said, gulping back a sob. 'What am I—?

Her question was left unfinished as someone shouted that the ambulance had arrived and then there was a flurry of activity as Bob was lifted onto a stretcher and, after a consultation with the doctors, carried away. Sally hurried after her husband.

Some of the guests had drifted away, others, closer to the Marshalls, had decided to help clear the food. Someone suggested they might as well eat it, but his suggestion met with little agreement. No one felt like continuing this party after what had happened.

'Have you got your car?' Miguel asked, and Jenny nodded. 'I'll follow you home.'

Jenny drove back to the villa. She was very concerned for Sally and Bob and felt that perhaps she hadn't done enough to persuade him to have further investigation when he'd sought a consultation.

She said as much to Miguel as they lingered outside the villa.

'You had better tell me what happened when he came to the clinic,' he said with a frown. 'Did you suggest that he should go to hospital for further investigation?'

'Look, what is this?' Jenny demanded. 'I'm a fully trained doctor. I don't expect an inquisition every time I make a clinical decision.'

'I wasn't criticizing, just asking.'

'The hell you weren't!' She glared at him. 'If you don't trust my judgement just say so right now and we can end our agreement.'

'Calm down, Jenny!' Miguel grabbed her arm, giving her a shake. 'I'm just asking you to give me a rundown of what happened when Bob came in. He complained of pain—and then what?'

Jenny took a deep breath. He had a right to know, of course. It was just that his attitude had begun to get to her. 'He told me he had only had the pain a few times and that it wasn't severe. I asked about other symptoms like constipation or changes in bowel movements, but he denied having any—and there was no sign of fever at that time. When I suggested a hospital visit he said he would prefer to wait until he got back to England. I spoke to Sally and told her to make sure he did go to a doctor when he got home. She replied that he was a coward about hospitals—especially out here.'

'Well, now he has been forced to go in a hurry,' Miguel said. 'We must hope that he comes through it OK.'

'I do hope so!' Jenny was thoroughly upset by now. 'Sally and the children...I wish I *had* pushed him harder.'

'You did what you were required to do,' Miguel said. 'I am not sure he would have gone whatever you did—besides, this could have happened before he was seen. He must have been having the pain for much longer than he told you.'

'Yes, I think he had. He just didn't want to admit it.'

Miguel's eyes were studying her intently, and there was an odd flicker in them, which she took for disapproval of the way she was dressed. 'It was just as well we were both around.'

'Yes. It's a pity the party was ruined. I'm afraid it leaves you all dressed up and nowhere to go.'

'The only place I want to be right now is home,' Jenny said. 'I'm just so concerned for Sally and Bob.'

'Let's just hope that peritonitis doesn't set in. I'll say goodnight, then—and don't worry too much, Jenny. It wasn't your fault.'

Jenny nodded her head but made no reply. She knew she would worry and, despite what Miguel had just said, she felt that he believed she ought to have done more.

Jenny rang the hospital first thing the next morning. To her relief she was told that though the patient had had acute appendicitis it hadn't burst and there was no infection in the abdomen. Bob Marshall's operation had been a complete success with no complications, and he was recovering nicely.

She telephoned Miguel, who told her he had already spoken to the surgeon personally. 'Apparently they got to him just in the nick of time,' he said. 'I tried to ring you to tell you, but your phone was engaged.'

'I must have been talking to the hospital,' Jenny said. 'I'm so relieved. I was restless all night.'

'I told you not to worry,' Miguel replied. 'But I must admit I was worried myself. I hate to lose a patient, especially through something that could have been avoided.' He laughed oddly. 'I'll see you later this afternoon. Excuse me now, I have an appointment.'

Jenny sighed as she replaced the receiver. It could have been an unpleasant incident. If anything had happened to Bob, Sally Marshall might have decided Jenny was guilty of neglect. The clinic was insured for such an eventuality, of course, and it was doubtful whether the case would have succeeded, but it wouldn't have done the clinic's reputation much good—or Jenny's either.

She *had* done what she could to persuade Bob, but perhaps her intuition had let her down this time. Second-guessing what was going on in a patient's mind played quite a large part in a doctor's work. Symptoms were often similar and could be misleading, or simply not severe enough to make an absolute diagnosis, which was why at times a patient could be sent home from the surgery or the hospital, and later collapse with a heart attack.

That had never happened to Jenny so far, and her intuition was largely responsible. Perhaps Bob Marshall had been too good at concealing his pain, or it might have been that the trouble had just flared up suddenly, as these things could.

All aspects considered, Jenny didn't think she had been guilty of neglect, but she would certainly insist on further investigation in future cases. She wondered for a moment about Juliana, hoping that the young woman had gone to her own doctor as promised.

Sighing, Jenny put the worrying incident of Bob's emergency operation from her mind and spent the next half-hour helping her father with his exercises.

'My shoulder is less stiff,' he told her, 'but I still can't raise my arm very far—and it is rather painful.'

'I'll talk to Miguel about that injection,' Jenny promised. She kissed him, then went through to the kitchen to talk to her mother. 'I'm just off, Mum.'

'Take care of yourself, love,' Beth said and looked at her anxiously. 'You seem down—are you?'

'Just a bit tired,' Jenny replied. 'But, please, don't worry. I'll be fine once I get going.'

'It was a shame about last night,' her mother said. 'I was hoping you would make some nice friends.'

'I'm sure I shall as time goes on,' Jenny said. 'I'm already getting to know lots of people.'

'I was thinking more of gentlemen friends...'

Jenny laughed. 'Oh, Mum,' she said. 'Don't worry about my love life. I've only been here a couple of weeks. There's plenty of time...'

'That's a new outfit,' Jenny said as Isabelle came into Reception the following afternoon. She felt it was time she tried to break through the barrier of hostility between them. The receptionist was a few minutes late and looked flustered. 'The colour suits you. Where did you buy it?'

'At a boutique in Marbella,' Isabelle replied after some hesitation.

'You have some lovely clothes.' Jenny persisted in the attempt, which seemed not to be meeting with much success. 'Are you going out later?'

'I like to look smart for work. Dr Sanchez expects me to look presentable.'

Jenny wondered if Miguel ever noticed any of the fantastic outfits his receptionist wore for his benefit, and thought he probably didn't. It was becoming more and more obvious to her that Isabelle was carrying a torch for her boss.

She wondered about the little scene she'd witnessed, when he'd arranged to pick Isabelle up the other evening. Perhaps she was wrong, perhaps they did go out socially, and yet she didn't get the impression that Miguel was interested in his receptionist other than in his role as a friendly employer.

Oh, well, it wasn't her business either way. Miguel's relationships were his own business. Jenny certainly had no right to question him. She wasn't sure he even liked her, though there was a look in his eyes at times... She put that thought right out of her mind. She would be crazy to let herself get emotionally involved.

Miguel hadn't contacted the clinic all that day. Jenny supposed he must have been busy. They had seen a stream of patients with minor ailments, and Soraya told her they hadn't been so busy in ages.

'I think it is because you are here,' Soraya said thoughtfully as they had a coffee-break. 'More holiday-makers are choosing to come to us with their problems.'

'It is just because there are more people here at the moment,' Isabelle said sulkily, and took her cup into the kitchen, where she could be heard running water and making a clattering noise.

'Oh, dear,' Jenny said. 'I'm afraid Isabelle doesn't like me much.'

'She will get over it.' Soraya shrugged. She looked at Jenny awkwardly, then went on to tell her something else, something worrying. There were three packs of opiate-based tablets missing. 'Our system has always worked before,' she said, looking most upset. 'I sign or the doctor signs the list when drugs are used. I cannot understand what has gone wrong this time.'

'I've signed three times since I've been here,' Jenny said. 'I'm sure I haven't forgotten, Soraya. Perhaps Dr Sanchez took something in a hurry and meant to write it up later?'

'He is always so meticulous,' Soraya replied. 'I

checked this list three weeks ago. It wasn't due to be checked again for a month. I only did it because of what you said about the cabinet being left unlocked.'

'I've wondered since if I heard something that night—while I was with Sarah. At the time I hardly noticed, but I wish now that I'd come out of my room and checked or told you about finding the key the next day. I didn't want to seem as if I was criticizing the minute I got here, but if there has been a theft it's serious. Not for the value of the drugs, but for the damage pethidine might do in the wrong hands.'

Soraya nodded. 'I shall speak to Dr Sanchez. If that key was left in the cupboard I am to blame.'

'No one is to blame,' Jenny said. 'But we must all be even more careful in future.' She glanced towards the kitchen. 'Does Isabelle ever have access to the drugs?'

Soraya looked shocked. 'No, of course not. She merely deals with phone messages, accounts and Reception when I'm busy.'

Jenny nodded. 'I thought not. Well, we shall just have to make sure things are checked more carefully in future, shan't we?'

Isabelle came back from the kitchen at that moment, and the conversation became more general as the phone began to ring and another patient entered Reception.

Jenny thought about the missing drugs as she drove home that evening. People did sometimes forget to sign if they were in a hurry, of course, but it was odd that it was three packs of the same strong painkiller—pethidine was a drug that addicts had been known to try all kinds of tricks to obtain. Some people even turned up at hospital claiming to be in pain from a kidney stone in the hope of getting an injection; there had been cases where a stone had shown up on a first X-ray, only to disappear magically in half an hour or so.

Isabelle had given Jenny an odd angry look when she'd left that evening, which wasn't unusual, yet she felt there was more behind it this time. Had Soraya told her that she'd asked if Isabelle ever had access to the drugs? The question had been in confidence, and she would be disappointed if Soraya had broken it.

Putting the niggling worry to the back of her mind, Jenny helped her mother with the evening meal.

'Ellen Dickson came to see me today,' she said. 'You remember you sent her husband into hospital? Well, he's much better and she was talking about ideas for various activities. We're going to have a keep-fit morning here once a week—exercises in the garden followed by coffee and biscuits.'

'Well, that should keep you busy,' Jenny said, and smiled as she tossed the salad.

'Yes.' Beth nodded agreement. 'And she's trying to drum up interest in Spanish lessons one afternoon a week. We'll have them by the pool in the sports complex, which should encourage more people to come. We're also hoping to get a whist drive going at the club once a month.'

'That all sounds rather interesting,' Jenny said. 'Once Dad is on his feet again properly you'll be able to get out more again.'

'Yes.' Beth looked pleased. 'He's come on a lot since you've been here, Jenny.'

'Yes, I've noticed an improvement.' In her mother, too! Her faint air of anxiety had completely disappeared.

Once Beth was happily settled in front of the latest episode of the period drama she was watching on TV, Jenny changed into a navy blue bikini and added a multicoloured sarong. She walked down to the swimming pool, pleased to discover that she had it all to herself.

It was pleasant to swim, and she completed several lengths before climbing out to towel herself vigorously. It had been warm in the water, but cooler out now that the sun had almost gone. She was shaking out her long hair and holding her face to the last rays of that sun when a man's voice spoke from behind her.

'Your mother said I would find you here.'

Jenny swung round to face Miguel, her heart suddenly racing wildly. His dark eyes were very intent and seemed for a moment to smoulder with heat as they swept her from head to toe. The bikini was very revealing, making the most of her, high full breasts, slender waist and long, long legs.

Something passed between them in that moment. Jenny felt her throat tighten, and her heart was hammering wildly. She couldn't help noticing how thick his eyelashes were, the sensual softness of his mouth and the way his eyes appeared to devour her. She felt that he was very much aware of her sexually, as she was of him, and even her toes started to tingle.

'I am sorry if I startled you.' Miguel's voice sounded slightly hoarse. He looked as if he was the one who had received a shock. 'I wanted to talk to you.'

'Yes, of course.' Jenny pulled on her wrap. She gathered her scattered thoughts, realizing they had important business to discuss. This wasn't the time for indulging her fantasies! 'Would you mind waiting while I go home and dress?'

'That would seem to be a sensible idea.' Miguel cleared his throat. Snatching a quick peep at his profile, she thought he looked almost angry. 'You don't want to get cold.'

Jenny was very conscious of him walking beside her as they returned to the villa. She excused herself at once, going swiftly to her own room to change out of her wet things. Some devilment in her made her choose the white jeans she had worn the previous evening, teaming them with a pink cotton top and matching canvas mules. She wrapped her hair in a white scarf bandanna style and went out to join Miguel.

He was sitting on the patio, drinking coffee.

'Mrs Talforth was just making some,' he explained, looking apologetic. 'She said she would bring one for you later if you would like it.'

'Not at the moment,' Jenny replied. She sat down in a basket chair opposite him, crossing her legs. 'You wanted to see me—was it about the missing drugs?'

'Yes and no,' Miguel said. 'They are a worrying factor, of course. I certainly haven't neglected to sign. I haven't prescribed the drug for weeks. We've never had this problem before...'

'So you think I must be responsible?'

'I didn't say that.' Miguel's mouth thinned. He seemed annoyed with her, but she wasn't sure why. Was it over the drugs or something else? 'It is just odd that it has happened now.'

'I am always very careful,' Jenny said. She felt chilled, upset that he seemed to blame her for what had happened. 'Soraya is sure she didn't make a mistake in her last accounting—so that means a theft must have occurred.'

'Yes, it would seem that way.' Miguel looked thoughtful. 'Which is worrying. We haven't had a break-in at the clinic so...'

'Someone must have entered, found the cabinet unlocked and taken the drugs while no one was about.'

'Yes, but Isabelle is always in Reception. How could someone have slipped past her into the treatment room?'

'When I first visited the clinic there was no one in Reception,' Jenny reminded him, her mind working at the problem. 'Soraya was dealing with a noisy child, I seem to recall. I don't know where Isabelle was—perhaps in the bathroom or kitchen. I didn't steal the drugs that day, but someone could have. There may have been other times when the reception area was left unattended.'

'Yes.' Miguel frowned. 'I suppose it must have happened that way. I shall have to warn her to be more careful—and Soraya must make sure she doesn't leave the key lying around.'

'Soraya is sure she didn't—but that would mean someone who knew where the key was kept must have taken it and used it.'

'But...Isabelle? That's rather unkind, isn't it? To accuse her, when you hardly know her.' He frowned. 'No, I cannot believe it. Why should she?'

'I don't know.' Jenny shrugged. 'There has to be some explanation. 'I trust Soraya...'

'But not Isabelle? Why do you dislike her, Jenny?'

'I don't dislike her, and I'm not accusing anyone,' Jenny said, and blushed as he gave her a hard stare. 'I'm just wondering aloud. Either someone left the cabinet unlocked or...'

'Yes.' He looked grim. 'Not very pleasant either way. We must certainly all take more care.'

'Yes, we must.' Jenny's feelings were ruffled. He seemed prepared to blame her but not Isabelle or Soraya.

There was silence for a few moments, then Miguel looked at her. 'I called to see Mr Talforth. His mobility is better since you've been working with him, but he says the shoulder is painful and that you suggested an injection of cortisone might help.'

'I told him I would speak to you so that you could decide. He's your patient, I wasn't interfering.'

'We could try it,' Miguel agreed. 'You know that these things don't work for everyone.'

'Yes, of course. I have explained that to Dad.'

'Well, I should be going...' Miguel got to his feet. Jenny rose, too. He hesitated, looking awkward. 'About dinner this weekend...'

'I'm not sure,' Jenny said, and could have bitten her tongue off the next moment.

'Nor am I,' Miguel replied. 'Elena wasn't well this morning. I am a little worried about her.' He sighed and combed his thick, wavy hair with his fingers. 'If I've seemed a bit off this evening, put it down to personal worries. The last thing I need at the moment is trouble at the clinic.'

'Oh, I'm so sorry,' Jenny said. Her annoyance faded instantly as she saw he was really concerned. 'Do you think it's another bout of her illness?'

'It might just be tiredness. She went out with Andrew last night, so this could simply be reaction.' He smiled. 'I'm sorry. I shouldn't take it out on you, Jenny. You've made life very much better...'

The look of appeal in his eyes at that moment made Jenny do something she would not normally have dreamed of. She reached out and touched the side of his face, caressing it gently with the tips of her fingers. Her touch seemed to ignite a fire, and before she knew what was happening Miguel pulled her close and kissed her on the mouth. The feel of his lips against hers was delicious, making her shiver with delight. She allowed herself to melt into him, her hands caressing the back of his neck as his tongue explored the soft interior of her mouth. Her breasts were hard against his chest, her body tucked into his so that she could feel the heat of him. It was a delightful, very sensual experience and Jenny enjoyed it very much.

She was aware of his hands moving down to her hips and pressed hard against his body by the pressure, she could feel his arousal. It sent shock waves tumbling through her, and she was swept away by the fierce need rising up like a torrent inside her. She couldn't ever remember having been this aroused by a kiss before!

When Miguel let her go, her eyes were smoky with passion, her lips parted in a slightly breathless look. Miguel smiled, his earlier tension gone as his gaze dwelt on her. She looked about seventeen!

'I'm sorry,' he murmured huskily. 'I did rather take advantage, but I needed to do that. I think it must be those jeans. They are very, very sexy, Jenny.'

She laughed. 'I know. I ought not to have bought them, but I thought some of my clothes were too stuffy for here.'

'You should definitely have bought them,' Miguel said, a wicked gleam in his eyes. 'I don't suggest you wear them for work—the heart-attack rate would shoot up—but I definitely approve.'

'Oh...' Jenny blushed. 'I thought perhaps you might not.'

Miguel's laughter was soft and provoking. 'I may be a doctor, Jenny, but I am also a man. Make no mistake about that. Provoke me and you may get more than you bargained for.'

Jenny felt his hot gaze on her, and suddenly she liked it—she liked it very much.

'Perhaps I shall see you tomorrow evening?'

'If I can manage it,' Miguel replied, and the blaze of desire had gone, to be replaced by anxiety again. 'About this weekend, Jenny. If I can't manage dinner on Saturday evening you might like to come to Elena's again.'

'Yes, I would,' she replied with a lightness of heart. 'We'll just take things as they come and see how they work out, shall we?'

CHAPTER SIX

MIGUEL took Jenny for a drink the following evening. He told her that Elena was better than she had been the previous day, but still seemed a bit down.

'I'm not sure if she's feeling ill or sorry for herself,' Miguel said to Jenny. 'I suppose you've gathered that Andrew is interested in her?'

'Yes, she told me herself,' Jenny replied. 'To be honest, I don't think she knows what she wants. Perhaps she still loves Juan despite what he did to her.'

'Yes, perhaps,' Miguel agreed. 'The human heart can play a lot of odd tricks—that's if you believe in love, of course?'

'I think I do,' Jenny said, taking him seriously. 'There are many different kinds, aren't there? You love Elena and Joachim. I love both my parents very much.'

'You know what I meant.' His dark eyes challenged her. Her eyes lingered on his mouth, remembering that kiss and the way it had made her feel. 'Passionate, all-consuming love between a man and a woman. Have you known that kind of love, Jenny?'

'Sexual desire?' Jenny asked. 'Oh, yes, I believe in that—it's what makes the world go round, isn't it?' This was said with a teasing note in her voice.

'But what about the love that drives men to murder and women to tears—do you believe in that, Jenny?'

Her heart was racing wildly as she sought for an answer that wouldn't be too revealing. 'I'm not sure,' she said at last. 'Humans are very emotional creatures. That kind of love must be very terrifying, don't you think?'

'But also very satisfying if it is felt on both sides.' He looked thoughtful. 'So do you approve of a relationship based on mutual trust and respect?'

'Yes, perhaps,' she replied, wondering where this was leading to. 'As long as there is also affection and understanding.'

'Yes, I see,' Miguel murmured, and sipped his drink. 'Arranged marriages were once the expected thing in this country. My father's parents were very angry that he chose an English girl—though in time they came to love her as he did.'

'I wish I could have known your parents, Miguel.'

'I also wish you could have,' he said, and smiled at her. 'I am sure they would have liked you.'

He changed the subject to the clinic, asking Jenny what progress she had made on their various ideas for new services, and they talked shop for some minutes. Then Miguel glanced at his watch.

'I must be going,' he said. 'I have a patient to see—just a routine check-up after a gall-bladder operation—then I'm going to call on Andrew Sinclair. He asked if we could have a chat and this evening seemed good as Elena has a friend with her.'

'Yes, I mustn't delay you,' Jenny said. 'I have letters to write. A friend from England asked if she could come out and stay for a week of her holiday. I'm going to let her have my room and sleep on the sofa-bed for a few days.'

'A particular friend?' Miguel asked. She nodded. 'If you want to take a couple of days off while she is here, let me know.'

'Oh, Moya won't expect that,' Jenny said. 'We'll go

out in the evenings and at the weekend. She'll laze by the pool most of the time during the day.' Knowing Moya, she would soon have a man in tow!

Jenny drove home after Miguel left to keep his appointment. She felt a little disappointed that their talk hadn't gone further. For a while she had thought Miguel might be suggesting some sort of an intimate relationship between them.

Something had changed between them the previous night when he had kissed her, bringing down the barriers. At least it had for Jenny. Until then, she hadn't been quite sure that he approved of her—or even really liked her. Now she knew that he found her physically attractive, of that there wasn't a shred of doubt. His eyes had practically devoured her! But what kind of a relationship was he looking for—something purely sexual? And if that was so, did she want to get involved?

It wasn't always easy to read his thoughts. Sometimes it was almost as if he were two people—the very serious doctor and devoted brother, but also someone rather exciting and even a little dangerous.

Jenny was intrigued by the fascinating glimpse of this other man. She had liked and respected Dr Sanchez almost from the start, but she thought her feelings for Miguel might be very different.

They had a rush of patients at the clinic over the next few days, and several evening calls, a couple of which were real emergencies, which meant that there was little time for Miguel and Jenny to meet and talk. They managed a few words on the telephone, and Miguel confirmed that Jenny was expected for lunch at Elena's that Sunday.

'She asked if you could get there at eleven-thirty so

that you could have some time before Andrew and the other guests arrive. We have several friends coming this week, Jenny.'

She had gathered that Sunday lunch at Elena's was a bit of a ritual, because it was much easier for Elena to have people there than travel to their homes, though she did occasionally go out if she felt up to it.

'Yes, of course I will,' Jenny said to his request to go early. 'I shall look forward to it.'

On Saturday she went into Marbella just before the shops shut at one-thirty and bought a long white crinkle cotton skirt and top, a wide gold belt to cinch in at the waist and gold sandals—which were almost obligatory in Marbella.

Afterwards, she called at Sally Marshall's apartment to see how she was getting on.

'Oh, Jenny!' Sally greeted her with a brilliant smile. 'I was coming to see you this afternoon. Bob wanted to thank you and Dr Sanchez for what you did for him.'

'We only did what was necessary,' Jenny said. 'I'm just sorry he had to go off in a rush like that.'

Sally laughed. 'It was probably the best way. He was so drowsy after that injection that he hardly knew what was happening, and didn't have time to be frightened. He's such a coward! The reason he wanted to go back to England was because he was scared of being ill out here.'

'But there's no reason, Sally. The medical service here is very good.'

'He's realized that now,' Sally said happily, 'so we're going to stay on after all—and when Bob is better we're going to have another party to celebrate.'

'I'm so glad,' Jenny said. 'I was very worried about him.'

'So was I,' Sally admitted. 'I may have been a bit sharp with you, but I never blamed you. Bob should have told you how bad the pain was becoming.'

'Yes, but it might not have made much difference. He wasn't an emergency then, and I would only have sent him for investigation. Appendicitis is one of those things that can flare up suddenly.'

Sally nodded. 'How are you settling in? Clive was very impressed, by the way. He wanted your telephone number, so I gave him Beth's. I hope that was all right?'

'Yes. Yes, I see no harm in it,' Jenny said. She wasn't sure she wanted Clive Jacobs to ring her, but she wasn't going to make a fuss about it.

'What are you doing this evening?' Sally asked. 'Only the children are going to a friend's house. Do you fancy going to Club Miraflores? They have a live group there. We could have a couple of drinks—or dinner if you like?'

'A couple of drinks would be nice,' Jenny said. 'Shall we meet there?'

'At eight,' Sally said. 'It will make a change—and I'm sure to know everyone. I can introduce you to people.'

'I shall look forward to it,' Jenny said. 'Well, I'd better get back and help Mum with a few things, then I think I'll spend the rest of the afternoon by the pool.'

'Sounds lovely,' Sally said. 'I'm off to visit Bob in a few minutes.'

'Send him my best wishes.'

When Jenny got in her mother told her that Clive Jacobs had telephoned that morning. 'He asked if you would ring him back when you came in.' Beth looked at her curiously. 'He isn't a patient, is he, Jenny?'

'No, just someone I met last week. I was talking to him when Bob Marshall collapsed.'

'I think he wants to ask you out.'

'Don't get excited Mum.' Jenny laughed. 'I'm already going out with Sally this evening. Besides, I'm not really interested in Clive that way. He's not my type.'

'Well, you had better ring him back.'

'After lunch.'

'No, do it now. Everything is more or less ready. I just have to pop the jacket potatoes in the microwave.'

Jenny went into the hall and dialled the number her mother had written down.

'Clive Jacobs…'

'It's Jenny Talforth. You spoke to my mother earlier.'

'Oh, Jenny. Lovely to hear from you. I just rang on the offchance that you might be free for dinner this evening.'

'That was kind of you,' Jenny replied. 'But I have another engagement.'

'That's a shame,' he said. 'I suppose I might have known. It isn't every day that a woman like you turns up. Maybe another time?'

'Yes, perhaps.'

Jenny replaced the receiver. What did he mean—a woman like her? She glanced at herself in the long, gilt-framed mirror on the wall and was a little surprised at what she saw. Her skin was acquiring a pale golden colour without her really trying, and her hair was slightly ruffled by the breeze. She had taken to wearing her hair loose when she wasn't working and it suited her, made her look younger—more alive.

Jenny realized that she was feeling more alive than

she had for a long, long time. She had been so busy working these past years that she hadn't noticed what had been happening to her. She had allowed herself to become drab, settling for sensible clothes in plain colours. It was no wonder that James Redfern hadn't noticed his mouse of a colleague.

She was glad now that she had never got involved with James. It could never have led anywhere. Besides, there was a man who was very much aware of her now—and she of him.

Jenny wasn't sure where this feeling between her and Miguel would lead, but she knew she wanted to explore it further.

She was smiling as she went back to join her mother for lunch. She would be seeing Miguel the next day, and hopefully this time they would have time for more than just a snatched drink.

Club Miraflores was busy when Jenny arrived that evening, but Sally was already seated at a table outside the clubhouse.

'I got a couple of drinks in,' she said as Jenny sat down beside her. 'White wine spritzer—OK?'

'Yes, lovely,' Jenny said. She helped herself to a green olive from the dish on the table. 'Who's the group?'

'They're one of those copycat bands,' Sally replied, 'but they're very good. I've heard them before—last summer.'

Jenny nodded and sipped her drink. 'It's nice here. I've been here to dinner with my parents and their friends a couple of times. I shall probably bring Moya when she comes out—she's a nursing friend I share a house with at home.'

'Is she coming out soon?'

'Yes, the week after next.'

'If Bob is up to a party then you must bring her over. They say he can come out of hospital next week.'

'Yes, but he mustn't overdo it for a while. No heavy lifting or anything like that.'

'No, of course not— Oh, there's Clive. He's seen us. I expect he'll come over.'

He made a beeline straight for them. He was wearing smart denim and looked rather attractive. His eyes went over Jenny appreciatively.

'So that's where you are,' he said. 'You should have said your date was with Sally. We could have ditched her and gone somewhere on our own.'

'Thanks very much!' Sally said, but she was laughing. 'Just say if I'm in the way, won't you, Clive?'

'You're not,' Jenny said before he could reply. 'I think the band is going to start playing now.'

Clive sat down at their table. He signalled the waiter, ordering a bottle of wine and tapas, clearly intending to spend the evening with them. Jenny felt a little annoyed that he had invited himself, but Sally didn't seem to mind so there wasn't much she could do.

During the evening he asked her to dance, and she felt obliged to agree, but by this time they had been joined by several more of Sally's friends and Jenny was asked to dance by others, too.

It was eleven o'clock when she excused herself and drove home. Clive had wanted to take her, but she'd refused politely but firmly. He had pressed his knee against hers under the table and had held her a little too close during their dance, and she was wary of being alone with him.

Mr Jacobs enjoyed playing the field, and Jenny wasn't interested in being another conquest!

Jenny's mother was making a cup of hot chocolate when she got in.

'Ah, there you are, love,' Beth said. 'Did you have a good time?' Jenny nodded and her mother gestured to the mugs. 'Would you like one?'

'I'll make it,' Jenny replied. 'Take yours through and have it with Dad as you always do.'

Beth lingered for a few moments. 'Dr Sanchez called again this evening. He gave your father that injection. I think he was hoping to see you. He seemed disappointed when I told him you had gone out with friends.'

'He didn't mention that he might call this evening.' Jenny frowned. 'I thought he was going to his sister's.'

'He's been busy apparently—a couple of emergency call-outs this afternoon. He had to go to the hospital with a patient he was worried about and stayed there for hours. He said he would see you tomorrow. Oh, and there was a phone call from England—from James Redfern.'

'Really?' Jenny's brows arched. 'Did he say why he was calling?'

'Apparently he has a conference out here the week after next. It's in Malaga, but he's going to a yacht party in Puerto Banus on the Sunday. He wanted to know if you might like to go with him. I said you would ring him back tomorrow.'

'Yes, thank you. I will.' Jenny was surprised. James had never asked her out before. 'I'm not sure I'll be free,' she said, wrinkling her forehead. 'Moya will be here by then. You don't mind that she's coming to stay, Mum?'

'Of course not,' Beth said. 'I want you to feel free to

invite your friends. This is your home, you know that, darling.'

'Yes.' Jenny smiled and kissed her cheek. She was thoughtful as she made her drink and took it to bed. Why had James decided to look her up? He'd hardly noticed she'd been around when they'd met at the surgery every day.

Was there something he wanted from her?

Jenny wore her new white skirt and top the following day. It wasn't as sexy as the laced-up jeans, but it was exactly right for the occasion and she was pleased with her own appearance.

Elena was sitting in the garden as before when Jenny arrived. She had been drinking iced tea and there was a large pile of glossy magazines on the table beside her. Evidence of Joachim's presence somewhere lay in the abandoned toys on the grass.

It was a warm morning, but a little breeze wafting in from off the sea prevented it from being too hot. Jenny could smell the wonderful perfumes of roses, a trailing purple wisteria and something else she couldn't name.

'You came nice and early,' Elena said, greeting her with a smile as Jenny went over to kiss her cheek. 'That was kind of you. We shan't get much chance to talk once everyone else gets here.' She indicated the jug of iced tea and extra glasses. 'Will you help yourself—or shall I ask Maria for something different?'

'This is fine,' Jenny said, helping herself to a glass. She sat down in a comfortable chair next to Elena. Joachim came up to her, and she sat him on her knee as she talked to his mother, but after a few minutes he wriggled free and went running off somewhere. Jenny looked at Elena, noticing her air of strain. 'How are you feeling now?'

'Did Miguel tell you I wasn't well?' Elena pulled a wry face as Jenny nodded. 'He worries too much. I told him I had probably eaten something that did not agree with me.'

'Oh, yes, you went to a new restaurant—was it good?'

'It was all right.' Elena wrinkled her attractive nose. 'But I prefer Andrew's place, or having friends here. I hate strangers staring at me, wondering what is wrong with that odd woman when I walk in somewhere new.'

'You should ignore the ones who stare. It's the best way. They don't mean to be hurtful, they just don't understand.'

'I do try.' Elena sighed, looking unhappy. 'Andrew wants to try living here with us, but I'm not sure. Supposing I end up in a wheelchair in a few years' time? It is hardly fair to him, is it?'

'He must be prepared for that,' Jenny said. 'He understands about your illness, about what may happen.'

Elena nodded. 'Juan wants to see Joachim,' she said and bit her lip. 'He wrote to me. He wants to come here one day next week. What should I do, Jenny?'

'Have you spoken to Miguel?'

'No. He would say I should refuse—or that Juan should be allowed only limited access. Juan wants to spend a day here with us every week, and to take his son out sometimes once Joachim gets used to him.'

'How do you feel about that?' Jenny saw a glimmer of hope in her eyes. 'You want him to come back, don't you?'

'Perhaps if he came to see Joachim…'

'Supposing that's all he wants, Elena?'

'It's going to hurt all over again,' she admitted. 'But unless I see him I shall not know how I feel about Andrew moving in.'

'Then I think you've answered your own question.'

'Yes, I suppose I have,' Elena said, and laughed. She really was very pretty when she wasn't pouting. 'That is enough of me and my problems. Tell me about you, Jenny. You are not married—is there anyone hovering in your life?'

Jenny blushed slightly. She could hardly say that she thought she was falling in love with Elena's brother, so she told her about her busy life in England and the friends who were coming out in the next weeks.

They talked for half an hour or so before Miguel arrived to set up the barbecue. His dark eyes sought Jenny out, going over her with approval. She thought that he looked extremely attractive in black jeans and a matching shirt opened at the neck to expose a glimpse of lightly tanned skin. A little pulse was beating at the base of his throat and she had a sudden desire to kiss it, a desire which she naturally suppressed as Elena's guests began to arrive.

There were fifteen in all, several of them Spanish, one German and a couple English. They were all expensively though casually dressed, and the women wore lots of gold jewellery that flashed in the sunlight. All of them spoke excellent English so the conversation was general and easy for Jenny to follow. She found it hard to remember all their names at first, but they were a very friendly crowd and the time passed pleasantly.

Jenny was sorry when the party began to break up. Miguel followed her as she walked to her car.

'We have hardly had any time together.'

'It's always like that when you're entertaining.'

'But I want to talk to you, Jenny.' His voice was low and husky, his smouldering eyes conveying a message that she couldn't mistake. He reached out to stroke a finger down her cheek, setting a trail of fire running through her. What was it about this man? She'd never felt anything like this before. 'Andrew is staying on after everyone leaves. Could I pick you up this evening?'

'Yes. Why not?'

Miguel smiled at her. 'Bring a swimsuit. I know you enjoy swimming in the evenings.'

'Where are we going?' She was surprised, having expected to be taken to a bar for a quick drink.

'You will see,' Miguel said. 'Drive carefully, Jenny.'

'Yes, of course.'

She didn't know why, but those simple words were very warming. He sounded as though he really cared—or was that just wishful thinking on her part?

Jenny changed into a pair of light blue denims and a matching shirt for the evening, slinging a black sweater over her shoulders. It was a little cooler when the sun had gone and she might need it later. At the moment it was still very warm, and the breeze had disappeared as it often did in the evenings.

'Where are we going?' Jenny asked again as Miguel's car headed towards Malaga a few minutes after he had picked her up.

'To my own villa,' he replied. 'Want to change your mind and escape now?'

'No,' she said her mouth quirking as she heard the teasing note. 'Why—should I?'

'I might have something terrible in mind.'

'I very much doubt it,' Jenny replied. 'Somehow I don't see you as the type that needs to trap unsuspecting females by drugging their drinks. I imagine you might have trouble in holding them off.'

Miguel's throaty chuckle sent little tingles of pleasure down her spine. 'You are amazing, Jenny. At first glance you appear reserved, even a little staid sometimes—but underneath you are really quite different.'

'Thank you, sir.' Jenny bubbled with laughter. 'At least, I think that was a compliment?'

'Oh, yes,' he murmured. 'You can be sure of that.'

Jenny smiled. She noticed that Miguel had turned off the main road and was heading up the hill past thickly wooded slopes so that the sea was lost from view. The villa, when they reached it, was hidden away from the road by trees and a neat brick wall. The gardens were quite extensive and lush with lots of colour and flowering shrubs. She noticed a hard-court tennis area away to the right and, as they pulled round the side of the house, a large and very tempting-looking swimming pool, its water glinting in the evening sun.

'Now I know how you manage to get a tan despite being indoors so much of the time.'

'Swimming is excellent exercise,' Miguel said. 'I snatch as much time as I can out here, though obviously it isn't as often as I would like—but I think the best time is in the evening after the sun loses its power. The water always seems warmer then.'

'As long as you get dry quickly afterwards.' She was remembering the time they'd talked after she'd come back from the pool, interpreting that look in his eyes in a different way now.

'Yes.' He smiled at her, and she knew he was remembering too. Remembering the spark between them, which she'd thought might have been anger but which had plainly been a touch of fire. 'I'll show you the house first. Then we can swim—and eat afterwards.'

'I get food, too?' Jenny asked with a teasing look.

'Only if you help cook it.'

She laughed and got out of the car as he held the door for her. The villa was one of the largest she had seen on the costa. It looked as if it had been built some years previously, and the gardens and terraces were in immaculate order.

As Miguel unlocked the door and switched off the alarm, Jenny realized that this was very different from the holiday villas that her parents and their friends owned. More solidly built, it had heavy carved wood doors and the floors were of thick marble covered with rich, jewel-bright Persian rugs. These were the real things, not the copies sold to the naïve.

Some of the furniture was obviously Spanish and quite old, made of hardwood and very traditional. A glimpse of the kitchen and bathrooms told Jenny that these had been modernized recently and were luxurious, gleaming brightly. Two of the bedroom doors were open, and Jenny could see that these, too, were fresh and modern, with smart covers and lacquered furniture, but the lounge made her stop and stare.

The sofas and chairs were of black leather, and scattered with cushions of various blues and reds, which colours were picked up in the curtains or rugs. The coffee-tables were huge and made of heavy black marble slabs supported on impressive bronze stands with lion-claw feet. A three-foot-high bronze statue of a naked woman holding a torch aloft stood in one corner, a similar one of a man more modestly draped in a loincloth in another. Various other bronzes, including a beautiful gilded clock, which was obviously a valuable antique, were scattered here and there about the room, and there were several huge green plants in bold containers.

Miguel was watching her, an amused look in his eyes.

'Well, what is your verdict?'

'Impressive,' Jenny said. 'Aggressively male.'

'Yes, I suppose it does come over that way,' he said, and laughed. 'It wasn't intended as a statement. I inherited this place from my grandfather. Some of the stuff has belonged to the family from way back. I've changed the bedrooms and modernized the plumbing. Perhaps I should just throw out everything else and start again.'

'I didn't say it was awful, just overpowering, and surprising. You could tone it down a bit perhaps—throw that jungle out and have flowers.'

'Anything else?' Miguel was interested.

'Perhaps some plain cream curtains and cushions to give it a calmer feel, make it less busy.'

'More feminine?' Miguel suggested. 'I think that's a good idea for a start, Jenny. Will you help me choose them?'

'Yes, of course. If you really want me to.'

'I never say anything I don't mean. What will you drink?'

'Oh...a glass of white wine, please.'

'Feel free to use the pool,' Miguel said. 'You can change wherever you wish. *Mi casa es su casa.*'

'Thank you. I do know enough Spanish to interpret that.'

'You will have to take advanced lessons if you wish to live here. It isn't strictly necessary, but it will make things easier. You are bound to come up against someone who doesn't understand English—especially away from the costa.'

Miguel disappeared in the direction of the kitchen to

fetch their wine. Jenny went into the nearest bedroom, which was furnished in pretty shades of apricot and cream, and slipped into her bathing suit. She had chosen a one-piece this time in a bright turquoise colour. She put on the towelling robe she had brought with her and went out to the patio. The sun was still pleasantly warm as she dropped the robe onto a lounger and dived straight in at the deep end. She had swum three lengths when she saw Miguel.

He had changed into a pair of dark blue trunks. His body looked lean and hard, his skin slightly tanned. Jenny felt her throat spasm with what she knew was desire. She hauled herself onto the edge of the pool, watching as Miguel dived in, cutting through the water with clean, powerful strokes.

He swam several lengths then came over to her. She smiled down at him, then felt his strong hands about her hips as he pulled her into the water and hard against him.

As their lips met in a hungry, passionate kiss, his tongue flicked at her and she opened to him, allowing him to take possession of her mouth. Her body was melting with pleasure, her senses spinning out of control.

It wasn't just that she hadn't been in a relationship for a long time. No man had ever made her feel like this. Her response to him was instantaneous, urgent with need as her body came thrillingly alive. He had set her on fire and there was no putting it out—neither did she want to!

'I want to make love with you, Jenny,' he murmured against her ear. 'Do you want it, too?'

'Yes...' Her voice was hoarse. She was trembling with this desperate need inside her crying out to be fulfilled. 'Yes, please.'

Miguel carried her up the wide sloping steps at the shallow end, kissing her as he did so. Then he set her on her feet. Leaving her for a moment, he fetched a large white towel and wiped off the excess water, rubbing her skin until it glowed, then he wrapped her in her robe. He slipped on a similar one himself.

Jenny watched and waited until he came back to her. She seemed incapable of independent movement. For the moment all she could think of or feel was Miguel.

He took her in his arms again, kissing her, possessing her mouth so that she became liquid fire in his arms, her little moans of pleasure mingling with the rasp of his breathing. She knew he was very aroused and half expected him to take her there against a wall.

Instead, he lifted her in his arms once more and carried her inside the house. He was so strong! She knew that he carried her effortlessly, without strain, but when he laid her down on what she instinctively knew was his own bed, he was so gentle, tender. He untied the belt of her robe, easing it off her shoulders, kissing them, then her throat and her lips.

She kissed him back, murmuring in a teasing voice that he tasted of the swimming pool.

'I haven't got time to shower,' he said huskily. 'I want you too badly.'

Jenny smiled with delight. Had he suggested leaving her even for an instant she would have screamed in protest. She needed, wanted this so very much. Her body was burning up with desire, but her heart was rejoicing. This was love—the kind she had always longed for. She had no qualms about what was happening between them because it was so right. Everything that Miguel was doing to her felt so perfect.

Her hands slipped up into his hair, her fingers stroking

the sensitive nape of his neck. She heard his throaty growl of response, then their bodies were straining together, their breathing becoming more excited as they let go of all reservations, giving themselves up to the pleasure of loving.

She whimpered with pleasure as he explored and tasted every inch of her with his lips and tongue, giving herself up to the delight of his loving.

'Are you ready, darling?'

'Yes...' she whispered. 'I want to be completely yours, Miguel.'

Her body welcomed him, meeting his urgent thrusting with an equal need of her own, their bodies joined as one in the age-old dance of delight. Their skin was still cool from the water, which made the heat inside feel even more exciting and delicious.

And when they reached a sudden, tumultuous climax, Jenny clung to him with tears of joy slipping down her cheeks.

'I've never felt like this before...'

He kissed her nose and smiled. 'That was only the beginning. I believe I did warn you that I might have wicked things in mind.'

Jenny laughed up at him, eyes glowing. 'So do I,' she said. 'Why don't we have that shower together? Then perhaps I might cook you some dinner.'

CHAPTER SEVEN

IT WAS Miguel who cooked their supper—a magnificent one of cheese on toast—while Jenny curled up with a glass of wine and listened to soft music.

'This wasn't quite what I had in mind,' Jenny said. 'Not that it isn't very good, but I was thinking I might impress you with my cooking skills.'

'Another time,' he murmured. 'I have other skills in mind at the moment, and heavy meals don't go with making love.'

'You weren't thinking of repeating what happened just now?' Jenny teased, a gleam in her eyes.

'I was thinking maybe I could improve with practice.'

'I shall look forward to that.'

'Oh, you will, my darling,' Miguel told her wickedly. 'Quite often when we are married.'

'We are getting married, then?' Her brows arched as her heart began to skip like giddy hares in spring.

'You're a marriage-or-nothing kind of girl, aren't you?'

'Yes, but...' She was going to say that they needed to talk but the telephone shrilled before she could finish.

Miguel frowned as he answered. 'Elena? Calm down! You're rushing too much. Tell me what happened. Yes, I see. And you are where? Is Andrew with you? Why not? All right, I will be there as soon as I can.'

He switched off his mobile and looked at Jenny apologetically.

'Is something wrong?'

'Joachim has had an accident. They've taken him into Emergency. Elena is frantic—I could not really make out what she was saying half the time.'

'Yes, of course she would be.' Jenny stood up. 'I'll get dressed properly.'

Miguel swore, clearly annoyed. 'I thought we were safe this evening, but apparently she has quarrelled with Andrew and he is not with her. I have to go to her, Jenny.'

'Yes, of course you do. I'll come with you.'

'Are you sure you want to?' He looked bothered, harassed, as he raked his thick hair with his fingers. 'I was thinking I could get a taxi for you before I left.'

'I'm coming to the hospital with you,' Jenny said firmly. 'I may be able to help—and if I'm in the way I'll get a taxi from there.'

She left him to sort out everything else while she dressed and fixed her make-up, then she rang her mother on Miguel's mobile as he locked up and set the alarm. He glanced at her as he got into the car, and she saw that his expression was grim.

'Ready?'

'Yes, of course. Let's just hope it isn't too serious,' she said.

But unfortunately it was. Elena was weeping when they arrived. She grabbed Miguel as he reached her, beating at him with clenched fists and screaming. From what she could hear of Elena's incoherent words, Jenny gathered that Joachim had fallen and hit his head and was still unconscious.

'You've got to do something, Miguel!' Elena screamed. 'They took him away and won't let me see him...'

'She was hysterical, that's why they won't let her in there.'

'Jenny looked at the man who had spoken. He was perhaps thirty or so, tall, athletic, extremely good-looking, but his eyes were hard and there was a sour expression on his face.

'Shut up!' Elena turned on him viciously. 'This is all your fault. I hate you! I never want to see you again.'

'He fell, Elena.'

'You let him fall.' Her eyes blazed. 'I could kill you! You are careless and selfish—and you will never see your son again if I can help it.'

'In that case, I want a divorce so that I can marry and have another family,' he said, then turned on his heel and walked out.

So *that* was Juan! Elena's husband. Jenny thought she would be better off without that selfish man.

'I hate him,' Elena cried, subsiding into tears as Miguel held her in his arms, soothing her. 'You were right, Miguel. I should never have let him near Joachim.' She looked up fearfully. 'Will Joachim be all right? I'll die if he isn't.'

'I'll find out what I can,' Miguel said and glanced at Jenny. 'Look after her for me. I'm going to see what's happening.'

Jenny put her arms around Elena. She was sobbing uncontrollably, and there were no words of comfort to offer. Joachim was all she had, and it would destroy her if she lost him.

'I'm so sorry,' Jenny murmured when the sobs began to ease at last. 'Can you tell me what happened?'

'Juan was playing with him, making him over-excited,' Elena said bitterly. 'I warned him to stop but he wouldn't listen, then Joachim fell and hit his head against one of the pots.' She gave a little cry of despair. 'Juan said it was my fault for having them everywhere, but nothing like this has ever happened before…and Joachim is so little. He was so white and still, Jenny. I can't bear it if he dies.'

'We don't know how serious it is yet,' Jenny said. 'Perhaps he's just concussed. He may come round and— Here's Miguel.' She looked at him anxiously as he came up to them. His expression was grim, and she knew the news wasn't good.

'He's still unconscious, but holding his own for the moment,' Miguel said. 'You can see him if you promise to be calm. You have to think of him, Elena, not yourself. Joachim is the important one at the moment.'

'Yes, I know,' she whispered, her eyes wide and dark with fear. She wiped her face with the handkerchief he gave her. 'Don't scold me, Miguel. There's only you now. I need you to love me.'

'I shall take you to him,' Miguel said, then glanced past her to Jenny. His manner was cool, detached. She felt as though she were looking at a stranger, not the man she had been making love with less than an hour ago. 'We shall be here all night. There is no point in you waiting. Have you money for a taxi home?'

'Yes, of course.' Jenny was hurt by the way he suddenly seemed to shut her out. 'You will ring me?'

'When I have news.' His face was white, his mouth harsh.

Miguel had his arm about his sister, supporting her slightly unsteady gait as they walked away. Jenny watched them and felt upset. She would have preferred to have stayed and offered what help or comfort she could, but it seemed that neither of them needed her.

* * *

Jenny was unable to sleep for most of the night. She lay staring into the darkness, feeling tense and upset. Why had Miguel shut her out? Why had he not wanted her to go to the hospital with him in the first place? Her heart ached as she waited for the call that would tell her the crisis was over, but it didn't come.

In the morning there were shadows beneath her eyes and she felt terrible. She was drinking her fourth cup of coffee when her mother came into the kitchen, still wearing her dressing-gown and looking anxious.

'No news yet, then?' Beth asked.

'Not yet.' Jenny glanced at her uncertainly. 'Should I ring the hospital and ask?'

'Dr Sanchez said he would ring. Perhaps you ought to wait. The child isn't your patient and he's not a relative.'

'No, I know...' Jenny jumped as her mobile suddenly shrieked. 'Yes. Miguel? How is he?'

'Not much better. They think there may be a blood clot near his brain. I believe they are going to operate soon.'

'Oh, Miguel! I am so sorry.'

'Look, I cannot leave Elena. She will not go home. I am worried about what all this is doing to her. I am cancelling all my hospital appointments for the next few days. Can you look after things at the clinic—cope with the evening house calls?'

'Yes, of course I can. Don't worry about that side of things, Miguel.'

'I have to go back now. They want to talk to me. I am not sure when I will be able to ring again.'

Jenny stared at her mobile as he rang off. She was glad that she was able to help in some small way, yet she felt as if he had somehow closed a door on her.

'Was it bad news?'

Her mother's question brought her back to reality. 'Yes, pretty rough. They seem to think there may be a small clot pressing against his brain—it means an operation.'

'That's terrible, Jenny.' Beth's eyes filled with sympathetic tears. 'That poor woman—as if she hasn't got enough to bear!'

'It makes things worse,' Jenny agreed. 'With her illness it's unlikely she could or would want to have another baby. If she loses Joachim...'

She was too upset to continue. Mother and daughter stared at each other in distress.

'If I had lost you...' Beth wiped away a tear. 'Well, we mustn't look on the black side. Perhaps it won't be as bad as it sounds.'

'It's bad enough,' Jenny replied. 'Any operation of this kind carries a high risk. All we can do for the moment is wait and pray.'

Jenny couldn't stop thinking about what Miguel and his family were going through. She carried her anxiety with her all day, though she didn't let it affect her work. Patients were entitled to her full attention, and she completed each examination with meticulous care.

It was almost better when she was with a patient. The atmosphere in the clinic was sombre. Soraya looked as if she might burst into tears at any moment, and Isabelle was looking less than her glamorous self with red eyes and a blotchy nose.

There was no news until late that afternoon, and then the phone rang and somehow Jenny knew it was Miguel. Soraya answered and handed it to her with an agonized look.

'Miguel—how is he?'

'He has come through it,' Miguel said tersely. 'It was a long operation and we thought we might lose him. He may have some slight brain damage, but he is alive. He hasn't come out of the anesthetic yet, but I feel pretty certain he is going to be OK.'

'Thank God,' Jenny said, and nodded to the anxious Soraya. 'Where is Elena? How is she?'

'She collapsed from exhaustion this morning. They gave her a bed on the medical ward and she is under sedation. It is probably the best thing for her at the moment.'

'Yes, I expect so,' Jenny said. 'And you? You must be so tired. You should go home and rest.'

'I am going home to change and eat something, then I shall come back to the hospital. I have to be here if…when he wakes up.'

'Yes, of course. This has been terrible for you, too, Miguel.'

'Yes.' He was abrupt, shutting out her sympathy instantly. 'You are sure you can manage? It is a lot to ask—the clinic and the house calls.'

'Don't give it a thought,' Jenny said. 'I shan't let you down, Miguel. I promise.'

'I know that. I was thinking of you. I am sorry, Jenny. It is no good. I have to go.'

'You will ring again?'

'When I can.'

Jenny replaced the receiver with a sigh. She told Soraya and Isabelle the latest news on Joachim.

'They can't tell yet whether he'll have any permanent ill-effects from the operation. I think it was quite difficult to get the clot and he may have suffered some damage—but at least he's alive.'

'But he was so perfect,' Isabelle said, and fled into the bathroom, where she could be heard sobbing.

'We were all so fond of him,' Soraya mumbled, and blew her nose. 'Dr Sanchez brought him to the clinic sometimes. He adores him. I don't know what Elena will do if... She thought the world of that child, worshipped him.'

'Yes, I know. It's very hard for all of them, and I know it must hurt to see a beloved child damaged,' Jenny said. 'But none of that will change. Even if Joachim isn't quite so perfect in the future we shall all still love him—perhaps even more.'

Soraya nodded, but it was clear that she was too upset to think about it in a calm way. Jenny was very upset herself. She didn't know the child well, but she had been charmed by him, as everyone who had encountered him had been. But it was of Miguel's pain that she was thinking, of what he must be suffering. He couldn't give way to tears—or only in private.

'Well, we have to keep things running here,' Jenny reminded the nurse. 'If we get any calls for house visits you'll have to provide me with a map, Soraya. Now, I think we ought to have a cup of coffee to keep our spirits up, don't you?'

'You talk as if what has happened means nothing,' Isabelle said from behind her. 'You do not understand what a child means to us. How could you? You are English. The English are unkind to their children.'

Jenny turned to face her. She saw the spite in Isabelle's face and wondered what she had done to arouse such dislike in the other woman. She had always been pleasant to her but, then, the hostility had been there from the beginning.

'I may not be Spanish,' she said quietly, 'but I understand how Miguel feels about his nephew. Perhaps better than you think.'

Isabelle glared at her. 'I wish you had not come here! We do not want you.'

'Be quiet!' Soraya said sharply. 'We need Dr Talforth and I am very glad she is here. If you are rude to her again I shall tell Dr Sanchez that I cannot work with you.'

Isabelle gave her an angry glare, then turned away as the phone rang. Soraya began to apologize for her, but Jenny shook her head.

'It doesn't matter,' she said. 'If we argue amongst ourselves, everything will go wrong. We all owe it to Miguel to make sure we do our jobs as well as we can.'

She turned and went into her consulting room. Alone, she almost gave way to tears, but the thought of what Miguel was going through gave her the strength to conquer them. It was her responsibility to make sure the patients didn't suffer—and she had to be ready when Miguel needed her.

Surely he would turn to her for comfort at some point? Jenny couldn't believe that the time they had spent together at his villa meant nothing to him. For her it had been the most wonderful moment of her life when he'd spoken of them spending their lives together—for he *had* begun to speak of marriage before Elena had phoned.

Jenny knew that she was very much in love. If she were in Miguel's shoes she would want him to comfort her, to put his arms about her and tell her it was going to be all right. Surely he must need her, too?

She realized that he had been used to standing tall, to carrying the burden of his family's needs alone—but he must know that there was no longer any need for that?

* * *

The next week was one of the worst of Jenny's life. She did her work as calmly and efficiently as ever, but she was consciously waiting for Miguel's telephone calls the whole time. They were always brief, giving the minimum of information, but at least he did ring. It was usually in the evening, when she was at home, asking how her day had gone, if she was coping.

'How is Joachim?' she asked every night, and the answer was always the same.

'Holding his own. Very sleepy. It's the drugs...'

'Yes, of course. Is Elena better?'

'They are keeping her on the ward under observation. She hardly speaks—unless I sit with her and force her to answer. I have taken her in a wheelchair to see Joachim, because she is incapable of walking at the moment. She cried so much that they asked me not to take her again until he is stronger.'

'She was bound to be upset, seeing him like that, with all the drips and things. Relatives find that so hard to bear because it looks so frightening. You must be so worried yourself, Miguel. Are you getting some sleep and enough to eat?'

'I am managing. I just hope he will be OK in the end, because I do not know what Elena will do if he isn't. It will kill her if—'

'He's going to be fine,' Jenny said. 'He is alive—and he will still be Joachim, whatever. Love doesn't disappear because a child is brain-damaged, Miguel—in fact, it often deepens, becomes more precious. I've seen that with my patients. You must have, too.'

'Yes, of course. But Elena isn't like other parents, Jenny. I have to go now.'

Jenny understood why he was so worried. Joachim had been such a bright child, always into mischief. It would be hard to accept if his personality had changed, if he had some paralysis or was unable to communicate.

But there was nothing anyone could do except wait and pray.

Jenny telephoned Moya in England, explaining how things stood.

'You're still welcome to come over. I should love to see you, but I shan't have much time to spare.'

'That doesn't matter, as long as I'm not in the way.'

'No, of course not. It just means I won't be as free to be with you as I would have been. I'm sorry, but it can't be helped.'

'Then I'll come out as planned. I've booked the flight and it would be a shame to waste the ticket. Don't worry, Jenny. I can find plenty to amuse myself.'

'I'll see you on Saturday, then.'

Jenny wished in a way that Moya wasn't coming, but she hadn't got the heart to turn her friend down. And when Moya did arrive she was suddenly glad to see her. She hugged her and shed a few tears.

'Hey! It's only a few weeks since you left,' Moya said, and gave her an intent look. 'What have they been doing to you out here?'

'Nothing,' Jenny replied, and wiped away her tears. She gave Moya a watery smile. 'I'm being daft! It is just that it's been so tense this past week, that's all.'

'This kid really means a lot to you—or is it his uncle?'

'Both...' Jenny laughed. 'Am I that easy to read?'

'Only to me, kid.' Moya grinned cheekily at her. 'So you finally went and found yourself a man. The saints be praised! He must be something special.'

'Yes, I think so,' Jenny said, her mouth softening with love as she thought of Miguel, of the way he had held her and made love to her. Oh, how she wished she could believe it would happen again! 'Everything was going so well and now...it's as if I'm a stranger to him.'

'He's worried to death,' Moya said. 'Who wouldn't be, in his shoes? You can't expect romance from a man in his situation, Jenny. Give the poor guy a chance!'

'I'm so glad you're here.'

Moya's straight talking did Jenny a power of good, blowing away the clouds that had hung over her all week. She felt more cheerful than she had since Joachim's accident, and on Sunday she took her friend to Club Miraflores for a meal.

'This is nice here,' Moya said. 'Yes, I like it—I like the friendly atmosphere. I think I ought to find myself a job out here.'

'I wish you meant that,' Jenny said.

'Well, you never know.' Moya grinned at her. 'Tell me, who's that ladykiller staring at us so hard?'

Jenny glanced in the direction she indicated and grimaced.

'Clive Jacobs. I hope he isn't coming over...'

But, of course, he did, and after seeing how the wind was blowing Moya did her best to transfer his interest from Jenny to her. She was successful, and by the time the evening was over he was showing signs of drooling. He had asked Moya for a date, and they had arranged to have dinner on Tuesday evening.

'You are sure you don't want him?' Moya asked as the two friends walked home later.

'Quite sure, thank you.'

'In that case, I shall feel free to bedazzle and ensnare him,' Moya said, laughing.

They were still laughing when they entered the villa.

Mrs Talforth was making her bedtime drink and smiled as she saw them.

'That's nice to hear,' she said. 'It sounds as if you both enjoyed yourselves.'

'It was great,' Moya said.

'That's good. I like to see young people happy,' Beth said. 'Dr Sanchez rang, Jenny. I told him you'd gone out with a friend for the evening, and he said it wasn't important.'

Jenny nodded. She'd hoped he might ring earlier, before she'd gone out. Now he would probably think that she had just gone off somewhere and didn't care about Joachim—or him.

No, of course he wouldn't! He must know how she felt.

She made a drink for herself and Moya, and her friend sat on talking for another hour. By that time Jenny thought it was probably too late to ring Miguel. She would try first thing in the morning.

Miguel sat in the dark, staring out at the pool, which had underwater lighting and looked very tempting. If only there was someone here with him to share a late night swim. He thought he would never be able to look at the pool again without thinking of Jenny, remembering the softness of her skin, the way she'd felt in his arms and the scent of her.

'Damn!' He swore as the desire burned inside him, making him very aware of his need, physically and emotionally. It had been a long time since he'd felt this way about a woman. In fact, he wasn't sure he ever had. 'Damn! Damn it!'

This was the first time he had come home to sleep since Joachim's accident. He had been snatching odd hours on a bed in his consulting room at the hospital. It had been a traumatic week, but the hospital had now cut down the painkilling drugs that had been constantly pumping into the child since his operation, and for the first time that afternoon Joachim had given Miguel a sleepy smile. It was a smile so like the ones that had captured his heart of old that Miguel had almost wept.

It seemed that Joachim was still there, his warm, loving personality waiting to reassert itself. Surely it was a sign that he was going to be OK? For all his years of training and dedicated service as a doctor, Miguel was as unsure and terrified as any relative whose loved one had nearly died. It did look as if the signs were good. Although Joachim wasn't out of the woods yet, he was making progress.

Miguel had wanted to tell Jenny the good news. He had been going to try and explain his behaviour over the past week. It was inexcusable, of course. He had made love to her, talking about marriage and then abandoned her. But what else could he have done?

Shared his fears with her, told her how much he missed her?

Jenny would have been willing to listen, he knew that. The lack—if that was the right word—was in him, not her.

Miguel was used to carrying his burdens alone. It had begun with the death of his father and had carried on through his mother's painful illness. Elena had been unable to cope, so he had sheltered her from as much as he could. He had been there for her when the news of her own problem had come as such a shattering blow, talking to her, explaining what it all meant, easing her terror. His had been the shoulder she'd cried on when Juan had walked out on her.

Miguel had hoped she was beginning to accept Andrew, not as a substitute, because her brother would always be there for her if she needed him, but as another person she could trust. She had so far refused to tell him why she had quarrelled with Andrew, but he suspected it had been because of Juan.

He thought her marriage was now finally over. Divorce wasn't an easy thing for a Catholic, but if both sides were willing to persevere something might be arranged. Would Elena want a new relationship then? Was there even a chance of her getting together with Andrew?

It would make it easier for Miguel to develop his own relationship with Jenny. Of course, he could simply get married—but what woman wanted to play second fiddle to her husband's sister?

Jenny was far more understanding than Maribelle had ever been, but did he have the right to ask so much of her?

If Elena became slowly worse she was bound to make more and more demands on his time because he couldn't simply abandon her to paid carers. She needed someone to love her.

Perhaps it would be fairer to call a halt with Jenny now? He hated to do that, both because he had discovered that he wanted her more than he had realized at the start and because it made him look as if he had been using her. She would naturally be angry, and she would probably walk out of the clinic—but the alternative was to give her so much less than she deserved. And with her looks and that wonderful smile, she would easily find someone else.

After all, she had told him that she didn't believe in romantic love.

* * *

Jenny was relieved that Moya was going out with Clive the following evening. She could not have been sure of being free until after nine and she was feeling tired. They seemed to be getting busier all the time at the clinic and another sleepless night had taken its toll.

She had tried ringing Miguel a couple of times, but there was only an answering service that asked her to telephone the emergency centre if her need was urgent. Otherwise, she was requested to leave a message. On the third occasion she did so.

'This is Jenny—please, ring me. It's personal, not the clinic. Everything is fine there so don't worry. Give my love to Elena and Joachim, and take care of yourself.'

She waited all day and all evening for him to ring her back, but there was no call. Jenny swung between anxiety that there had been some kind of setback with the little boy and anger that Miguel hadn't bothered to get in touch.

What did he think he was playing at, for goodness' sake? She wasn't just a colleague—there was more than that between them. Or had she read a lot more into what had happened that night at his villa than had really been there?

As each day passed without a word from Miguel a sick feeling began to grow inside Jenny. She knew he had been in contact with Soraya at the clinic, but he hadn't asked to speak to her—why? What had she done? He could surely have replied to her message! Why was he ignoring her? Was this Miguel's way of telling her that that evening at his villa had been a mistake?

Surely that wasn't true? They had been so happy until Elena had telephoned. Miguel had spoken of marriage— or had she imagined that part? Had he merely been teasing her? Everything that had happened afterwards had been so traumatic that their time together had begun to seem like a dream.

Somehow Jenny managed to get through the week. She went out a couple of times with Moya, taking her mobile with her.

'If Miguel rings here tell him to try my mobile,' she told her mother. 'Please, Mum. Make sure he knows I want to speak to him.'

'Of course I will, Jenny. I'd have thought he would have rung you before this.'

Jenny nodded but didn't answer. She couldn't bring herself to blame Miguel, even though his neglect was hurting her. He was just so wrapped up in what was happening at the hospital that he hadn't had time to think about her.

On Friday night, Jenny had a couple of drinks at a bar with Moya and then went home. Moya was going on to a nightclub in Puerto Banus with Clive.

'I want to make my last night special,' Moya said. 'You are sure you don't mind?'

'Of course not.' Jenny smiled at her. 'I'm afraid I haven't been much company for you.'

'No worries! I've had a great time,' Moya said. 'I might even come out here to live. Clive offered me a job yesterday.'

'You mean you'd give up nursing?' Jenny was shocked and disbelieving. 'But it's your life. You've always said it was more important than anything...'

'Sometimes it's good to have a change,' Moya replied. 'I haven't made up my mind yet. We'll see what this evening brings forth.'

Jenny shook her head and said no more. Clive wasn't her type, but he might be Moya's.

She was sitting on the terrace at home a little later

when she heard the phone ring in the house. Her mother came to call her.

'Is it Miguel?'

'No—James Redfern.'

Jenny took the phone reluctantly. 'James? Where are you?'

'In Malaga. I'm coming your way tomorrow afternoon. Are you free?'

'Well, I'm on call, but you could come to the villa if you like.'

'Yes, I would like to if that's all right. I wanted to have a little chat—and I'm going to a rather nice party later. Would you be interested in coming with me?'

'It's kind of you to ask,' Jenny said, 'but I'm afraid I can't manage it.'

'That's a shame. Still, never mind. There's always another time. I'll see you tomorrow at about three, OK?'

'Yes. Yes, of course. I'll look forward to it.'

Jenny replaced the receiver, feeling puzzled by his previous remark. What did he mean about another time? He was hardly likely to be out here often—was he?

'Are you going to the party tomorrow?' Beth asked as Jenny wandered into the kitchen in search of a drink.

'I told him I couldn't manage it.'

'Why? Moya will have left us by then. You'll only sit here on your own, waiting for the phone to ring.' Beth frowned. 'I must say I'm surprised at the way Dr Sanchez has behaved over this, Jenny. He could have phoned you—it's only polite.'

'Yes, he could,' Jenny said. 'But he hasn't—which must mean that he has nothing particular to say to me, mustn't it?'

She took her drink back outside. It was almost dark, just the faint glow of the lights from the road below her winding away along the coast. The air was still warm, faintly perfumed with the scent of roses. In a few minutes she would go in and wash her hair. Miguel wasn't likely to come now.

'Jenny...' His voice startled her. She swung round, straining to see him in the half-light, and then he walked forward so that the light from the house fell on his face and she thought he looked drained, exhausted. 'I am sorry if I frightened you.'

'No, I wasn't frightened, merely startled. I wasn't expecting you.' Her voice had gone cold. She wasn't sure why but she felt very angry suddenly. 'Why didn't you return my call?'

'You said it was not urgent.'

'I said it was personal.'

'Yes, I am sorry. I should have called but I have been very busy. I have had to divide my time between the patients I cancelled last week, Elena and Joachim.'

He'd had time for them, of course! Well, that ought to tell her something—where she came in the order of what was important to him. And that was last!

'I've been worried. How is Joachim?' She managed to sound calm, almost impersonal.

'Better, thank God. He seems to respond to people when they talk to him, though he has not spoken yet and he is very poorly still. Elena is the one causing a problem now. She will not eat or talk—except to Joachim. She wants to take him home but, of course, the hospital will not allow it yet. They will not even consider it until she starts to eat and behave normally. They don't believe she is capable of looking after herself, let alone a very sick little boy.'

'Surely Maria can help? And you could get a nurse in...'

'Yes, but Maria is not always able to be there at night. It means I may have to move in for a while—when they are prepared to let Joachim go home.'

'I see...' Jenny understood what he was telling her. His commitment to his sister was going to increase, and he wouldn't have time for her.

'I came this evening to apologize,' Miguel said huskily. 'I have behaved badly as far as you are concerned.'

'Yes, you have.' She wasn't going to let him get off lightly. 'I wanted to help and you shut me out.'

'I know. I am sorry, believe me,' Miguel said. 'I am not asking you to forgive, only to understand.'

'Understand what?' She raised her eyes to his, forcing him to meet her gaze.

'Why I have to put whatever was beginning between us on hold. I cannot commit to a relationship at the moment, Jenny. Not until Elena is back to what she was...if ever.'

Jenny's eyes were intent on his face. His expression was harsh, impenetrable. He couldn't stand there like that if he loved her, saying things that he must know were breaking her heart! Surely he must know that this was ripping her to shreds?

But she wasn't going to show it, she wasn't going to cry and beg for him to love her.

'Well, that's that, then, isn't it?'

'For the moment, yes.' Miguel's dark eyes seemed to glitter with a silver flame in the light of the moon, which had just sailed out from behind a bank of clouds. 'I am very sorry, Jenny.'

'Yes,' she said softly. 'So am I.'

The tension between them was almost unbearable. Jenny felt as if she couldn't breathe. Why couldn't he see what his stubbornness was doing to them?

'Miguel...'

His eyes seemed to snap with fire. He gave a strangled cry, then reached out and grabbed her, his kiss harsh, brutal, bruising her lips with its intensity. Then, just as abruptly, he let her go. The fire had gone out of him, and he was as cold as ice.

'It was just sex,' he said. 'We are grown-ups, Jenny. I cannot give you any more right now.'

Then he turned and walked away, leaving her staring after him as the pain began. Jenny wanted to run after him. She wanted to scream and shout as Elena had, to beat at him with her fists, make him think about her feelings, her pain. Of course, she didn't do anything so uncivilized.

She wasn't important enough to him. Miguel had decided he had to choose between her and Elena, and his sister had won.

It was natural enough. He loved Elena and his nephew very much, and she could understand that—but why couldn't he share his love with her too?

The answer wasn't very pleasant but she had to face up to it. He had just told her quite bluntly. The other evening, when he had made love to her so magically, had been about sexual desire—nothing more. Jenny was simply a woman he had shared an amusing interlude with, someone to spend a little time with when he'd had nothing better to do.

She knew she was probably being unfair to him. He was in an awkward situation. Both Elena and Joachim needed him—but he could have shared his problems with her. She could have helped to care for his sister and that poor little boy.

Jenny's heart ached for the whole family. But what could she do when Miguel had deliberately shut her out?

CHAPTER EIGHT

'I DON'T believe it! You, getting married?' Jenny stared at her friend in disbelief. 'But you've always said it wasn't for you, that you were married to your career.'

'I've fallen in love,' Moya said. 'It's that simple, Jenny. I never expected it to happen, and I can't explain why Clive is the one—but he is and I'm happy.'

'I am so glad for you!' Jenny hugged her. 'Where will you get married—out here?'

'No way,' Moya said, and gurgled with pure joy. 'My mother would never forgive me. No, I'm going home to tell her the good news when I get back. Clive is flying over next week. We'll have a special licence and a family do at a hotel, then come back here to live. You will come over for the wedding?'

'Yes, of course,' Jenny promised, and hugged her again. 'I've got to clear my things from the house. Oh, poor Angie! She's going to need two new friends to share the house with her.'

'Her boyfriend will probably move in with her,' Moya said. 'He's been asking about your room. You've made up your mind to stay here, then—even after this last week?'

'Yes. Nothing has changed at work. I need hardly see Miguel if I prefer not to. Besides, I can find another job if I have to. Yes, I shall stay. I like it here.' She smiled bravely. 'Ring me when you have a date for the wedding?'

'Yes, of course.'

They kissed and Moya went out to her waiting taxi. Jenny drove to the clinic. She was delighted with her friend's news. Perhaps she had misjudged Clive. He couldn't be all bad if Moya loved him.

But, then, women often fell for men who let them down! Jenny was still feeling hurt after the way Miguel had told her they were finished. He had spoken of putting their relationship on hold, but that had just been an easy get-out. What he'd really meant was that he was prepared to have a casual fling, but anything else was out of bounds. Anger rushed in, smothering the hurt. How could she have thought he was so special? He was the same as all the others!

When she arrived at the clinic, her problem suddenly got worse. Isabelle was standing outside, waiting.

'Where is Soraya?'

Isabelle shrugged. 'She doesn't tell me what she does.' She muttered something in Spanish under her breath. Jenny couldn't catch it, but she suspected it was rude.

She unlocked the clinic with her keys. The light was flashing on the answering machine. Jenny played back the recorded message.

'I am so sorry,' Soraya's voice was breathy with anxiety. 'My husband was fixing the roof and fell off the ladder. He has hurt his leg. I am at the hospital. It may be a few days before I can get back to work.'

'Oh, poor Soraya,' Jenny said. 'It looks as if we shall have to cope on our own, Isabelle.'

Isabelle's only answer was a black look. Jenny frowned. Clearly the receptionist was going to make things as difficult as possible.

The rest of the morning proved that she could expect

no help from the girl, who was clearly sulking over something. She answered the phone and took messages, but made no attempt to do any of the things Soraya usually did. Jenny had to ask the patients to come through when she was ready, and to dispense medication when necessary. She kept the key to the dangerous drugs cabinet firmly in her pocket.

Fortunately there were no emergency call-outs. Jenny had never been so relieved to see the end of the morning's work. She took a little time to make sure that everything was locked, and she counted the boxes of pethidine. They tallied with the list.

It was as she was about to leave that the phone shrilled. Jenny sighed. If she left it, the automatic transfer to the emergency service would take over—but it might be urgent. She went back and answered it.

'Jenny? I've just heard about Soraya's husband. She is going to be away for at least a couple of days. Can you manage?' Miguel asked.

'I should imagine so. I've coped this morning.'

'I could get a temporary nurse but she might not speak English as well as Soraya.'

'I told you, I can manage. For a while anyway.'

There was a pause. 'You are angry.'

'Yes, yes, I am,' Jenny said. 'Was there anything else? Only I do have a private life...'

'We must talk...'

'I think you said all there was to say last night.'

Jenny put the receiver down with a bang. It started to ring again but she left it and went out, taking care that the door was properly locked. If anything went wrong while Soraya was away, Jenny would be to blame. She was angry, but she still didn't want to cause trouble for Miguel.

Her mobile rang as she drove home. She had it set so that she could see who was calling. It was Miguel and so she didn't answer. She wasn't prepared to talk to him at the moment—she'd had enough!

However, when her mother's phone rang soon after she got home Jenny had calmed down enough to think rationally. She couldn't go on ignoring his calls. She answered the phone, and it was Sally Marshall on the other end.

'Jenny, it's Sally. I'm ringing to invite you to a party in three weeks' time. It's on the Saturday evening—will you be able to come?'

'I should be able get there,' Jenny said. 'Unless there's a dire emergency—like my host collapsing with flu or something.'

Sally laughed. 'Bob is fine and so am I. Isn't it good news about Clive and your friend Moya? I met her one evening and I think she's perfect for him. Clive needs someone to keep him in line and I think she has him taped.'

'Yes, it's wonderful news,' Jenny said. 'It will be nice having her out here. Moya is a lot of fun to know.'

'We shall have lots of parties,' Sally said. 'Well, the children are clamouring for their lunch. What are you going to do today?'

'Fall asleep in the sun, I should think.'

'Well, enjoy,' Sally said, and rang off.

Jenny sighed as she glanced at herself in the mirror. She was feeling low, but it wasn't really lack of sleep that was bothering her. She had thought she might be able to stay on at the clinic but now she wasn't sure it would work. She couldn't argue with her boss all the time—and, however badly Miguel had behaved, he deserved respect as far as work was concerned.

She supposed she could find a job at one of the other clinics on the costa. There were enough of them, for goodness' sake! The thought of starting again was singularly unappealing. Besides, she imagined the contract she'd signed was binding. If Miguel wanted to be difficult...but he wouldn't. He had behaved badly towards Jenny, but it wasn't really his fault. He would see that it was best for all concerned that she should go. She would wait until he could replace her, of course.

As her anger waned so the pain began. Memories of the way they had been together that night and others of the friendly, happy family life that had seemed to beckon in the future came back to haunt her. She felt the sting of tears, but blinked them away. Crying never helped. And she was a fool to care about a man who only wanted her for a casual affair!

Jenny suddenly remembered that James Redfern was calling that afternoon. She had completely forgotten about it! She stacked the dirty dishes for her mother, started the dishwasher and then went to take a shower.

Looking at herself in the bedroom mirror half an hour later, Jenny wondered why she had chosen to wear the white jeans and the skimpy pink top. She had brushed her heavy, straight hair loose and applied a shimmer of matching pink lipstick. She didn't need any other makeup now that her skin had acquired a golden tan.

She wondered what James would think of the change in her. She was sure he would be surprised, but would he approve of her new image?

She laughed at her reflection. It didn't matter what James thought—it didn't matter at all!

She answered the door to him herself. He stared at her for a moment, his eyes opening wide in surprise. He was wearing the kind of business suit he had always wore, his only concession to the weather being that he had left the jacket in his hired car.

'Good grief! Is that really you, Jenny?'

'Yes. Do I look so different, James?'

'Very. The air out here must suit you.'

'I think it's the tan—and the clothes,' she said. His expression gave her a feeling of satisfaction. Maybe he was beginning to realize she wasn't such a mouse after all! 'Will you come in? I thought we would sit in the garden. There's an umbrella if you want to be in the shade.'

She led him through the house, introducing him to her mother.

'It is nice to meet you, Dr Redfern.'

'Thank you, Mrs Talforth. You have a nice place here.'

'We like it. Let Jenny show you the garden and the view.'

James exclaimed as he saw their view. 'This is delightful. I must look for something similar if I decide to buy out here.'

Jenny invited him to sit in one of the comfortable basket chairs, which was shaded by a bright yellow umbrella. 'Are you thinking of buying a holiday home?'

'It may be rather more than that,' James replied. He was looking at her with more interest than he had ever shown before. 'I've been invited to set up a private clinic on a prestigious new complex further up the coast. A friend of mine has a controlling interest in the commercial section—it's big business, Jenny.'

'Yes, I suppose it must be for him. But it's surely not for you, is it, James? You wouldn't consider giving up your own practice?'

'At first I was inclined to turn the idea down flat,' James admitted. 'But then I decided to attend the conference in Malaga—that's a separate matter entirely. Just another AIDS awareness thing.'

'Rather important, wouldn't you say?'

'It would be if they ever did anything,' James said with a wry grimace. 'I'm afraid I get bored with hearing the same old arguments. It's time someone did something instead of talking!'

'I agree with you,' Jenny said. 'Something has to be done. Far too many people are dying, particularly in Africa. It's an international scandal.'

James nodded. 'I couldn't agree more. I've already written a paper on the possible alternatives. Well, I'm in danger of becoming a bore on the subject. Are you sure you won't come to this party, Jenny?'

'Quite sure,' she said, and smiled. 'I'm sorry you've had a wasted trip out here— Ah, here's our coffee.' She looked up at her mother and thanked her.

James was watching her as she poured for them both. 'Yes, milk and sugar, please. It wasn't a waste of time, Jenny. You see, I wanted to ask if you would join me if I decided to have a go at this thing.'

'The clinic?' He nodded and she was surprised. 'I'm not sure...' She wanted to say no at once, but caution held her back. She might be looking for a job in a few months, and working with James hadn't been so bad in the past. She was no longer under any illusions about her feelings towards him, which would make it very much easier this time around. 'I would have to think about it carefully if you decided to go ahead.'

'But you're not definitely turning me down?' He arched his brows, a faint smile on his mouth.

'No, I'm not turning you down, James,' she said. 'Nor

am I saying that I would join you if you went ahead. I'm saying that I would think about it.'

'Well, that's fair enough,' James agreed. 'I did rather spring the whole thing on you.'

'Yes.' Jenny smiled. 'What has made you think about making a change in your working life?'

'Perhaps because you did,' he replied honestly. 'I kept thinking about you after you left, Jenny. I didn't expect to miss you, but I found that I did…rather a lot.'

How much those words would have meant once! Now she was able to laugh and shake her head at him. Spain and meeting Miguel had done that for her. She knew what being in love really meant now, and would never settle for less.

'Having woman trouble, James?'

He gave her a rueful look. 'That's putting it mildly. My own fault, of course.'

'Now I know why you've come,' she teased. 'You're escaping.'

James threw back his head and laughed. 'I never realized what a treasure you were, Jenny. Why didn't I see it when you were under my nose?'

She gave him a considered look. 'Why not indeed? Perhaps you were too busy chasing all the others, James.'

They were laughing together with the ease of old friends when Miguel walked round the side of the garden. He stood watching them for a moment, frowning. Jenny glanced up and saw him as he was about to turn away.

'Miguel!' she called. 'Come and meet my friend from England.'

Miguel hesitated, then came towards them. Jenny and James had risen to their feet.

'James, this is Dr Sanchez. Miguel, this is Dr Redfern. We were colleagues at home.'

The two men shook hands, but neither of them smiled. Jenny sensed that they had taken an instant dislike to one another and wondered why.

'Will you have coffee, Miguel?' Jenny asked. 'Or something cold?'

He looked as if he meant to refuse, then changed his mind. 'I'll have a cold drink,' he said. 'Water or fruit juice. I have to drive later.'

'Yes, of course,' she said. 'I'll fetch some drinks. I'm sure you can find something to talk about while I've gone.'

Her heart was thumping wildly as she went back into the house, but she was determined to remain calm, even a little distant. Miguel wasn't going to start an argument while James was there, and somehow she meant to keep him there for the next hour.

The two men were talking about the conference when she returned with her tray. They both jumped up to take it from her, but James was the nearest. Miguel glared at him and at her.

He was very angry. Why was he angry? He had made it clear he wasn't ready to have a relationship with her so why should it annoy him to see her talking to another man?

'I've just been asking Sanchez what he thinks the chances are for the class of place we're setting up, Jenny. When I told you about it, I neglected to explain that I meant the kind of exclusive clinic we have at home, with facilities for patients to stay. We shall do routine treatments, plastic surgery and health and fitness routines, as well as medical consultations.'

'Oh, I see. I hadn't realized you meant that kind of

clinic.' He was talking about what most people would call a health club, she supposed.

Jenny was annoyed. He had obviously been talking about his plans to Miguel, perhaps implying that she was considering joining his team. She imagined that people who could afford it would enjoy coming to Spain for such treatments. Now she understood what was being planned, it was an interesting concept—if she wanted to work in that kind of medicine.

What Jenny liked about Miguel's clinic was that it had the common touch. The patients paid for treatment, but those on the insurance panel were far more like the people she would deal with at home on the NHS. People like Mrs Jeffries and her own parents.

She handed out drinks, and then sat down to watch and listen as the two men talked. How shallow James seemed compared to Miguel! She'd sensed it when she'd first met Miguel, but now she could see and hear it. She would be mad to even think of leaving Miguel's clinic to work for James!

Leaving personal considerations aside, she still knew where she wanted to be—but she couldn't be sure Miguel would want her to stay on after her behaviour that morning.

She kept thinking that at any moment he would say he had to leave, but he seemed not to be in a hurry for once. Neither was James, but at four-thirty he glanced at his watch.

'Well, this has been very pleasant, but I really must go, Jenny. I have to change and I have an appointment at six.'

'It was nice to see you,' she said, and stood up, walking to the side gate with him.

'You won't change your mind about the party?'

'No, thank you—not this time.'

James hesitated, then leaned towards her. He gave her a brief kiss on the lips, which left her totally unmoved. 'I'll telephone you from England. You will think about what I asked?'

'I will James. Have a safe journey tomorrow.'

Miguel had wandered away to look at a rose bush while they'd said their farewells. He was scowling as he came back to her.

When she sat down again he stood towering over her. 'I hope you remember you signed a contract for six months?'

'Of course,' Jenny said, and smiled. 'Sit down, Miguel. You look like a caged tiger.'

'What the hell do you expect?' he demanded. 'I suppose he was the man you had a thing for before you came out here?'

'I hardly think that's any of your business,' Jenny snapped back.

'No?'

Miguel glared at her, then reached out and grabbed her by the upper arms, pulling her against him. Her first reaction was to jerk away. Just what did he think he was playing at? She wasn't a machine that could be turned on and off at will.

'Damn you...' she began, but the look in his eyes was so hot it was melting her resistance. As his lips sought and found hers, she knew a rush of overwhelming love and desire, and suddenly all that mattered was that she was in his arms and it was where she wanted to be.

'Sorry,' he muttered as he released her at last. 'You seem to bring out the worst in me, Jenny. I'm not usually such a selfish brute.'

She nodded, sensing the suppressed frustration in him.

'James isn't important, Miguel. He never was—not really.'

'You're not going to work for him?'

'Why not?' Jenny looked cool and calm, but her insides were in turmoil. 'I worked with him for two years at home.'

'You must have needed that job!'

It wasn't like Miguel to say something so—so rude.

'James isn't so bad.'

'He's shallow and selfish.'

'Yes, perhaps he is,' Jenny replied, seeming unruffled. 'But a lot of men *are* selfish.'

'Is that directed at me?'

'No. It was just a general statement.' Jenny was suddenly tired of arguing. She didn't want to be angry with him. She wanted to reach out and kiss the tiredness away from his face. She wanted to take him in her arms and love him, but caution and pride held her back. 'I think you're probably too unselfish for your own good. Sit down, Miguel—unless you have to leave?'

He sat down, but his eyes still held that angry, smouldering expression. 'I wasn't exactly unselfish the other night. I should have thought more before I began something I knew might not work out.'

'How are Joachim and Elena?' she asked, ignoring this provocative statement.

'I took them home this morning. I've arranged for a private nurse for the boy day and night, and Maria will take care of Elena during the day as usual. I shall stay there at night until she is back to normal. I am hoping she will pick up now that she has her son home.'

'Yes, I see,' Jenny said. 'What about your work? Will that suffer?'

'I'm more or less back to normal at the hospital. I am

not sure about evening calls. I may have to get a locum to help out for a while.'

'I can manage as we are for a week or two,' Jenny said. 'Not indefinitely, of course, but long enough for you to take your time over finding someone you can trust.'

Miguel nodded. He looked at her broodingly, still apparently annoyed at finding her with James. 'Do you want to leave?'

Jenny hesitated, then decided to tell the truth. 'No, I don't, Miguel. I wasn't sure what James meant at first, and I thought I might have to look for something else. But I don't want to work in that sort of medicine. I like the clinic—but I wasn't sure I would be able to stay on there.'

'Did you think I would make things difficult for you?'

He already had. Didn't he realize what he had done to her—to her poor, bruised heart?

'I wasn't sure we could continue to work with each other.'

'Because of the other night?' She was silent and his gaze narrowed. He nodded as if he had only just realized something. 'I've hurt you, Jenny. I am truly sorry. I never meant it to be this way.'

'No, I don't suppose you did, but just what did you intend, Miguel? You spoke of marriage—was that to be a marriage of convenience? Because you want a wife and children?'

He inclined his head, his eyes never leaving her face. 'I suppose it was something like that,' he admitted. 'My last relationship failed because I wasn't able to give her enough time. I am not sure what I was thinking or even if I was thinking at the time. I imagine I must have thought you would understand—about the work.'

'Because I'm a doctor?'

'Yes. And you had spoken of something like that yourself—mutual respect and affection. I thought we had those, Jenny.'

'Yes. Yes, of course we did.'

Surely they had had much more? Didn't he realize how much he was hurting her by treating their lovemaking as something mundane or ordinary? It certainly hadn't been that way for Jenny. She'd thought they'd had something special, but apparently it hadn't been the same for him—though he *had* been jealous of James.

Miguel was frowning. 'I still think we might have made it work—but at the moment it is impossible. I have to be there for Elena. Please, understand, Jenny. She needs me. She just couldn't cope alone at the moment.'

'I do understand that, Miguel. Certainly, she needs someone to love and care for her. She has been through a terrible experience.'

Jenny felt cold all over. Why couldn't he see that she needed him, too, that she would be willing to share his problems, to help both him and Elena? She cared about his sister, too!

'I ought to go. I just wanted to be sure you understood. I wasn't using you. I am sorry you have been hurt.'

'I'll get over it!' She was flippant, head up, eyes bright with defiance.

'Give me a little time to work things out, Jenny. Please?'

Her heart started to thump madly as he looked at her. What did he mean? Was he still hoping there could be something between them? His eyes seemed to convey that, but she couldn't trust her own senses any more. He seemed to promise one thing and do another!

'Yes…'

It was all she could manage. They both stood up. She stared at him, at his mouth, hungry, longing for him to kiss her, to tell her he wanted her and nothing else mattered. And she thought that he wanted the same, but he merely reached out to touch her cheek before walking away. Jenny watched him go. Her heart was aching. Why couldn't he see that she would do anything to be with him?

Why hadn't she told him that?

Jenny spent Sunday with her parents. Ronald managed to make it to the garden on his daughter's arm. He looked so pleased with himself and life that Jenny's own heartache no longer seemed quite as important.

She enjoyed being with them, looking after them, and making lunch while her mother had a lazy day.

'Have you made up your mind about settling here?' her father asked. 'You are happy, aren't you, Jenny?'

'Yes, I am,' she replied. 'I'm going back to Norwich the week after next for Moya's wedding. Angie has promised to send some stuff I don't want to the auction for me and I'll pack the rest to be sent out here. It's best to get it all done at once. I shall fly out on Friday evening and get a return flight on Sunday. If Soraya is back at work she can manage for one Saturday morning. If not, Miguel will arrange something. I shall have to talk to him.'

'I'm glad you're on good terms with him again,' Beth said. 'I think you were upset because he didn't ring you—but I expect he was busy.'

'Yes. He's had to move in with Elena for a time. She's just too depressed to be alone.'

Beth nodded and smiled. 'Just until things get back to normal.'

'Yes, I expect so.'

'You'll enjoy Moya's wedding. It all happened so quickly for her, didn't it?' Beth sighed as she looked at her daughter but didn't say anything.

Jenny laughed. 'Don't despair, Mum. You might get your grandchild one of these days.'

And sooner than any of them expected if Jenny's suspicions proved correct!

Jenny hadn't given her period a thought until that morning, when she had suddenly realized she was late.

Jenny put off doing the test that would confirm her suspicions. If she didn't know for sure she didn't have to think about what she was going to do when it started to become obvious.

She didn't even consider an abortion. There was no way she would let them take Miguel's baby out of her—the thought that she might be pregnant was too precious to be analysed or discussed with anyone just yet. She wanted to hold it to herself, to savour the prospect before it became public property.

So she wouldn't do the test until—until after Moya's wedding. She would wait and let herself dream for a while.

It was very busy at the clinic that week, though fortunately Soraya came back on the Wednesday.

'Are you sure you are ready to start work?' Jenny asked her. 'I can manage if you want to be with your husband for another day or two.'

'He is bad-tempered with the pain of his leg,' Soraya said, and pulled a face. 'All the time he sits in front of the TV and complains. I tell him he is lucky. He could have broken his neck—and all because he will not pay for a repair to the roof.'

'You just have to be thankful that he *was* lucky,' Jenny said. 'It's strange that sometimes a fall like that can do so little damage while a bang on the head can be severe.'

'My husband has a head of wood!'

Jenny laughed. It was good to have the friendly nurse back, and it eased her workload, as well as making the clinic a nicer place to be. Isabelle's mood hadn't improved. She sulked all the time and was rude to Soraya as well as Jenny.

'If she continues this way I shall ask Dr Sanchez to let her go,' Soraya said after Isabelle had gone that evening. I do not know what is wrong with her. She used not to be like this.'

'I'm afraid she doesn't like me.'

Soraya shook her head. 'I think it is more than that—but she will not tell me what is wrong.'

'Could it be man trouble?'

Soraya frowned. 'There was someone...a year or eighteen months ago. He was bad, a criminal. The police caught him trying to bring drugs in from Morocco. He went to prison.'

'He couldn't be out again, I suppose?'

Soraya's eyes narrowed. 'You think...she might have taken those drugs for him? No! She would not be such a fool. She could lose everything.'

'Women will do foolish things for love. She hasn't had a chance to take anything recently. I've kept the key in my pocket the whole time.'

'Isabelle has her own keys to the clinic,' Soraya said, and frowned.

'But she was waiting outside the day you didn't come in.'

'She often forgets to bring them,' Soraya said, looking anxious. 'We must be very careful in future, Jenny.'

'Yes. We must—but don't say anything to Miguel just yet. He has enough to think about for the moment. We'll keep an eye on things ourselves and see what happens. We may be wrong. It may never happen again.'

'I shall check the list every week,' Soraya said. 'And one of us must keep the key to the drugs cabinet—and lock it away at night. Dr Sanchez has all his own keys.'

Jenny nodded and the subject was changed. She told Soraya that she was going back to England for her friend's wedding, and the nurse said that she would be very happy to hold the fort for a couple of hours.

'It is possible that Dr Sanchez will feel able to come in by then,' she said. 'Elena should be feeling better soon—do you not think so?'

'Perhaps,' Jenny replied. 'I believe it is more a case of feeling unhappy than actually being ill.'

'Dr Sanchez should be firmer with her,' Soraya said, her mouth prim. 'He has always given her her own way. It is time she realized that he has a life of his own.'

'That's really his decision,' Jenny said. She glanced at her watch. 'You'll be late if you stay any longer, Soraya.'

'Yes, I must go.' The nurse raised her brows. 'Are you leaving, too?'

'No, not for a while,' Jenny replied. 'I have some case notes to enter in the computer, and I want to do a little research on the Internet for one of my patients who may need a heart bypass. He has seen a consultant, but he wants to know if they can do his op by microsurgery. Apparently, he's read that it's possible now and I want to refresh my mind on the possibilities before I advise him.'

'You work too hard,' Soraya said. 'But at least there are no house calls for you this evening.'

Soraya left after carrying their coffee-cups to the kitchen. Jenny made sure the front door was firmly locked behind her, then went back to her office and switched on the computer.

She had been working steadily for half an hour when she heard something. She stiffened. Someone had come in. She was sure of it. Yes, she could hear movement. Was it Miguel? She didn't think so. Whoever it was seemed to be trying not to make a noise.

Jenny got up and went to her door, opening it carefully. She couldn't see anyone in the reception area, but the door of the treatment room was open—and so was the top drawer of Soraya's desk. The key to the drugs cabinet wasn't there—they had decided on a new place to keep it.

Jenny ran her tongue over dry lips as she heard a sudden loud banging noise—someone was trying to break open the metal drugs cabinet! She hurried to the treatment room and looked in at the open door. Isabelle had some kind of tool in her hand and was trying to force the door of the cabinet.

'What are you doing?'

Isabelle gasped and swung round, staring at her in horror. The colour drained from her face, her eyes dark with shock.

'I thought you had gone...'

'I was working late. What are you doing, Isabelle?'

'I—I wanted something for a bad headache.' The lie was so obvious that Jenny dismissed it instantly.

'You don't expect me to believe that, do you?' she

asked. 'It's useless to lie, Isabelle. I know you took those missing drugs. You came back that night, thinking everyone had gone home, didn't you?'

'I thought there was no one here,' Isabelle said, a look of defiance in her eyes now. 'I took the drugs and I was going to sign Soraya's name on the list—but then I heard voices and I was frightened.'

'So you left the key in the cabinet and ran away?' Jenny nodded as the other woman was silent. 'Why did you take them, Isabelle? Don't you realize you could lose everything?'

'What have I got to lose?' Isabelle asked, her mouth twisted with bitterness. 'A job that I dislike and being ignored by everyone here.'

'That isn't true, Isabelle.'

'What do you know of my feelings?' Isabelle glared at her. 'You do not understand what it is like to love someone who does not know you exist.'

'I probably understand more than you think. I felt like that once—for almost a year. James didn't even see me, not the real me. And in the end I realized that it didn't matter. I wasn't in love with him. I was just lonely.'

'I don't care about you!' Isabelle blazed suddenly. 'Carlos loves me. He has promised to marry me if I get him the drugs he wants. Why should I not do what he wants?'

'Don't be a fool,' Jenny cried. 'Can't you see he's just using you? He'll take all you give him and then abandon you to the trouble you've brought on yourself for his sake.'

Isabelle ignored her. She had begun to attack the cabinet furiously, jabbing viciously at the strong metal door with a sharp chisel in an attempt to force it open.

'Stop that!' Jenny ordered. 'If you don't stop at once I shall call the police.'

'I'll kill you! It is all your fault. *He* liked me before you came.' Isabelle whirled on Jenny, darting at her suddenly with the chisel held aloft. 'I hate you!'

Jenny put her hands up to protect her face, which was the part Isabelle seemed to be intent on attacking. She felt a sharp sting as the blade scored the back of her hand, then, even as she cried out in alarm, there was a shout from behind her and someone rushed past her.

Miguel fought with Isabelle for a few minutes, the girl kicking and screaming as he struggled to subdue her. At first she seemed not to realize it was him and stabbed frantically at him with her weapon, but after a fierce tussle he managed to twist her wrist so that she dropped it. She gave a sob of despair and then burst into noisy tears.

Miguel frowned at her. 'What is the meaning of this, Isabelle? Why were you attacking Dr Talforth?'

'Ask her!' Isabelle dodged past him to the door, then paused. Taking a key from her suit pocket, she threw it at Jenny. It struck her body and fell to the floor. 'Keep it! I shall not need it any more. I am not coming back here. I hate you all.'

'Isabelle!' Miguel shouted at her to stop but she ran off, slamming the door of the clinic after her. He turned to Jenny with a frown. 'What was going on?'

'She attacked me with that chisel when I tried to stop her breaking open the drugs cabinet.'

'Yes, I had gathered that much,' he said. 'But what was all that before—about someone using her, ignoring her?'

Jenny had noticed blood on his shirt. 'Are you hurt? You had better let me take a look—slip your shirt off.'

'It is just a scratch,' Miguel said, but he did as she said, leaning against the table and watching as she worked. 'A drop of antiseptic will do.'

Jenny washed her hands at the sink before getting what she needed. She cleaned the wound in Miguel's left arm, which was little more than a deep scratch, then applied a little antiseptic cream and a gauze dressing.

'Is your tetanus jab up to date? That chisel doesn't look too wholesome to me.'

'Yes, thank you, Dr Talforth.' Miguel's mouth softened as she gave him a strict look, then stripped off her disposable latex gloves. He frowned as he saw there was fresh blood on the back of her hand. 'You were hurt, too. I didn't realize. Let me do it for you, Jenny.'

'A plaster will do—it's nothing.'

'It is equally as bad as mine was.' He used clean wadding to bathe the wound, then applied a smaller dressing than that she had used for him. 'Are you covered for tetanus?'

'I had my booster before I came out.'

Miguel nodded, his dark eyes intent on her face. 'Why don't you tell me about Isabelle? Just what has been going on here—and what made you suspect her? Because you did from the start, didn't you?'

Jenny bit her lip. 'I wasn't sure until this evening—but Soraya had also noticed something was wrong. Isabelle has been unhappy and sulky recently. We thought she might have had trouble with her boyfriend. Apparently he was in prison for possession of illegal drugs. I think he made her do it.'

'But what was all that stuff about understanding how she felt?'

'You didn't notice she had a thing for you, of course?' Jenny arched her brows at him. 'You didn't take her out, pick her up for a drink or anything that might have given her reason to hope?'

'No—at least, only once or twice when her car was in the repair shop.'

'You didn't see her eyes light up whenever you smiled at her?'

'No—well, I imagined it was just something that would go away in time. I didn't want to be involved with her—she was too much like Maribelle, my previous girlfriend, pretty and spoiled.' He frowned. 'I suppose that makes what happened my fault?'

'Yes, in a way it does.'

'I was too busy to notice. I've been careless and selfish, haven't I?'

'Your attitude may have contributed to her unhappiness, but I think her boyfriend is to blame.'

'What do I do about her?' Miguel asked. 'Should I report this to the police?'

'In theory the theft of the drugs ought to be reported,' Jenny said. 'But I imagine what she took before has long gone, and she didn't get anything this time. I think Isabelle and her boyfriend will make themselves scarce—why make things worse for her? I noticed a nasty bruise on her arm just now. She has probably been through a rough time…' She picked up the keys Isabelle had thrown at her and gave them to him. 'She won't use these again, but it might be as well to have another lock fitted.'

'I'll certainly do that,' Miguel said. 'Though I doubt Isabelle will come back. She will expect me to report her, which I ought to do, of course. Yet, as you say, she will probably be too scared to come back here. So, if you agree, I think we shall just forget it this time, though if she does try to make more trouble I shall have to do something then.'

'Yes, that sounds about right to me. We'll have to be careful who has these keys in future. We can't allow a similar theft to occur. The drugs we keep here could be dangerous.'

Miguel nodded. 'I see that. I'm sorry I dismissed your suggestion that Isabelle might be responsible in the first place. I should have trusted your judgement, Jenny. You're not spiteful, and you don't suggest something like that without good reason.'

'You didn't know me then.' She smiled at him. 'I wasn't sure I was right—it was just intuition.'

'Why don't you make a fuss when you're hurt?' he asked, the look in his eyes causing her stomach to lurch. 'Why don't you scream and shout and make demands, Jenny?'

'Too damned independent, I expect.'

Miguel laughed. 'Well, if that's what it is, I like it.' The burning look he gave her made her feel weak at the knees. 'You know, I think we should—' He cursed as his mobile shrilled. 'Yes, Dr Sanchez speaking. Yes, I see. I'll be there in a few minutes. Yes, thank you for letting me know. No, it is no trouble at all.' He gave Jenny an apologetic look as he ended the call. 'It's Mr Jeffries. He says their daughter is really very unwell this time, and his wife is frantic.'

'Of course you must go.'

'Yes, I must.' He sighed. 'Mrs Jeffries is neurotic and she worries too much about that child—but this sounds serious. I have to respond just in case. May I telephone you this evening? It may be quite late.'

'Yes.' Jenny was in complete agreement. 'I understand that, Miguel. Please, don't apologize. I'll go for a swim after supper, but I'll definitely be at home after nine if you want to contact me then.'

'Good. I'll ring you. Will you lock up here for me, please?'

'Yes, of course. You ought to go.'

'That seems to be the story of my life,' Miguel said, and gave her a rueful smile. 'One of these times I shall manage a whole evening without interruptions. I promise, Jenny.'

'I'll look forward to that,' she replied, and smiled as he rushed out.

It took her a few minutes to clear up the treatment room, and then she, too, left the clinic for the night. She was thoughtful as she drove up the hill towards the villa.

What had Miguel meant by his promise to 'manage a whole evening'? She thought he'd decided that it was just too difficult for them to be together?

Had he changed his mind?

CHAPTER NINE

MIGUEL did telephone Jenny that evening, at about half past ten.

'How are you?' he asked. 'I am not sure that I told you how magnificent you were earlier. In fact, I am not sure I said any of the things I ought to have said. It was a shock, seeing you struggling with Isabelle. If I hadn't happened to come in she might really have hurt you.'

'Oh, I doubt it. I'm pretty tough.'

'Well, it scared me, I can tell you.'

'How's your arm—is it sore?'

'I expect I shall live.' He paused, then went on, sounding hesitant, 'Can we try again, Jenny? Not just yet, but later—when I have fixed things up here?'

Jenny's heart was racing, but she kept her tone light and casual. 'I don't see why not. I'm a forgiving sort of a girl.'

'You would need to be. I haven't treated you as I should have done. In fact, I have said some pretty rotten things.'

'You certainly seemed to distrust me at first.'

'Yes, I got something wrong, Jenny. Something someone said quite innocently when I wasn't listening properly.'

'I'm an adult, Miguel. If sex is all you want, I would rather you told me now.'

'It isn't—but it was pretty good between us, wasn't it?'

'I thought it was fantastic.'

159

He laughed. 'Amazing, actually. I keep thinking about the way we were together. As a matter of fact, it is the only thing that has kept me going since then.'

'Why didn't you ring me before? I mean, to talk like this—to let me help, if only by talking?'

'I am not sure,' he said. 'I had some stupid idea of it not being fair to you—that it would be better if you were free to do your own thing. I thought I ought to finish it before we were involved.'

'Perhaps I'm old-fashioned, but I thought we *were* involved,' Jenny said. 'That night meant something to me, Miguel.'

'It meant a lot to me, too,' he admitted. 'I have been a fool, haven't I?'

'Yes, I would say that's a fair estimation of your recent behaviour.'

'Ouch!' He laughed. 'You certainly do not pull your punches, Jenny. I shall have to learn to duck.'

'Just let me in another time, Miguel. I do understand your commitment to Elena. If it were my family I would need to spend time with them, too—but I would want the person who was special to me to be there as well.'

'Am I special to you, Jenny?' His voice had suddenly gone husky and her stomach curled with desire.

'Yes. If you don't know that you don't know me.'

'I think I am beginning to. You're something of a revelation, Jenny.'

'What does that mean?'

'I'll tell you another time.' His voice was full of promise, which made Jenny ache to be with him. She wanted so much more than a phone call, but she knew she had to be patient for a while. 'I'm sorry, darling, but I do have some work to do...'

Jenny felt a slow trickle of warmth begin to spread through her from her toes up. 'How was your patient when you got there?'

'Sarah has a very virulent stomach bug. I put her on fairly strong antibiotics, but she should be fine within forty-eight hours. I told Mrs Jeffries you would call in and check on Sarah tomorrow, just to make sure she is all right. If that is OK.'

'Yes, of course it is. You know I want to help as much as I can, especially while things are so difficult for you. I hope we shall be able to work together more in the future, and discuss our problems. And I wouldn't mind taking on some hospital work once we really get going.'

'I think that is great. You know I shall help all I can.'

'Of course.'

'I really want things to work out. Can you forgive me for shutting you out? I think it was a self-defence mechanism.'

'Just don't do it again!'

Miguel chuckled as he caught the teasing note in her voice. 'Dream about me,' he said. 'I shall dream of you.'

Jenny's eyes stung with tears as he closed the connection. She realized that it had been difficult for Miguel to admit that he needed her. He had always been the one to do the caring. He would need to learn to share his problems, but at least he was trying.

'It's good news,' Jenny said as Mrs Richards took a seat and looked at her anxiously. 'Your blood test was completely normal. You shouldn't have any need to worry about spina bifida at all.'

Tears sprang to Mrs Richards's eyes. 'I'm so relieved,' she said. 'I don't know what I would have done if you'd said I needed to have the amniocentesis test.

My husband said I shouldn't have come in the first place.'

'Well, so far everything looks fine,' Jenny reassured her. 'But it wouldn't hurt to have an ultrasonic scan. It's something we arrange for lots of mothers.'

'You've really set my mind at rest. Whatever you think best, that's what I'll do.'

Jenny typed up some details after she left, then glanced at her watch. It was almost time to pack up for the evening. She had just decided to close up the computer when Soraya came to tell her there was someone to see her.

'It is Señor Martinez,' Soraya said, looking puzzled. 'He says it is a private matter.'

'You had better ask him to come in,' Jenny said. 'Perhaps he's a salesman or something.'

Soraya gave a little shake of her head but made no comment as she went out. Jenny got to her feet as a very smart man in his early fifties came in. He was obviously a businessman and looked affluent.

'Forgive me,' he said. 'I should have made an appointment, but I have just come from the hospital and I called on the chance that you could see me.'

'Yes, of course,' Jenny said. 'Please, sit down. What is it that I can do for you? If you have just come from the hospital...'

'I have been visiting my daughter—Juliana,' he said, and cleared his throat. 'She has just had an operation to remove one of her ovaries...'

'Oh, I see...' Jenny felt a cold shiver go down her spine. 'I'm very sorry. I had hoped it was merely a benign cyst.'

'It was cancerous, but at a very early stage, so she will not need chemotherapy. The consultant told me we were very lucky that it had been caught, and that prompt diagnosis had probably saved my daughter's life...'

He sounded very emotional, and Jenny nodded. 'I'm very glad Juliana took my advice,' she said. 'I thought it best she should see her own doctor in case it turned out to be serious.'

'Juliana has told me why she came to you first,' her father said. 'I want to thank you for the advice you gave her.'

'It was the same as I would give to anyone in her situation,' Jenny said. 'I am just glad they were able to help her.'

'I am assured that she will be fine,' he replied, 'and that is more important to me than anything. I might have been angry if Juliana had become pregnant, Dr Talforth, but I can assure you that I would not have treated her harshly.'

'I am sure she knows that now,' Jenny said, and smiled.

'She does... Thank you again.' He got to his feet and they shook hands. 'If I can ever do anything for you, simply ask.' He placed one of his cards on the table in front of her. 'I shall not take up any more of your valuable time. Good evening.'

Jenny smiled as he closed the door behind him. It was sad that Juliana had had to have one of her ovaries removed at such a young age, but good that the illness had been caught in time. She had been right to insist on further investigation, even though she had thought at the time of examination that it had probably been only a benign cyst.

Miguel was right when he said further investigation was always the best policy. *Miguel...* Jenny felt a warm glow as she looked forward to his call. He rang her every night now, though he still hadn't found time to get over, telling her about his day, listening to what she had to say.

'It has been pretty hectic,' Miguel said on the following Thursday evening. 'Sometimes I wonder how so many people manage to get sick at the same time.'

'I don't suppose they do it on purpose.'

'No, of course not. How did you get on today? It was your free clinic this morning, wasn't it?'

'We were busy,' Jenny told him. 'Several routine blood tests and blood-pressure checks. I also had a young man who wanted a test for prostate trouble. I think there's cause for further investigation, so I've referred him to the hospital. That was besides the usual crop of the morning after the night before.'

Miguel chuckled. 'I've persuaded Elena to have some friends round this Sunday. She was reluctant at first, but she agreed in the end. How do you feel about coming?'

'I would love to,' Jenny said, 'but Moya is getting married this weekend and I'm flying over tomorrow evening. I'm sure I told you.'

'Yes, of course you did. I had forgotten. Soraya is going to hold the fort at the clinic, isn't she?'

'Yes. Unless you can manage to get in for a couple of hours?'

'I'm not sure.' He sounded evasive. 'I may have something else on. 'It's probably best to leave it with Soraya for once. She can refer anything she isn't sure about.'

'How is Elena—and Joachim?'

'Joachim is wonderful,' Miguel said. 'I told you he had begun to talk a bit more, didn't I? He is slower than he used to be and, of course, he doesn't run about yet, but he is getting better, Jenny. He said thank you for that lovely picture book you sent him. He has been asking when you are coming to see him.'

'Tell him very soon,' she paused. 'As long as he's getting better. You've seen no improvement in Elena, then?'

'She seems physically back to where she was—it's her mental attitude. I can't get through to her, Jenny. She is so listless...uninterested in anything other than Joachim.'

'It's natural for a while. She could have lost him. Give her time, Miguel.'

'Yes, that's all I can do, my darling.' He hesitated, then said, 'What time will you be back on Sunday?'

'It's a late flight. It should get in at around eleven.'

'I wish I could come to England with you.'

'Yes, so do I. Another time.'

'Yes, another time. Take care of yourself, my darling.'

'You, too. Don't work too hard.'

Jenny disconnected, smiling as she went to take a bath before climbing into bed with a book. Earlier that evening she had given in to temptation and carried out the test she had been putting off.

She was quite certain now that she was carrying Miguel's child. She hugged her secret to herself. She would have to tell him sooner or later, of course—but she wanted it to be face to face.

Jenny would have been nervous of his reaction if it hadn't been for those late night calls. Some of them had been more intimate than others, and she was confident that Miguel intended them to be together. It was just a case of waiting until things were easier for him.

* * *

Jenny threw rice over Moya as she and Clive came out of the register office, then kissed both of them.

'You're a lucky man,' she told Clive. 'Make sure you take care of her.'

'Yes, I will,' he promised. 'This hit me like a bolt out of the blue. I've never known anyone like Moya before.'

'She's pretty special,' Jenny told him. 'But, then, she thinks you're special too.'

After the reception at a prestigious hotel in Norwich, Moya and Clive drove off to an undisclosed destination. Jenny returned to the house she had shared with her friends and began to pack the things she wanted sent out to Spain. She had arranged for a carrier to pick the boxes up that afternoon, and when the doorbell rang she imagined it must be the van driver.

She stared in surprise as she saw Miguel standing there, one small suitcase in his hand. He was wearing a dark business suit and looked devastatingly handsome, which made her catch her breath as her knees went wobbly.

'Miguel! I don't believe it—how?' She laughed with delight. 'How on earth did you manage to get away?'

'I told Elena I was coming over to join you. She said it was about time I started to think about my own life and let her get on with hers.'

'Elena said that?'

'Well, not quite in those words. We'd had a flaming row the previous night. I told her she had better start pulling herself together or she wouldn't live long enough to see her son get much older.'

'Oh, Miguel, you didn't—you shouldn't have!' Jenny said, drawing him inside the house. She stared at him. It just didn't sound like Miguel. He was always so patient with his sister, so protective of her feelings—perhaps too much at times. 'That was a little harsh, wasn't it?'

'She needed a shake-up, Miguel said. 'Believe me, it wasn't easy. I don't think I've ever been that harsh with her in my life. But it seemed to work. She was almost back to her normal self before I left.'

'But will she be all right alone?'

'She isn't alone, Jenny. She has a nurse for Joachim day and night—and Maria.' He looked a bit like the cat that had swallowed the cream. 'Besides, I phoned Andrew and asked him to go and see her.'

'Will she be pleased about that?'

'He was. Apparently, he was the one who walked out on her after their row. It was over Juan, of course. I told him that was definitely finished, and he couldn't wait to get there.'

'I do hope they make it up,' Jenny said. 'He thinks the world of her.'

'Andrew is in love with her,' Miguel said, and his eyes held a serious, thoughtful expression now. 'Elena could not bring herself to believe it. Juan had hurt her too badly, but it is my belief that she has missed Andrew terribly. I think that is what has been making her so miserable—as well as the worry over Joachim, of course.'

'It would be so good for her if they got together at last.'

'And for us,' Miguel said. 'You do realize what a difference it would make to us? I should still be there for her, of course, but she wouldn't need me all the time.'

'You mean we might get to finish what we started that night at your villa?' Jenny asked, teasing him.

'We just might,' Miguel replied, and a silver flame

leapt up in his eyes. 'At least we are safe from interruptions tonight. I didn't even bring my mobile with me.'

'Nor did I,' Jenny admitted. 'I forgot mine—what's your excuse?'

'Deliberate truancy,' he replied with a wicked look. 'So, what shall we do this evening—dinner and dancing? We've never had a proper date, darling. I should like to make the most of this one.'

'Dinner and dancing,' Jenny murmured. 'That sounds wonderful, but I need a shower first. How about you? You must be warm after your flight.'

'Does that mean what I think it means?' His eyes gleamed. 'Are you asking me to share it with you?'

'Why not?' Jenny murmured, a wicked smile on her lips. 'Angie went off somewhere for the evening with her boyfriend. We have the house to ourselves and an answering machine...'

'You taste so good,' Miguel said, looking down at Jenny as she lay amongst the tangled sheets. 'I think I could gobble you up.'

'You had a good try,' Jenny replied, and he laughed. She reached up to kiss him lingeringly on the mouth. 'But I seem to remember you promised me dinner and dancing.'

'So I did,' Miguel said with an indulgent smile. 'Where shall we go? You know Norwich better than I do.'

'There's a rather nice hotel where we can have dinner, and a couple of nightclubs. I trust you brought your glad rags with you?'

'I'll have you know I wear Armani,' Miguel said, giving her a mock scowl. 'Are you always this bossy, my darling?'

'Invariably,' she replied. 'I dare say you'll get used to it in about twenty years or so.'

'I think I might grow to like it,' he said. 'Now, who goes to the shower first? If we do it together we shall never manage to get to the hotel in time to eat.'

Jenny pushed him away as he began to caress her breasts once more.

'I'm hungry,' she said. 'Feed me or I may bite.'

'Promises, promises!'

Somehow they did manage to dress, summon a taxi and get to the hotel for a late dinner.

It was the most delicious meal Jenny had ever eaten, though she hardly noticed what was on her plate. She thought that anything would have tasted good with Miguel's eyes seeming to burn into her that way!

After they had eaten, they took another taxi to the nightclub Jenny thought was probably the best. It was crowded, but there was just about room to dance. It was fun, dancing with Miguel, and she discovered that he was far more into this kind of thing than she had imagined. Because of that, Jenny let herself go more than she normally would have, laughing and having fun as she wiggled her hips seductively to the music.

'Where did you learn to dance like that?' she asked as they went back to their table.

'In my wicked youth,' he replied. 'I did a bit of flamenco. But I might ask the same of you, Jenny.'

'Oh, I just followed you,' she murmured.

She left him for a few minutes then, making her way to the powder room and cooling her warm cheeks with a little water. It was as she was on her way back to their table that a man approached her. She didn't notice him until he took hold of her arm, trying to swing her round to face him. She sensed immediately that he had been drinking too much and tried to pull away, but he held onto her, insisting that he wanted to dance with her.

'Please, let go,' she said. 'I don't know you—and I have no wish to dance with you. I'm with someone.'

'Stuck-up bitch!' he muttered, and leered at her. 'I know you—you live with that nurse. She's anybody's...bet you're the same.'

'How dare you speak to me like that?'

Miguel was heading towards them and the murderous look in his eyes spelt trouble. Jenny was afraid that things might turn violent and managed to wrench herself away from the drunk just as Miguel reached them.

'Take your filthy hands off my fiancée,' Miguel ordered coldly. 'Or I shall have to teach you a lesson in manners.'

The drunk spat at him, then, before Jenny realized what was going on, he snatched an empty wine bottle from an ice bucket and raised it threateningly. Without thinking, Jenny moved between them and the drunk smashed the bottle against the side of her head.

She felt the pain, then gave a little moan and fell into Miguel's arms as all hell broke loose around them and the minders came rushing up to grab the drunk. As the blackness folded about her, she neither heard nor saw what happened next.

When Jenny came to, she was lying in a hospital bed in what seemed to be a little side ward. There were two beds in it, but she was the only patient. It was Sunday morning, though, of course, she wasn't aware of that at that moment, only of the ache at her temple. She put up her hand and encountered a thick bandage. Her head hurt and a little whimper of pain issued from her lips.

'Water...' she muttered.

'Not yet,' a nurse said. 'You can have some ice chips to suck if you like.'

'Yes, please.' Jenny's mouth felt very dry. 'What happened?' she asked. 'Did I have an accident?' A sudden terrible fear gripped her and she caught at the nurse's arm. 'I didn't lose my baby? Please, you must tell me! I haven't lost the baby?'

'You just had a bang on the head—ah, here is Dr Sanchez. He sat with you all night. I'll leave you to talk while I fetch that ice.'

'So you are awake,' Miguel said. He perched on the edge of the bed. 'How is your poor head? Does it hurt terribly, darling?'

'Miguel?' Jenny stared at him. 'What happened? I can't remember.'

'We were at a nightclub. That drunk was causing trouble. I tried to intervene, he picked up an empty wine bottle and you got in the way of what was meant for me.'

Jenny sighed and closed her eyes for a moment. She vaguely remembered now that he had told her, though it all seemed a bit hazy. She touched the side of her head again.

'I haven't had an op, have I?'

'No, just a few stitches. I'm afraid they've made a bit of a mess of your hair—and you will probably have massive bruising above your right eye.'

'That's all right, then,' Jenny said, and attempted a smile. 'Ouch, it hurts to smile.'

'My poor darling,' Miguel murmured, and bent to kiss her gently on the lips. 'I've telephoned your parents and let them know you won't be back for a couple of days. I told them not to worry because I am going to be here, taking care of you.'

'But you can't stay on here,' Jenny protested. 'You have patients to see, Elena to think of. You should go back this evening as you planned.'

'I can rearrange my appointments,' Miguel said, frowning. 'I wouldn't think of leaving you here alone after what happened. I took you to that place, I should have taken care of you…'

'Don't start blaming yourself,' Jenny said. 'I'm a big girl now, remember?'

'I want to be with you, Jenny.'

'Bless you for that,' she said, and squeezed his hand. 'But I don't want us to start out this way, as if you have to be there all the time, watching out for me. If I were fighting for my life that would be different, but I've just had a bang on the head. There were obviously no complications or we wouldn't be having this conversation—so I want you to catch your plane this afternoon. You can telephone me from Spain, and when I'm feeling better I'll follow you.'

'Independent lady!' Miguel said, but she could see that despite his desire to stay with her he was relieved. 'Are you sure, Jenny?'

'Quite sure. I shall miss you, but it won't be for long. They won't keep me here for a little knock on the head.'

'It was worse than that,' he said, and frowned. 'But if you think you can manage…'

'I'm certain I can!'

He laughed. 'Is there anything I can do for you before I leave?'

'Ask Angie to send me some things.' She glanced down at the hospital nightgown. 'I must look a sight in this!'

'You look beautiful to me.'

Jenny pulled a face. 'Flatterer! Miguel, there's something—' She broke off as the door of the small side ward opened and the nurse she had asked for some water came in with a large bunch of yellow roses. 'Oh, how lovely—thank you, Miguel. I just love roses.'

'I didn't send them,' he said, and looked for the card. 'I rang your friend Angie and left a message in the machine—perhaps she sent them?'

Jenny read the card he had given her and gave a cry of surprise as she saw the signature. 'They are from James Redfern—how on earth did he know I was here?'

'He happened to be in A&E after seeing a patient when you were brought in last night,' Miguel said. 'He was very helpful and naturally concerned for you.'

'Yes, I suppose so. We were colleagues for two years. It was nice of him to send the flowers.'

'I should have thought of it first.' Miguel looked regretful and perhaps a little annoyed.

'You had other things on your mind,' Jenny said.

She had been about to tell him that she was pregnant, but the nurse was hovering with a vase for the roses, and Miguel seemed to have withdrawn slightly. She wondered what was on his mind—it couldn't be because of the roses, could it? Surely he wasn't jealous?

'I don't need flowers,' she said. 'But I do need a phone call, Miguel. You won't forget?'

'Of course not.' He bent to kiss her softly on the lips, then glanced at his watch. She sensed that he was still brooding about something. 'If I am going to catch that plane...'

'I know. Go on—and don't worry. I'll be fine.'

'I shall miss you, Jenny.'

'Have a good flight. I'll be back before you have time to notice I'm not there.'

He kissed her again and went out of the door. It had

hardly closed behind him before the nurse noticed a wallet lying on the floor.

'This must belong to Dr Sanchez,' she said. 'I'll run after him.'

'Yes, catch him if you can. He'll need it.'

Jenny lay back and closed her eyes as the nurse went out. She had to concentrate hard to banish her foolish desire to weep. It had taken all her strength to send Miguel on his way, but she knew it was the right thing to do. She wasn't a clinging vine and she could manage—and he had enough problems without sitting around, waiting for her to get over a bump on the head!

'It's all right, I caught him,' the nurse said when she came back. 'He told me to take special care of you, because you're a very special lady. Wasn't that nice?'

'Yes, it was,' Jenny said, her moment of self-pity banished. 'Do you think I could have those ice chips now?'

'Yes, of course.' The nurse beamed at her. 'He must think a lot of you to send you those flowers.'

'Oh, they were from a friend,' Jenny said, and sighed.

She closed her eyes again as the nurse went out. Her head ached like mad, but it wasn't as bad as her feeling of loss. She had been a fool to send Miguel away when she needed him so badly!

CHAPTER TEN

IT WAS the following Saturday before Jenny felt like flying back to Spain, though she was released from hospital after two days. She used the extra time to sort out the rest of her possessions and say goodbye to a few friends.

She rang James to thank him for the flowers.

'I didn't come to see you because I thought I might be in the way. I suppose congratulations are in order?'

'What do you mean?'

'You are going to marry Sanchez? It's obvious he's in love with you, Jenny. He looked terrible when they brought you in. I think if I hadn't got things moving quickly he might have started a riot in Accident and Emergency.'

'James! Miguel isn't like that.'

'He was that night. At first I thought he might have had a drop too much to drink, but then I realized he was half out of his mind with worry over you.'

'You're kidding me!'

'No, really—I felt sorry for the poor guy.'

Jenny puzzled over James's revelations. Miguel never lost his cool. He was always so strong, so sure. Even when Joachim had been injured, he'd merely taken control in a very calm, almost remote manner. James must have been exaggerating!

Jenny was a little shocked when her bandages first came off. About two square inches of her hair had been shaved away so that they could stitch the wound inflicted by the drunk, and her right eyelid and half of her cheek had a bruise which gradually turned yellow and purple.

She felt a bit self-conscious, but solved the problem of her bald patch by winding a scarf round her head like a wide Alice band. There was nothing she could do about the bruising so she decided to tough it out and not bother with trying to cover it up.

People stared at her as she queued to load her luggage at the airport, and an elderly man offered to help her.

'You look as if you've been in the wars,' he said kindly. 'If there's anything my wife and I can do to help you need only ask.'

'You've made me feel better simply by asking,' Jenny said. 'But I am really much better now, thank you. It was just a little accident. Nothing too terrible.'

She was still getting the odd headache now and then but, as she'd told Miguel every night when he'd phoned, she had pills for that.

'Don't worry about me, she'd said, first from the hospital bed and then from the house. 'The doctors tell me my head must be made of iron. I was lucky, Miguel. Of course I wouldn't win any beauty contests just yet, but I wasn't thinking of entering.'

'The bruises will go,' he'd said. 'I'll kiss them away when you get back—and your hair will grow.'

'How are Elena and Joachim?'

'Very much better,' he'd said, sounding cheerful. 'Elena is happier than she has been for a long time. Joachim's recovery is slow but sure. He still doesn't say much, though, and he doesn't laugh the way he used to. Poor little devil! He has been so brave, Jenny...'

'Be patient,' Jenny had said. 'He will laugh and play again. You'll see. In a few months he'll be running around as if nothing ever happened.'

'When you say it I almost believe it. How did you get to be so brave and so wise?'

'With a lot of backsliding and perseverance,' she'd quipped. 'Just wait until you know me a little better!'

'I am looking forward to it,' Miguel had replied, then added, an odd note in his voice, 'Did Dr Redfern come to see you in hospital?'

'No. I phoned him to say thank you for the flowers, but I haven't seen him.'

'Ah, yes, the flowers. What time does your flight arrive? I'll meet you at the airport.'

'I can hire a car. I shall be needing one. I had a contract last time, but I cancelled it before I left. I'm going to buy something. I sold my Golf here. The garage took it back for a decent price so I can afford something similar there.'

'I'm still going to meet you,' Miguel had said. 'Don't be so damned independent, Jenny! I want to drive you home.'

'OK—sorry.' She'd given a nervous laugh. 'I want to see you, too, of course.'

'We have a lot of talking to do.' Again she'd caught that odd note in his voice. 'But it will keep until you get here.'

'I'm on the Monarch flight from Luton.'

'I'll be waiting for you,' Miguel had promised—and he was.

She saw the huge bouquet of red roses first, and then his concerned expression as he searched the crowd for her. She waved and called his name and his face lit up with pleasure as he saw her.

'Jenny! I was beginning to think something must have happened.'

'Did you think I had been kidnapped by white slavers?'

Miguel pulled a wry face. 'I see that bump on the head made no difference to your sense of humour. It wasn't so funny that night you were attacked. I thought you might be seriously hurt.'

'Just teasing, Miguel. Don't scold me. I've missed you.'

'I've missed you, too.' He kissed her. 'How are you—really?'

'I'm really fine. Just a headache. I could do with a cup of tea.'

'I'll make you one when we get home.'

'Home?' Jenny looked at him as he took charge of her trolley.

'To my place,' Miguel said. 'Your parents know. They understand I want you to myself for a while.'

'Are you going to cook my dinner, too?' Jenny asked. 'I'm also hungry.'

'I am going to give you everything you want,' Miguel replied, smiling at her. 'Anything your heart desires.'

Jenny suddenly felt very happy.

'It's good to be home,' she said.

Jenny curled up in the evening sun, watching as Miguel swam a few lengths of the pool. She had done justice to the delicious meal he had cooked for her—sole in a piquant sauce that tasted of wine, creamy, fluffy potatoes which had been sautéed to make them brown and crisp outside, tiny peas and a dish of crisp salad. Afterwards, she had eaten fresh peaches with cream, followed by a rich dark coffee and delicious chocolates.

'I don't know how you can swim after all you ate,' she said as he came back to her and stood shaking the water from his hair. 'It's not good for you on a full stomach.'

'I know.' He flopped down on a sunbed beside her and pulled a wry face. 'But sometimes you have to be brave enough to break the rules.'

'Yes.' Jenny sighed. 'You should get dressed. The sun has almost gone behind those clouds.'

'In a minute,' Miguel said, his dark eyes regarding her thoughtfully. 'Is there anything you want to tell me, Jenny?'

'What do you mean?'

Jenny felt a jolt of surprise as she saw his expression. He was clearly in the grip of some strong emotion. What was he thinking? She sensed a suppressed anger...hurt.

'I think you know.' His gaze narrowed. 'Why didn't you tell me you were having our baby? It is mine, isn't it?'

Jenny's cheeks went hot. 'Yes, of course,' she said. 'Who else...? You don't think it's James Redfern's?'

'It did cross my mind,' he said, frowning. 'You were involved with him before you came out...'

'No, I wasn't! Why do you say that?'

'You said something to Isabelle the night she attacked you—about having had a thing for him. And your mother mentioned that you'd been unhappy—something to do with a male colleague. I got the idea it was a love affair that went wrong...'

Jenny sat up indignantly. 'And you put two and two together and made five?' She glared at him. 'Well, thank you very much! If you imagine I'm the sort of woman who hops out of bed with one man and straight into bed with the next, you definitely don't know me!'

'I didn't say that...'

She continued to glare at him. How could he think

she would do something like that? 'But you implied it. For a while I was interested in James, but at that time he didn't know I was around. I realize now that I was never in love with him, that, in fact, I was merely lonely—but I admit I did find him attractive for a while. Perhaps because he was around, and I didn't have much of a social life. I was always too busy working or attending meetings to think about my love life.'

'Then...why didn't you tell me about the baby?'

'I was going to—anyway, who did?'

'The nurse at the hospital. She said you had been worried about losing the baby—she told me when she chased after me with the wallet.'

'Oh...' Jenny nodded as she remembered. 'Yes, I was confused when I first came round. I thought I might have been in a car accident and I was anxious in case I had lost the baby.'

'But why not tell me?'

'I haven't told anyone else. Because at first I wasn't sure. I kept putting off doing the test in case it was just a false alarm, and then I—I didn't want to put pressure on you, Miguel. You had other, more important things to worry about.'

'You weren't thinking of—? No, of course not.'

'If you mean a termination, certainly not. You don't have to be responsible, Miguel, but I'm not giving up this baby. I can take care of it myself.'

'It is our baby, and I would be very hurt and angry if you imagined for one moment that I did not wish to be responsible for him.'

'Or her,' Jenny said. She realized she had been swift to flare up and gave him an apologetic smile. 'Yes, of course I know that. I jumped too soon and I'm sorry.'

'If you have one fault, Jenny, it is your independence. It is an admirable quality—but not if carried to excess.'

'I know.' Her eyes flashed at him. 'You do it, too. You shut me out when Joachim was injured.'

'And I have tried to make amends.'

'Yes, you have. Sorry.' A little smile touched her mouth. 'Shall we start again? I'm having your baby, Miguel. I'm very happy about it, and I'm glad you are, too.'

'That's better.' His frown relaxed. 'I left you in hospital and came back here because I had taken too much time off recently, and I needed to catch up on my appointments. It does not mean I didn't care. I have been thinking of you all the time. If you had needed me I would have stayed.'

'But I did,' Jenny said, and laughed ruefully. 'I regretted it the moment you had gone and I missed you like hell—but I'm still glad I forced you to go. I want you to care about me, Miguel, but I am not a clinging vine, nor do I expect you to give me one hundred per cent of your time. You don't have to worry every time a patient needs you and you have to cancel dinner. I'll understand.'

'I think you should know that I am in love with you,' Miguel said. 'When I first thought about asking you to marry me, I didn't realize how much you would come to mean to me—but then Isabelle attacked you and I was frightened because of what might have happened. When you were hurt at the nightclub...' His eyes went black with emotion. 'I was terrified, Jenny. I thought I might lose you. And I had never told you how much I love you...never given you the things I wanted to give you or made love to you all night.'

'No...' Jenny's throat was tight. 'Why was that,

Miguel? Why didn't you tell me you cared before? Surely you must have guessed how I felt about you?'

'Sometimes I thought you might love me,' Miguel replied. 'But you were always so—so in control. So damned independent!'

'I didn't want to be a burden to you,' she said softly. 'I think you've had enough of that in the past.'

She got to her feet and opened her arms to him. Miguel jumped up and moved to pull her close to him. Their kiss was deep, passionate and full of promise.

'Does your head ache now?' Miguel asked huskily. 'I can wait if it does...'

'You may be able to,' Jenny murmured. 'But I can't...'

Jenny was wearing a new white sheath dress she had bought in Norwich when Miguel took her to have lunch at Elena's the next day. They had been to see her parents for an hour or so earlier that morning to tell them the good news. Jenny's father hadn't been in the least surprised, and her mother had produced a bottle of champagne from the fridge.

'We've been waiting for this day for a long time,' she'd said, and had kissed her daughter and then her future son-in-law. 'I couldn't be more delighted, my dears. You are perfect for each other—Ron and I have thought it all along.'

Jenny hoped Miguel's family and friends would be as pleased. She glanced at the large teardrop diamond ring on the third finger of her left hand as they turned into the gateway of Elena's villa. Miguel had given it to her the previous evening after they'd made love and had been sitting together, watching the light fade from the sky.

'I hope Elena will be pleased for us,' she said.

'It doesn't matter one way or the other,' Miguel said tersely. 'She is going to have to learn to share, Jenny. I cannot give her all my time in future—and I don't want to.'

Jenny nodded. She knew that there had to be changes, but she didn't want to hurt Elena or to take anything from her. She hoped that she could add something, that they could be happy as a family.

She smiled at Miguel. 'Be gentle with her, darling. We have so much.'

'Yes, we do. I never dreamed I would ever feel like this about anyone.'

They had now arrived at the villa. Miguel opened the car door for her and she smiled up at him as he put his arm around her. She felt a little nervous as they walked out on to the patio where all his friends were standing, talking, sipping cool drinks and laughing in the sunshine, but as they were noticed a ripple of spontaneous applause broke out.

Jenny looked at him in surprise. 'How did they know?'

'I telephoned Andrew shortly before we left for your parents' home.' He had wanted to give his sister time to get over the shock, but he need not have worried for she greeted them both with a warm smile.

'It is about time,' she said, and looked up at Jenny teasingly. 'I hope you are going to keep this brother of mine in line? It is totally beyond me.'

'It may be beyond me,' Jenny said with a wry look, 'but I promise I shall do my best for you, Elena. Perhaps with two of us we shall be able to manage it.'

After that there was a deluge of congratulations and

demands to know when the engagement party was going to be.

'As a matter of fact, the wedding has already been arranged,' Miguel said. 'You do not think I'm going to feed all of you twice, do you?'

There was general laughter and lots of cheeky remarks as Jenny sat in the chair next to Elena. She could see that Miguel's sister still looked tired, which was understandable after the strain of the past few weeks.

'How are you?' she asked.

'Oh, you know…' Elena shrugged. She had been going to say more but Andrew emerged from the house, holding Joachim by the hand. The child tottered unsteadily but determinedly, holding tight to the large, comforting hand that would never let him fall.

As he drew close to Jenny, he stopped, tugging on Andrew's hand.

'*Hola*, Joachim,' Jenny said. 'I'm Jenny—do you remember me?'

His large eyes stared at her in wonder, then he pointed to the bruising on her face. 'Poor Jenny,' he said in a clear voice. 'Just like Joachim.'

'Yes, darling,' Jenny said. Then she did a very brave thing. She reached up and took off the scarf she had wound round her head to hide the bald patch and scar left from her accident. 'Look, Jenny's head had a bump, too.'

Joachim reached out to touch her scar as she bent towards him, his fingers running over it in wonder before going to his own head to trace the line of his own, much more serious scar. All at once a huge smile broke over his face.

'Joachim and Jenny,' he said. And then the tiny miracle happened. Joachim laughed—the high, delighted, innocent laughter that no one had heard since his accident. 'The same...Jenny the same.'

'Yes, Jenny is just the same.' Jenny kissed his cheek and for a moment his arms closed about her, and then he toddled a little further to his mother, who had tears running down her cheeks.

'Mama not cry,' he said stoutly. 'Mama smile. Mama come for walk with Joachim.'

Elena hesitated. She almost never left her chair when she had visitors because she was so conscious of the way she walked. Now she looked at Jenny for a moment, before pushing herself awkwardly out of the chair to take hold of her son's other hand. Together, she, Andrew and the little boy walked around the garden together, and Jenny thought she had never seen a more beautiful sight, even though the woman's steps were perhaps even more awkward and unsteady than her son's.

Miguel came over to Jenny, his eyes warm and loving as he gazed down at her. 'Two miracles in one day,' he murmured. 'How do you manage it?'

'Oh, you know,' she quipped. 'The impossible we do at once—miracles take a little bit of love.'

'Rather a lot of love,' Miguel said. He pulled her to her feet and into his arms, kissing her while everyone watched and smiled. 'You know, my darling, I think you are a rather special lady.'

'That's OK, then,' Jenny said, 'because I think you're special too.'

0606/108/MB038 V2

Escape to...

Escape to CARIBBEAN KISSES
Susanne McCarthy
Joanna Neil

19th May 2006

Escape to GREEK AFFAIRS
Sara Craven
Margaret Mayo

16th June 2006

Escape to SPANISH SEDUCTION
Sharon Kendrick
Anne Herries

21st July 2006

Escape to ITALIAN IDYLLS
Sara Wood
Diana Hamilton

18th August 2006

Available at WH Smith, Tesco, ASDA, Borders, Eason, Sainsbury's and all good paperback bookshops

www.millsandboon.co.uk

M&B

Sexy!

Three steamy, sultry reads to get the temperature rising this autumn

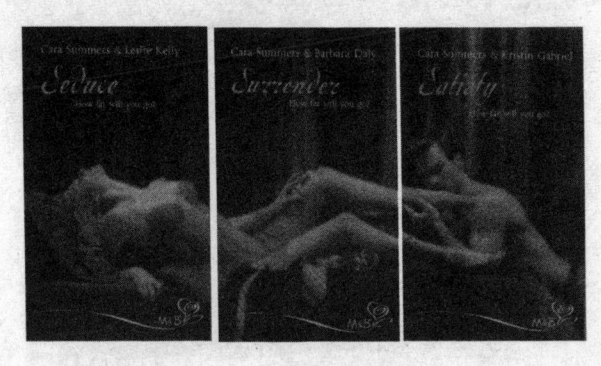

Seduce

The Proposition by Cara Summers &
Wickedly Hot by Leslie Kelly
Available 21st July 2006

Surrender

The Dare by Cara Summers &
Kiss & Run by Barbara Daly
Available 18th August 2006

Satisfy

The Favour by Cara Summers &
Good Night, Gracie by Kristin Gabriel
Available 15th September 2006

www.millsandboon.co.uk

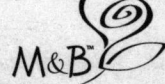

The child she loves...is his child.

And now he knows...

HER SISTER'S CHILDREN BY ROXANNE RUSTAND

When Claire Worth inherits her adorable but sad five-year-old twin nieces, their fourteen-year-old brother and a resort on Lake Superior, her life is turned upside down. Then Logan Matthews, her sister's sexy first husband turns up – will he want to break up Claire's fledgling family, when he discovers that Jason is his son?

WILD CAT AND THE MARINE BY JADE TAYLOR

One night of passion doesn't make a marriage, but it could make a child. A beautiful daughter. Cat Darnell hadn't been able to trample on her lover's dream and kept her secret. Joey was the light of her life. And now, finally, Jackson Gray was coming home...was going to meet his little girl...

On sale 4th August 2006

www.millsandboon.co.uk

Seductive, Passionate, Romantic
There's nothing as sexy as a Sheikh!

THE SHEIKH'S BRIDE

Featuring *The Sheikh's Virgin Bride* and *One Night with the Sheikh* by Penny Jordan

Available 1st September 2006

THE SHEIKH'S WOMAN

Featuring *The Arabian Mistress* by Lynne Graham and *The Sheikh's Wife* by Jane Porter

Available 15th September 2006

Collect both exotic books!

www.millsandboon.co.uk

0806/121/MB043 V2

Coming soon from No. 1 *New York Times* bestselling author Nora Roberts…

Atop the rocky coast of Maine sits the Towers, a magnificent family mansion that is home to a legend of long-lost love, hidden emeralds— and four determined sisters.

Catherine, Amanda & Lilah
available 4th August 2006

Suzanna & Megan
available 6th October

Available at WHSmith, Tesco, ASDA, Borders, Eason, Sainsbury's and all good paperback bookshops

www.silhouette.co.uk

THE SERIES YOU LOVE IS GETTING EVEN BETTER!

This September, Tender Romance™ is becoming Mills & Boon® Romance. You'll find your favourite authors and more of the stories you love—we're just making them better!

Watch for the new, improved *Mills & Boon Romance* series at your favourite bookseller this autumn.

MILLS & BOON

Romance

Pure romance, pure emotion

Exciting new titles on Mills & Boon® Audio CD coming in September 2006

Two passionate Modern Romance™ titles

Stay Through the Night
The Italian Tycoon's Bride

And two elegant Historical Romance™ titles

The Bride's Seduction
The Warlord's Mistress

Available 1st September 2006

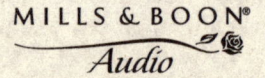

MILLS & BOON®
Audio

www.millsandboon.co.uk

M027/BH/PB

"I was fifteen when my mother finally told me the truth about my father. She didn't mean to. She meant to keep it a secret forever. If she'd succeeded it might have saved us all."

When a hauntingly familiar stranger knocks on Roberta Dutreau's door, she is compelled to begin a journey of self-discovery leading back to her childhood. But is she ready to know the truth about what happened to her, her best friend Cynthia and their mothers that tragic night ten years ago?

16th June 2006

M029/BIIS/PB

"People look at me and they see this happy face, but inside I'm screaming. It's just that no-one hears me."

While breaking the news of Princess Diana's death to millions, reporter Isabel Murphy unravels on live television. *But Inside I'm Screaming* is the heart-rending tale of her struggle to regain the life that everyone thought she had.

21st July 2006

MIRA